I0717401

The Last Hoffman

The Last Hoffman

Gwen Tuinman

RP

RUBY PUBLICATIONS
WHITBY ONTARIO

A RUBY PUBLICATIONS ORIGINAL, March 2020

Copyright © 2020 by Gwen Tuinman

All rights reserved. Published in the United States by IngramSpark.

ISBN: 978-1-9991759-2-4

Printed in the United States of America

Whitman, Walt. "Perfections". *Walt Whitman: Leaves of Grass*, Signet Classic, New American Library: Times Mirror, 1980, pp. 227.

The Last Hoffman

1.

The day after his wife should have turned forty-two, Floyd Hoffman finished sorting mail at the post office, then strode south along Narrow Falls's main street to meet with his lawyers. He took shallow breaths to avoid tasting the fetid air, which, on that warm June afternoon, reminded him of eggs left in a hot car. A good rain could remedy the situation, but as luck would have it, the sky was cloudless and blue.

Farther along the sidewalk, a woman was pushing a baby carriage towards him. Her ill fitting T-shirt and pants, chopped off below the knee, made him long for the days when women still wore dresses. His Bonnie could have taught her a thing or two about looking presentable. As the gap between them closed, he feigned interest in a passing truck and the stack of pine logs chained to its flatbed. Floyd never knew how to handle these situations, whether to acknowledge a person or look away. When proximity forced his decision, he gave a polite nod. A look of recognition flashed in the woman's eyes, and she jerked her head to the right as if to study the wares in a shop window.

An elderly couple walking an aged mutt followed close behind the woman. The husband scrutinized Floyd and muttered something to his wife. Her smile hardened and her eyes narrowed. Until they'd passed, Floyd drilled his gaze at the library, situated between the river and the spot at which Main T-boned Water Street. As a refuge, he ranked it one notch above Tony's Pub.

Townspeople fell into one of two camps: they either gawked at Floyd or ignored him. Which was worse, he couldn't decide. A midrange reaction would have been preferable—something between mild curiosity and disguised repugnance.

Since he'd begun walking, Floyd had passed three empty storefronts whose windows were covered over in brown paper and eight others displaying placards that championed the local paper mill. *We* ♥ *McLelland* signs had become the rage all over town, appearing in residential areas and even in the back windows of cars. The sight of one felt like salt poured in an open wound.

His glance flicked to across the street where Smith and Harper's law office nestled between the stationery shop and the shoe store. With a rolled-up copy of that day's newspaper clenched in his right fist, Floyd stepped off the sidewalk and passed between a station wagon and a sedan parked at forty-five degree angles to the curb. He took a cautious step past their bumpers and into the street, gauging the advance of the white service truck approaching from the right. Its driver hunched forward, both hands gripping the top of the steering wheel. The truck slowed to a near stop, and Floyd leaned into his next stride. No sooner did his heel strike the pavement than the engine revved. The truck vaulted ahead, tires squealing. Floyd sucked in his breath and scrambled back between the parked cars. As the truck shot past him, the driver's face contorted in an ugly tirade, and his fist shook a raised middle finger at Floyd. The vehicle sped north in the direction of the river. Bold lettering across its back doors read, *McLelland Pulp & Paper Mill.*

Floyd's heart banged inside his chest, and the newspaper shook at his side. After several seconds, his brow relaxed and his mouth drifted shut. He thought he'd seen it all. The tactic was new, the message old. *Back off.*

Two more cars rolled by him, but the third stopped. When the driver waved him on, Floyd loped across both lanes, not slowing until he'd reached the safety of the opposite sidewalk in front of Smith and Harper's gold-stenciled window. He gripped one of the brass pulls, hefted the door open, and then stepped inside. A mildew smell permeated the air, but still, it was a relief to escape the foul odour in the street.

The interior office doors remained closed. No one came out to greet him. The steno chair behind the secretary's desk sat empty, on an angle facing towards the front door. Had he misunderstood the meeting time? Then he noticed the blank sheet of letterhead waiting in her typewriter and a half-full teacup in the centre of the blotter. She'd be back. With a handkerchief from his pocket, Floyd cleaned his glasses, then mopped the prickle of sweat from the back of his neck. He tucked the folded cloth back into his pocket and took a seat on one of the oxblood leather chairs on the other side of the room.

Framed photographs of the first and second generations of Smith and Harper lawyers hung on a prominent spread of wall in the waiting area. On many occasions, Floyd had paced the office examining the collection of oil paintings that depicted aspects of Narrow Falls's history—a view of Brewster's Gorge, lumbermen felling pines, and an open-air sawmill. An original town survey dated July 1825 filled the space above the first chair. Although he'd seen the drawing during scores of previous visits, he leaned in for a closer look at the blank patch north of the penciled-in river. In those days, no one could have conceived the nightmare of a pulp-and-paper mill in such a pristine location. His own street southwest of Smith and Harper had still been farmland when this survey was completed.

Finally, a door opened. Gerald Smith, head down, his silver-rimmed glasses resting on his forehead, walked out of his office. Even at three in the afternoon, his shirt looked fresh from the hanger. He swung right, leafing through a handful of documents, and crossed the short hallway that led to the conference room. "The paperwork has arrived," he announced upon reaching Clive Harper's office door. His weight shifted to one foot, and he leaned a shoulder against the doorframe.

Floyd strained to overhear Gerald and Clive's hushed exchange. Good news for his case, he hoped. His shoulders drooped when Gerald mentioned someone else's surname following the word *divorce.* After five minutes of idly tapping the newspaper roll against his knee, curiosity overtook Floyd. He cleared his throat.

Gerald straightened up and looked over his shoulder. "You're early," he remarked with mild annoyance.

Floyd shrugged.

With the sweep of an arm, Gerald ushered him into Clive's office. Floyd chose his customary seat just inside the door. While Gerald pushed a pile of books aside to create a seat on the credenza, Floyd unrolled his newspaper and waited for the go-ahead to begin.

The hinges of Clive's office chair groaned as he pressed away from his desk. A necktie hung loose around his unbuttoned collar, and his fingers were laced across the front of his vest. "How are you, Floyd?"

"I've been better," Floyd said. "Have you heard about the swimming ban? It's on the front page of today's *Sentinel*."

"Yeah. I've got it right here." Clive shifted a stack of folders and laid his own newspaper copy on the desk. He traced a finger below the print as he read aloud. "Questions about the integrity of Narrow Falls's water have resurfaced. Last summer, several people reported skin rashes, nausea, and headaches following direct contact with water at Riverside Park."

"Great stuff," Gerald said.

Clive looked past Floyd and clapped his hands together. "Carol! Thank God you're back. I'm starving."

The secretary sailed towards him carrying a soft drink in one hand and a paper bag stamped *Narrow Falls Diner* in red print in the other. The smell of fried food instantly flooded the office. She set the takeout lunch on the centre fold of the newspaper and hastened out of the room. Within seconds, Clive had peeled the foil from his burger and was woofing down his first bite.

"Where's my salad?" Gerald asked.

Clive tipped the bag and looked inside. "It's not here," he answered with a cheek full of food.

"For the love of—"

"The article. It's insulting," Floyd interjected, leaning forward in his seat. He paused for a moment, distracted by the condiments dripping from Clive's burger. "The public works department is warning people to stay out of the river between the McLelland mill and the gorge. But nowhere in the article does their spokesperson suggest a link between the mill's activities and water quality!"

Gerald folded his arms. "The *Sentinel* can print whatever it likes. Bottom line, Clive and I are going to prove that the mill knowingly operates without regard for ministry regulations."

"We need to stick to our original strategy—stay calm, present the facts, and keep hammering at the accuracy of the numbers on McLelland's emissions reports," Clive said, wiping ketchup from his chin with a napkin. "At every opportunity, we circle back to Bonnie's autopsy report and the level of dioxins present in the blood and tissue samples."

"He's right," Gerald chimed in. "It's slow going, but the ministry will start pressuring the mill, and change will happen."

"Sure." Floyd rolled the newspaper and tossed it onto the adjacent chair. His jaw clenched as he spun his wedding ring around his finger.

It was Gerald who finally broke the silence. "Trust the system to do its job."

"She's been gone eight years," Floyd said softly. His voice shook as he fought against the lump rising at the back of his throat. "McLelland Pulp and Paper needs to pay, but I'm no closer to making that happen than the day I sued them four years ago." He slumped on the chair and raked a hand through his hair.

The other men waited for Floyd to gather his emotions.

Gerald spoke first. "You've known Clive and I since we were all kids. You can count on us."

"We want this win as badly as you do," Clive added.

Floyd lifted his glasses and wiped his eyes with the back of his hand. They were right. He needed to get hold of himself and focus on the bigger picture. Gerald and Clive would prove the mill's negligence. Folks in town would have to face the truth.

"How's your son doing?" Gerald asked in a reserved tone.

"Dean's fine." Floyd leapt to his feet. "I'm going to the library to comb through the microfiche one more time. Maybe I've missed something."

"Leave that to us. You should go home." Clive smiled reassuringly. "There's a ball game on television tonight. Dean's a ball player, right?"

"But if you really want to . . ." Gerald said with a shrug

"No, Floyd." Clive reached for his drink. "Work can wait. There's always tomorrow."

Not for everyone.

Floyd levied a weak smile and walked to the door. "Guess I'll head home."

"Great." Clive rasped the drinking straw against the hole in the plastic lid of his soft drink. "We'll be in touch."

In the outer office, the typewriter clattered at a steady tempo. Staring at the floor, Floyd trudged past the secretary's desk. His pace quickened as he neared the front doors. One solid push returned him to the street. He turned a sharp right and marched with dogged determination towards the river.

First stop, the library. And the second—Tony's Pub.

The veil of twilight had begun its descent by the time Floyd returned home that evening. He walked slowly along the front walk and glanced worriedly at the gloom behind the living room windows. One step after the other, he hauled himself up the porch steps. The hinges groaned when he pulled the screen open to unlock the interior door. Inside, the kitchen smelled like toast. There was neither a plate nor a scattering of crumbs on the counter or table, which could only mean Dean had eaten in his room again. Floyd lined his shoes up against the wall in the entranceway. From his vantage point next to the kitchen, he peered down the hallway to his son's bedroom door. It was shut. A thin line of yellow light ebbed from beneath its bottom edge. The boy was still awake.

Floyd quaked inside like a building caving in on itself. Should he knock on Dean's door? Talking usually led to more trouble, so he decided against it.

Instead, Floyd played one of his father's treasured albums on the hi-fi and hoped that the sound of music might coax the boy from his room. While the soothing melody of violins swelled in the stillness, Floyd sagged into an armchair and waited. And waited.

The telephone rang just as he'd begun to nod off. When the persistent jangling continued above the strains of Pachelbel's Canon in D, Floyd lifted the needle from the album. With trepidation, he crossed to the hallway where the phone hung on the wall. No one he knew would call this late in the evening. He picked up the receiver and pressed it to his ear.

"Hoffman, is that you?" a gravelly voice said.

"It is."

"Quit stirring up trouble, or you'll be sorry. I'll come over there and—"

Floyd slammed the receiver down.

It immediately began to ring again. He eyed the rotary telephone and rested an index finger against his chin. His burdens were heavy enough, he decided. One more stick of trouble might break him. Floyd turned and shuffled past the landing and turned the light on above the stove to save Dean from stumbling when he roamed the darkened house. Then he retreated up the stairs.

It was just past ten o'clock when Floyd climbed into bed. He stared at the ceiling and worried about how peculiar he'd grown, lying in the dark with his wrists fastened to his sides like clasps on a suitcase. Even his ankles were welded together so his legs couldn't stray onto his wife's half of the mattress. She'd claimed it as her own on their wedding night, pouncing onto the bed with legs kicking inside the circumference of her white dress.

If Bonnie were still alive, she would have laughed at his habit of not allowing anything, inanimate or human, to touch her side of the bed. *Oh, Floyd, you sentimental fool. Sit here while you pull on those socks. I don't mind.*

The clarity of her voice inside his head nearly convinced him to abandon this regimen. He longed to spread himself across Bonnie's half of the sheets and crush his face into her pillow. But his eyes squeezed shut, and he resolved to mind enough for both of them. He would fold the top sheet over the upper edge of the bedspread again the next night and ease the covers away from the bed as he had for the past nine years.

When sleep evaded him, Floyd switched on the bedside lamp and reached for his eyeglasses. The back of his head rested against the plaster wall, and his spine pushed into a feather pillow. He opened the top drawer of the nightstand and drew a white cotton handkerchief, starched and sharply pressed, from the six others piled inside. After wiping his eyes, he pulled a strip of scrunched paper from the breast pocket of his pajama shirt and read the word scrawled there in shaky blue pen. *Themselves* was all it said. Floyd returned the note to his pocket and patted his chest. The scratch of paper against the cotton fabric settled him. He swung his legs over the side of the bed and rocked onto his feet. From a stack of file boxes in the corner of his room, he retrieved a file of papers he'd been working on.

Floyd skimmed the column of names scratched in pencil on the first page. Over the past two weeks, he'd clocked twenty-seven hours at the Narrow Falls Public Library, looking over the obituaries of mill employees and retirees. He knew every name on the page: *Morton Andrew, Hisdale, 42, of 32 Oak St. Died May 7, 1968.* He knew Morton's sister, Phyllis, from grade school. And then, of course, there was her cousin Marian, who'd been Bonnie's friend. The whole town was interconnected if you dug deep enough.

The telephone rang again, and its shrill clamour set Floyd's eyes to darting around the room. Who the hell could be calling? "One Winston Churchill. Two Winston Churchill . . ." Floyd counted off twelve seconds and stopped. Still, the phone rang. "Things with bells," he muttered, wishing the caller would give up. "Streetcars, Toronto Stock Exchange, bicycles, doors, alarm clocks, cathedrals."

Downstairs, floorboards creaked along the length of the hallway. The last ring was cut short by Dean's voice.

"Yup," he said, then his voice dropped to a soft murmur. The receiver clunked into the cradle, and seconds later, his bedroom door clicked shut.

"Huh," Floyd said aloud. There'd been a tenderness in his son's voice, one Floyd hadn't heard for a very long time. Could his son have been speaking with a sweetheart? *Maybe.* Floyd had never seen a girl around, and Dean had never mentioned anyone special. But then, Dean didn't say much of anything conversational these days.

Before Bonnie died, Dean had been a chatterbox. "Where's Mommy? What's she doing?" Now seventeen-year-old Dean rarely engaged in small talk. Instead, he preferred to launch grenades at his father. "Why did Mom need to sneak me out of the house for midnight swims at the gorge? I think you scared her. I think you and all your stoic German shit sucked the life out of her."

The big question wedged itself between them. "There's something you're not telling me about Mom." Floyd's evasive answers drove him and Dean further apart. He felt Bonnie's secret leaning hard against the inside of his teeth. It fought for the light of day, but he held it hostage. Floyd loved his son, but the answer Dean sought would not bring him the peace he wanted.

Sequestered on his side of the bed, Floyd spoke into the darkness. "Don't worry, Bonnie. I've not told him anything. I'll not betray you, darling."

2.

Tammy King's mouth tasted like vomit. Her hands shook, and tears rolled off the tip of her nose as she hovered over the plastic garbage pail. When her gut settled, she wiped her mouth on a crumpled Garfield T-shirt that read, *Have a Nice Day* across the chest. She turned it inside out, balled it into a lump, and buried it deep inside her laundry basket.

After easing her bedroom door open, she looked left then right. Her socked feet skimmed the surface of the hall carpet as she sprinted to the bathroom with the garbage pail hugged tightly against her chest. She flushed its contents down the toilet and wedged the garbage pail under the faucet. Before running water in the sink, she waited for the length of time required to zipper a fly and tuck in a shirt. When the last sour bits of her dinner had disappeared down the drain, she brushed her teeth and shoved the toothbrush into the back pocket of her jeans.

She laid an ear against the bathroom door before darting back to her bedroom with the garbage pail in hand. As she passed her parents' room, her right knee banged into the corner of the wrought-iron telephone stand tilting out from the wall.

A burst of pain sent Tammy hobbling into her bedroom with tears gathering in her eyes. "Shit, shit, shit." She closed the door carefully over the telephone cord that snaked across her carpet, then slid to the floor with her back pressed against the side of her bed. A stream of air whistled through her lips while the muffled applause of a television audience rose up from the room below. *This can't be happening.*

The telephone stared up at her in taunting silence. She'd been trying to reach Dean for two days. Had his feelings changed? Tammy wasn't sure. In recent weeks, when she'd glanced up to find him studying her, Dean had frowned and looked away. Perhaps this new sullenness was a passing mood. He hadn't been feeling well lately.

For the next fifty-three minutes, she sat cross-legged on her bedroom floor, twisting strands of shag carpet around her fingers. When she last dialed Dean's number before dinner, he hadn't answered. Sleeping again, no doubt. After their first rendezvous, Dean had made her promise to call during his father's work hours. "I don't want Floyd knowing anything about us," he'd said. "Trust me, I'm protecting you." She'd never before risked calling his house at such a late hour for fear that Mr. Hoffman might answer.

But things were different now.

Tammy held the receiver tightly against one ear and dialed his number. The ringing sounded distant, as though it was travelling from the far end of a tunnel. *Pick up. Pick up.* She pictured Dean sitting on the edge of his bed, gauging her impatience in the shrillness of each ring. Is that why he wasn't answering? She was about to hang up when she heard his voice on the line.

"Yup."

"Hey, you're there."

"Yeah."

"I've missed you." She picked flakes of pink polish from her nails.

"Me too."

"Look, I know it's late but we really need to talk. Can I come over?"

"Sure. I was thinking the same thing," he said. "We should talk . . . about the future."

Relief flooded Tammy's heart. Talk of the future could only mean one thing. Dean still loved her. "What about your dad?"

"He's in bed. Come around to the back, like usual."

Tammy dumped the contents of her school bag onto the floor and repacked them along with a change of clothing, her toothbrush, and Dean's football jersey. She slept with the shirt folded under her cheek each night, but during the day she concealed it in the back of her closet under some old sweaters.

When butterflies circled the inside of her stomach, she rested her forehead against the window screen and inhaled the cool night air. Her parents were downstairs watching *Columbo* on television. In all likelihood, her father's head was tipped back against the headrest of his recliner, and rumbling snores were rolling out through his slack mouth. Always preparing something for the women's auxiliary, her mother would be preoccupied with her latest crocheting endeavour. They had no idea. Tammy imagined their explosions of anger followed by bursts of disappointment, then shame settling like dust on the furniture.

She planned to slip through the front door with her overnight bag slung across her shoulder. But first, she would write a letter to leave on her parents' bed. Tammy hovered over the paper and squeezed the pen. It all needed to be perfect.

Mom and Dad:

I am leaving this note to tell you about something really important. I thought it would be easier this way than in person.

I have a boyfriend. We've been seeing each other for some time now. You don't know him, but trust me when I say we are in love, and it's the real thing. By the time you read this, I will be at his place. I'm going there to tell him the same thing I'm telling you now.

Tammy closed her eyes and whispered the next line. She could scarcely believe she was saying the words, even after rehearsing them for days.

I'm pregnant.

It had happened two months earlier. She and Dean had tried to be careful, but on one occasion, the heat of the moment had erased all common sense. Later, in a quiet moment, she'd voiced concern. He'd said something funny, although right now she couldn't remember what, and she'd laughed until she cried.

Please be happy for me. This is not the usual order of things, but we'll make it work out somehow. We've got plans for the future. I'll be home tomorrow. I'm hoping that you will have calmed down by then so we can talk it over.

She signed the letter, *Love, Tammy.* It was a natural closing that she had written as an automatic reflex to ending a message. Now she realized that it was more of a request. Could they still love her? Would anything be the same?

P.S. Don't worry, Mom. I'm not doing this alone. I know he will always be there for me. He loves me.

Twenty minutes later, Tammy stole along the side of Dean Hoffman's house. She stuck to the shadows until she reached the backyard, where Dean leaned through his bedroom window. He raised a finger to his lips, then pointed upwards to the second story, where lamplight filtered through his father's bedroom curtains. Her brows lifted, and she mouthed a silent, "Okay."

Tammy passed her overnight bag into Dean's outstretched hands. His fingers, long and slim, resembled those of a pianist or an artist more than a defensive lineman's. She loved these hands that had stroked her cheek and pressed their heat against the space between her shoulder blades.

While Dean dispensed of her bag, Tammy stepped onto the cinder block they'd concealed behind the masses of lavender growing along the foundation of the house. Her running shoes crushed the purple blooms beneath her feet and released their familiar scent into the night air. She hoisted herself onto the sill and swung one leg and then the other through the window. All at once, she and Dean were facing each other in awkward silence. Not exactly the Romeo-and-Juliet moment she'd pictured.

A book sprawled face down in the centre of Dean's bed. Its cover was half the size of binder paper and covered in faded denim the colour of old blue jeans.

"What's that?" she asked, reaching for the book.

"It's private," he warned in a sharp tone that stung her.

"Sorry," Tammy said.

Dean's eyes lowered, and his voice softened. "It's a journal. My grandmother got me started on it after Mom died."

"Oh."

"Grandmother called it a remedy for melancholy."

Tammy's nails dug into the soft flesh of her palms. "Are you sad now?" she asked.

Dean shoved the journal into the top drawer of his nightstand, then fell back on the bed and folded his arms behind his head. "So what's up?"

"You wanted to talk about the future," she said. Her throat constricted, and her heart ached with a yearning to hear the words *I love you.*

"No, you first. You called me, right?" Dean patted the mattress. He reached for her hand as she sat, but his dark eyes drilled holes in her confidence.

Tammy had no idea how he'd take the news. She'd practiced all of the ways she might tell him, but none of the phrases she'd rehearsed would step forward to be spoken.

"I'm late," she finally said.

"You're late," Dean repeated slowly. He released her hand and sat up as waves of realization rolled across his face. "Pregnant?"

"Yes." Tammy sagged forward, and tears dropped onto her lap. She pulled a used tissue from her pocket to wipe her nose while she waited for Dean to process her announcement. Each new moment of empty silence only heightened her anxiety. She shredded the edges of the tissue and laid the pieces in a line across her knee.

Dean eased from the bed and scuffed out of the room. Tammy watched the hem of his pajama pants dragging along the floor at his heels. When the door closed behind him, the tension that had been coiling in every part of her body migrated to a singular point at the centre of her forehead. The spot pulsed with alarm. What was happening?

"Everything okay?" a deep male voice called from upstairs. Tammy bristled. She'd forgotten about Dean's father.

"Yeah. Go back to bed," Dean responded abruptly.

She heard rummaging in the kitchen followed by the unlatching of the refrigerator door.

A moment later, a whisper, "Tammy, let me in."

She crammed the tissue into her pocket and scrambled off the bed. Dean swept past her when the door opened, clutching a glass of milk in each hand. He extended one to her, then raised his own in a toast.

"You are going to be a great mother, babe. Cheers." He took a long drink, then turned away to cough into his sleeve. His shoulders shook. Milk slopped over the rim of his glass and splattered on the floor. "Wrong pipe," he said after regaining his composure.

"You do love me," Tammy said. And the tears began to fall as if they'd never stop. Dean produced a bag of store-bought cookies from the waistband beneath his T-shirt and tossed it underhand onto the bed behind Tammy. Then he looped his arms around her and pulled her close.

"Tammy King, I will love you until the day I die."

They lay on top of the bed, fully clothed and staring at the ceiling. Tammy lifted her head from the pillow and looked across the landscape of Dean's face to the alarm clock on his nightstand. His cheeks were drawn, and she thought he looked a bit thinner. He'd caught some kind of bug and hadn't been feeling well since late spring.

"What time is it?" he asked.

"Just after midnight."

"So they've definitely read the letter by now?"

"Yup." Tammy pictured the scene in excruciating detail. Her mother would have turned the television off after the evening news and nudged her father's shoulder. She would have trudged up the stairs, pausing on the top step to call his name again. He never could wake up on the first warning. Straightaway, she'd notice the envelope in the centre of their bed. It didn't belong there. She'd read twice, her brows squeezing together and her mouth flopping open like a beached fish. Then she'd yell, "Lawrence," and Tammy's father would thump up the stairs. "Where's the fire?" he'd ask. That's when she'd tell him. Their world would shatter, and Tammy knew she was to blame.

"How am I going to face them?" she asked.

"They're going to be pissed."

"That's an understatement. What about your dad?"

"Let me worry about Floyd." Dean rolled towards Tammy and rested a hand on her belly. "Maybe I should come home with you tomorrow."

"No. Not a good idea. My parents blame your dad for stirring up trouble at McLelland's."

"The entire town blames him. I guess that'll make me an asshole by default, huh?"

"I'm sorry." Tammy's face crumpled. "The whole thing's a mess." She dabbed at her eyes with a ball of tissues and sniffled. "I'm going to get so fat. How am I going to finish school? People will know."

Dean frowned. "Big T-shirts. They hide a lot of secrets." His arm threaded around her, and she laid her head on his shoulder.

"Your chest is still rumbly," she said with a yawn. "Sounds like there's ten cats purring in there. When do you see the doctor again?"

"I dunno." His arm hung over the side of the bed while he fished a hand inside the squashed cookie bag resting on the floor. "Want one?"

Tammy nodded. He took an oatmeal cookie for himself and passed one to her. She laid it on the bedcover.

A framed photograph of Dean's mother dazzled from the top of his dresser. The camera had captured her mid-sentence as she looked back over her shoulder. One hand gripped her wide-brimmed hat, and a sheer scarf streamed from the other.

"What do you recall most about your mom?"

Dean finished chewing the cookie and licked the crumbs from his fingers. Then he sat upright and hugged his knees to his chest.

"Memories come to me in pieces, you know? Music blaring in the middle of the night. Laughter. Late night swims. Mom bawling in her room." Dean thrust an index finger at the ceiling. "There's only one person who could help me put it all together, and he's not talking."

He lifted the bottom edge of his T-shirt to wipe his eyes, and for the briefest of moments Tammy witnessed a new thinness about his midriff. He reached for a blanket hanging over the foot of the bed and spread it over them.

"You look tired, babe." Dean flicked the lamp off. "Try to rest. You're sleeping for two." He pressed a kiss to her forehead and lay down.

"Dean?"

"Yup."

"What did *you* want to tell *me*?"

"Nothing that won't keep until tomorrow."

• • •

Sunlight through the window and the ache of a full bladder pulled Tammy from a deep sleep the next morning. She stretched and yawned, then laid her arm over Dean's side of the bed. Her eyes shot open. It was empty.

Water running through the pipes of the old house preceded feet padding down the stairs. Light steps, not heavy Dad steps like Mr. Hoffman would probably make. Seconds later, a drawer closed and then the refrigerator opened. Dean must be in the kitchen.

Tammy paced the room as the urgency to visit the bathroom continued to build. Until she could be certain that Dean's father had left for work, she'd need to stay hidden in the bedroom. Thoughts of dashing upstairs to the toilet took over her mind. What she needed now was a distraction.

She could strip the bed and make it up properly. It seemed like the grown-up thing to do. Tammy dragged the sheets and blankets onto the floor, then tiptoed to Dean's side of the bed to smooth the fitted sheet. That's when she saw the white plastic cap wedged between the mattress and box spring. She knelt on the floor to read the raised print: *PUSH TO TURN.* Tammy instantly understood what she'd discovered. She pulled Dean's secret from its hiding place and read the label.

Patterson's Pharmacy
23 Main St. Narrow Falls, ON
RX 9369224 Ref: 3
D. Hoffman
Take as needed
Not to exceed 4 per day

Pale blue capsules nested like robin eggs inside the plastic. She sank to the floor and set the pill bottle between her feet. Dean had hidden medication from her. What did this mean? What else could he be hiding?

Fine hairs stood up on the back of Tammy's neck as she eyed the nightstand where he'd stashed his journal the night before. Snooping might be wrong, but hiding information from someone you love didn't seem right either. She needed to know if she could count on him.

Tammy lifted the journal from the drawer and laid it open on her lap. She stared intently at the back of Dean's bedroom door and strained her ears towards the sound of chair legs dragging across the floor. She needed to skim through the journal quickly and put it back into the drawer before Dean returned.

An inscription scrolled across the inside of the front cover in eloquent script: *From Grandmother Brookman, August 1972.* The brown ink bled into the paper with no sign of ballpoint scratches. He'd drawn two stick figures riding bicycles on the opposite page and coloured them with pencil crayons. The caption, written in his grandmother's hand, read, *Mother and Dean biking to the park.* Mr. Hoffman didn't appear in any of the pictures, but Dean's grandmother's handwriting appeared on every page.

Tammy skipped forward to recent entries near the end of the journal.

Note to Self   February 12, 1981

I hate this crap town. I'm getting the hell out of here, and I'm taking T with me. There's nothing for us here. We're done with high school in June, and we'll be cutting out on grad. I'll never come back to this one-horse town. For what? A job at a diner? A hardware store? End up like the old man . . . miserable piss tank. Peace out.

Note to Self   March 3, 1981

I missed most of school this week. Too bad, eh? No calculus for me. Boohoo. It's a sweet gig. T comes at 7:30 each morning to read to me. She sneaks over at lunch hour to slip between the sheets. The old man is at Tony's Pub, working on a beer. He doesn't even know I've got a girl. God, I love the smell of her hair.

Tammy's thumb traced the heart Dean had drawn around the letter *T.* Her eyes cut to the door when she heard crinkling and the sound of a toaster lever being pressed down. She had only a minute or two to skim over the most recent entries.

Note to Self   June 4, 1981

Regrets. Haven't written for a while. I've been feeling like shit. Tired all the time. Doctor Killjoy told me this would happen. I had to bus it all the way to North Bay for that bit of info. Graduation? Leaving this dead-end town? Well, the road to hell is paved with good intentions. Hell. I guess I will need to ponder that realm soon. T keeps calling.

Tammy went numb. It was as if her head had filled with cotton batten and her tongue had been weighed down by lead. She pressed a hand to her chest and read the note again. She thought back to the weeks he'd been absent from school. A virus, something like mono, he'd told her. But you don't go all the way to North Bay to see a doctor about that. No, this was something bigger.

The overwhelming implication seized Tammy and shook her hard. She thought she knew what it meant, but she wanted to be wrong. They were so in love. Dean was everything to her. He couldn't leave her alone, not with a baby. Who would look after her? She clapped a hand over her mouth to keep from sobbing.

The bedroom door flung open. Dean hurried inside, struggling to suppress a coughing fit as he set a plate of toast on his nightstand. The urgency stamped on his face frightened Tammy. His nostrils flared and his eyes flashed as he wheeled away from her to brace both palms against the wall. His shoulders lurched forward as he released a few croupy barks. When it finally ended, he drew a hand across his chin and turned to face her again.

She looked up at him from among the twisted bedsheets strewn on the floor. There was a bright red smudge at the corner of his mouth and across the back of his hand. Three drops of blood had begun darkening on the chest of his T-shirt. Air rushed from Tammy's lungs.

Dean's gaze traveled to the journal lying open next to the bottle of pills on the floor. His eyes darkened.

"I was making the bed . . ." Tammy said apologetically. She pointed to the last *Note to Self* entry dated June 7, 1981. It simply read, *Tell Tammy.*

"Tell me *what?*" her voice broke.

"Oh Jesus." And Dean slumped to the floor.

3.

Floyd lay on his side, counting blurry rosebuds on the bedroom wallpaper. He'd been measuring the space between coughs since Dean's first attack that morning. At twenty-seven rosebuds, he wiped the tears from his eyes with a corner of the bedsheet and shifted his attention to the colourless sky outside the window.

How Floyd would survive what lay ahead, he'd no idea. Bonnie's ordeal had ruined him. Dean's would finish him off. His chest ached at the thought of, once again, masking his grief while someone he loved slipped further away from him. At the end of it all, he'd be called upon to watch another casket being lowered into a grave. The worst was yet to come, but already he could barely face Dean. Each day, it was more difficult for Floyd to look into his son's eyes, so full of belligerence and underscored with dark circles.

In twenty minutes, his alarm clock would ring. Floyd rolled onto his back and stared at the ceiling. He didn't feel much like facing people today, least of all his boss. The house needed his attention. Last night, he'd overheard Dean struggling to open his bedroom window again. It wouldn't take much effort to chisel layers of old paint from the sash, but like a lot of other things, Floyd had been putting it off. He could fake being sick, but he was already getting the stink eye from his boss for the last three times he'd called in just before start time. Best not to risk it.

When a sob reached his ears, he stopped breathing and his eyes widened. Floyd had heard Dean's muffled crying before. This sob was high pitched—like Bonnie's.

Somewhere in his house, a girl was crying!

Floyd's jaw dropped. Surely, he would have heard the front door open when she arrived. *The rattling window.* Dean had snuck her in.

Why all the secrecy? Floyd had never inflicted parameters on Dean. In fact, they coexisted more like roommates than father and son.

He swung his pale legs over the edge of the mattress. The situation required careful diplomacy. He could act casual and knock on Dean's door. *Come for breakfast and bring your friend along.* Floyd reconsidered. The girl had been crying, so perhaps she'd just heard the news, in which case Dean would resent an interruption of any kind. Floyd stretched his neck to the right and then to the left. Better to leave things alone. He'd start his day as usual and wait to see what unfolded.

Floyd cinched the belt of his worn bathrobe about his waist. With heavy footsteps meant to broadcast his presence, he proceeded along the hall to the bathroom for a quick shower. When he finished, he ran a comb through his hair and shaved in record time.

The smell of fresh brewed coffee rose to the upstairs landing. Floyd could hear the percolator shaking against the stovetop as he returned to his room. Already, a wonderful turnabout. Dean seldom ventured into the kitchen before Floyd left for work, and the boy had never made coffee before.

A splash of worry tainted Floyd's optimism. Dean wanted something.

"Relax," Floyd told himself, "it's only coffee, and he *is* my son, after all." Still, his mouth went dry as he buttoned his work shirt and tucked it into his navy polyester pants. If they stuck to safe subjects—nothing to do with Bonnie or death— it would be okay. And then there was the girl. A female presence might take the edge off of Dean so Floyd could talk with him.

After granting himself a last reassuring look in the mirror, Floyd went downstairs to the kitchen. "Morning," he said, rounding onto the linoleum floor.

Dean glanced up at him and then continued reading the funny pages left over from the weekend newspaper.

"This is a nice surprise." The corners of Floyd's mouth turned upwards in what he hoped resembled a smile. He concealed his disappointment that the chair next to

Dean's remained empty. Nothing in the boy's behaviour suggested that he was hiding anything. Floyd began to wonder if he'd imagined the sounds of a third person in the house.

"Have you eaten yet?" Floyd asked as he filled a mug with coffee.

"No," Dean said.

"I'll make you some toast with lots of butter. That's how you liked it when you were little." Floyd pulled the bread bag from the cupboard and dropped two slices into the toaster.

"Mom's the one who made my toast." Dean's words were razor sharp.

Silence inflated the awkwardness between them. Floyd took his reprieve when the bread popped up. He scraped the butter back and forth until it melted into the toast.

"School today?" Floyd asked.

Dean squinted and curled his lip. "No."

With a sinking heart, Floyd sat down and nudged the plate of toast across the table. "Plans?"

"What the fuck?" Dean fired back. "It's Tuesday! Everyone I know is at school."

"I know you must be feeling—"

"You don't know shit." Dean lunged from his chair, but instead of railing on, his mouth began to gulp at the air. His breath sounded as if it was being sucked into his lungs through a narrow straw.

Floyd sat paralyzed by the panic flaring in Dean's eyes. Movements rolled past him, frame by frame, until the boy's right hand reached towards him from across the table. Primal instinct kicked in, and Floyd vaulted from his chair to position himself behind Dean. His arms slipped around his son's chest and lowered him onto a chair. "Lean forward and take little breaths."

Dean's elbows rested on his knees, and his shoulders rose and fell in time with his wheezing breath.

"It's going to get easier. Give it a minute." Floyd rested a hand on his son's back. It had been a long time since he'd touched Dean. The geography of his body had eroded into something sparse and angular. If only Floyd were a cancer sponge. He imagined the black X-ray shadows lifting away from Dean's insides and permeating his own by osmosis.

Dean wrenched away from Floyd's hand. He turned in his chair and looked up at Floyd. Fear had left his face, and anger had slid into its place.

"You're coming straight home after work?" he asked.

"Yeah," Floyd said. "I've been thinking you should move back into your old room upstairs. It might be easier for you when—"

"No more stonewalling bullshit. I want us to talk about Mom." Dean's index finger punched holes in the air that hung between them. "I deserve to know things."

Floyd said nothing. His eyes locked on the blood smear at the corner of Dean's mouth and the darkening drops on his shirt.

"Coward," Dean said. He stormed out of the kitchen.

And Floyd watched him go.

It was as if he and his son had awakened one day unable to speak each other's language. No matter the conversation, Floyd always said the wrong thing. Their relationship was complicated, with too many feelings disguised as something else. Without Bonnie to bridge the gap between them, Floyd didn't stand a chance.

July 1953

Floyd raced his Schwinn Spitfire onto the gravel drive. At six o'clock sharp, his parents would eat dinner—with or without him. The rumble in his stomach told him he was late. He stood on the left pedal and swung his opposite leg over the seat as the bike ground to a stop. The chain across the carriage house doors was padlocked, so he jogged the bicycle in a wide arc around his father's Packard and continued into the backyard. He leaned the handlebars against the back of the building, then untied the stack of books from the carrier and hurried towards the house.

Once inside, he cocked his head and listened. Silence greeted him instead of the usual kitchen sounds and classical music. Unnerved by the absence of fried-onion aroma and the scent of his father's pipe, Floyd kicked off his shoes and walked slowly along the hallway.

He paused at the kitchen door to search for his mother, but the room was empty. The stovetop was clear, and the table hadn't been set for dinner. Everything felt wrong. He hugged the books tightly in the crook of one arm and turned towards the living room.

Floyd's father stood in front of the fireplace. With rugged good looks and a bearing reminiscent of a statue in an old public square, he struck an intimidating figure. In a chair next to him, Floyd's mother, with eyes downcast, smoothed her apron. Unable to read either of their facial expressions, Floyd felt at a disadvantage.

"Mutter and I have been waiting," his father finally said.

"I've been busy making afternoon deliveries for Mr. Patterson."

"And gossiping with the old man." His father regarded Floyd's books and sighed heavily. "Sit."

Floyd took a seat in the middle of the sofa and fumed silently. He'd long given up on convincing his father of the merits for lingering in the store after hours to discuss history and politics with Mr. Patterson.

"If this is about being late . . ." Floyd began, but his father raised a hand to silence him.

"Mutter and I are going home to live with your grandfather."

To live with Opa? The old man was little more to Floyd than a face in a picture frame. They'd met only twice in Floyd's early childhood, and he could remember nothing of either visit. Opa's house was not home. *This* place was home. "For how long?" he finally asked.

"Permanently," his father replied.

A lump burned in Floyd's throat, and tears filled his eyes. His parents rarely left Narrow Falls, and certainly not without him. "What about me?"

His father bristled at the show of emotion. "Opa has lived many years now without the care of a wife. He's become a child once again and needs help. There's only us." He tipped his head towards Floyd's mother. "In two days time, we return to Kitchener to be with him."

"Two days?" Floyd repeated.

"The house is yours now," his father continued. "The cupboards are stocked, and the electric is paid up to the end of next month. We are leaving everything for you."

"I-I can't take care of a house," Floyd stammered, the tears now rolling down his cheeks. "I'm only seventeen!"

"The needs of the weak come before the needs of the strong. Your tears and words change nothing." Floyd's father glowered down at him.

"Why not sell our house? We can all go to Opa's," Floyd pleaded.

"You would spit on my gift to you? After how hard I've worked for this house and everything in it?" His father stepped closer to him. "No stranger will live under this roof."

"Then bring Opa here!"

"He is too old for such change."

"Father, please—"

"Put schoolboy foolishness behind you! No more pedaling your bicycle around town to deliver old women's pills. Find a job suited to a grown man. Work at Brewster's Brickworks and make something of yourself, as I did."

"I've no interest in making bricks." He flicked a discreet glance at his mother, who issued a wide-eyed look of warning.

"It's Brewster's that kept you fed and a roof over your head!" he said.

Floyd leaned over his knees and spoke directly to his mother. "Mutter. This is your home. Come back when Opa is well again."

His mother blinked and shook her head.

"You think only of yourself, Floyd," his father continued. "The change will be good for her. She will have friends again—other women who speak our language, Germans connected to the old country. For too long, we have been separated from people like us, and now we are eager to go back. There is nothing for us here."

Nothing for us here.

Floyd wished that *he* were his father's people, more rugged and old-world. But in the bottom of his heart, he'd always known, without question, he was not.

The following day, Floyd asked Vic Patterson if he might be excused from making the next afternoon's deliveries. He couldn't bring himself to explain that his parents were leaving town without him. Why he felt such shame over their decision to desert him, he couldn't discern. They'd made their choice. He'd no say in the matter. Perhaps that was the source of his disgrace. They hadn't considered him at all. Instead, they were tossing him over the side of the lifeboat with nothing to cling to. This was worse than their not attending his high school graduation ceremony. Was it his fault somehow? Had he done something wrong? He felt awkward not offering Mr. Patterson a concrete reason for his request, so he said, "It's personal." The older man regarded him with concern but claimed he'd somehow manage and did not push for further explanation.

• • •

Even on the morning of his parents' departure, as Floyd lined their suitcases up next to the Packard, he couldn't believe they were really going. Something would surely stop them. Perhaps his mother would insist on staying behind. She'd remained in the house thus far, unable to look at him without pulling a handkerchief from her apron pocket to wipe her eyes.

His father came outside wearing his best suit and set his hat on the roof of the car. He regarded Floyd with a hard glint, as though daring him to balk, and unlatched the trunk of the car.

They first wedged the suitcases in place, then Floyd passed into his father's hands the boxes of treasured books and knickknacks, a sewing basket, and an overstuffed bag of yarn and knitting needles. When they finished, his father slammed the trunk closed and went inside for a final check of the house.

With his hands resting on his hips, Floyd waited next to the car. A sensation came over him like he was being watched. The little boy who lived across the street sat on his tricycle at the end of his family's driveway, eyes trained on Floyd. He wore a brimmed straw hat and a pair of red cowboy boots. His mother knelt nearby in the uncut lawn while she weeded a flowerbed. Their front yard was strewn with toys— an orange ball, plastic shovels and sand pail. Floyd frowned at the Hoffman yard of severely cropped grass and straight-edged flowerbeds.

Floyd's father came down the porch steps with his mother following haltingly behind. He continued to the sidewalk and made a last grim-faced survey of the street. "The Frenchman is spying again."

At the house left of tricycle boy's, a barrel-chested man drinking from a mug stood on display in his front window. Instead of turning away when he'd been caught gawking, he grinned and raised the mug in a gesture of cheer. Floyd's father turned away with a grunt. "Beware of any man who smiles too much. He's hiding something." He walked around the Packard, kicking at each tire, then nodded sharply at his wife and tossed his house keys to Floyd.

"We go now," Floyd's mother said, weeping. "You are a good boy. Stay a good boy." She opened her fleshy arms wide and hugged Floyd until the air squeezed from his lungs. Her cheek smelled like soap. Over her shoulder, he could see the woman across the street resting a trowel across her knees while she looked on with curiosity. Shame rose in Floyd like bitter sap, and he looked away.

When his mother released him, his father stepped forward with his right hand extended and clasped his son's in a firm grip. His eyes grew moist, and, in a puzzling twist, his bottom lip trembled slightly as he cleared his throat. "Pay the bills on time. Don't let the grass grow too long before you mow it."

The display of sentiment came too late.

"Yes, sir," Floyd said flatly. "I'll do things just as you've taught me."

His father's eyes widened slightly, then his stoic comportment snapped into place once more. He released Floyd's hand and reached for his hat. "Mutter and I have a long drive ahead. We'll be leaving now."

The Packard backed out of the driveway and onto the street. His father stared straight ahead, but his mother turned in her seat and waved good-bye to him through the shallow rear window. Floyd raised his right hand feebly and let it drop to his side when the car vanished from his sight.

He'd always assumed he'd be the one to leave Narrow Falls, not his parents. Too early, he was taking on the role of house steward. The icebox was crammed with cabbage rolls and meat pies, but those wouldn't last forever. And then what? Floyd sat on the front steps of the porch. His emotions were muddled. Shouldn't he be reveling in his newfound freedom? He was king of his castle, free as the birds warbling from the branches of his neighbour's oak tree.

The neighbour woman sauntered to Floyd's side of the street, trailed by her son, whose red boots pumped madly at the pedals of his tricycle. Together, they followed the sidewalk to the Hoffmans' gate.

Floyd rested his forearms on the top of his thighs and lowered his head. It was too late to duck into the house. She'd already lifted the latch and let herself into the yard. He focused his attention on an ant winding its way across the toe of one sneaker. As the squeak of the tricycle wheels drew nearer, he rolled his eyes upwards to glimpse the checkered pants that stopped just above the woman's ankles and the flowered gardening gloves folded in her left hand.

"Is everything all right?" she asked softly. When Floyd didn't answer, she made herself at home on the lowest porch step and stared up into his face. He wished she'd go away. "You look so sad," she said, speaking to him as teachers had in grade school when they attempted to draw him out to join the other children.

"I guess," he replied, his eyes drifting to her son's red boots. Floyd could feel her motherly scrutiny, analyzing his responses for cracks she could squeeze through.

"I saw your parents leaving. They had a lot of suitcases. And boxes."

Floyd studied her face, trying to decide if he should confide in her. He wanted to escape her attention and run towards it at the same time.

The woman reached into the breast pocket of her blouse and pulled out a lighter and a pack of cigarettes. "You want one?"

Floyd shook his head and watched her light up a smoke.

The little boy left his tricycle and leaned against his mother's thigh. Her arm slid easily around his shoulder. The woman pulled him towards her and kissed the top of his head, then turned her face away to blow out a stream of smoke. She looked back at Floyd expectantly, then with a tilt of her head said, "You'll feel better if you talk about it."

So Floyd took a deep breath and told her everything. When he explained that his parents weren't coming back and that he'd been left to fend for himself, her brows pinched together in disbelief.

"Why, that's perfectly awful. I could never walk away from my little guy and leave him saddled with all of this." She gestured towards the house and took an agitated drag from the cigarette.

She was right. They had *saddled* him to the house. Not once did they ask if it was what he wanted. He should have spoken more strongly against their plan. But he didn't know what he wanted from life, so he'd been ill equipped to conjure a strong defense.

"Honestly, what does a boy your age know about budgeting for property taxes and home repairs? They've left you without a car." Her mouth dropped open. "Oh my gosh, do you even know how to cook?"

Her words tied Floyd's belly in knots. In a move that would have infuriated his father, the woman stubbed her cigarette out on the step and flicked it into the flowerbed.

"If you need help with anything at all, just knock on our door. We're here to help." She patted the tops of Floyd's sneakers and nudged her son towards his tricycle. Once he'd pedaled onto the sidewalk, she closed the gate and they crossed the street.

A few steps into her driveway, the smiling Frenchman called her over to the hedge that dissected their yards. A few seconds into their conversation, she glanced in Floyd's direction. The man nodded his head slowly as she spoke. A grey-haired woman, carrying a grocery paper sack in her arms, strolled past the end of the hedge. The man waved for her to join the conversation as well. The first woman embellished her story with wide sweeps of an arm. When she reached into her pocket for another cigarette, the Frenchman and the older lady turned in tandem towards the Hoffman house. The man smiled ear to ear, and the woman issued a piteous expression.

Floyd's cheeks burned red. He stalked inside, slammed the door, and drew the curtains across the front windows. He walked the house from end to end—first downstairs, then up—exploring each room with a critical eye. In the living room, there were gaps that gave him pause. A blank spot on the floor where his mother's knitting basket normally sat. On the bookshelf, a yawning space previously occupied by his father's favourite books. Floyd sluggishly climbed the stairs and surveyed the half-empty medicine cabinet in the bathroom. Then he sat on the foot of his parents' bed and stared into their closet at the single wire hanger lingering there like an abandoned child. *What have I done to deserve being left behind?*

For the next two days, Floyd barricaded himself inside the house. He thawed an apple pie on Saturday afternoon and ate half of it for dinner along with a scoop of ice cream the size of a man's fist. Late into the night, he read an encyclopedia and fell asleep fully dressed, listening to the radio. Music distracted him from the nighttime sounds of the house that had caused him to sleep lightly the previous evening. The inexplicable creaking that had gone unnoticed while his parents lived there now raised his alarm.

He slept late on Sunday, an indulgence his parents would have never permitted. At half past eleven, he went downstairs for breakfast. While he perused the refrigerator for something appealing, he detected feminine chatter coming up the walkway. Panic squeezed his chest. He couldn't bear up under any more looks of sympathy. Floyd swung the refrigerator door closed and eyed the stairs. Too late to sprint up the steps and hide. If the women peered through either the kitchen or the living room windows, they'd see him before he reached the first landing. So instead, he dropped to his hands and knees and scrabbled across the linoleum. He managed to crouch against the inside of the front door just as shoes stomped up the porch steps.

"I tell you, the sermon today was a rerun," the first voice said. The tricycle boy's mother was back.

"That's unlikely, don't you think?" a second woman replied. Floyd recognized the heavy accent of the Frenchman's wife.

Knock. Knock. Knock.

Floyd hugged his knees to his chest and held his position.

"The minister is getting old. He should hand the reins over to that guest preacher who visited last month. Findlay, I believe is his last name. No one drowsed off that Sunday," the boy's mother said.

"Try knocking again," the Frenchwoman said. "The window screens are open. He must be here."

Bang. Bang. Bang. Footsteps crossed the porch to the kitchen window. Floyd held his breath.

"I don't see him," the mother said.

Please go away.

"My goodness," she exclaimed, "it's barren in there. Nothing at all homey about the place."

"Someone else must have beaten us to the punch and invited the tragic boy for dinner. God love 'em," the Frenchwoman said.

"I'm so sorry for that boy," the mother replied. Her footsteps returned to the door.

"Perhaps it's better this way. His father ruled with an iron fist. And did you ever see a more browbeaten woman than Mrs. Hoffman? I never heard a full sentence out of the poor thing."

"The boy takes after her, sadly," said the Frenchwoman. "Afraid of his own shadow. A little peculiar, that one."

Floyd's hands slid from his knees. His palms rested against the coolness of the linoleum flooring. Tears welled in his eyes. His humiliation was complete.

In the coming weeks, neighbours popped out of houses like gophers from burrows each time Floyd stepped onto the front porch. They feigned surprise at having intercepted him, but he knew they'd been lying in wait for him to surface. Each one slathered him with looks of concern and offers of assistance. When asked about his parents' intended return date, people's frowns and looks of dismay stabbed at Floyd's heart. He surmised they were fishing for details not already circulating the neighbourhood. Fresh news traded like currency in a small town.

Floyd learned to avoid these uncomfortable encounters by riding his bike everywhere. When returning home, he'd pedal hard up the driveway, zing past the carriage house, unlock the back door of the house, and disappear inside before anyone could accost him. He routinely ignored knocks at the front door. Eventually, people gave up trying to help him. Some took affront to his resistance and ceased waving when he sped by.

On a sweltering afternoon in late August, Floyd set off to make his last pharmacy delivery of the day to an elderly woman who lived on Francis Street, a few blocks away from the high school. When the traffic surge generated by the mill's four o'clock shift change calmed, he pedaled along Main Street with casual vigilance. Later, as he travelled side streets lined with tidy houses and squared-off flowerbeds, the scent of frying potatoes wafted from someone's kitchen to escalate his already building hunger.

He rounded the corner onto Francis Street and immediately slowed his bicycle.

Directly across from the home to which he was delivering a prescription, a red Cadillac convertible was parked at the curb. Music blared from its radio. Two of the school bullies he'd been most relieved to escape upon graduating now stood on either side of the car, each holding an uncapped bottle of beer. The third sat behind the steering wheel, revving the engine to the delight of both friends. They were all wearing employee uniforms from McLelland Pulp and Paper Mill. Like most boys from his class, they'd followed their fathers' footsteps to McLelland's and the promise of easy money. Floyd's father, pragmatic as he was, refused to work there. *No good can come from breathing in McLelland's putrid chemical soup for eight hours a day.* On that point, he and Floyd could both agree.

"Hey, it's Hoffman!" shouted the thick-necked ogre standing on the sidewalk on the right side of the car. Throughout high school, he'd done all the smacking and shoving around. Floyd had secretly nicknamed him *Minotaur,* after the mythological Greek character that had the body of a man but the head of a bull.

Sheep, so branded for his go-along nature, stepped away from driver's side door. "Oh yeah," he said, eyes snapping with anticipation.

The car door swung open and *Narcissus,* the cruelest of the three boys, emerged. Like the character who loved his own reflection, his blond pompadour was slicked perfectly in place. He swaggered towards the centre of the street, and Sheep closed the car door behind him.

Ignore him. Say nothing. Floyd steered his bike away from the car and veered towards the customer's house. From the corner of one eye, he saw Narcissus speeding towards him. A sharp tug on the back of his shirt unseated Floyd from the bike. When he collided with the pavement, pain exploded through his right shoulder and elbow. The three tormentors laughed as he struggled to his feet with the crumpled pharmacy bag still clutched in his hand.

"You should be more careful, Hoffman," Sheep tittered.

Floyd shook with anger as he brushed bits of gravel from his elbows.

"Still doing that sissy job, taking pills to old people, eh?" Narcissus sneered.

Minotaur lumbered into the street. "He's not man enough for the mill. Not cut out for real work, like us."

Floyd turned away and pushed his bike towards the sidewalk. There was nothing to be gained by talking. He'd tried that before only to be rewarded by a sharp punch to the gut and two weeks of ridicule. The birdlike figure of the elderly woman appeared in a window of the house to which Floyd was delivering. He wouldn't disappoint Mr. Patterson by fighting in front of a customer.

"We're not done talking yet. You haven't even looked at my new car," Narcissus said. "What do you think? She's nice, right? Nicer than your kiddie bike."

Minotaur, with his arms folded across his chest, stepped in Floyd's path.

"Sure," Floyd said. "Real nice." He turned the handlebars sharply with the intent of passing Minotaur on the right, but the brute only stepped sideways to block him again.

"What are you hoodlums up to?" a thin voice called out. "Leave Floyd be." The old woman, wearing white braids pinned at the top of her head and embroidered slippers on her feet, waggled a boney finger from her front stoop.

"Oh, Floyd," Sheep mimicked in falsetto.

"I thinks I hear yer mother callin' ya," Minotaur said. More laughter.

"Don't worry," Floyd called out, raising a hand to reassure the woman. "I'll be right there."

"Nope, couldn't be his mother calling," Narcissus continued. "His parents left town for good without him. They couldn't stand Hoffman either."

Floyd's eyes narrowed at the boys' laughter, and he imagined his fist crunching into the centre of Narcissus's pretty face, right between the blue eyes that the schoolgirls went mad for.

"Maybe they went back to Germany to live with all the other scheming Krauts," Narcissus added.

Floyd had heard it all before. He looked past Minotaur to the wisp of a woman, now tilting slightly against the handrail.

"I'd like to deliver the lady's heart medication, if you don't mind."

"If you don't mind," Sheep taunted.

"I don't mind at all," Minotaur replied. "But first, let me fix your bike. There's something wrong with the front tire." He knocked Floyd aside and threw the bike to the ground. Then he lifted one of his steel-toed work boots and bore down on the front wheel. The metal rim twisted under the crush of his weight.

The young men waited for Floyd to strike back. Instead, he collected himself and righted the bike. He pushed past Minotaur, the wobbly tire scrubbing against metal with each rotation, and continued across the old woman's lawn.

"Oh, you dear boy. You're bleeding. Should I call someone to come get you? Your father, maybe?"

"There's no one," Floyd said. He passed the pharmacy bag into her hands and stared at the brick front of her house. "Sorry about the bag." He turned the bike around and made for the sidewalk. To his relief, the three bullies were preoccupied with looking under the hood of the Cadillac. He'd passed two houses before Narcissus shouted at him.

"Hey, Hoffman! You got no parents or teachers left to help you. Who's left to stand between you and us now, eh?"

Floyd clenched his jaw. It was true that he was completely on his own. He wouldn't suffer the indignity of calling his parents with news that he was still being harassed. His father was right about one thing. Floyd wasn't a schoolboy. He'd also said that cruel men only understood the language of violence, and he must learn to speak their tongue. But Floyd wouldn't retaliate for fear they'd thump him the moment he drew his fist back. Neither could he tolerate adolescent behaviour from other young men who found sport in mistreating him. In future, he would remove himself as a target, keep to himself, and avoid conflict at all costs.

As he pushed the bike closer to the Hoffman house, he reviewed the merits of his plan. By cutting himself off from other people, he could avoid the feelings that had been scraping him raw since his parents' departure—the embarrassment of being pitied and the voyeurism of people expecting him to fail.

Floyd lowered his eyes as he shoved the bike past his gate. He turned into the driveway and peered up just as the Frenchman slunk out of the carriage house carrying an armload of tools belonging to Floyd's father. The chain and padlock lay in a heap on the gravel. The Frenchman's chin was tucked downwards in an effort to trap the topmost item, a box of nails, against his chest. Carefully, he reached a hand over his head to return the padlock key to the top of the door frame. He walked with careful steps to prevent the remainder of tools from spilling to the ground.

Floyd planted himself firmly in the man's path and waited for him to realize he'd been caught. When at last the Frenchman glanced up, his eyes shot wide open.

"What are you doing?" Floyd demanded.

"I'm just borrowing a few things," the man answered nervously.

"More than a few."

"Oh, I just thought . . ." The man stumbled over his words at first, but then the permanent smile that Floyd's father so despised returned to his face. "Well, your parents moved out of town, and I don't suppose they'll be using these tools much."

"I'll be using the tools." Floyd glared at him, fueled by anger and frustration, until the man slumped back into the carriage house and returned the pilfered tools to the workbench.

The Frenchman came outside, smiling broadly. "See, no harm done, boy. Next time, I'll ask first." He jetted past Floyd.

Beware any man who smiles too much. He's hiding something.

"Wait a minute!" Floyd called out, surprised at his own brashness.

The man halted and, without turning around, responded, "Yes?"

"Is there anything else you'd like to *unborrow*?"

The Frenchman muttered something indiscernible and rifled through his pants pockets. He pulled a set of Allen keys from one and a handful of metal washers from the other, then pitched them onto the driveway and stormed across the street.

From its hiding place above the door frame, Floyd retrieved the padlock key and tucked it into his pocket. He fed the chain through the handles of the carriage house doors and hooked the padlock shackle through a pair of links, then squeezed until the lock shut with a satisfying click.

Why must people be so disappointing?

4.

Tammy stood outside Dean's living room window, waiting for his signal before departing. While he scouted the sidewalk from an upstairs window, she leaned against the weathered batten board and picked at a curl of white paint. Overgrown shrubs at the south corner of the porch shielded her from neighbours' prying eyes. It was all very cloak-and-dagger, she thought, but necessary to keep their relationship a secret. She used to worry about being grounded for life if her parents learned that she was dating the son of the much-hated Floyd Hoffman. Now her biggest fear was facing their certain wrath upon learning that their first grandchild would be a Hoffman. Things would get worse. Her mother would seek to punish Dean. Tammy couldn't let that happen.

At last, Dean appeared at the window and rested his forehead against the raised sash. "All clear," he said, pressing a hand flat against the screen. "You're going to be great." His bottom lip trembled. "I love you."

"I don't want to leave," Tammy said.

"I know."

"I'll call you." With her backpack slung over her shoulder, Tammy plodded towards the sidewalk. This soon after lunch, she'd blend in with other students returning to school. She glanced back at the house one last time before leaving the yard. Dean stood at the window, his right hand laid over his heart. Tammy paused to return the gesture. It wasn't until Dean receded into the shadows that she let her hand drop to her side.

Tears slid from her eyes. How could this be happening when she loved him so much? She began counting the months on her fingertips. "April to May, May to June, June to July . . ." The baby would come in January. Dean may already be gone by then, and along with him, Tammy's dream of escaping her parent's house.

Along the tree-lined streets of Narrow Falls, she shuffled like a sleepwalker. One foot stepped ahead of the other, carrying her past children playing on front lawns, women reading books on verandas, and men leaning against parked cars. She ignored their curious glances and muffled conversations.

It came as an unwelcome surprise to find herself standing in front of her parents' house, eyes puffy and scalp prickling. Nausea welled in her stomach; skipping breakfast hadn't helped. She sat on the curb with her forehead resting on her knees and her hands clasping her head.

"Warm enough for you?" a voice said from above her. Tammy shielded her eyes against the sun and looked up into the face of Blanche Clark. She and her husband lived two houses up the street.

"Morning." Tammy managed a weak smile.

"Afternoon, more like it." Mrs. Clark tipped her head to one side. "You've seen better days. Are you coming down with what your father has?" A wide smile settled across her lips when Tammy's eyes darted to the driveway. Her father's car sat where he'd parked it the previous night. No doubt he was sick, but not the way Mrs. Clark meant. "My Vern says there's some kind of big news coming for the mill." She shook her head. "Not a good time to be missing work, if you take my meaning."

"I'll be sure to pass that along."

"You do that," Mrs. Clark said. "And a word to your mother." She watched Tammy stand and brush off the seat of her pants. "Arlene says if Mirabelle is going to miss her wash and set, she could at least call the salon to say so." She patted her own freshly curled hair, then continued on her way.

The dull click of Mrs. Clark's heels against the sidewalk raised the heat in Tammy's face. Little wonder her mother held no fondness for this woman.

Tammy sighed and took up her backpack. She walked the crumbling driveway, past her father's car and around the chipped lawn jockey standing at the corner of the garage. When she arrived at the cement steps covered in green outdoor carpeting, she noticed something unusual. The front door of the house had been left ajar. A sliver of peach-coloured wall peeked out from inside.

Her guts liquefied as she climbed the front steps. She wanted to bolt, run back to Dean's house or somewhere beyond the Narrow Falls town limits and not come back. Instead, Tammy eased into the disarming quiet of the King house and closed the door behind her. She stepped out of her huarache sandals and allowed the backpack to slide from her shoulder to the floor.

She tiptoed along the collage of gap-toothed school photos hanging in the hallway until the wall ended, then peered into the living room. Her knees buckled at the sight of her parents waiting there with faces pale and drawn, as if they'd been notified of a death.

Her father's eyes refused to meet hers. Still wearing rumpled pajamas, he slouched in his recliner, reduced to half his normal size. Her mother sat bolt upright, dead centre of the sofa, resting her folded hands in the lap of her flowered housecoat. The coffee table in front of her was strewn with wads of used tissue. An open phone book, some paper, and a pen rested on the cushion next to her.

"Well?" Tammy's mother leveled a piercing glare. Her chin vibrated, and the cords stood out from her neck. "Who is he?" she shouted.

"Now, Mirabelle—" her father said.

"Lawrence," she snapped, and her husband sank farther into the upholstery. "I want the name of the little shit who did this to you!" Mirabelle's arms folded across her chest. "Where, pray tell, did these little soirees take place?"

Tammy's shoulders dropped, and tears rolled steadily down her face.

After a lengthy silence, Mirabelle said, "For a smart girl, you do stupid things." She blew her nose into a fresh handful of tissue.

Lawrence dragged the cuff of his pajama shirt across his eyes. "What about college in the fall?"

"I can defer my acceptance," Tammy answered.

"To when?" Mirabelle turned to Lawrence. "She thinks better days are coming." She swiveled back to Tammy. "You don't know what you've brought on yourself and this family, but you'll be finding out in a damned quick hurry. There aren't going to be any more *better* days.”

“I’ll get a job, then,” Tammy said.

Lawrence closed his eyes. “Where?”

“It’s not like when we were young,” Mirabelle said. “You can’t step out of high school and expect to land a job. The brickworks over at Brewster’s Gorge is gone. Shops downtown are closing left and right. You can’t count on the mill anymore. They aren’t going to be hiring when the pink slips start coming.”

“I’m sorry, Mom,” Tammy whispered.

“Well, how pregnant are you?” Mirabelle asked.

“A couple of months . . .”

“Another month, you’ll be popped out to here. Can you just hear me saying to the churchwomen, ‘Do you have any maternity dresses in the poor bin?’ Then they’ll ask, ‘Who might that be for?’ And I’ll tell them it’s for my unmarried honours student daughter who got herself knocked up and ruined the family.”

Every word was a bullet ricocheting off a wall.

“Maybe I could ask the women down at the salon,” Mirabelle continued. “Oh, my good God, won’t Arlene and the girls have fun with this one. It’ll be all over town, and when Eva finds out . . .” She rolled her eyes, “She’ll have all the bragging rights then. It will be *cousin Jessica this* and *cousin Jessica that.*”

Tammy broke down and sobbed. She’d become the dark horse in a race she never chose to be part of. Jessica would become the benchmark of perfection she’d failed to reach. Aunt Eva would surely lord Tammy’s failings over the King family in some mean-spirited fashion. Tammy held her breath to ward off the bile simmering at the back of her throat.

“The neighbours . . .” Lawrence rested his elbows on his knees and his face in his hands. He made no sound, but his shaking shoulders gave him away. The sight of him crying gutted her.

“Look at what you’ve done to your father!”

The crush of guilt equaled Tammy’s confusion as her eyes darted from the spark of satisfaction burning in her mother’s eyes to her father’s distress and back again. Her stomach wrung itself out like a wet towel, and her gorge rose. Tammy doubled over and vomited. A splatter of clear yellow bile shot onto the beige carpet. The springs of the recliner groaned. Lawrence's slippers crossed her field of vision as he escaped to the kitchen. Her upper body shook as she righted herself, and a strand of mucus stretched from her chin.

How could she feel worse than she had five minute earlier? She'd evaporated, been reduced to her lowest form. There she stood, eyes closed and her arms folded instinctively over her belly. The room fell silent except for the tick, tick, tick of the clock hanging on the wall behind her father's recliner.

"I suppose I'll be mopping up that mess too," her mother said. Tammy opened her eyes and found Mirabelle evaluating her from head to toe. Tammy's heart withered under her mother's cold stare.

"Mom, I'm—"

"Go clean yourself up." Mirabelle's head shook in disgust. Tammy turned away and headed for the stairs. When her hand reached for the banister, her mother called out. "Have you been to the doctor yet?"

"No."

"You'll see him this week." Mirabelle lifted her glasses from the bridge of her nose and wiped her eyes. Tammy fled up the stairs to escape before her mother could release the next arrow.

Late-afternoon sun shone through the bedroom window. Stale air hung above Tammy's face, and heat pressed against the walls. Her sleep was fitful at best. When the oven door hinges squawked from the kitchen below, Tammy's eyes sprang open, and she lifted her head from the pillow. According to her wristwatch, it was nearly five o'clock. Her stomach growled in response to the aroma of roasting meat wafting through the air grate.

When Tammy sat up and stretched her arms above her head, she became acutely aware of her own stench. She pulled the day-old shirt over her head and dropped it on the foot of her bed. On the way to her bureau, she paused to study her profile in the full-length mirror that hung on the back of her bedroom door. Her breasts ached. That was something new. She tilted her head to one side and passed her hands slowly over her belly. Puffy, she thought, or was she conjuring something that wasn't there yet? The notion that cells were multiplying and fashioning themselves into a new creature in there was altogether unbelievable. She turned away from the mirror in search of a fresh T-shirt and pair of clean cutoffs. Surely, tomorrow she would awake to find this had all been a dream.

The mouthwatering smell of frying potatoes and onions now floated up from the kitchen along with the worrisome hum of her parents' voices. What were they saying about her? She was caught between wanting to punish herself and protect herself. *Forewarned is forearmed,* she decided. Tammy pulled a pillow from the bed and lay down next to the heating grate. The floor creaked beneath her as she settled, and the voices stopped abruptly. She lay still, holding her breath, until they resumed.

"If Hoffman keeps nosing around, he's going to ruin things for all of us," her father said.

"A ministry vehicle was parked next to the library after lunch yesterday. Arlene saw two fellas collecting samples at Riverside Park."

"Vern Clark says they were down at Brewster's Gorge too."

"Next thing you know, there'll be more lawyers involved," her mother added. A lid clanged against a pot, then water dumped into the kitchen sink.

"The *Sentinel* published another one of Hoffman's letters this morning," her father said.

"Pitiful character. I've lived my entire life in Narrow Falls without as much as a sneeze. He's going to complain everyone right out of a job. If that mill closes . . ." More silence, then the clatter of silverware.

"A baby. I can't fathom it," her father said. His comment pierced Tammy's heart more deeply than any one of her mother's barbs. Worries dropped like pennies into the back of her mind. She needed to hear Dean's voice, even for a minute, before they called her downstairs for dinner.

Tammy grabbed the telephone from the hallway and carried it into her room, closing the door over the cord. She dialed Dean's number.

"Yup."

"It's me. Is everything okay?"

"He didn't show—" The line went dead.

Her bedroom door swung open. There, with the unplugged telephone cord dangling from her right hand, stood Mirabelle. She glowered at Tammy, then at the pillow lying next to the grate. Her shoulders drew back, and her eyebrows pressed together. "Dinner," she said.

Tammy's stomach dropped. She passed the telephone into her mother's waiting hands, then followed her along the hall and down the stairs. Tammy's eyes fixed on the collar of her mother's blouse and the stiffness of her neck. Mirabelle marched ahead, the telephone tucked beneath her arm like the spoils of war.

Lawrence left for work earlier than usual the next morning. Tammy waited for the sound of his car grinding out of the driveway before shoving change into her pockets and padding slowly down the stairs. She dropped her backpack at the front door and proceeded into the kitchen, peering sideways through a curtain of long hair.

Mirabelle sat at the kitchen table leaning over a folded newspaper, a pencil pressed to her lips. Without looking up, she asked, "Are your grades sliding?"

"No."

"Good." Mirabelle raised a teacup to her lips and studied the crossword. The cuckoo clock chirped from the living room. "Seven fifteen. You're ahead of schedule." Whether it was an observation or an accusation, Tammy couldn't be sure. A spoon and cereal bowl were set out for her on a placemat and, in the centre of the table, a box of Cornflakes, a plastic milk pitcher, and a bag of brown sugar.

"Exams start next week." Tammy shrugged. "Thought I'd find a quiet spot to review my notes." She concentrated on the tinkling sound of the first flakes hitting the bowl as she poured the cereal. Her mother scrutinized the two heaping spoons of brown sugar and generous dousing of milk she added next.

"Your lunch is in the fridge," Mirabelle said. "Same amount as always." She paused. "Eating for two is a myth."

A mouthful of cereal lay at the back of Tammy's tongue like wet paper. Although her stomach cried out for more, she laid her spoon against the inside of the bowl and pushed away from the table. She grabbed the brown paper lunch bag from the top shelf of the refrigerator, and when she closed the door, she noticed the telephone sitting on the kitchen counter, bound in its own cord.

"The phone company is sending a man around today. I've always wanted a line in the kitchen," her mother said.

Tammy concealed her dismay behind a veneer of feigned disinterest and continued to the hallway. She jimmied her lunch into the backpack. "Bye," she whispered.

"I'd tell you to behave, but it seems like a moot point," her mother said. And there it was—the parting jab. Tammy winced and closed the door gently behind her.

Within a few minutes of leaving the King house, Tammy had hustled past the street where the high school stood and headed south towards the stretch of century homes that eased visitors into the downtown district. With only two cars parked in front of the diner, Main Street was quiet and would remain so until vendors started trickling in to open their shops at nine o'clock.

She slipped into the phone booth on the street corner next to Patterson's Pharmacy, and dropped a quarter into the slot, then waited for the dial tone. Her fingers raced through Dean's telephone number. After one ring, he answered.

"Dean, it's me."

"Hey."

"What happened last night—with your dad?"

"I don't wanna talk about it." The sharpness of Dean's tone stung her. "What about you? How were your parents?" A cough rattled on the other end of the line.

"Pretty much as I expected, but worse," she said.

"Where are you?"

"Downtown. I'm walking back to school after we talk. No idea how I'm going to get through exams." She felt immediate guilt for mentioning something so insignificant.

"You'll do fine. You're the smartest person I know."

"People are going to figure out that I'm pregnant."

"Who gives a shit? Bunch of losers. They're just jealous because you're smart *and* pretty."

"Not for long. I'm going to get fat."

"I wish I could see that . . ." A prolonged silence stretched between them. "I've been talking to Doctor Gillespie. You don't have to worry about the baby."

"Why would I worry?" she asked above the sound of a passing car. She turned her back to the street and pressed a finger to her ear.

"I was thinking that what I got might be hereditary, passed down, you know. So I talked to the doctor. He threw a lot of numbers at me and said not to worry."

"Oh," Tammy said, a little breathless. It hadn't occurred to her to worry.

"Turns out it's more of an exposure thing."

His words filled her with unease. "I don't get it."

"My old man has been kicking up a fuss about pollution from the mill making people sick. Turns out, there's something to it."

"Glad you told me about that," she lied. Problems were mounding up, and she didn't need one more thing to worry about. Another car passed the booth, and a woman had arrived to unlock the rear entrance to the pharmacy. Tammy couldn't risk being seen. "Our time is almost up," she said, anxious to be on her way. "I only put a quarter in the phone."

"Call me again soon?" Dean said

"Okay."

"Tammy, you can do this. You're stronger than you know."

She certainly hoped so.

By three o'clock, Tammy could only think about escaping the drone of the teacher's voice. She'd rather be sleeping than reviewing exam schedules and calculus notes. All around her, students shifted in their seats, eyeing the clock from behind opened books. The dismissal buzzer finally sounded, and they all surged into the hallway.

The current of people carried her past the home economics kitchen and the tantalizing scent of baked goods. When her stomach growled loudly, she imagined neon signs above her head flashing, *Pregnant. Pregnant. Pregnant.*

With books hugged to her chest and her head hung low, she maneuvered to the edge of the crowd and stopped at her locker. Two girls from homeroom stood in front of an opened locker next to hers.

"After grad in July, I'm outta here," the taller girl said.

"Lucky," her friend replied. "I'm stuck here in town."

Tammy spun the dial on her combination lock and tugged it open. Both girls turned to face her.

"What about you?" the first girl asked.

"I'm not sure," Tammy answered. Heat rose in her face. She leaned into her locker and continued to fill her backpack with textbooks.

"I heard you got accepted at three colleges," the second girl said.

Tammy gripped her locker door and stared the girl straight in the eye. "I'm keeping my options open."

Both girls nodded as if they understood completely. Tammy clicked the lock shut, then with eyes downcast, she grabbed her backpack and strode towards the foyer. As she passed the gymnasium, the custodian hauled a skid of chairs from beneath the stage. Rows of examination desks would span the gym floor in a few days. Her arms folded across her belly. She couldn't think about exams now.

Tammy shouldered the school door open and barreled past couples lounging under trees and smokers gathering along the curb. It wasn't until she reached a quiet side street east of the school property that her pace slowed. After she turned north at the next corner, Tammy sucked in her breath.

The King family car ambushed her from the opposite side of the street. From beyond its expansive grill and chipped windshield, Mirabelle leaned against the steering wheel and flashed the headlights. Tammy cast a look over her shoulder, then scooted across the street. As she neared the car, her mother cranked the window down. "You have an appointment," she said flatly. "Get in."

The passenger side door whined when Tammy pried it open. She climbed in and slid her mother's purse to the centre of the front seat as the car chugged away from the curb.

"It's warm in here," Tammy said, picking at a hangnail.

"Well, don't roll your window down. The wind will muss my hair."

The left turn signal blinked on the dash. "Doctor Gillespie's?" Tammy asked.

"At four o'clock," Mirabelle replied. "You're having your blood iron checked, if anyone asks." Six blocks later, she parked the car across from the phone booth Tammy had used to call Dean that morning. Mirabelle dropped the car keys into her purse before checking her hair in the rearview mirror.

Tammy wished she were anywhere but here. Hunger twisted the inside of her stomach—or was it nerves? She couldn't be sure.

Mirabelle's hands suddenly dropped to her lap. "Floyd Hoffman." She spat the name out like sour milk in response to Dean's father crossing the street ahead of them. "I ought to start the car up and run him over."

Too close for comfort, Tammy thought. Her heart pounded against her T-shirt. "Who is that?" she asked, hoping to bait her mother.

"A know-it-all thorn in my side." Mirabelle shook her head. "Thinks he's better than the rest of us. Been that way since we were kids in school."

The moment Mr. Hoffman disappeared from view, Mirabelle left the car and began walking towards the pharmacy. Tammy followed along, staring at the sidewalk until she caught up to her mother. While they waited to cross Main Street, she stole a discreet glance in the direction he'd been travelling. Her breath caught in her throat.

Mr. Hoffman was looking down at her from the top step of Patterson's Pharmacy. Their eyes met for only a second before she spun away and darted across the street to the doctor's office.

Dr. Gillespie's waiting room was modest. Louvered window blinds muted the afternoon sun, and if not for the green leather upholstery, the chairs would have disappeared against the dark wood paneling. Tammy slumped in a corner chair. Mirabelle stared straight ahead and periodically dabbed at her eyes with a tissue.

The creaking of an office chair preceded quiet footsteps on the other side of the wall. Seconds later, Dr. Gillespie opened the door to his inner office and leaned into the waiting room. "Tammy?"

She breathed deeply and rose to her feet. Mirabelle gathered her purse, expecting to follow, but the doctor raised a finger to stop her.

"Just Tammy," he said.

Mirabelle's face reddened as she dropped back in her seat. Dr. Gillespie's expression remained pleasant. The arm of his white coat extended in welcome as Tammy brushed past him. After he followed her into his office, the door gently clicked shut behind them.

Once settled in the chair on the opposite side of the doctor's desk, Tammy quelled her nerves by focusing on the motion of his hands as they turned pages in her medical file. Upon finishing, he picked up a pen and smiled with a fatherly warmth that put her at ease.

"Your mother tells me that you've found yourself in the family way, Tammy."

"Yes, sir." Her shoulders drew up to her ears.

"Let's start off easy with a few questions."

"Okay," Tammy said quietly.

"First day of last period."

"April second."

He removed a device from his desk drawer, two plastic wheels that rotated on a brass pin. He turned them until he appeared satisfied and said, "The baby is due January sixth." Tears rained down Tammy's face. "Let's just make sure you're both fine," he added. "We don't have to figure everything out today."

"I know," she said, reaching for a tissue box at the corner of his desk.

Doctor Gillespie stepped into the adjoining examination room and returned with a hospital gown which he laid across her knee. She looked up at him in surprise.

"Put this on in the other room, Tammy. Remove your panties. The brassiere can stay on. Sit on the table when you're ready. I'll give you a minute to get settled before I come back." He paused in the doorway. "Do you have any questions before your mother joins us?"

"Do I have to identify the baby's father? Legally, I mean."

When the doctor shook his head, a seed of courage began to germinate.

5.

Twenty minutes of standing idle on the pharmacy steps left Floyd agitated. He tugged at the door one last time. Still locked. Never would have happened in the old days, when Mr. Patterson ran things.

Floyd knew he should go straight home as he'd promised Dean. The moment his feet touched down on the sidewalk, he should have marched north to his house. He should have swung the front gate open, climbed the porch steps, and took to the kitchen. He could have made tea for Dean, prepared a meal, and initiated some kind of meaningful conversation. Yet there he was, trekking south towards the library with his hands shoved in his pockets and a canvas bag full of notebooks slung over one shoulder.

A young woman brushed past Floyd. Her scarlet dress reminded him of something Bonnie might have worn. Was Bonnie watching him now? He pictured the tilt of her head and her furrowed brow. *Buckle down*, her expression said. *This foolishness has gone on long enough.*

Dean was a brittle trapdoor that Floyd feared testing with the full weight of the truth. How could he appease his son's curiosity without dishonouring Bonnie's dying request? He needed somewhere quiet to think his words through.

An hour spent in a study carrel was nearly as good as a stiff drink. A little calming research, then he'd double back to the pharmacy to pick up Dean's medicine and head home. Hopefully, he'd be spared from bumping into Mirabelle King again. She and her friends had made his life a misery when they were kids. Little wonder that her daughter resembled a scared mouse. He couldn't pin it down, but something about that girl unnerved him. On his way across Water Street, he pushed thoughts of her from his mind. After all, she wasn't his problem.

The library visit did nothing to relax Floyd. To the contrary, it deepened his misery. He'd combed through his notebooks without knowing what he hoped to find. Maybe an unexplored avenue would leap off the pages. The silver bullet must be hiding among the lines of blue ink, something that vilified McLelland's with one hundred percent certainty.

Floyd pulled the newest notebook from his bag and turned to the news clipping he'd slipped between the pages. Just the kind of thing to reignite his determination should it falter.

Narrow Falls Sentinel

June 12, 1981

Free Swimming at the Brookman Public Pool

NARROW FALLS – Families can enjoy a free swim at the Brookman Public Pool from 1:00 p.m. to 4:00 p.m. on Saturday June 27 and Sunday June 28. Popsicles will be provided to all children twelve and under. The event is sponsored by Mrs. Rose Brookman.

Mrs. Brookman continues the philanthropic legacy of her late husband and past president of McLelland Pulp and Paper, Gene Brookman. "My husband initiated several community projects," she said, "but closest to his heart were the ones that brought joy to children."

Additional free swim dates are set for July 25 and 26, August 22 and 23. The Brookman Public Pool is located at 23 Centre Street. Visitors will be asked to show proof of residency.

"Oh, come on," Floyd mumbled, rubbing the back of his neck. A rich stakeholder throwing money at a problem to protect her investment. People like her didn't care one iota about the truth. Years of being her son-in-law had taught him that.

His forearms rested inside the carrel. It must be close to five o'clock by now. He'd go home soon. But not yet. Dean would be chomping at the bit to talk about Bonnie, but Floyd couldn't see his way through that minefield. More time to think. That's what he needed. The hour had passed too quickly.

He tried to focus his mind on going home, but Mirabelle King and her daughter kept pushing their way into his thoughts. The years had certainly caught up with Mirabelle. Her face had settled in a constant grimace, as if she'd just smelled something rancid. For a few seconds on the street, the girl had locked eyes with him. Her jaw had dropped, and she'd turned away sharply as if she'd been caught at something. No doubt she'd heard gossip about him, especially now with all the strife concerning the mill.

But he couldn't imagine how his presence could generate such alarm in someone he'd never met. Maybe Dean was right. He was horrible. Floyd raked a hand through his hair and squeezed his eyes shut. Forget the library. He needed a drink.

At Tony's Pub, the after-work crowd had begun drifting in from the mill. Men congregated around bar stools and tables closest to the front door and the window overlooking the street. Country music spilled from a radio above the bar, and thick clouds of cigarette smoke blanketed the room. As Floyd wove through the gauntlet of patrons, several men continued in conversation, but others paused to watch him pass by.

"Asshole," someone shouted.

The pub grew quiet. Floyd's eyes remained fixed on the floor until he reached his mark, a worn stool at the farthest end of the bar. He dropped onto the seat and placed his canvas bag on the adjacent stool. His shoulders rolled in on themselves until he hunched over the bar like a mountain slide of misery.

One by one, the men turned back to their conversations.

Floyd knew each one of them by name. They'd all been children together, though never friends. In grade school, the other boys had flashed decoder rings and collected comic books while Floyd uncovered the quiet treasures found on bookshelves.

Instead of pursuing hockey and girls, he'd directed his attention to reading and conversations with Vic Patterson about politics and figures of historical significance.

Lawrence King's reflection appeared in the mirror above the bar. What were the odds? The whole clan was out today. Mirabelle's husband sat alone at a booth against the far wall, nursing a beer. Looked like he had his own problems.

Floyd knew Lawrence, but not well. They saw each other periodically at the pub after the day shift let out at the mill. Quiet guy, kept to himself. Although not originally from here, he'd managed to infiltrate the native Narrow Falls crowd. Marrying one of the local girls had helped.

Tony Monteiro responded immediately to the tapping of Floyd's fingertips on the bar. He'd been pouring drinks in Narrow Falls for over twenty years, and in that time, he'd mastered the shorthand of nods and winks that minimized the need for speech. Tony set a glass in front of Floyd and poured two fingers of whiskey. He wiped his hands on the front of his apron while he studied Floyd.

"Don't mind those goons. Some guys got axed from the mill today," Tony said. His eyes cut to the growing crowd at the other end of the bar. "You should think about going home."

Floyd answered with a shrug.

"Grab a shower. Eat something."

Floyd's head tipped back with a jerk, then he set the empty glass on the counter. "Again," he said.

Tony placed both hands on the bar and leaned towards Floyd. "Go home and see the kid."

"What's the point?"

"He's still here. He could beat this thing," said Tony

"It's unlikely—given the history."

"Well, go home and just be there. Talk to him."

"He hates me." Floyd's voice caught in his throat.

"Maybe, but he *needs* you," Tony said.

Floyd sank deeper into himself. The weight of that kind of needing was too heavy to bear. Again. He downed another mouthful of whiskey before turning his gaze to a fixed point beyond Tony's shoulder.

"Jesus, Tony, you should see him. He's a shadow. Sleeps all the time. It's going just how it did for his mother." Another swallow and Floyd returned the glass to the ring of condensation on the bar. "I don't know. Maybe if I get him to a doctor in Toronto, we *could* turn this thing around." He paused to swirl melting ice around the bottom of the glass.

"Money talks," Tony offered as he shined up a glass.

"I've got money. It's influence I'm short on."

The bartender sighed.

Floyd traced a finger along the edge of his coaster. "Doc Gillespie doesn't have the clout to get Dean to the head of anyone's lineup. I could call Dean's grandmother. She knows people."

At the sound of breaking glass, Tony dashed for the broom and dustpan. A man wearing grey coveralls sat in a cluster of onlookers, his elbows on the bar and his face in his hands. Two friends consoled him with pats to the back and a fresh drink.

"What the hell are you looking at?" A red-faced youth took an uneven step towards Floyd.

The best response was no response, Floyd decided. He held his glass with two hands and studied a group shot of last year's softball team hanging next to the mirror.

"Hey, I'm talkin' to you, Hoffman."

Heads turned in Floyd's direction.

"A bunch of the fellas went home with pink slips today. If we lose the newsprint contract with the Yanks, there's more of us that'll be let go." Murmurs of ascent rose from the crowd. "So just you keep your mouth shut."

"No more letters to the Sentinel," a new voice called out.

"Yeah, push off, *Kraut*," the first man shouted.

The crowd cheered and then turned back to their beers.

Tony finished wiping a glass and flipped the towel over his shoulder. He cast a worried look at Floyd and shook his head. With a shaky hand, Floyd nudged his empty glass across the counter. He held up his index finger. When Tony raised a questioning brow, Floyd said, "Just pour."

Floyd waited for the scrum of men to thin before crossing the room to leave. Relief and sadness overcame him when he stepped into the cool evening air. Across the street, a small group of high school kids had gathered at the riverside park. A trio of girls occupied the bench while the boys tossed rocks into the current and smoked cigarettes.

Dean should be among those boys. He should be swaggering with confidence in a body that hadn't betrayed him. Floyd leaned his back against the brick face of the pub and worked to gather his emotions.

One of the girls separated from the bench. She skipped over to the riverbank and threw her arms around the neck of a boy dressed in a sleeveless shirt. She kissed him on the mouth, then scampered back to rejoin her friends on the bench.

Floyd reached into his back pocket for a folded handkerchief, but instead pulled out a wrinkled square of paper. Dean's prescription. Floyd wiped his eyes with the heel of one hand and set off to Patterson's Pharmacy. Good thing he wasn't forgetting to pick up the medication. For the past two nights, he'd shown up without it. Dean had been furious the first time Floyd forgot—and rightfully so. After the second offense, the boy punished him with silence.

Things needed smoothing over. Floyd considered buying a package of the butterscotch candies Dean liked so much. He'd leave them on the kitchen table, a peace offering of sorts—before all the talking. It may be prudent to open with a story from his own childhood before easing into deeper waters. What trouble could come from telling about his friendship with Vic Patterson? Other people had found redeemable qualities in Floyd. Why couldn't Dean do the same?

Floyd still missed the old man. Vic was the third and last generation of Pattersons to operate the store. The first time they met, Floyd had been a shy boy hiding in the folds of his mother's coat while she paid for a tube of Camphor Ice. After she'd put her wallet away, Vic had taken a butterscotch swirl from a glass jar next to the cash register and passed it across the counter. Just as Floyd had reached for the candy, his mother slapped his hand away. *"Wir kriegen sarnichts für freii!"* She'd deposited an extra handful of change on the counter. With a smile, Vic had told her that candies were half price that day and had pressed a second butterscotch swirl into Floyd's palm.

Now, forty years later, Floyd approached the pharmacy stairs wondering why he couldn't apply the same diplomacy where Dean was concerned. That settled it. He'd pick up the pills and some candy and figure the rest out on the walk home.

From the bottom step, a *closed* sign was visible inside the front window. Floyd's jaw dropped. He raced to the top step and pulled on the door handle. Another punch to the gut. It was locked. "Oh no," he moaned. Banging on the glass, he shouted, "Open up, damn it. It's before seven."

But then he pressed his forehead against the glass and glimpsed a clock on the back wall. He was five minutes late.

October 1953

The hush left by the absence of kin was crushing in comparison to the silence Floyd was accustomed to. Evenings were the worst. Minutes crept by like hours. He'd often break the monotony of isolation by venturing to Vic Patterson's place. The old man would answer the door after the first knock and usher him into the dining room. The chessboard would already be set up on the table, and next to it, two mugs and a pastry box from the diner.

"How are you set for money?" Vic asked one evening.

"All right, I guess," Floyd said. He toyed with a chess piece and avoided looking Vic in the eye. Actually, he'd just enough savings to cover the cost of food and utilities for two months.

Vic spooned sugar into his mug of tea. "The mill is hiring. I read about it in the paper. You interested in that?"

"Thanks, but I don't think so, Mr. Patterson." The young men who'd tormented Floyd through high school had been working at the mill since July. They'd make his life a misery.

"You know, I could put a word in for you over at the post office. Martin Randall is an old friend of the family. He does the hiring over there."

A slow smile spread across Floyd's face. The post office was peaceful, like the library, and its history appealed to him.

His job interview was scheduled two weeks later. Floyd sat ramrod straight waiting for Mr. Randall to review his application for a mail carrier job. The office was disproportionately small in comparison to the man's height. Although toppling binders lined the shelves, his desk top lay bare except for an ashtray, two blue pens, and Floyd's paperwork.

"So why the post office?" Mr. Randall asked. He rocked back in his office chair and clasped his hands over the expanse of his sweater vest.

"It's a noble pursuit, sir. I'd like to be part of it." Floyd's earnest reply surprised the older man, and he snorted aloud.

"A noble pursuit, eh?"

"The earliest known postal service dates back to the ancient Romans. Wars have been won or lost based on the delivery of a message."

Mr. Randall laid his glasses on his desk.

"Benjamin Franklin served on Canadian soil as Deputy Postmaster of the British Post Office."

"Son, the job is yours. See my clerk on your way out. There are some details that need sorting out—paperwork and such." He reached across the desk to shake Floyd's hand.

"Thank you, sir."

"Don't thank me yet," Mr. Randall said. "We'll see how *noble* you feel when you're freezing your arse off in January."

Floyd shrugged, and his face reddened. He'd just turned to leave when Mr. Randall called after him.

"How in God's name did you know all of that—about the Romans and Benjamin Franklin?"

"I picked it up here and there," Floyd said.

By Christmas, he'd begun door-to-door mail delivery. Homeowners attempted small talk, like, "Nice weather we're having," or "More bad news, huh?" They quickly gave up when all they could levy was a nod.

Some days came and went with little more than a complete sentence passing between Floyd and another living soul.

6.

Something was off. Floyd knew it the moment he pushed the front gate open and glimpsed Dean through the screen door. Trepidation weighed on him as he climbed the porch steps.

"Do you have my pills?" Dean asked when the door swung open. He squared off against Floyd with his chin thrust forward and his eyes brimming with tears.

Floyd was gutted. His head swam, recalling the chain of events that had thrown him off track. To explain that he'd remembered the prescription and then forgotten it until the last minute wouldn't help the situation.

So he shrugged.

"Again? Are you fucking kidding me?" Dean's voice rasped. He hinged forward to cough with one arm wrapped around his ribs and the other bracing the weight of his upper body against a bent knee. He glowered at Floyd as he righted himself.

Floyd studied his son's face and tried to find pieces of himself there, but to no avail. Everything about Dean was turning sharp—the ridge above his brow, his cheekbones, and the collarbone that showed when the neck of his T-shirt was pulled askew. Even his shoulders had become corners.

"I took my last pill at noon," Dean said.

"Tomorrow morning, I'll call Patterson's and arrange for delivery to the house," Floyd offered. The insufficiency of the words struck him once they'd left his mouth, so he reached into his pocket. "Here," he said, holding out a fistful of change and some crumpled bills. "This should cover it."

Dean huffed and rolled his eyes. Tears dripped from his chin while Floyd stood, rooted to the floor. After a lengthy silence, Dean wiped his eyes on the sleeve of his shirt and headed for the living room.

The reprieve pleased Floyd until he considered the inappropriateness of his relief. Shame regressed him into a small boy, circling his mother's skirt in hope of absolution. The withholding of words was an heirloom that passed through the hands of every Hoffman.

Floyd set a kettle of water on the stove to boil. His mother's cast-iron fry pan warmed on a second burner while he searched the refrigerator. He pulled out a carton of eggs, a bag of dark rye bread, and some boiled potatoes.

"Have you eaten?" he called out halfheartedly.

There was no response.

Floyd dropped a pat of butter into the centre of the pan and set about dicing the potatoes in the palm of his hand. After he tumbled the cubes into the bubbling grease, a hiss erupted and quickly settled into a low, steady crackling. He'd begun pushing the potatoes around the pan with a spatula when Dean appeared at the kitchen door with both arms folded across his chest.

"Hungry?" Floyd asked.

Dean gave a curt nod.

Floyd wiped his hands on a tea towel, then stepped over to the table and turned a chair towards the stove. He looked at Dean and patted the backrest, as if coaxing a small bird to eat from his hand.

Dean's gaze slid to the floor, then he tipped away from the doorframe, shuffled across the linoleum, and plopped onto the seat. Above the sagging neckline of his shirt, vertebrae pushed against his skin like a row of shrink-wrapped marbles.

"Comfortable?" Floyd asked quietly.

Dean shrugged.

Floyd returned to the stove. He shifted the potatoes to the edge of the pan and added another dollop of butter. The crescendo of popping grease filled the vacuum of silence in the kitchen.

"How many eggs?" Floyd asked.

Dean stared at his feet and held up two fingers. Floyd cracked four eggs, one after the other, and let them drop into the pan.

"When's the last time you were outside?" Floyd asked.

"I dunno."

"We could take a couple of chairs out back and eat dinner in the yard."

The boy scowled.

"Like we used to when your mother was here," Floyd added.

Dean's brows pinched together as his eyes narrowed. "All right."

Floyd carried a chair outside and set it in a patch of fading sunlight at the centre of the yard. As he returned to the kitchen, he met Dean carrying a second chair down the hall.

"You all right there?" Floyd asked, backing up to hold the door open.

"I'm fine—Dad."

Floyd stopped short and cocked his head. He hadn't called him *Dad* for months. Dean looked equally surprised that the word had slipped from his mouth, similar to when he was eleven and said "shit" in Floyd's presence for the first time. The curtain of bravado had parted to reveal a boy filled with uncertainty.

Dean edged past him and stepped barefoot into the grass. Although the boiling kettle whistled from the stove, Floyd remained at the back door until Dean set the chair down. When he began turning towards the house, Floyd hastily retreated along the hallway.

From a low kitchen cupboard, he retrieved Bonnie's favourite tray, the one with an embossed rose pattern on the handles. Then he mounded two plates with buttered toast, fried eggs, and potatoes, and placed them on the tray along with cutlery. He shook a generous amount of ketchup onto Dean's plate. After wedging a tumbler of milk and a mug of hot tea between the plates, he hoisted the tray and carried it outside.

As he squeezed through the door, Dean lifted out of his chair. "I'll get us something to use as a table."

"Stay put," Floyd insisted. "I'll do it." He bent over and set the tray on the ground, then disappeared around the side of the house. A moment later, he returned with an empty garbage can, which he flipped upside down. Floyd then set the tray on the bottom of the can and declared, *"Eine tabell!"*

"What's this about?" Dean held a piece of paper between his fingers. He thrust it towards Floyd. *Themselves* was printed in the centre in shaky letters. "It fell from your pocket when you put the tray down."

"It's something your mother wrote." Floyd took the paper from Dean and returned it to his pocket. "I carry it everywhere, like a lucky penny."

"Why that word?"

"It's from a Walt Whitman poem called 'Perfection.'"

"So?"

"Your mother loved Whitman. We used to read to each other from his book, *Leaves of Grass.* 'Perfection' was her favourite."

"That's so cheesy," Dean said. A smile tugged at the corner of his mouth.

"It made her happy," Floyd replied. "'Only themselves understand themselves and the like of themselves, as souls only understand souls.'"

"Huh," Dean said. He reached for his dinner plate and rested it on his knees. "Do you still have that book?"

"Oh yes."

"Where is it?" Dean asked as he speared a chunk of potato and dragged it through the ketchup.

"Bottom shelf of your mother's nightstand."

"Cool."

For a moment, Floyd wasn't disappointed in himself.

Sleep was a stranger that night. The intermittent rasp of Dean's coughing and the image of pill bottles waiting in a plastic tray pervaded Floyd's thoughts. How could he have been so scattered? He pictured a taxi driver pounding at the front door with the pharmacy bag in one hand, and Dean answering the door, groggy and squinting into the morning sun. It wasn't right. Floyd rolled over and laid an arm across Bonnie's side of the bed.

Something had changed between himself and Dean that afternoon. He'd seen the flicker of warmth in the boy's eyes when he'd spoken about Bonnie. A window of opportunity had opened, and Floyd needed to climb through it.

Floyd pressed his lips against his fingertips and laid the kiss on Bonnie's pillow. He reached for his glasses on the nightstand, then folded the covers back and went downstairs to the kitchen. He switched the light on above the stove and collected a flashlight from the pantry, along with a set of silver keys and a jug of distilled water. He snugged the belt of his housecoat and went outside to unlock the shed.

On his first trip back to the porch, he lugged the dead car battery he'd been storing under his workbench for the past few years, and on the second, he carried a charger and a long extension cord. He removed a rubber stopper from the top of the battery and poured the water inside. After hooking the charger cables to the proper battery terminals, he connected the whole affair to the extension cord, which he then ran beneath the front door and plugged into an outlet in the living room.

Floyd stood at the front door, smiling at the loud hum on his porch. His plan was set in motion. He'd charge the battery overnight, and tomorrow he'd be the perfect father—or at least act the part.

Dean scuffed into the kitchen the next morning, yawning and scratching his head. Damp ringlets coiled against his forehead, and pillowcase folds were imprinted on his cheek. He bristled when he saw Floyd leafing through the newspaper at the kitchen table.

"It's past nine. Shouldn't you be at work?"

"I called in this morning," Floyd answered.

"Playing hooky?" Dean's upper lip curled. He opened the refrigerator and rested an arm on top of the door while he surveyed its contents.

A sick feeling settled in Floyd's belly. This was all wrong.

"There's never anything to eat," Dean said. Condiment jars clinked against each other when he closed the refrigerator door. His face suddenly filled with concern. "Are you sick? Is that why you're home?"

"No," Floyd replied.

Dean closed his eyes and sighed. "Then what's up?"

Floyd strove to evenly modulate his voice. "I thought we could spend the day together."

"Together?" Dean repeated slowly.

"We could take a car ride out to the gorge."

Dean's mouth fell open, and his eyes widened. "But you haven't taken the car out for years. What about the battery?"

"Charged and waiting. We just have to pop the backseat and hook everything up." Floyd shut his mouth tightly for fear his bottom lip would tremble or that he'd scare Dean off by saying something horribly wrong, like, "I love you," or "Don't leave me, you're all I have left in the world."

"Can I drive on the back roads?"

Floyd nodded.

"Can we talk about Mom?"

"I think we should."

"Yes!" Dean fist-pumped the air. "Let me get some pants." Two steps into the hall, he wheeled back and leveled an index finger at Floyd.

"My pills."

"We'll swing downtown to pick up your pills and some takeout on our way to the gorge."

Floyd listened for the dull clunk of the latch closing on Dean's bedroom door, then he sprang into action.

An hour later, Floyd was waiting at the back of the pharmacy beneath a dangling cardboard cutout of a sun wearing dark glasses. The artificial cheeriness amid the chrome and glass surroundings made his head ache. Remnants from the original apothecary sat on display in the front window for the benefit of the old-timers. Except for those few rescued items, all signs of Vic Patterson's existence had been erased. Perhaps this was what Floyd disliked most of all.

In the pharmacy of his childhood, a bank of small oak drawers had covered the lower half of the south wall from the end of Vic's service counter to the dispensary. On the front of each drawer, a small metal bracket had held a label. *Aaron-Adams,*

Adrien-Afton, Agent-Ailsworth. It was orderly, factual, and reassuring. Floyd could understand lives filed on index cards.

"Will there be anything else, sir?" A young woman smiled at Floyd from behind the counter. She wore a white polyester jacket with a Patterson's Pharmacy crest stitched on the chest. Floyd presented two rolls of butterscotch candies along with a pair of mirrored sunglasses. She held Dean's medication in a plastic bag and keyed the new items into the cash register. When Floyd passed the exact change into her palm, his fingers brushed against her skin. He pulled his hand away as though he'd been burned. The woman's cheeks reddened when she wished him a good day.

Floyd walked to the front of the store and paused a few feet from the glass door to look out to where his car sat in front of the building. Dean rested in the passenger seat, drumming to the beat of the radio, his hands alternating between his knees and the dashboard. He bobbed to the music, happily distracted, like any other boy his age.

Nietzsche was right, Floyd thought. *God is dead.* The throne was empty, and no one's hand was guiding this earthly farce. What other explanation could there be for sons predeceasing their fathers? He wiped his eyes with the back of his hand and walked outside.

Music booming from inside the Volkswagen garnered a disapproving look from a woman crossing the sidewalk. "Kids, huh?" she said, rolling her eyes as she clipped past Floyd.

He grimaced as he stepped next to the passenger's side door and tapped on the glass. Dean lowered the radio volume and cranked the window down. After Floyd handed the bag through the opening, Dean rifled through its contents and pulled out the sunglasses. He looked up at Floyd with uncertainty.

"It's a sunny day," Floyd said with a shrug.

"I have no water . . . for the pills," Dean said.

"I'm going to run up to the diner for some food. You want some orange juice?"

"Apple."

"You can come with me," Floyd ventured.

"I'll wait here."

"There's a southwest wind today, so the mill is blowing this way. Keep the window rolled—" Floyd struggled to look unaffected when the music volume shot up again. While Dean raised the window, Floyd stared across the roof of the car. Maybe spending the day together was a mistake, but he would at least make the effort of going through the motions. He turned towards the diner and started walking.

The *Sentinel* had run an article that morning, "Another Failing Grade for McLelland Pulp and Paper." They'd quoted from one of Floyd's recent letters to the editor. *We should be able to trust that the air we breathe won't bring about our death.* The mill's wet scrubbers repeatedly malfunctioned, allowing the main boiler to spew contaminants into the air. R.J. McLelland stood by his claim that the problem was fixed, but all a person needed was a nose and a walk outside to smell the truth. The odour of rotten eggs laced with a faint note of chlorine regularly wafted through the downtown area. This morning was no exception.

Floyd took shallow breaths and increased his pace. By the time he stepped into the diner, the morning rush had ended. There were two women sitting at a table next to the plate-glass window. One held a small child in her lap. Its head rested against her chest while she drank coffee and listened to her friend. An older child, a boy, maybe four years old, knelt on a chair with his chin perched on the backrest. He studied Floyd unabashedly, then turned back to the table to reach for a slice of toast.

The waitress bustled past Floyd carrying a tray of egg-crusted plates and coffee-stained mugs.

"Morning, Floyd. I'll see if your order's ready," she said and disappeared into the kitchen.

He puzzled over how she knew his name. He did not know hers. Two old men occupied vinyl stools at the far end of the service counter. One lowered his newspaper and glanced at Floyd, then elbowed his friend. With a stubby finger, he pointed to the page he'd been reading, then their bland faces turned towards Floyd.

"Nice day," the first man called out. His words sounded more like a question than a statement.

"Yes," Floyd said as he fumbled for his wallet.

The waitress burst through the kitchen doors with a brown paper bag in each hand. "Anything else?" she asked.

"Apple juice," Floyd answered, staring at the lineup of earrings along the outer edge of her right ear.

She took a bottle from an upright cooler and tucked it inside one of the bags.

"Eighteen even," she said cheerily. She watched Floyd fish through his wallet for exact change. "You ordered breakfast and lunch. You must be going on an adventure today."

"Yes," Floyd replied. He deposited payment next to the register.

The waitress frowned and issued the standard line, "Have a good day, sir."

Floyd kept his head down and pushed his wallet into his pants pocket. He exited the diner, cradling a bag in each arm.

His anxiety flared as he neared the car. The sight of Dean's rigid profile through the passenger side window turned Floyd's hands clammy. To speak or not to speak. Here he was, broiled in uncertainty and fearful of making a misstep, just as he'd been twenty years earlier when he first saw Bonnie. He opened the car door.

"Hey," he said to Dean as he set the bags on the backseat of the Volkswagen. He slid into the driver's seat and pulled the door closed. The warm air inside the car mixed with the rising smell of grease and onions.

Dean's head leaned against the backrest. The mirrored sunglasses made it impossible to know if he was awake or sleeping.

"Have I ever told you how I met your mother?" Floyd asked.

Dean's face rolled towards him.

Floyd saw his opportunity and seized it.

June 1961

Floyd's days settled into an uneventful pattern of events, all contained within a ten-mile radius of his home. Months passed, and then years, without deviation. The catalyst for change arrived one June afternoon in the form of a young woman. She sat dead centre of the top step at Patterson's Pharmacy, absorbed by the book that lay open on her lap. As Floyd approached, he drew a stack of elastic-bound letters from his mailbag and tapped them against his leg as he whistled a few bars of Brahms. Instead of moving aside as he expected, the young woman remained unwavering in her disregard.

Perspiration collected on Floyd's upper lip, and his heart fluttered with an odd mix of irritation and curiosity. Had he not been entrusted to deliver Vic's mail, he might have willed himself to look away and walk past the three steps leading up to the pharmacy door. Floyd sucked in his breath and pushed the canvas mailbag behind his hip so he might pass through the narrow gap left between the woman's shoulder and the adjacent handrail. He stole discreet glances as he scaled the first step and the next. Slim ankles showed below the hem of her dress. Her skin was tanned. At the top step, he cautiously edged around her and noted her left hand resting lightly on the open pages of the book. No engagement ring.

"Excuse me, miss, you're blocking the door," he wanted to say, but his throat held the words captive. Instead, Floyd contorted himself and squeezed through the space she'd left him.

Once inside, he set the letters next to the till and rested his hands on the edge of the oak counter. Vic stood in front of the dispensary, engaged in sombre conversation with a customer. Floyd dried his palms on the dark fabric of his pant legs and studied the sweaty handprints left behind on the wood. He couldn't reconcile his desire to know more about the strange woman against his natural inclination to avoid her. What if she looked up at him? What if she didn't?

Floyd turned back to the door. Two strides separated them now. She wore her black hair in an orderly fashion, smoothed behind her ears and secured against the nape of her neck.

He pressed outdoors and craned forward to see what she was reading. As he stepped past her, a sound crossed the edge of his awareness. *Thunk. Thunk. Thunk.* At first, he perceived it to be far away and disconnected from any action on his part. But then he saw the cola bottle, half-full, rolling onto the sidewalk at the bottom of the wooden steps. He'd kicked her drink. A trail of cola bled across the hem of her dress and dotted her ankle.

The young woman looked up at Floyd. It was the moment he both dreaded and yearned for. Her eyes were sky blue. Not the watery blue of a temperate day, but the intense cerulean blue he'd only seen in library books.

Floyd's mind scrambled to compose the optimal response. He needed to deliver an eloquent apology using just the right number of words. Too many may sound overdone; too few could seem dismissive.

"I would like to replace your soda," he finally offered.

"That is very kind but totally unnecessary. I'm not really thirsty. Just filling time while I wait for someone."

Floyd's shoulders dropped. He followed her gaze to a mature couple emerging from the lawyer's office on the other side of the street. The gentleman tucked some folders under his arm and buttoned his suit jacket. He hadn't noticed Floyd yet. His wife had. Her eyes measured him as she drew a pair of white gloves from the handbag draped over her wrist. She lifted her chin and called, "Darling!"

"Duty calls," the young woman said, rising to her feet. "Mother is dragging us off to some dreadful event." In a blink, she was standing on the sidewalk, looking up at him. "Floyd." She pronounced each letter like she was tasting it.

It took a moment for him to realize that she'd read his name from the embroidered patch above his breast pocket. When he didn't ask for her name in return, she simply offered it.

"Bonnie Brookman from Toronto. Pleased to meet you."

She laughed and joined her parents. After she slipped into the space between them, her father's pinstriped sleeve stretched across her narrow back to usher her down the street.

As the Brookmans walked away, Floyd hoped for some sign of interest from Bonnie. She did not look back over her shoulder for a last glance at him—but her mother did.

For two weeks after Floyd first met Bonnie, she returned to the pharmacy steps with a book in hand. He arrived to find her there at two o'clock sharp each day. While passing her on the stairs, he'd smiled shyly, but nothing more. How could a girl so beautiful be interested in him?

On Monday of the third week, Floyd stood at the bottom of the empty steps and checked his watch. He looked up and down the street. *Where is Bonnie?* Floyd found himself awash with the same sense of loss he'd experienced when his parents had left him.

Vic waited inside with a look of condolence. He pushed a tall stool to the front of the counter and motioned for Floyd to sit. "Do you know a woman by the name of Ann Wright?"

"No, I don't."

"And for good reason. She hasn't lived here for nearly forty years."

Floyd lifted his mailbag onto the counter and sat down.

"Ann was the girl next door. She used to tag along when I went fishing. Threw a softball as well as any of us boys. Somewhere along the line, we started seeing each other through a new lens. She resembled Mary Pickford," Vic said with a faraway look. "One thing led to another and she got to pressing me about going steady. I wasn't having any of it. She went off to visit an aunt in Renfrew County one summer and never came back."

"What became of her?"

"Ann met up with a schoolteacher and they married within the year. She's a grandmother now, but in my mind we're still seventeen and dangling our feet over the riverbank at Brewster's Gorge." He looked directly into Floyd's eyes. "She could have been Ann Patterson—but I hesitated and lost."

"You loved her?"

"I love her still."

On the walk home, Floyd ruminated over what he should have said to Bonnie. He tried phrases on like sweaters to see which one felt right. *Join me for a soda? What are you reading? Might I escort you home?*

Head down, Floyd plodded through his front gate without realizing that Bonnie was seated on the porch steps. "Hello," she called out cheerily.

He formed a stupefied grin and replied, "One second." The words he'd practiced earlier flew from his mind as he made his way past her. She continued to read the book that lay open on her lap, even as the back of Floyd's heavy leather shoes brushed against her thigh.

Floyd hurried into the house and dashed upstairs to strip off his postal uniform and change into a short-sleeved shirt and a pair of dungarees. He splashed his face with water, smoothed his hair, then raced down the steps again.

Floyd returned to the porch to find Bonnie waiting on the spot where he'd discovered her earlier. She closed the book and hugged it to her chest. They stared at each other for a moment before Floyd spoke.

"How did you—"

"Mr. Patterson told me where you live. I like him," she said. "So where are we off to?"

"The library."

"Perfect. I need to trade up. Jane Austen is boring me to tears." A smile filled her upturned face.

Floyd looked into Bonnie's eyes, and his insides melted like butter. In that moment, he was completely lost in the beauty of being seen by someone else. She looked past his dreary exterior, through his layers of shy awkwardness, and straight into his very heart.

• • •

In the days to come, Bonnie continued to greet Floyd on his porch after work. They shared cucumber sandwiches from the same plate and sipped lemonade from chilled glasses.

During their walks to the library, Floyd would start twenty different conversations in his mind. But the words swam inside his mouth until he swallowed them again. Bonnie filled the silence with stories about vacationing in the Adirondacks and horseback riding at her uncle's stable in Prince Edward County. She introduced Floyd to words like *dressage* and *tack*.

"Father is ridiculously wealthy. The first generation makes it, the second generation enjoys it, and the third generation loses it. That's what they say. Well, I'm the third generation." She laughed a little too loudly. "Fingers crossed."

"What brought your family to Narrow Falls?" Floyd asked.

"Father invested in the paper mill. Otherwise, Mr. R.J. McLelland would have lost his shirt, and most of the town would have been out of work." Bonnie laughed. "Father being president was all Mother's idea. He hates it, really."

"What about siblings?"

"Absolutely not. Mother believes in quality over quantity. Frankly, I don't think she'd have the patience for a second Bonnie. She barely has enough for the first one."

Floyd doubted that his pedigree would pass Mrs. Brookman's inspection. He thought back to how she'd looked at him that first day on the steps of Patterson's Pharmacy and wondered how he would bear up under her scrutiny.

The Narrow Falls Public Library was Floyd's terra firma. His shoulders relaxed and his pulse slowed whenever he and Bonnie crossed the threshold. They settled into the same study carrel at three o'clock each day, in much the same manner that worshippers claim the same pew each Sunday. Floyd would squeeze two chairs into the tight space. He relished the sensation of their knees brushing together.

"This silence is suffocating," Bonnie said one afternoon. She kicked her shoes off and jounced her feet on the front rung of her chair. "I wish somebody would make noise." She stood up and padded barefoot between the library stacks and returned with a new selection of books about hot air balloons, Hawaii, fashion, and poetry. When it was time to leave, Floyd reshelved his books with care. Bonnie left behind a tower of unexamined literature.

A few afternoons later, Bonnie dozed off at the library. She'd said little to Floyd that afternoon except to apologize for her sluggish pace. He settled back in his chair to watch her sleep. She reminded him of the Friedrich von Amerling paintings he'd discovered in an art history book.

Long past their usual departure time, the librarian tapped on the carrel and pointed to the clock. Library hours ended in ten minutes.

"Bonnie," Floyd whispered. No response. He gently nudged her shoulder. When she continued to sleep, he shook her knee with some vigour. "Wake up," he said firmly.

Bonnie woke with a start. "You let me sleep?" she asked in a tone that both questioned and accused. "What time is it?"

"Nearly seven," he answered.

"We've got to go," she said. "Now!"

When Floyd cocked his head to one side, she reached for his right hand and pulled him to his feet. They hurried to the street and barely spoke to each other during the trek through town. By the time their shadows lengthened on the sidewalk, they were soldiering along next to the stone wall bordering the Brookman estate. A stand of oak trees and bushes blocked Floyd's full view of the house until he and Bonnie reached the centre of the wrought-iron gate. His heart sank when he realized the full grandeur of the property. Floyd cast a look at Bonnie and then back at the splendour of the house—the ornate front door, the banks of tall windows, the fancy wood trim. He imagined his father whispering, "Find a new girl."

Coach lights flicked on beneath the portico, and the front door swung open in a slow arc. Mrs. Brookman stepped outside. She wore a powder-blue skirt, a tailored white blouse, and perfectly sculpted hair.

"See you tomorrow, then." Floyd raised the latch and pushed the gate open.

Bonnie sighed and flashed a weak smile as she trudged past him. She continued around the edge of a circular flower garden, then stopped at the bottom of the cement stairs leading to her mother. There was a moment during this pause when Floyd thought Bonnie might turn on her heel and come back to him. Instead, she pulled herself up one step at time, then rested again just below the landing.

Mrs. Brookman's arms folded across the front of her blouse. Her chin lifted, and she spoke quickly. When she finished, Bonnie's back straightened, and her head turned slowly from side to side. Her mother's face tightened, then she leaned forward and shook Bonnie by the shoulders.

Should he intervene? It was hard to tell. Floyd squeezed the iron gate frame until his knuckles turned a bloodless white. He stood down when Bonnie's mother released her grip. It appeared that some kind of agreement had been struck. Mrs. Brookman placed something in the centre of Bonnie's right hand. Bonnie looked over her shoulder at Floyd and raised the hand to her face. She put something in her mouth, then turned away and proceeded into the house without waving.

Mrs. Brookman sagged against a column under the portico and closed her eyes briefly. But when she noticed Floyd watching from the front gate, her steely countenance returned, and she glared at him until he lost confidence and turned away.

On his walk home, Floyd replayed the day's events in his mind until he could no longer be sure what was real and what he'd imagined.

7.

Along a side road outside the town limits, Floyd drove the Volkswagen onto the gravel shoulder and let Dean slide behind the wheel. The boy rolled the driver's side window down and jacked the radio volume to full blast. He pulled onto the road, ground the gears, and accelerated too quickly for Floyd's taste. Loose gravel pummeled the underside of the car, and a dust cloud billowed in the rearview mirror. Dean howled into the wind with abandon, and worry faded from his face.

A lump burned at the back of Floyd's throat. He wanted to hang his head through the window and shout with happiness. He wanted to take Dean driving again, see him graduate college and fall in love. Without Bonnie, Floyd was a widower. Who would he be without Dean?

They steered onto an old logging road and parked the car in the tall grass next to a dirt path that led into the gorge. Floyd carried a blanket over his shoulder and a bag of diner takeout in either hand. He paused periodically along the way so Dean could rest against a tree and catch his breath.

"I had to stop for your mother twice as often as I do for you," Floyd said after they had descended a steep slope to the river.

"Why's that?"

"She hiked in silly shoes—sandals, actually. We needed to stop constantly so she could extract pebbles from beneath her heels." Floyd could picture Bonnie standing in Dean's stead with a hand braced against a pine. "Oh, Floyd, this is exciting!" she'd said. "The water is so fast here!"

"Did you come here a lot? With her?"

"Often."

"I was here before. A bunch of times."

Floyd nodded.

"With Mom," Dean added.

Floyd sensed the trap being laid with those two words. He set the takeout bags on the ground and pointed farther upriver. "Can you make it to the top of the falls, or should we stop here?"

"Keep going." Dean stepped past Floyd and picked his way along the bank for several yards. Then he stopped suddenly and turned on Floyd. "You're playing it cool now," he sniped, "but I remember how angry you were that night when you came here to get us. I was just a little kid, and it was a long time ago, but I know what happened."

"I was concerned, not angry," Floyd answered, setting the takeout bags on the ground again and rubbing the back of his neck.

"Your *concern* kept Mom locked in her room for three days."

"It was her choice, Son. She wanted the quiet time to work out her thoughts."

"Don't call me *son*." Dean's voice was full of venom. "You frightened her. You didn't really love her, and you don't love me either."

"That's not how it was!" Floyd said with mounting frustration.

"I hate you. I can't believe I'm stuck with you for a father." Dean's words flew like rocks.

Floyd wheeled away from Dean. He balled his fists into tight knots of bone and sinew, and an angry howl shot from his mouth. Emotions he'd managed to wall off behind politeness and self-control broke through. His lungs expressed a final drawn-out note of grief, and then the gorge fell into abrupt silence.

How could he move past this moment? Vindicating himself would mean betraying Bonnie's secrets and knocking her from the pedestal Dean had placed her on. He scrambled for the right words as he turned towards Dean.

The boy's placid expression unnerved him.

"Huh. So you're not a chunk of ice," Dean said. "There's hope for you, Floyd. Real hope." He chucked a rock into the river and continued towards the sound of fast-moving water.

Floyd pursed his lips. *What the hell did that mean?* Better to let sleeping dogs lie and move on.

There were two separate waterfalls in Brewster's Gorge as the result of a flat rock, the size of a king-sized mattress, dividing the river before its fifteen-foot drop. A thick curtain of water surged over the wider of the two falls, obscuring the craggy rock face and unyielding granite that waited in the river below. In a less deceptive manner, the protrusion of several worn boulders interrupted the tumble of water over the second fall.

By the time he and Dean made the ascent to the crest of the falls, Floyd's stomach was rumbling. He chose a partially shaded stretch of rocks overlooking the falls and spread the blanket. He then opened a Styrofoam carton of scrambled eggs from the diner and promptly closed it again.

Dean sat on the edge of the blanket and busied himself with snapping dried twigs into tiny bits. "Eggs cold?" he asked.

Floyd nodded and peered over the top of his glasses. "Maid Marian packed great picnic lunches."

"I haven't seen Marian in forever."

"She used to cover for your mother and me."

"Cover?" Dean pointed to the bag of sandwiches.

"Grandmother Brookman didn't share your mother's fondness for me." Floyd passed Dean a chicken salad sandwich on whole wheat.

"No kidding."

They both smiled at that.

"So we had to sneak around a bit," Floyd said.

"Been there," Dean replied with a smirk that caused his father do a double take.

"Tell me about the first time you brought Mom here—Dad."

Floyd smiled and hugged his knees. Things were back on track. "All right. It's a good story."

Events played in Floyd's mind like a movie on a screen. Some scenes he determined to keep for himself, and some he'd hold back for Bonnie's sake. What remained were the details that affirmed Dean's likeness to his mother. These parts, Floyd shared freely.

That first day Floyd brought Bonnie to the gorge, she wore a white dress and flowered sandals. With her hair tied back in a red ribbon, she resembled a dark-eyed Elizabeth Taylor. Floyd couldn't believe his luck.

She'd arrived at their rendezvous with cheeks slightly flushed from the exertion of toting her wicker picnic basket for several blocks. "Marian insisted on preparing a lunch." Bonnie's eyes sparkled as she leaned towards him. "If Mother found out, Marian would be in such trouble." Mrs. Brookman had hired a maid close in age to her daughter, never considering that the woman may become Bonnie's accomplice rather than the informant she'd intended.

Floyd reached for the handle and made a show of testing the basket's weight. "Does Marian think we're staying for a week?"

"If there's enough food, maybe we should." Bonnie took him by the hand and pulled him towards the road.

Floyd rattled off facts about the natural history of the gorge as they followed the winding river. Bonnie clapped her hands and giggled at the splash of water dodging through the rapids below the waterfalls. She was in high spirits that day, animating stories with her hands and punctuating sentences with laughter.

When the falls came into view, she kicked off her sandals and dashed ahead of Floyd to a sloped granite slab. She held on to the low branch of a spindly pine and leaned over the churning water, her arm stretched towards the falls. "I love this place!" she yelled into the spray.

"Be careful!" Floyd sprinted to catch up. He winced when a piece of loose wicker from the basket jabbed into his leg.

Bonnie suddenly wobbled, and her feet slid downward along the rock. She let out a squeal. The slick granite beneath her feet made it impossible to backtrack and resume her grip on the pine without falling.

In the nick of time, Floyd's left arm slid around her waist. The counterweight of the full picnic basket clenched in his right hand saved them both from tumbling into the river several feet below. She recovered her balance and, hand over hand on the pine branch, pulled herself to higher ground.

"Sir knight, claim your prize!" Water droplets rested like dew on her lashes when she moved in to kiss his mouth. Her skin was warm, and her lips tasted like fruit-flavoured candy. When the kiss ended, she looked up at him with a sly grin that held his gaze. He felt a hand firmly pressed against the zipper of his shorts. Floyd's breath caught in his throat, and his body stirred under Bonnie's touch.

"Oh my," she purred.

When she released him and turned away with a peal of laughter, Floyd worried that he'd done something wrong.

They climbed to the top of the gorge and spread towels on a granite plateau looking across the falls. After lunch, they held each other's hand and lay down with their faces turned towards the sun.

"Close your eyes and count to twenty," Bonnie said excitedly.

"Why?"

"Just do it."

Floyd shut his eyes, "One, two, three . . ." He continued shouting numbers above the roar of the falls. "Nineteen, twenty." The only sign of Bonnie was her dress, lying in a crumpled ring at the foot of his towel.

"Over here!" she called.

Her lemon-yellow bathing suit drew his eyes to the centre of the river above the primary falls. His heart pounded in his ears when he saw her there, arms waving above her head.

"I'm surfing," Bonnie whooped. The current surged against her thighs, forcing her closer to the edge of the falls.

Floyd leapt to his feet just as she tipped forward sharply. One of her hands swept the surface of the river, sending up a plume of spray, before she righted herself again. Her hair had come loose, and wet curls tumbled over her shoulders. With outstretched arms, Bonnie continued forward.

"No! Go back," Floyd hollered. He waved his arms wildly, but it was too late. She'd already leapt from the crest of the falls.

"Geronimo!"

In the space of a heartbeat, Bonnie slid beneath the current and disappeared. A sliver of yellow flashed from behind the curtain of falling water, then a leg or an arm. As Floyd hurried to the base of the waterfalls, his mind began turning over possible scenarios, none of them good. Could he find her? What if she was injured? How long would it take to run for help?

He found no sign of her in the river as he hurried along the embankment, eyes scanning the water. Just beyond the rapids, where the current slowed, he glimpsed Bonnie's yellow bathing suit. Quick as a shot, Floyd raced along the riverbank until he reached her. He stood, gasping for air, and watched Bonnie trailing her fingers across the surface of the water as she sat in the shallows.

"That was fun," Bonnie said when she finally noticed him. Blood streamed from a split in her forehead.

Floyd paced the shore, raking a hand through his hair. "Fun?" he exclaimed. "Bonnie, I thought you'd drowned."

"Oh, come on," Bonnie crooned and opened her arms wide. "Don't be upset."

Floyd stepped off the grassy bank and waded into the knee-deep water, removing his shirt as he went. He plunged it below the surface of the river, then wrung it out and wiped the blood from Bonnie's face. He sat next to her and circled an arm around her shoulders while he applied pressure in an attempt to staunch the bleeding.

They rested against each other, studying the patterns and swirls in the current. Bonnie nestled against Floyd's chest, and his chin came to rest on the crown of her head. He would be her protector, he decided, even if it meant shielding her from herself. He became acutely aware of her body pressing against his and the way her wet hair lay against his belly.

Bonnie raised her chin and kissed him, lightly at first, then with determination. She whispered in his ear and pulled away from his embrace.

He thought he'd dreamt the words at first. But she'd really said them. "Floyd, I want you."

She rose slowly out of the water, her eyes burning with mischief. Her gaze locked with his as she pulled the bathing suit strap from one shoulder and then the other.

So many times, he'd dreamed of this moment. And now it was really going to happen. Wide-eyed, he watched as she rolled the suit down to her waist.

She cupped her breasts with both hands and stared down at him with a saucy smile.

"I love you, Bonnie. I promise I do." Floyd began fumbling with his belt. He leaned back and half floated in the water as he worked himself out of his shorts and boxers. Cool water rushed against his tender flesh as he wadded his clothes into his right fist and lobbed them onto the riverbank.

Bonnie wriggled her suit past her hips and kicked it free from around her ankles. She placed a foot on either side of Floyd's legs and lowered herself onto his lap.

Floyd reached forward to touch her breasts and the curve of her bottom. He was filled with passion and wanting everything at once.

"Not yet." She pushed a hand against his chest.

He leaned back, arms bracing his weight against the riverbed and fingers digging into the silt. Then he noticed the blood trail along her right brow and how it had begun spreading down her cheek. He wished for everything to be just right and to forget her earlier recklessness. Now all he could do was think of it.

Bonnie sank one hand below the water and clasped it around him. Floyd observed a flicker of surprise. For a moment, he worried that his partial arousal had disappointed her. But then a sultry look darkened her eyes, and she leaned closer to him so her breasts pressed against his chest. In a husky voice, she whispered, "Not to worry, darling. I know precisely how to fix this."

8.

The car trunk slammed with a thud. Tammy felt the impact of metal on metal through the fleeting vibration that passed from the steel frame of the car to where her temple rested against the window. She wondered if the baby had felt the tremor ripple through her womb.

Tammy's eyes cut to her mother's image in the side-view mirror. Mirabelle stood at the back corner of the car, wiping her hands on a tissue while Tammy waited. The garish floral pattern of her Sunday dress made her appear clownish. As she walked along the passenger side of the car, the span of her hips filled the entire mirror. In a flash, she passed Tammy and tromped up the cement steps to the front door of the house.

"Lawrence!"

The screen door burst open, and Tammy's father poked his head outside, much like a turtle venturing out of its shell. His head bobbed up and down while her mother spoke, and when she steamed towards the car again, he backed into the house without acknowledging Tammy.

And so it had been since announcing her pregnancy. She'd attempt to catch his eye while he looked anywhere but at her. Tammy's father had never been described as a talkative man, but when he would invite her to join him in tinkering with a carburetor or changing a spark plug on the lawn mower, that was conversation enough. Passing a tool substituted for affection.

Tammy missed that.

"Well, if he's not coming with us, he should at least be useful and mow the lawn," her mother said as she slid behind the wheel.

"Why can't we just walk to church, Mom?"

"I'd prefer not to flaunt your condition, thank you very much."

"Nothing's showing yet." Tammy stared out over the dashboard.

Her mother snorted and turned the key. "The Clarks are walking that damned dog again."

"Dad never goes to church."

Blanche Clark smiled broadly and waved as she passed behind the car. Tammy's mother revved the engine.

"Look at them taking their time." She sucked her teeth. "They can see I want to back up."

"Why do I have to start going again?" Tammy asked.

Her mother swiveled towards her.

"Because the trunk of this car is full of items for donation. Things we don't want. Things that could be enjoyed by other people. After the service, you're going to put every piece of it into the poor box behind the church."

Her mother paused to reload with a final comment aimed directly at Tammy's heart.

"It's time you acquired the discipline necessary to pass the things you once loved on to a better home."

Tammy's eyes stung with tears as she turned her face to the window. She did not look back when the indignant puff of air escaped her mother's lips.

Parishioners funneled towards the Narrow Falls United Church as the King family car rumbled past. Families advanced along the front walk like ants filing off to a picnic. Tammy recognized a boy following his parents across the church lawn; he'd sat next to her in tenth grade calculus. When he looked in her direction, she scrunched down in her seat.

Farther down the street, her mother pulled along side the curb and killed the engine. Tammy rested her hand on the door latch and waited for an elderly couple to pass by on the sidewalk. As they neared the front bumper, walking arm in arm, the husband winked at Tammy, then reached across to pat his wife's hand.

Life is unfair, she thought. *Dean will never be that old.*

When Tammy finally emerged from the car, her mother was already waiting on the sidewalk. She cast a skeptical eye over her daughter's wardrobe. Tammy had dressed in a denim skirt and a loose-fitting peasant blouse, which she'd left untucked.

"You'll fool people until the end of August, but after that you'll blow up like a balloon." Her mother tugged at the hem of Tammy's blouse and shook her head. "Your mystery boy doesn't have to worry, does he? He's getting off scot-free."

"Not really," Tammy muttered as they headed towards the church.

"And how's that?" her mother demanded. Her voice pulled tight as a bowstring when Tammy didn't answer. "You walk like a flat-footed duck in those hideous things." She pointed at the huarache sandals on Tammy's feet. "Might as well have worn my old house slippers."

Tammy rolled her eyes.

Her mother's demeanour transformed as they neared the swell of organ music flooding past the church doors. She delivered a sugary smile to the deacon who greeted them at the top step.

"Morning, Mrs. King." He shook her hand first and then Tammy's. The scent of his aftershave followed them into the empty vestibule.

"Pray for the Lord's forgiveness," Tammy's mother hissed. "And while you're at it, ask him to throw some luck my way. God knows I'm going to need it to clean up this mess before the whole town figures out what you've been up to." With a quick nod, she turned and set off down the aisle in search of empty seats.

Tammy trailed a few steps behind, her eyes fixed on a loose thread dangling from a seam in her mother's dress. Perhaps the brightly coloured print that preceded her down the aisle might draw attention away from her own forlorn appearance.

A vacancy awaited them on the aisle, eight rows from the front. Tammy dropped onto the pew next to her mother. Nothing had changed in the chapel since the last time she'd attended a service. Same hymnals. Same communion cup holders.

The organ music paused. On both sides of the recessed area behind the pulpit, the doors eased open, and choir members dressed in burgundy robes began spilling out to fill the opposing bench seats. Reverend Findlay followed them with a Bible pressed to his chest and his face frozen in concentration. The organist resumed playing, and the choir rose to their feet. The reverend remained seated and prayerful until their hymn ended, then he crossed the floor to stand on the dais.

"The call to worship is listed in your bulletin." The reverend steadied his Bible above the pulpit. "Come, all you who are weary."

"Come, all you who have sinned and are fearful," the congregation responded in a low murmur.

A figure of Jesus stared out from a stained-glass window at the side of the church. The bottom panel had been tipped open for ventilation. Tammy wished she could escape into the piece of blue sky beyond that narrow space.

When the service concluded, Tammy and her mother merged into the aisle and began shuffling towards the exit. As they neared the last pew, a voice called out, "Mirabelle!"

"Eva?"

"Look at you, Tammy. So grown up."

"What are you doing here? Don't they have churches in Ashfield?"

"Yes, and much less provincial, but the long drive was worth it. I'm visiting Mother today," Aunt Eva said with an imperious tone.

"The woman can't remember her own name. She certainly doesn't know who you are anymore."

"That's not the point, Mirabelle. Mother and I have a special bond. Her joy is my only reward." Aunt Eva's eyes twinkled.

Tammy's mother stiffened. She locked an arm around Tammy's and pulled her close. "Where are your girls? Couldn't get them to come with you?"

"Oh, Mirabelle. Jessica is vacationing with her fiancé's family for two weeks at their lake house. Beautiful place. Cyril and I are joining them midweek. They have two guest houses and a full staff." Aunt Eva clapped her hands together. "Imagine that, I won't need to lift a finger. And Andrea is facilitating a camp for disabled children this summer. Such a darling she is."

"My girl will be doing some Christian work for the church this summer."

"Ha!" The sound darted from Tammy's mouth before her mind caught up to her mother's game.

The grip on her arm tightened.

"She's meeting with the reverend this morning to discuss details."

The three women looked to the front of the church, where Reverend Findlay stood facing a small crowd of worshippers. He glanced past his audience to the back of the church, then he excused himself and motioned for Tammy to come forward.

Mirabelle turned to Eva with a satisfied grin. "Daughters need a role model of charity, and they should find it in their mothers. Raise them right and they'll follow you to the end." She smirked as if she'd had the last word.

"See you, Aunt Eva." Tammy leaned towards her mother's ear and whispered, "I'll walk home."

Red patches bloomed on her mother's neck.

"God bless," Aunt Eva called out gleefully.

"A stray sheep returns to the fold," Reverend Findlay crooned as Tammy drew closer. "Your mother said I should expect you. Come this way." He gestured to the door on the right side of the pulpit. "It's best that we speak privately in my office."

Tammy bit her bottom lip.

The reverend's hand lingered on the small of her back as he ushered her along. When the warmth of his skin penetrated the gauze of her blouse, Tammy's back arched slightly. Her sandals slapped against the soles of her bare feet as she hastened her step.

She pressed through the doorway and into the corridor, followed closely by Reverend Findlay. She could navigate this stretch of maroon carpet with her eyes closed. As a child, she'd made a game of counting off the number of steps between places. Eleven paces straight ahead and a sharp turn left would take her in the direction of his office.

Upon rounding the corner, a mother and father smiled politely and squeezed past her and the minister. Children trailed behind with Sunday school papers clutched in their fists. There remained only five more paces to the stairwell leading down to the Sunday school classrooms in the musty basement. Directly across the hall was the entrance to the church nursery. The wailing of a baby assaulted her ears as they neared the windows overlooking the row of cribs in the nap room. A sense of alarm washed over Tammy. In six months, her own child would be broadcasting its dissatisfaction to the world. A baby. Her baby. This was really going to—

"Tammy."

She jumped and wheeled around upon hearing her name. The reverend stood planted outside the doorway to the nursery. His chin lifted slightly, and he stretched an upturned palm towards her. When she hesitated, his eyes grew cold and hard. She stared at his meaty hand and blunt fingers.

"Tammy," he said with authority. The baby continued to bawl in the background.

She trudged reluctantly to his side, eyes trained on the floor. The weight of his arm came to rest on the back of her shoulders. He smelled like the church basement.

"See what can be done here," he said, nudging her into the room. "Come to my office when you finish. I'll be waiting." Then he was gone.

The nursery was not a place where Tammy had spent time. Babies weren't her thing. She stood awkwardly among the baskets of stuffed animals and pondered the three cribs lined up against the end wall. Above them, hand-stitched clouds were thumbtacked to the ceiling. Did babies really like this stuff? Not knowing for sure panicked her.

"Sorry for all the racket," a voice called from the other side of the room. A woman smiled wearily over her shoulder. On the changing table in front of her, the baby's dimpled legs flailed in the air. "My son's diaper rash is flaring up *and* it's feeding time," she said apologetically.

"Do you need anything?" Tammy asked.

"Can you get rid of this?" The woman passed a soiled diaper into Tammy's hands. Then she lifted the baby to her shoulder, settled into a rocking chair, and began unbuttoning her blouse.

Tammy averted her eyes and searched the room for a garbage can. She was surprised to be handed a bundle of human excrement in such a casual manner. By the time she disposed of the diaper in a can near the hallway and returned to the woman, the crying had ended. A crescent of pale breast was visible as the baby nursed. When the woman noticed Tammy staring, she smiled.

"Diaper, feed, diaper, feed," she whispered. "Half the time I don't know if I'm awake or walking in my sleep."

Tammy nodded and tried to picture herself in the woman's place.

"We're okay now, if you have someplace to be."

Tammy blushed and headed for the reverend's office.

Squeaky floorboards beneath the hall carpet betrayed Tammy. Reverend Findlay called out at the first sound of her approach.

"Come in."

She stepped haltingly into the room, hands clasped before her. The reverend sat behind his desk, bowed over an open Bible and a sheaf of lined paper. With a silver pen in hand, he wrote a few lines at the top of a fresh page while Tammy waited, uncertain about what to do next. When he'd finished, he laid the pen horizontally in the centre of his notes. Then he lifted the frame of his glasses, rubbed his eyes briefly and exhaled a slow stream of air.

Reverend Findlay wore his white hair slicked back in a thinning pompadour. His sideburns were unfashionably long, and flakes of dandruff peppered the shoulders of his black polyester suit. He thrummed his fingers on his desk and looked at her thoughtfully.

"Close the door and have a seat." He pointed to a straight-backed chair in front of his desk.

Tammy complied immediately.

"Your mother has informed me of your situation." He allowed the words to stand for a moment, then added, "How disappointing."

Tammy blinked back the tears. His directness caught her by surprise.

"Is the father a Christian?"

She shrugged.

"I expected as much. Is there talk of marriage?"

"No," Tammy replied.

"Do you have experience with children?"

She thought back to the harried woman she'd met in the nursery and shook her head.

"How far along now?"

"Two and a half months."

"What are your plans? You must have some details worked out," Reverend Findlay said. Every word became a rock hurtling towards Tammy. "How will you financially support your child? Do you have a job? What about college?" His elbows rested on the desk and his chin on the steeple formed by his fingers. "Are you equipped to manage the stresses of parenthood alone?"

Tammy slouched in the chair.

"Will the child grow to resent you if there is no father in its life? Could you raise a *son* alone?" he asked.

When Tammy began to sob, Reverend Findlay left his chair to sit on the front edge of his desk.

"There, there," he said, patting her shoulder. "Not to worry. I have a solution that will be comfortable for all of us."

She wiped her eyes and looked up at him.

"I've contacted a home for unwed mothers. They have an opening at the end of August. You'll stay there for the remainder of your confinement. The home will charge a nominal fee, of course." His grey eyes studied her closely as he continued. "The staff will arrange for adoption to a deserving Christian couple. Rest assured the child will be raised in a God-fearing home. You need only sign the paperwork and the home will look after the rest."

"You make it sound so easy."

"It's a system that works. If you're anesthetized, you won't even see the child. It will be as if the baby never existed," the reverend boasted. He folded his arms across his chest and huffed when these words made Tammy cry harder. "The timing is perfect," he insisted. "People will assume you've gone off to college. "

"Is the home far away?" she asked.

"Two hours' drive. It's the Beatrix Home in Hattersburg," he replied. "There is no need to worry. You are unlikely to see anyone who will recognize you."

Soon after escaping Reverend Findlay, Tammy squeezed through a gap in the cedar hedge behind the building. As she tiptoed through the neighbouring yard to the sidewalk, she wiped her eyes with a fistful of toilet paper she'd grabbed from the ladies room in the church basement. She'd gone down there to freshen up, then returned to the ground floor and ducked out through the Sunday school entrance at the rear of the building.

Her mother had undoubtedly planned to nab her in the chapel following the chat with Reverend Findlay. She'd have demanded a blow-by-blow account of the discussion so she could interject her own commentary about the wonderful insights of the reverend. She'd marvel over the wisdom of his proposal as if she weren't the original architect of his vision. But all Tammy could think of was the complications posed by the Beatrix Home. Dean had said she'd make a great mom. Clearly, he wanted her to keep the baby. And she couldn't think of being two hours away from him. They had so little time left together. If she went away, they'd have even less.

Tammy had walked aimlessly for a while, and her stomach was growling. With the church several blocks behind her and her mother nowhere to be seen, she began to sort through her thoughts. She knew nothing about babies—that was true. Attending college would be impossible. Her prospects would be limited, and she'd be alone.

She desperately needed to see Dean. First, she'd call the house to make sure his father was out. Being questioned by another adult was the last thing she needed. Tammy looked over her shoulder, then set off to the pay phone next to Patterson's Pharmacy.

Tammy stepped up on the cinder block in the Hoffmans' flowerbed and tapped lightly on Dean's window frame. Through the screen, she could see him lying back on the pillows with his eyes closed.

"Psst. Dean," she whispered.

He awoke with a start and broke into a fit of coughing.

"Are you all right?" Tammy asked. Dean's features were vague and difficult to interpret through the mesh.

"I'm fine," his voice rasped. "Come on in."

Tammy scooted to the back door and slipped inside. She kicked off her sandals and carried them into Dean's room. The air was heavy with the tang of body odour. Spent tissues littered the top of his nightstand, and among them a pill bottle lay on its side next to a partial glass of water.

She sat cross-legged at the end of the bed and rubbed the soles of his feet. "You look tired," she said.

Dean smirked. "We had a father-and-son day this week. I'm still recovering."

"Really?"

"Yeah. Turns out all I had to do was call him *Dad*, and the vault swung wide open. He was telling stories all day. Once he started, he couldn't shut up. I found out new stuff about Mom."

"That's great," Tammy said, folding her hands in her lap. She *was* pleased for him, but she registered the hint of something dark in Dean's manipulation of his father.

"Dumb bastard forgot to pick up my pills the night before."

"Dean," Tammy groaned.

"What?" Dean snarled. "Whose side are you on?" He studied Tammy's face as though he was seeing it for the first time.

"Yours." Tammy chewed the inside of her bottom lip to keep from crying.

"That's more like it," he said, leaning his back against the headboard. "So let me tell you what happened. First off, we took the car out, which is huge 'cause that thing's been sitting idle like a lawn ornament since forever. Once we got of town, the old man pulled over and asked if I wanted to drive. Hell yeah, I wanted to drive. So I hopped behind the wheel and drove it like I owned it. You should have seen me, babe. I was a real pro."

"Hmm." Tammy nodded.

"We parked on a side road near the old brickworks and walked through the bush to Brewster's Gorge. So we carried some takeout and a blanket along the river and hung out for most of the day at the top of the falls. The last time I was there was with my mom." Dean's eyes flashed. "Oh my God, that was an adventure." He started laughing.

"What's the joke?"

"Well she woke me up in the middle of the night. I think it was the summer before second grade. We snuck out of the house with our bathing suits and a couple of towels. She had to piggyback me most of the trip, but we walked all the way to the gorge. She sang Beatles tunes at the top of her lungs, and she even did cannonballs off the top of the falls."

"That's so dangerous." Tammy's brows pinched together. "What were you doing the whole time?"

"Playing in the river. Perfectly safe, Officer. There was a lot of moonlight. We had a blast until Floyd showed up." Dean paused for a moment. "He was really pissed. I remember them fighting, then we all got in the car and drove home."

"Sorry."

"My mom went to her room, closed the door, and didn't come out. She stayed in bed for three days. All Floyd's fault." Dean jabbed his finger into the air. "That's the shit I remember."

"You sound hoarse. Maybe we should stop talking," Tammy said.

Dean leaned forward and grasped both her hands. "Promise me you won't let Floyd near our kid, even after I'm gone. Our baby is the only thing that will be left of me. I can't stand the thought of Floyd being in my kid's life."

How could she make a vow that implied she was keeping the baby when she was still undecided? "You're not going anywhere," Tammy finally whispered.

"Promise me!"

Tammy dragged the corners of her mouth into the semblance of a smile.

"That's my girl." Dean let go of her and reached across his nightstand for the glass. He gulped a mouthful of water and asked, "Are you feeling okay? You look a little pale."

"I'm fine. I've got to be going though. My mom . . ." Tammy rolled her eyes and shrugged. She swung her legs over the edge of the mattress and stepped into her sandals.

When she stood to leave, Dean grabbed her wrist and pulled her back onto the bed. He pressed his body against her back and rested his chin on her right shoulder. One arm slid around her ribs while the other laid a book on her lap. "This belonged to my mom. Now it's yours. And our baby's."

"*Leaves of Grass* by Walt Whitman," she read aloud and flipped to the inscription on the inside of the book cover.

To my Bonnie,

Every day with you is poetry.

Love, Floyd

Tammy's chin trembled. "I can't possibly take this. I mean, your father . . ."

Dean snorted. "He won't miss it."

"Really?"

"Floyd is my father, but she was my mother. I am her son," Dean said, splaying his fingers across Tammy's belly, "and this—is my son. He is the last Hoffman, and he deserves to have this book."

"How can I say no to that?" she said with a heavy sigh. "You can't."

9.

Today, Floyd would tell his mother-in-law that history was repeating itself. Without her help, another life would be torn from the family tree. For two days, he'd been straddling the past and present, scraping together the courage required to face her. They hadn't been in the same room since Bonnie's funeral eight years earlier. A peace offering seemed appropriate, so he'd cut some stalks of lavender from behind the house and bound them with butcher twine.

He tossed the bouquet onto an empty park bench at Riverside Park. The constant mechanical hum of McLelland's Pulp and Paper Mill from across the river underscored the splish of the current. Twenty-four hours a day, the mill churned out the combined roar of drying fans and pulp refiners along with the jarring racket of wood chippers. With the wind blowing away from town, the odour was tolerable.

Floyd plopped down on the bench, then rested an elbow on each knee and wove his fingers together. Time ticked by while he ruminated over what he'd say to Bonnie's mother. And what she'd fire back at him in return.

At noon, he looked over one shoulder and across the park to where the blinds were rising in the front window of Tony's Pub. A rye and coke would levy temporary boldness, he thought, but a visit to Mrs. Brookman called for a different brand of fortitude.

This was a Sabbath for contemplation—not praying. Floyd had adopted the tenets of Murphy's Law in the place of religion, and the past had become his Bible. Life had divided itself into two testaments, the world before and after Bonnie.

Lingering in her favourite places helped to strengthen Floyd's resolve. If he allowed his mind to drift and his vision to blur, he could still conjure his wife's image from those early days after they first met. She wore carefully ironed dresses then, some days boldly striped and on others, pastel or floral.

A pair of children skipped past the end of Floyd's park bench on their way to the beach area. The parents followed close behind, lugging a picnic basket and an oversized canvas bag brimming with plastic toys. The clanging of church bells sounded from across town. Floyd checked his watch. It was one o'clock already.

"Stay away from there," the mother called out. She pointed to where the current had deposited tiny islands of yellowish suds along the shoreline. "Just play in the sand." The father smiled apologetically at Floyd as they swept past.

While the parents spread their blanket next to the beach area, the children kicked their shoes into the sand and began pulling plastic pails and shovels from the bag. The tallest child, a boy, stood at the river's edge with a bright orange ball tucked beneath one arm. He glanced back at his parents, then at the current again. *He's going in,* Floyd thought. But instead, the boy's shoulder blades pinched together, and he scampered off to join his sister.

When Dean was that age, no amount of warning could have kept him from the water. His mother either, for that matter.

"Oh, Floyd, life is a juicy peach. Take a bite," she'd said once with an impish grin. Even after he'd shown her the toxicity reports containing chemicals with multi-syllabled names, she'd laughed and swooped Dean up in her arms. "We're not scared, are we, baby?"

Perhaps it was that day the army of belligerent cells had begun its march through her body and Dean's.

Floyd sank into his memories and relived the day Doc Gillespie had pulled him aside to say that Dean had been in to see him. He'd recognized the symptoms immediately—lethargy, lack of appetite, radiating pain, faint nausea. Floyd had wanted to vomit when he was handed the oncologist's phone number. Doc had tried so hard to instill confidence. "He's top notch. I've referred two other patients to him this month." The oncologist was blunt. Dean wouldn't make it past Christmas.

"Knock it off," Floyd admonished himself. Dean still had a chance. Bonnie's mother had big-city connections that could change everything. He picked up the bouquet of lavender from the bench and vowed that he would start walking to the Brookman house in the next few minutes. But the sight of tanned youngsters digging in the sand reminded him of Dean, so he put off his departure and tossed the flowers back onto the bench.

When a second family began spreading their blanket at the beach, Floyd knew it was time to go. The new children quarreled and chased each other through the park while the parents laid claim to a patch of grass by the river.

He shifted off the bench, clutching the lavender bouquet in one fist. Anxiety marched through his stomach at the very notion of darkening Mrs. Brookman's doorway, hat in hand. He'd rather eat broken glass than explain the full extent of Dean's illness to his mother-in-law. But her affluent social connections to Toronto doctors could be the ticket to Dean's survival, so it had to be done.

Once she'd digested the news, Rose Brookman would skewer him with that look of disdain he'd seen each time their lives had intersected. She blamed him for Bonnie's demise. "I knew you weren't up to the task. Bonnie needed more." Rose never once considered her and her husband's culpability. Gene Brookman had taken over as president from fiscally irresponsible Sam McLelland, while the heir apparent, R.J. McLelland, was being groomed for the position. The mill regained its profitability during Gene's years at the helm, but at what cost? Since her husband's passing, Rose's telephone calls and correspondence had become even less amicable.

Floyd started walking. Halfway across the park, he tossed the flowers into a trash can. He'd face Mrs. Brookman empty-handed. She never went in for that sentimental tripe anyway.

August 1962

Before the end of summer, Floyd decided to make things official with Bonnie. He suspected their afternoon trysts had become fodder for the gossip mill amongst his neighbours. He'd noticed women along the street casting sideways glances at Bonnie and their husbands' knowing grins when he passed by. A proposal of marriage would be the gentlemanly thing to do. All this kibitzing around without a formal commitment wasn't right. And besides, he loved her to death.

Vic insisted on passing his mother's engagement ring to Floyd. Old Mrs. Patterson had worn it through sixty years of happy marriage to her husband. The same kind of luck could rub off on Bonnie. For days, Floyd carried the ring in his pocket, mulling over ways to orchestrate the perfect proposal.

One evening, Floyd and Bonnie walked arm in arm from the library to the Brookmans' home. Autumn winds shook the trees, and a chill in the air cautioned of winter's stealthy approach. With his free hand tucked inside the warmth of his left trouser pocket, Floyd spun the engagement ring around his baby finger.

"People will talk if you insist on tinkering with things in your pocket," Bonnie said teasingly. "What've you got in there that's so valuable you can't let go of anyway—a diamond ring?"

"I don't know," Floyd mumbled. He hadn't arranged the right words for a proposal yet. Everything needed to be just right. What if she said no?

"Oh my gosh." Bonnie sucked in her breath and wheeled around to face him. "It *is* a ring! Oh, Floyd, let me see it."

He didn't want to. Not yet.

"Come on! Come on!" She squealed and thrust her right hand towards Floyd in anticipation.

Floyd took the ring from his pocket and hitched his pant legs so he could drop to one knee. "Bonnie," he began slowly, but before he could kneel, she plucked the ring from his hand and popped it on her finger.

"Yes, darling. Yes, I'll marry you!" Her arms locked around his neck, and she planted wet kisses over his face, his neck, and his ears.

Throughout their embrace, Floyd fought to maintain his balance against the force of her affection. The thrill of her exuberant acceptance left him overjoyed. But as the days wore on, a pinch of disappointment niggled at him, and he regretted not having asked her to marry him with carefully chosen words dispensed in accordance to his own methodical tempo.

It was the second week of December when Mrs. Brookman invited Floyd to dinner. She could have relayed the invitation through Bonnie or asked one of the house staff to contact him. Instead, she'd telephoned to make the invitation herself. After the seconds it took him to recover from the shocking warmth of her voice, he responded *yes*. He was to come to the estate on the following Saturday. A few family friends would be joining them as well.

After months of broadcasting her disappointment, Mrs. Brookman must have resigned herself to the romance between him and Bonnie. Since the humiliation of her mother weeping openly at the news of their engagement, Bonnie insisted that date nights be spent at his house—soon to be her own, she oft reminded him. Aside from her desire to be alone with Floyd, he suspected she sought to shield him from the sting of her mother's disdain.

The dinner invitation would be his opportunity to show Mrs. Brookman that he could fit into her world of social dictates, etiquette, and finery. Never before had he the occasion to attend a fancy dinner. Guests had never been invited to the Hoffman table, nor had his family ever, in his recollection, been asked to dine at someone else's house. So, with only three days to prepare, he borrowed a library book containing a labeled diagram of a formal place setting and learned to differentiate between a salad fork and a dessert fork; a water goblet and a wineglass; and a soup spoon and a coffee spoon. He'd lay the napkin across his lap and pass food to his right.

It felt like a chance at a new beginning.

The air was crisp on Saturday evening. Snowflakes like tufts of gauze descended through the darkness to blanket the shoulders of Floyd's tweed overcoat as he walked to the Brookman estate. Christmas tree lights twinkled through the front windows of houses he passed, and the soft glow of coloured bulbs trimmed the edges of snowy rooftops. He hugged a paper-wrapped poinsettia to his chest, and for the first time in ten years, felt the joy of the season.

When at last Floyd reached the estate, he paused inside the wrought-iron gates of the snow-covered driveway and took in the spectre. A white spotlight illuminated the face of the house, and from each window a set of electric candles glowed yellow against the night. A grand wreath with an equally impressive red bow hung from the front door. He'd anticipated the mansion would be impressively decorated, but this display exceeded his expectation. The appearance of the Hoffman house was sadly lacking by comparison. Bonnie would be thrilled to find strings of coloured lights wrapped around the railing on his porch. He'd visit the hardware store next week.

Floyd crossed beneath the portico and paused a few feet before the towering front door. His mouth dried out like a twisted sponge. He wanted so desperately for things to go well with the Brookmans, for Bonnie's sake and his. Floyd checked his watch. *Right on time.* He'd just knocked at the door when a butler swung the door open wide.

"Good evening, sir. May I?" The man bowed slightly and took the poinsettia, then stepped aside to wait for Floyd's coat.

Floyd eyed the looming Christmas tree that dominated the foyer. Its top stretched above the banister of the second-floor balcony. He'd only begun unbuttoning his coat when Bonnie, in a strapless cocktail dress, emerged through the parlour doors to the right of the tree.

His smile melted away when she was joined by another man. The stranger's left arm draped across her back, and his hand cupped her bare shoulder as she dabbed her eyes with a tissue. They'd walked a few steps across the white marble floor before Bonnie spotted Floyd.

"You're here!" she cried out. A dazzling smile replaced her doleful expression, and she rushed toward him, leaving her male companion to sulk in the shadows. "I was so worried." Her arms locked around Floyd's neck and pulled him close.

"About what?" Floyd asked in confusion.

The stranger slid a hand inside his suit jacket and produced a pack of cigarettes. "You see, *Bunnie*," he said smugly. "I'm always right about these things. A poor bachelor never passes on a free meal. He was bound to show up sooner or later."

From over Bonnie's shoulder, Floyd measured the other man, now bowing his head over his hands to light a cigarette. He wore a tailored suit and gleaming black leather shoes. Cuff links flashed at his wrists. When he exhaled, a thin line of smoke knifed through the air. Floyd disliked him already.

"I thought you weren't coming." Bonnie sniffled.

"Your mother said dinner was at seven," Floyd said.

Bonnie finished unbuttoning his coat. "Yes, you goose. When a hostess says dinner is at seven, people gather for cocktails at least an hour earlier. The other guests have already moved to the dining room."

"I wish you'd told me," he whispered to Bonnie. Floyd handed his coat and scarf off to the waiting butler, who promptly disappeared through a door on the left side of the foyer.

"That's how it's done. I thought you'd know," she shot back.

The dark-haired man sauntered towards to them. "Not even married and already squabbling." His smile never reached his eyes. "Allow me to introduce myself since Bunnie's not going to. I'm Richard."

"And this is Floyd, my betrothed," Bonnie said with dramatic flare.

"Good to meet you," Floyd said warily.

Richard's chin lifted, and he chuckled. "Well, Bunnie, as you are no longer in need of rescuing, I'll join the others in the dining room." He ground his cigarette into an ashtray sitting on a nearby hall table.

It was a relief when Richard left them alone. Bonnie hadn't paid him much attention, but still, his familiarity with her chipped away at Floyd's confidence. To top things off, Floyd had miscalculated the dress code of the evening. They were much more elegantly dressed than he. A clerk at Harding's Family Clothiers had recommended a festive red turtleneck and chocolate-brown dress pants. "Just the ticket," the woman had promised. Now Floyd wasn't so sure.

Bonnie performed a slow twirl. A rhinestone necklace sparkled across her collarbone, and her flared skirt lifted slightly, revealing layers of crinoline against her shapely calves. "Well?" she asked. "What do you think? I had my hair put up today, same as Grace Kelly did for her wedding."

"Very pretty," Floyd said and then smiled apologetically. "I should have worn a suit."

"Nonsense. You look fine," she said. "Let's hurry. Mother loathes tardiness."

Floyd unzipped his rubber spats and peeled them away from his salt-speckled shoes. "The butler made off with the poinsettia I brought for your parents," he said.

"Mother will see it later. Come on!"

They linked arms, and Bonnie led him around the Christmas tree to a set of French doors that opened into the dining room. Floyd's step faltered when he heard the hum of voices lifting above the violin music. Worry bubbled up inside his gut. "Your mother said a *few* friends." The idea of conversing with more than two or three people made him nervous enough. But to be cast among a room full of strangers would be paralyzing.

"This is nothing. Wait until you see her New Year's Eve party." Bonnie squeezed his arm and pulled him across the threshold.

The dining room, nearly the same length as his house, was more magnificent than anything Floyd had ever seen. A chandelier, the likes of which he'd only witnessed in movies, dangled hundreds of glittering crystals above the dinner guests. The blood-red tablecloth was set with silver-trimmed china—dinner plates, salad plates, soup bowls—and the full spectrum of silver cutlery he'd studied in the book illustrations. Tapered candles burned in candelabras along the centre of the table, heightening the twinkle of light reflected by wineglasses and water goblets. The east and west walls of the room were hung with gilded mirrors and equestrian oil paintings, each adorned with garlands in honour of the holiday season.

Richly attired guests continued their banter as they glanced up with curiosity at Floyd and Bonnie, scanning the table for a pair of adjacent seats. Bonnie's father raised a hand and waved to them from the end of the table nearest the door.

"Glad you could make it!" Mr. Brookman said, jumping up to pump Floyd's hand. "Watch out for this crew," he added loudly, as if to draw the attention of guests within earshot. "They've all got sharp teeth, every one of them, and they bite!"

When his eyes widened, Mr. Brookman clapped a hand on Floyd's left shoulder and roared with laughter.

"Don't scare him like that," Bonnie scolded. She kissed her father's cheek, and he returned to his chair.

"You know all these people?" Floyd asked.

"Oh sure," Bonnie said excitedly. "Mother's on an art gallery board with Monsieur Raymond and the Knowleses. We know the Weltons from the yacht club. Mr. Fitzgerald manages Father's real estate holdings. Both my parents golfed with the Thompsons and Hobarts when we lived in Toronto." She pointed to a couple sitting opposite one another at the centre of the table. "We buy season tickets for the ballet with the Davies, and for the theatre with the Spencers. We're still getting to know the McLellands. They seem like nice people. Their son, R.J., is with that redhead. And then there's the Carsons, Richard's parents, seated next to Mother. We've summered together since I was a child. They're practically part of the family."

For the first time, Floyd wondered how Bonnie's marrying him might affect her. Would he be isolating her from this network of people of privilege? He had neither friends nor family to gather around her. His parents didn't even know she existed.

Along the table, a few heads turned conspiratorially towards one another and then back to the young couple. Floyd didn't need to hear words to know what people were saying. *What an unlikely match. She's far too good for him.*

Mrs. Brookman held court at the far end of the table opposite her husband. Decadent cakes and platters of sugary pastries covered the surface of a polished sideboard behind her. Engrossed in conversation with a similarly aged woman seated to her left, she paid no notice to the server bowed forward and tipping a wine bottle above her glass.

Floyd counted twenty-two seats at the table, and of those only two were vacant. As he and Bonnie neared her mother, Richard tipped his chair back and issued a sly grin. "I've been saving this spot for you, Bunnie," he said, patting the seat at the corner of the table between himself and Mrs. Brookman. The sole remaining chair was on the other side of the table, directly across from him. Floyd was beginning to detest Richard.

At the sound of her daughter's name, Mrs. Brookman ended her conversation and turned her attention towards them.

"Richard," Bonnie said, "would you mind terribly shuffling across the table so Floyd and I could sit next to one anoth–"

"Oh nonsense," Mrs. Brookman interjected. "He's already settled."

A butter knife and a torn-open dinner roll lay on Richard's plate. When he raised his wineglass to Bonnie, she flashed a helpless look at Floyd.

"It's fine," he said with a smile meant to shield his annoyance from Richard.

The woman who'd earlier been speaking to Bonnie's mother piped up. "Do sit down, Bonnie. It'll give us a chance to catch up."

Floyd circled behind Mrs. Brookman's chair and her friend's. By the time he slid into the vacant chair, Bonnie was already seated and laying a dinner napkin across her lap.

"Bonnie, aren't you going to introduce us?" the woman said, tipping her head towards Floyd.

"Of course, Mrs. Carson," Bonnie replied. "This is my fiancé, Floyd Hoffman. We're to be married in June."

"Oh," Mrs. Carson squeaked. "I hadn't heard."

One corner of Mrs. Brookman's mouth twitched.

"I'm Frank Carson. Richard's father," said the man seated on Floyd's left. "Good to meet you." He swirled ice cubes in the bottom of his squat glass. "Hoffman? The name's familiar. Do you have people in Toronto?"

"No, sir," Floyd replied glumly.

The server stepped forward to fill Bonnie's wineglass. At the halfway mark, Mrs. Brookman snaked a hand, palm down, across the tablecloth, then raised her index finger, signaling the man to stop pouring. Bonnie glowered, and her mother cocked a warning brow in response.

Their exchange was fleeting, but Floyd had seen it.

"When *were* we last all together?" Mrs. Brookman asked.

"Waikiki, Royal Hawaiian Hotel," Richard answered. Then he looked at Bonnie. "Dinner on the beach, blue sundress, and a gardenia in your hair."

"Richard, how do you remember such things?" A blush rose to Bonnie's cheeks, and her eyes cast downward at the table.

If Mrs. Brookman were a cat, there'd have been feathers hanging from her lip. She and Richard were conspiring to unsettle him. Floyd dried his palms on the bottom edge of the tablecloth and did his best to appear nonchalant.

Mrs. Carson sighed wistfully. "We all thought Richard and Bonnie would marry one day."

"Don't give up yet, Mother. I have six months to steal Bunnie away," Richard said, reaching an arm around the back of Bonnie's chair.

Mrs. Brookman raised a wineglass to her lips. Although her smile was hidden, the creases at the corners of her eyes belayed her satisfaction.

"Oh, Richard, you haven't changed a bit," Bonnie said. "Still as incorrigible as ever."

Floyd was seething.

At Mr. Brookman's end of the table, a burst of laughter rang out followed by the clanking of glasses. R.J. McLelland lifted one hand to wipe his eyes while the other reached around the redhead's shoulders to hang precariously over her left breast. A member of the kitchen staff rolled a trolley, topped with a soup tureen, into the room. She served Mr. Brookman first, then began working her way along the table.

A thin silver-haired man sitting on Richard's left studied Floyd with an expression of dismay through black-rimmed eyeglasses. He wore a gaudily patterned cravat with a large amethyst pin in the centre. He leaned forward slightly and, in a heavy French accent, said, "Turtleneck . . ."

Floyd, unsure as to how to respond, waited for more words to ensue. But the man only sipped his red wine and then buttered a dinner roll. Richard looked at Floyd and smirked. Bonnie's conversation with Mrs. Carson kept her from witnessing the peculiar exchange.

"Monsieur Raymond. He's an artist," Mr. Carson mumbled to Floyd, as if that explained everything. "So what do you do, Hoffman?"

"Yes, tell us. What is it that you do?" Richard's eager expression told Floyd that he already knew. The server reached over Richard's shoulder for his soup bowl while he waited for a response.

The women's conversation had ended. They were listening too.

"Well, out with it," Mrs. Carson said. "We're all curious now."

"I'm with the postal service," Floyd finally answered.

Mrs. Carson's mouth crumpled.

"He's a mailman," Mrs. Brookman explained in a droll voice.

"But he's a very good one," Bonnie added quickly.

Floyd wished she'd said nothing. Her tone came close to apologetic.

"I tip our mailman every Christmas," Mrs. Carson said in a low voice. "They don't make much money, you know."

"Floyd does just fine. He has a lovely little house," Bonnie said.

A little house? *She might as well call it a shack.*

"This backwater town can't have anything to offer in the way of theatre and galleries. Bunnie, you adore the ballet," Richard said. "You must miss Toronto."

"Sometimes, but I've found simpler pleasures here." She drained her glass of wine, then hastily added, "And Floyd."

Before her hand left the glass, Richard grabbed a wine bottle from a passing server. He leaned easily against Bonnie while he replenished her glass.

"So, Richard," Floyd began, more forcefully than he'd intended. "You'll be leaving tomorrow, I suppose. Back to work on Monday."

"No, I drove the Mercedes up myself. I'll be staying on for a few extra days. Rose has arranged for an intimate group of us to go downhill skiing on Monday." He took a leisurely sip of his wine. "At the very least, the office owes me a day off after the deal I just closed."

"A significant deal," Mrs. Carson boasted. "He was the topgrossing broker in Frank's office."

Of course.

"Floyd, you should come with us," Bonnie said.

"I doubt he owns skis," Mrs. Brookman said. "Besides, he'll be delivering letters. Perhaps another time."

There'd be no *other* time, Floyd knew.

"I'll rent skis for you," Bonnie insisted. "Take the day off and join us." She gulped from her wineglass, and when she set it down again, Mrs. Brookman nudged it out of her reach.

"Blue-collar workers don't enjoy the luxury of spontaneous vacation days," her mother said.

Floyd's face heated. Mrs. Brookman had made her point. A working-class man didn't fit into Bonnie's life. He wasn't good enough for her. Eager for a chance to collect himself, he tore off a piece of dinner roll and pushed it into his mouth. *I could ask for the day off. Maybe.* When he drew a deep breath to speak, bread crumbs sucked into his windpipe. He coughed and gasped for air. As he fought to regain his breath, he reached for the glass pitcher in the centre of the table, intent on pouring himself a drink. His eyes watered. Everything before him turned blurry.

"Are you all right?" Bonnie asked.

Floyd nodded, but continued to cough. He returned the pitcher to the table, but when he mistakenly set it on the edge of a dinner plate, it toppled towards him. Water gushed over the front edge of the table and flooded his lap. He shoved his chair suddenly away from the table to avoid a further soaking.

The chair met with resistance. A startled cry sounded behind him along with the clatter of metal against the floor. He'd collided with the soup trolley and knocked the ladle from the server's hand. Lobster bisque had splashed the front of the woman's uniform.

"I'm sorry, so terribly sorry," Floyd wheezed. He stood up and wiped his eyes.

The lap of his pants was dark with water, as though he'd urinated himself.

Bonnie's hands flew to her face. Richard broke into riotous laughter. A round of applause rose up from Mr. Brookman's side of the dining room. The Carsons rolled the tablecloth away from the edge of the table and sopped up some of the water with dinner napkins.

Mrs. Brookman touched her dinner napkin to either corner of her mouth and addressed the server, now wiping soup from the front of her uniform with a kitchen towel. "Marian, take Mr. Hoffman to the laundry room. See to it that he dries his pants. And send someone to clean this up. We'll need a new place setting and half a dozen fresh dinner napkins."

"Yes, ma'am," Marian said. She pushed the trolley against the wall behind Floyd.

"I'm coming with you," Bonnie said, sliding her chair away from the table.

"Stay here." Mrs. Brookman clamped a hand over Bonnie's. "Chef has prepared Waldorf salad, your favourite. It should be coming out soon."

"I'll only be a moment," Floyd said. He smiled to hide his humiliation from Mrs. Brookman and Richard. If not for Bonnie, he'd have bolted for the door and put the entire event behind him.

"All right, then," she said.

The note of relief in her voice bruised him like knees hitting a sidewalk. He'd embarrassed her, which was worse than any embarrassment he felt for himself. With his head hung low so as to avert the eyes of the other guests, he followed Marian into the hallway like a scolded child.

The music and laughter of the dinner party faded behind them, replaced by the clanging of a busy kitchen as they neared the rear of the house. They stepped aside to make way for two servers carrying wide silver trays packed with salad plates. Once the other staff had squeezed by, Marian showed Floyd into the laundry room, the door of which was located just before the kitchen entrance at the end of the hall.

Marian regarded him with empathy. "In a few days, this will all be forgotten."

Floyd doubted that was true, but he thanked her anyway. After she left, he unlaced his shoes and hurled them across the room. Then he kicked off his soaked trousers and pitched them into the nearest of three dryers. He wanted to slam the dryer door shut, then open it, and slam it over and over again. But, mindful of not drawing more attention to himself than he already had, he opted to close the door lightly and cranked the timer to fifteen minutes. He paced along the line of washing machines in his stocking feet, acutely aware of what a pitiful sight he made in damp boxers and Christmas turtleneck.

He rested his elbows on the folding counter and cupped his face in his hands. How could he go back to the dining room and rejoin those people after making such an ass of himself? But return he must for the preservation of his dignity. He raked a hand through his hair. What was he doing here? He'd only succeeded in failing.

Suddenly, the laundry room door flung wide open. Floyd spun around to find himself facing Mrs. Brookman's stony glare. His hands folded in front of his groin. He stood tall with his heels pressed tightly together and waited for the onslaught.

"You won't make her happy," Mrs. Brookman said after a lengthy pause.

"That will be for Bonnie to decide," Floyd said.

"It will be impossible to provide her with a proper lifestyle on your mailman wages. You've no education beyond high school to carry you to greater opportunities."

"I can change that."

"If you love her as you claim to, you'll call off this charade. Let her have a real chance at happiness with someone who is her equal."

"Someone like Richard?"

"Yes." She produced a sardonic smile. "They have a shared history. The Carsons' values align with ours. Richard is a successful broker with a reputable firm. He can afford a house in the city, in a good neighbourhood near galleries, theatre, and vibrant people."

Although Floyd didn't want them to, her points made sense. He should have realized much sooner that Bonnie was far above him.

Mrs. Brookman's eyes gleamed as his veneer of false confidence began to dissolve.

"My daughter is a unique young woman. She requires constant excitement, the kind that only money can buy. Without it, she will become *restless.* I know you understand what I'm saying."

Floyd thought he did.

"Bonnie needs to travel, see the world," Mrs. Brookman continued. "When's the last time you left Narrow Falls?"

Floyd looked at her pencil-thin eyebrows and the diamond-ringed pearls fastened to either earlobe—and hated her.

"I didn't think so," she said smugly. "Consider what I've said. You'll see that I'm right."

The hell of it was—he was beginning to.

Floyd's telephone rang twice shortly after lunch on Sunday, but he didn't answer either time. It was most likely Bonnie calling. He didn't have the heart to talk since Mrs. Brookman had ripped it out the night before. Instead, he spent the afternoon ruminating over all the reasons why Richard was the better man. Floyd loved Bonnie, and it had taken so long to find her. The thought of sending her into the arms of Richard Carson was killing him. So when the telephone rang again closer to dinner, he snatched up the receiver and pressed it to his ear.

"Hello, Floyd?" The concern in Bonnie's voice was immediate.

"Yeah."

"You left so abruptly after dinner. We barely had a chance to say good night."

Floyd scrambled for a plausible excuse, but none came to mind.

"Are you still there?" she asked.

"I am," he said softly. Before hearing her voice, he thought he could do what needed to be done, but now he wasn't sure.

"Something's wrong. I can hear it in your voice." She paused. "Did Mother get to you?"

Floyd didn't answer. His heart was rend in two.

"She did! I knew it."

"Your mother's right. I'll never be Richard. You'll end up hating me." He listened anxiously, wishing he could unsay it.

The receiver slammed down on the other end of the line.

A numbness permeated his body, as though he'd been plunged beneath the surface of an icy river. He'd ruined the best thing that had ever happened to him. Floyd's back slid down the wall until he reached the floor. "Stupid, stupid, stupid!" His fists struck against his forehead, and tears streamed down his face.

Ten minutes later, feet pounded up the porch stairs, and a hail of fists sounded against the front door of the house. Floyd hurried to the front hall and jerked the door open. Bonnie stared back at him from below the ribbed edge of a bright pink toque.

"I don't want Richard," she shouted.

"But, Bonnie . . ."

"But nothing. It's you I want. I love you!"

"Think of it, Bonnie, he can provide for you in the way you deserve. Look at this house and how I live. It's a long way down from what you're used to." In spite of his words, Floyd wanted her to keep fighting for him, convincing him that he was the one. The wind blew strands of hair across her cheek. She was so beautiful it hurt to look at her.

"Mother, Richard, and all those snooty people—they want to change me." Bonnie's mittened hands mashed together as if shaping a snowball. "They want to mould me into the perfect high-society girl. But I won't let them turn me into someone I'm not." She threw her mittens on the ground and reached for his hands. "I want you, Floyd."

"But Richard—"

"I could never love Richard Carson the way I love you. There isn't a genuine bone in his body. He's a puppet, and his parents pull the strings. If not for his father, he wouldn't have that job he brags about. Besides, I don't like who I am when I'm around him."

"Come inside," Floyd said. "You must be freezing."

She stepped into the warmth of the front hall and pulled her hat off. "Richard and I were spoiled rich kids, and we behaved badly. He thought it was funny when I got tipsy. Richard spurred me on. And I loathe the way he calls me *Bunnie*. He only does it because I dislike it so.

"You would never do that. You love me enough to let me be who I am, and I trust you to steer me away from being *that* Bonnie who does foolish things. You're real and honest. And I know you have my best interest at heart, always. I feel safe with you." She stepped forward to kiss him. "There's no one else for me, only you."

"What about money? I'll never be rich," Floyd said.

"I know a lot of rich people. They're not happy people." With a coquettish smile, she unzipped her coat and let it slip to the floor.

She loves me. She really loves me.

"Are you going to ask me to stay?"

He slowly unwound the scarf from her neck. "Would you like to stay, Ms. Brookman?"

"Forever," she answered.

April 1963

Fall turned to winter, then yielded to spring. By April, plans were underway for a late June wedding. Bonnie and her mother sat on either side of an antique writing desk in the Brookman's parlour, debating every manner of detail concerning colour palettes, linens, crystal, floral arrangements, garden furniture, appetizers, and wine selection. Mr. Brookman smoked his pipe and looked on with calm detachment, as if watching a cricket match or a round of polo at a country club. The jarring experience of raised voices and heightened emotions made Floyd's stomach squeeze into a knot.

"I don't see the point of such a large wedding party," Bonnie argued. "Eight bridesmaids and groomsmen plus the maid of honour and best man?"

"You don't need to see the sense of it, my dear. It's how things are done," her mother said coolly. "Look at the list of names again, and choose."

Bonnie left the desk. She braced her hands against the edge of the baby grand piano in the corner of the room and let her head drop forward in exasperation. "I've seen your list, Mother. Most of these people aren't my friends. Floyd's never laid eyes on any of them."

"It's quite simple. Either you choose your wedding party or I will."

"Mother! You're not listening to me."

Mrs. Brookman ran the tip of her pen down the length of her lavender-coloured paper, then jotted a note. Without lifting her eyes from the page, she said, "We could discuss flowers for the house instead, if you prefer."

Bonnie's jaw clenched, and her eyes watered. When she turned on her heel and bolted from the parlour, Floyd stood to follow her.

Mrs. Brookman leveled a scathing gaze at him before gently addressing Bonnie's father. "Gene, would you be good enough to settle her down?"

"Certainly, dear." He winked as Floyd lowered himself back onto the sofa.

"Roses it is, then," Mrs. Brookman said, adding a check mark to her list. She looked up at Floyd as if daring him to contradict her.

Floyd burned with indignation at her treatment of Bonnie. The wedding party issue was not resolved. If he just approached the situation with tact and diplomacy, surely he could make some headway.

"I've given this a lot of thought, Mrs. Brookman. I'm going to ask Vic Patterson to be my best man."

Mrs. Brookman's shoulders lifted as she laughed. "Oh, for a moment I thought you really meant it."

"But I do," he said with determination. "Vic has been a steadfast friend. If not for him, I may have never asked Bonnie to marry me."

"Vic Patterson is old enough to be your father. Think of the wedding photos," she said with a shudder.

"I feel strongly on this point, Mrs. Brookman. Vic is my good friend. It's important to me that he is honoured in some way."

Mrs. Brookman rested an index finger against her chin. "He can sit in the front row during the ceremony and at the head table during dinner. It's unorthodox, and I don't like it. That's the best you'll get from me."

In light of her obstinate nature, Floyd viewed her concession as his victory. At least he'd gained something. "Thank you," he said.

"My father once told me that a fair negotiation is one where both sides come away hurting. And so, Mr. Hoffman, you must give me something in return. The best man will be Richard Carson."

The name was a punch in the gut. Floyd's mind churned through the implications of her request. He despised Richard, but the wedding would only last for one afternoon. Floyd had won the big battle. Bonnie would be his forever. He might even enjoy Richard's discomfort at standing so close to them during the exchange of vows.

"Done," he said with a lift of his chin.

She smiled and noted Floyd's decision on her paper.

Marian appeared at the French doors. She smiled at Floyd and waited for Mrs. Brookman to look up from her writing desk. "Reverend Findlay has arrived."

"Make him wait a minute, then show him in."

With a nod, Marian backed out of the room and pulled the doors closed.

"I wasn't aware we were meeting with the reverend today," Floyd said.

"Falling behind already?"

"No. Bonnie just didn't mention it," he answered, instantly regretting his defensive tone.

Mrs. Brookman sniffed and gave him a knowing look that made the tops of his ears burn.

The French doors parted, and Reverend Findlay strode into the room. He exchanged pleasantries with Mrs. Brookman and sat in her husband's chair. Floyd was ready with a polite smile, but the man never looked his way.

"The ladies' auxiliary would like a word with you, at your earliest convenience, Mrs. Brookman. It's a matter regarding the menu for the wedding supper," the reverend said.

Bonnie's mother smiled. "We don't require their services."

His face grew stern. "The ladies always prepare the meal when couples marry at the church. It's a tradition."

"My daughter will not be married at the church."

Floyd squeezed an arm of the sofa. No one had mentioned this change of plans to him.

"She'll be married here, in our garden." Mrs. Brookman shook the china bell sitting on a corner of her desk.

Patches of red splotched the reverend's neck above his clerical collar. "Marriage is a ceremony meant to be performed inside the sanctity of the church. Not a frivolous, giddy occasion to be held in a flower garden."

"You'll not find a hint of a smile at *these* nuptials," she countered.

Floyd glanced nervously in the direction of the French doors and wished Bonnie would step through them. Marian reappeared instead, carrying a large rectangular gift box, which she presented to the reverend. His lips parted and his brows knit together as he stared at the box resting on his knees.

"You may open your gift, Reverend." Mrs. Brookman smiled victoriously as he untied the ribbon and lifted the lid. "I had it specially made for you."

Wide-eyed, he passed a hand over the folded vestments. When he lifted the purple stole to thumb the embroidered cross, a cheque slid from its folds and fluttered onto the white carpet. Floyd hastily returned it to the reverend. *Payable to Narrow Falls United Church. Two thousand dollars.*

"For the mission field," she said.

"This is extremely generous," the reverend said slowly.

"Yes," Mrs. Brookman said as she rose to her feet. "Perhaps we should venture out to the garden. The arbour and the terrace are ideal for a wedding."

Floyd studied his shoes for a moment, then cleared his throat. "Mrs. Brookman, I have one other request—that Bonnie walk down the aisle to Pachelbel's Canon in D."

"A *German* composer?" Mrs. Brookman asked as if she hadn't heard properly.

"Yes, Johann Pachelbel is a favourite of my father's."

"Will your father be in attendance?" she asked.

For the hundredth time, Floyd imagined his parents gawking with disapproval at the opulence of the house. They didn't even know he was getting married. "No."

"Then he won't mind that we don't play it." Mrs. Brookman closed her eyes briefly and sighed with impatience. "Bonnie will prefer something of a French influence, or perhaps Italian."

With an unwavering gaze, Floyd replied, "Bonnie should be consulted. It's her day."

She returned the look with smug confidence. "A mother knows her daughter. In some cases, better than the husband does. Don't you agree, Reverend Findlay?"

"Absolutely," he replied.

• • •

A week before the big day, Floyd could no longer put off telling his parents about his plans to marry. He expected the conversation to be strained, but his parents' hostility jolted him. The late notice angered his father. Were he and his wife not good enough for the Brookmans? The bride's family deflected attention from themselves by flaunting such lavish trappings. What were they hiding? Floyd had reached beyond his station, they said. Why not a nice German girl? The final blow came when details about the engagement ring surfaced. They couldn't believe he'd put a stranger's ring on the girl's hand when his own grandmother's wedding band waited in a drawer. No one else would use it now. He was the last Hoffman.

"One son, I have. One son." There was a lengthy pause, then his father's deep-voiced condemnation, "You disappoint me."

Floyd hung his head.

On the evening before Floyd and Bonnie were to be married, the Brookmans hosted a wedding rehearsal in their garden. Members of the wedding party planned to trickle into Narrow Falls throughout the day before the wedding. The bridesmaids would be paired up in bedrooms on the upper floor of the mansion as the groomsmen would be in the wing facing the garden. Bonnie had telephoned midweek to tell him the kitchen was operating like a military base on high alert. Mrs. Brookman kept the house staff busy with preparations for the rehearsal party dinner and the wedding. Her mother's nerves had been taut all week, so he kept his distance.

That evening, Floyd walked around the west side of the mansion towards the garden. Through the low set parlour windows, he could see that the settee and armchairs had been rearranged to make room for some elbow-height pedestal tables. Mrs. Brookman may not be happy about his marrying her daughter, but she was sparing no expense to make the proper impression on her guests.

Once he'd rounded the corner of the building and passed between a pair of towering cedars, he paused amid a sprawl of waist-height shrubbery and peered tentatively at the terrace. The bridesmaids and groomsmen had already congregated there around a grouping of round tables. He spotted Richard Carson at the centre of the group with his arm slung around the shoulders of a long-haired blond woman wearing dark sunglasses and a blue mini skirt. "Hoffman!" he shouted. "Quit hiding in the bushes, you ole scallywag."

Floyd was at once the focus of attention, the very thing he most dreaded. He sucked his breath in and walked onto the terrace. "Hello."

"Everyone, this is Floyd," Richard said. "Floyd . . . everyone."

The women's voices droned together in a tepid greeting. One man said hello and stood to shake his hand.

"Bonnie's over there." One of the women pointed to the centre of the lawn, where Bonnie and her parents had gathered at the rose arbour with Reverend Findlay.

Mrs. Brookman's expression curdled when she saw Floyd coming towards them. Bonnie's eyes lit, and she skipped towards him. "We're going over ceremony details," she said, leaning in to kiss his cheek. She looped her arm through his and walked him to the arbour.

"And here he is, the man of the hour," Mrs. Brookman said.

The reverend turned to Mrs. Brookman. "We could begin rehearsal now, wouldn't you say?"

Their group moved to a wrought-iron garden chair stationed about thirty feet from the arbour and in alignment with a set of parlour doors that opened onto the terrace.

Mr. Brookman hooked his little fingers inside the corners of his mouth and loosed an earsplitting whistle. Bonnie's mother frowned. "Gene, really."

A man and woman zipped through the French doors along with two children—a boy and a girl—in tow. One by one, people left the terrace and set off across the lawn.

"The chair marks the beginning of the aisle," Reverend Findlay told the wedding party. "You men line up behind the groom according to the order Mrs. Brookman has set. Ladies, you will line up accordingly behind the groomsmen. Then the ring bearer and flower girl. And last but not least, Bonnie and Mr. Brookman." The reverend beamed as everyone fell in order. "All right, then, next we—"

"Reverend, if I might intervene," Mrs. Brookman said, ignoring his fading smile. "I've designated three rooms upstairs where the groom and the other young men will dress and wait for the ceremony to begin."

The arrangement was acceptable to Floyd. The less time he needed to spend among the throngs of wedding guests, none of whom he knew but Vic Patterson, the better.

"Pardon me, Rose," Richard said.

Mrs. Brookman smiled sweetly at him. "Yes, Richard, dear?"

"Groomsmen usually usher. The fellows and I spoke about it earlier today. Edward and John have agreed to fill that role, if it's agreeable with you."

"Indeed. Thank you, boys," she said.

Floyd imagined Richard gloating behind him.

"One of you must watch from an upstairs window for your cue. When you see the flautist and violinist have taken their place next to the arbour, the groom and his men will come downstairs, through the parlour doors, across the terrace, and along the aisle."

Reverend Findlay puffed his chest out. "The best man will usher the mother of the bride to her seat, of course, before the rest of you proceed up the aisle." He smiled at Mrs. Brookman and then returned to the arbour and pointed to a spot in the grass. "The groom will stand here."

Floyd felt a hand against the back of his right shoulder.

"Go," Richard said.

Floyd and the men trooped forward to the arbour and fanned out in a row.

"Once the men are in position, music will begin, and then the bridesmaids will come through. And then the flower girl and ring boy, followed by," Mrs. Brookman paused to sigh, "Bonnie and Gene."

"Mrs. Brookman, if I may?" Reverend Findlay said with a pained expression.

"Yes, yes," she said.

"Let us begin," he said with a wave of his Bible.

The bridesmaids walked the grassy aisle and lined up opposite Floyd and the groomsmen, then the ring bearer trudged uncertainly along the strip of grass while the flower girl dawdled along next to him.

Bonnie's father whispered something in her ear. When she shrieked with laughter, the reverend's brows mashed together, and his mouth flopped open as if he might protest. But his eyes flicked to Mrs. Brookman's, and he said nothing.

Throughout the rehearsal of vows, Floyd felt the pressure of being watched, as if by vultures waiting their turn to rip at carrion. How much worse would it be at the actual wedding? Certain people would be waiting for him to fumble his lines or drop the ring. Or maybe for Bonnie to change her mind and run for the house. At the very least, people would be looking at him and thinking, *He doesn't belong.* If only he and Bonnie could have dodged this grandiose affair in favour of a quiet ceremony.

After the rehearsal, a light dinner was served on the terrace. Across from Floyd and Bonnie, Reverend Findlay sat chatting exclusively with Mrs. Brookman. Bonnie laid her cutlery next to her plate and leaned against the back of her chair with her arms folded across her chest. Suddenly, she tossed a chunk of dinner roll at the reverend's plate.

Floyd's fork stopped halfway to his mouth.

"When are you going to stop treating Floyd like he's invisible?" she asked.

Reverend Findlay looked at Bonnie as if seeing her for the first time. "I beg your pardon?" he said, craning his head forward.

"Do you plan, at any point this evening," she said loudly, "to direct your conversation towards my fiancé?"

"Bonnie," her mother warned.

The reverend stared goggle-eyed at Bonnie.

"You've not spoken to him except to tell him where to stand and what words to repeat for our vows. He *is* the groom, and therefore," she said, "half of the reason you're here. You could at least make an effort to be social with him!"

"Here we go," Richard said, lifting his wineglass. "Dinner *and* a show. Oh, how I've missed this."

The reverend's face reddened with indignation, and he turned towards Mrs. Brookman.

"That's enough, Bonnie," she said.

"By this time tomorrow, I'll be a married woman. I'll say what I like."

Floyd touched Bonnie's shoulder. "It's all right," he whispered.

"No, it's not!" Bonnie said. She stood up and tossed her dinner napkin in the centre of her salad plate. Conversations along the table ceased. "He should be thanking you, Floyd. Without your proposal, he'd have never raked in that ridiculously large donation cheque my mother wrote to pressure him into performing the wedding here."

"That money was for the church," the young reverend protested.

"Gene, do something," Bonnie's mother hissed.

Mr. Brookman finished chewing a mouthful of his dinner and took a gulp from his water glass. "Sweetheart, what your mother is trying to say—"

Bonnie's eyes glistened as she leaned over the table and thrust an index finger at the reverend. "All I want is for this man to say something conversational to my fiancé."

For a moment, no one spoke.

Then Reverend Findlay, his eyes cold and squinting from behind the silver frame of his glasses, cleared his throat and said, "Floyd, are you looking forward to tomorrow's nuptials?"

"I am," Floyd replied, looking up at Bonnie.

A satisfied smile lit her face. "Wasn't that easy?" She sat down, returned the napkin to her lap, and began eating as if nothing had happened.

One of the groomsmen applauded, and the rest of the wedding party followed suit. Mr. Brookman chuckled and reached for a wine bottle to refresh the reverend's glass.

Floyd racked his brain trying to figure out how he might have given the impression that he was bothered by the reverend's arm's-length treatment of him. In fact, Floyd had been relieved by the distance between them. He looked left then right along the table. Everyone but the reverend went on eating as if nothing unusual had occurred. His look of uncertainty matched Floyd's. When their confused gazes met, they hastily looked away from each other and resumed their meals.

On the afternoon of the wedding, piano music emanating from the Brookmans' parlour could be heard in the upstairs bedroom where Floyd sat at a window overlooking the garden. He was already dressed in his black tuxedo and pinned with a red rose boutonniere. Behind him, two of his groomsmen sat on the side of a twin bed and smoked cigarettes over a shared ashtray. Two others rested in armchairs, and another pair had claimed the dressing benches at the foot of each bed. The room reeked of cigarette smoke, cologne, and flowers. There were more vases of roses and carnations in the house than at a funeral. At moments, the combined odours had turned Floyd's stomach.

His parents would have hated the formality and scale of the wedding. Two large columns of white chairs were arranged in front of the arbour. Early that morning, along the west side of the lawn, a raised dance floor had been constructed and a canopy mounted above it. After dinner, a band would assemble on a secondary platform next to it. On the terrace, a head table designed to seat twenty-four people stretched the length of the parlour wall. Large circular tables filled the remainder of the terrace and the surrounding lawn. Waitstaff darted between them to make final checks of the floral arrangements and place settings.

Couples were walking through the garden, stopping to talk with other guests. New arrivals continued to cross the lawn. The women wore flouncy brimmed hats with flowers pinned to them. Two hundred white chairs faced the arbour where Floyd and Bonnie would take their vows. Three quarters of the chairs were filled. It must be nearly time for the ceremony to begin. The attention of all those eyes would be trained on Bonnie. And him. He ran a finger around the inside of his collar and tugged to loosen his tie.

"Looking out the window won't make this thing happen any faster," Richard said. "Come have a Scotch with me." He raised his glass.

"Same answer as last time," Floyd said without turning away from the window.

"That's a *no*, then," Richard said. He took a drink and picked a piece of tobacco from his bottom lip. "I wonder how the girls are getting along."

"Don't bother them again, Richard," one of the other men laughed. "They're apt to throw something at you this time."

The piano music has stopped.

Floyd leaned into the window and scanned the yard. The two ushers were busy directing stray guests to their chairs. Reverend Findlay was already standing under the arbour with his Bible hugged against purple vestments. The violinist and flautist were making their way towards him.

"It's time," Floyd announced.

The men jockeyed for a last look in the mirror and smoothed their tuxedo jackets before heading to the parlour. They gathered at the bottom of the stairs and sorted themselves into order. Floyd would lead them out, with Richard behind him.

Mr. Brookman met them at the French doors leading onto the terrace. "Break a leg, boys. See you out there."

At least one of Bonnie's parents is happy about the marriage.

Floyd led the way across the lawn and stopped at the bottom of the grassy aisle where Mrs. Brookman waited in a pale green dress and matching hat. Richard stepped forward and offered her an arm, then ushered her to the front row. He smiled into the crowd and patted the shoulders of a few guests seated along the aisle as he returned to his place in line.

When Reverend Findlay gave the nod to proceed, Floyd's mouth went dry. After a moment, Richard leaned close to Floyd and, in a surly voice, said, "Well, what are you waiting for?"

Floyd's mind blanked completely as he walked towards the arbour. The words he was supposed to say fled his mind. Steps from the rehearsal evaded his memory. As he passed the front row of seats, Vic Patterson bolstered him with an atta-boy smile. Floyd clasped his shaking hands in front of him and waited for the groomsmen to fall into position.

The violinist and flautist raised their instruments and began to play. The line of bridesmaids preceded Bonnie and her father across the lawn towards the aisle separating the seated guests. The maid of honour blocked Floyd's view of Bonnie except for one edge of her dress and the top of her veil. Each of the bridesmaids held their bouquet in front of their raspberry-coloured dresses and, one by one, walked smiling along the aisle. The ring bearer and flower girl followed close behind, levying sounds of approval as they waved at the crowd and dropped flower petals in the grass. Once the maid of honour joined the other bridesmaids opposite Floyd and the children were seated in the first row, Bonnie and her father linked arms and took their first step forward.

Here she comes.

Bonnie was dressed in lace and layers of fabric that reminded him of sheer curtains lifted on a summer breeze. She appeared to float across the grass in a state more beautiful than he'd dreamed of.

Floyd's knees began to tremble. At first, it was just a slight shaking behind his kneecaps. But as Bonnie neared the arbour, and he could see those piercing eyes looking out through the lace of her veil, the quaking of his legs increased. People were looking at her but also looking at him now. All these people, watching and wondering, *Why him?* He loved her so much. Could he really do it—marry her and make her as happy as she was going to make him?

She stood next to him and smiled so radiantly he could barely breathe.

Reverend Findlay cleared his throat and stared out over the guests. "Into this union, Bonnie Eleanor Brookman and Floyd Aldric Hoffman have come to be joined in holy matrimony. If anyone here may show just cause why they may not be lawfully married, speak now or forever hold your peace."

When, after several seconds, no one spoke, the reverend continued.

"Bonnie Eleanor Brookman, do you take this man as your husband, to love him and keep him in sickness and in health, forsaking all others, be faithful unto him, for as long as you both shall live?"

"I will," Bonnie replied.

"Floyd Aldric Hoffman, do you . . ."

The reverend's words sounded distant, as if they were faint echoes travelling from the far end of a long tunnel. Floyd's head sloshed on the inside like water against the prow of a boat.

"Hey," Bonnie said with affection. "You just look at me." She pointed her right index finger at her chin and drew a circle around her face. "We're the only people that matter."

When she prompted him by mouthing, *I will*, Floyd offered a lopsided grin. He focused on her face, and the rest of the world receded. "I will," he said loudly.

Their eyes remained locked on each other during the remainder of their vows, looking away only to place the gold bands on each other's fingers.

"Now that Bonnie and Floyd have pledged themselves to one another through the giving and receiving of rings, I pronounce them husband and wife. You—"

Bonnie's arms flung around Floyd's neck, and her lips crushed hard against his. The full length of her tongue thrust into his mouth, and his eyes popped wide open.

"—may kiss the bride," the reverend finished with a tone of disapproval.

Discreet giggles erupted in the bridesmaid line. A sharp whistle pierced the silence and the groomsmen whooped. A smattering of reserved applause emanated from the seated guests.

"Oh, dear Lord," Mrs. Brookman muttered.

After the ceremony, the Brookman house surged with the busyness of an anthill. Floyd spent the afternoon sidestepping waiters dressed in neatly pressed uniforms. They wove through the garden balancing champagne flutes on silver trays. Women wearing black skirts and comfortable shoes darted back and forth from the kitchen to the terrace, hefting silver tureens filled with foods that Floyd had never eaten before.

Mr. Brookman introduced him to all of the *right* people. They shook Floyd's hand and waited for him to speak, but the pressure to make small talk silenced him. He doubted other people's interest in Russian history, local geology, or the migratory habits of geese.

Floyd was the only person at his wedding with *his* last name—except Bonnie. There'd been no telephone call from his parents. Served him right for hoping they'd change their minds and show up. How could he feel so lonely when so much life swirled around him?

He had Bonnie, he reminded himself, and that was enough. She was a vision, all fluffed out with crinolines. Mrs. Brookman was circulating her through the garden like a show pony, stopping to ingratiate her with the most prestigious guests. When Bonnie laughed, her chin lifted and her neck arched gracefully.

"I'm so lucky," Floyd whispered.

Vic joined him on the terrace. He took a cold drink from a passing waiter and pressed it to his forehead. "Ooh, it's a hot one, isn't it?"

"She's like a swan." Floyd leaned against the terrace balustrade and raised a glass of lemonade to his bride. Next to Bonnie, her mother was studying him with a look of disdain.

"Son, you're in deep water," Vic said. He was watching Mrs. Brookman. "Don't let the sharks sink their teeth into you." He grinned and doffed an imaginary hat to Bonnie's mother.

She grimaced and turned away.

10.

When you're halfway through hell, keep going. Winston Churchill's words looped through Floyd's mind as he trudged south along Main Street in the direction of the Brookman estate.

By his estimation, this visit to Bonnie's mother marked the midpoint between the initial ambush of Dean's illness and, hopefully, its defeat. He'd determined from the onset to divide the coming months into survivable portions of time. Scraping and bowing before Mrs. Brookman would be one of those isolated events. The name of one doctor was all he needed from her. Surely, old grudges against him wouldn't dissuade her from helping her grandson.

Muted laughter from farther down the street drew Floyd's attention. Two teenage boys emerged from the alley between the dry cleaners and the florist shop and then turned to walk in his direction. The taller boy looked familiar, a friend of Dean's, perhaps. His shirt lolled open, and he carried a guitar by its strap slung over one shoulder. His eyes narrowed as Floyd walked by.

"Hey!"

Floyd turned abruptly.

"You're Dean Hoffman's old man?" The guitar boy waited with keen interest, but his friend's eyes sparkled with suspicion beneath the creased peak of his Yankees ball cap.

"Yes," Floyd answered

"I heard he wasn't doing too good."

"He'll be fine."

"That's great, man." The boy tugged at the guitar strap and hoisted the instrument higher on the back of his shoulder. "Does he still play?"

"Sometimes." The lie caught in the back of Floyd's throat. Guitar music hadn't come from Dean's room in weeks.

"Cool. We should jam again sometime."

Floyd nodded. His lips pressed together, and his chest ached.

The second boy nudged his friend's elbow and whispered, "Allan, let's go."

"See ya." Allan and the other boy eased between two parked cars and onto the street.

Floyd painted Dean into the scene, with his scratched-up Gibson bumping against his back as he kept pace with his friends. He'd have been laughing easily with these boys, leaning forward as he walked with an eagerness to reach wherever they were heading off to.

Allan stopped in the centre of the street. "Storm's comin'!" A car slowed, and its horn honked. "You better pick up the pace, Hoff Man." Then he raised his fingers in a peace sign to the driver and fell back into step with his friend.

A wide slash of dark sky extended above Narrow Falls. Floyd pushed his shoulders back and resumed walking. Responsibility settled on him like a thousand anvils. His plea for Mrs. Brookman's help could mean the difference between life and death for Dean. He must succeed.

His own father had once told him that in medieval Germany, a *hoffman* was a steward of other men's property. Floyd labeled himself a poor caretaker. While his eyes had been trained on Bonnie, Dean had become a fallow field.

In a lucid moment before her death, Bonnie had begged, "Let me be his angel. Please, Floyd. Don't tell him I'm broken."

"I promise."

Floyd hoped that Dean would mature beyond his teenage angst, and the truth would become a whisper in his ear, that his mother had a disturbance of the mind beyond her control. He would realize that when she dragged him from bed to walk moonlit back roads and jump from waterfalls, his father had reacted with tolerance. He would remember there'd been no threats to have her committed when she carved a Shakespearean quote into a windowsill over and over again with a ball point pen. His father never complained when she rearranged the living room furniture at midnight, and he didn't insist on medication to end her malaise, even when she lay in bed for days. He would see that Floyd bore no resentment towards his mother for the complexities her illness brought to his life. Not when she railed inside the house or sank onto her knees, wailing in the yard. Not when the neighbours looked at his father accusingly or spread rumours that he'd driven her to despair.

If Dean guessed the truth, Floyd could release Bonnie's secrets like doves from a cage. But if Dean didn't live long enough for his realization to spark, he'd never figure the truth out on his own. The key was time.

Floyd reached the corner of Clarence and Main as the sky turned to slate grey and a cool breeze began to blow. The rain would catch up to him soon.

Conflict made his skin itch. If only this business with Mrs. Brookman were over. She'd want to control every detail of Dean's situation. Under pressure, words typically failed Floyd, but today he would surprise her. He hoped she wouldn't surprise him in return.

His quiet nature had fueled Mrs. Brookman's disdain from the beginning. "He'll never do. The man is a simpleton," she'd told Bonnie. Even his German heritage revolted Rose Brookman. One glance from her reduced him to a knee-knocking schoolboy.

Growing up, his parents spoke only when a situation demanded it, but rarely for the music of the words. Through two World Wars, his grandparents had cloaked themselves in hard work and kept their mouths shut. His mother and father mashed emotional issues into small jars and screwed the lids down tightly. *Bad things happened, but that's in the past. Don't speak on it now.* Stoicism equaled strength. That was the Hoffman way.

As he trundled down the street, Floyd reflected on his need to change. "A stone shows more emotion than you," Dean had yelled at him once. He needed more from a father than food on the table and a roof over his head. It was tough for Floyd to alter the fabric of who he was, but he would dedicate himself to trying, for Dean's sake.

He'd begin with optimism. After the Toronto doctors worked their magic on Dean, he and the boy would drive the Volkswagen to his parents' home in Kitchener for the first time in a decade. They'd picnic at Victoria Park and tour the Joseph Schneider *haus*. When Dean tired of his grandmother's sauerkraut and beef *eintopf*, they'd return to Narrow Falls and set about turning their own house into a home. He could spring for some paint and a new sofa. Enough time had passed since Bonnie's death to justify unlocking the room behind the kitchen.

Floyd advanced down the sidewalk with a renewed conviction to stop smothering the past. He'd been afraid for so long of saying the wrong things that he'd said nothing. He could change. He knew he could.

It took only a few blocks for Floyd's spirits to plummet again. Walking loosened the memories he'd allowed himself to forget. He had done his best to spare Dean from witnessing Bonnie's darkest days. "I want my mama," he'd cry, pounding on the bedroom door. Each time Floyd carried him downstairs, a ball of anger glowed hotter where trust used to reside.

Floyd had dreamed recently that he was standing beside Bonnie's sickbed. She'd looked up at him, dull-eyed and face drawn. Then, somehow, her face had changed, and it was Dean glaring up at him. Floyd had awoken with his damp pajama shirt plastered to his skin. He'd sat up, staring at the wall, and waited for the reassurance of coughing from downstairs. Each time Floyd's eyes closed, Dean's face haunted him.

He ashamedly admitted that when Dean stopped talking to him in the spring, he'd been relieved. It was a reprieve from that face, so much like his mother's. Maybe Dean would have been better off growing up at the Brookmans', farther away from the mill. Fingers of guilt squeezed his heart at the thought.

When he could no longer hear chains clanking together on flatbed trucks or the hissing release of air brakes, Floyd knew he'd reached the side of town where money fixes everything. Aged maples lined the streets like watchful sentries, their trunk circumferences measuring more than twice the span of a man's arms. Estate homes towered among bridal wreath shrubberies, perfectly edged walkways, and climbing roses on white painted trellises. These wooden castles with their turrets and coach houses belonged to families with names like Whittemore, Beaupre, and McTavish. No Hoffmans, Beckers, or Straubs.

A fine mist began to fall as Floyd neared the Brookman house, and thunder rumbled in the distance. Through his wet glasses, the wavy hulk of the Brewster-brick house appeared like a beacon of hope. It stood among its neighbours' gingerbread cornices as unapologetic as a boisterous third cousin at a family reunion. Brewster's Brickworks had given his father a job despite the anti-German sentiments of wartime. Sometimes people did the right thing.

He felt hopeful until he considered Mrs. Brookman's dogged attempts to gain custody of Dean following Bonnie's death. She'd testified that Floyd was emotionally absent and unfit to parent. In some ways, she'd been right. Bonnie's pattern of despondency and euphoria were the seasons Floyd had lived by. Her absence created a vacuum he could barely function in. At the time, Gerald Smith and Clive Harper were no match for Mrs. Brookman's legal team. Had it not been for Mr. Brookman, Floyd would have lost Dean. "Rose, you can't rip the boy from the only home he's ever known," Mr. Brookman had cautioned, "and just after losing his mother this way. It's not right."

Floyd reached the beginning of the Brookmans' garden wall as a light drizzle began to fall. He followed its stone face across the front of the estate, then took shelter beneath some low-hanging pine boughs twenty feet from the main gate.

Tears streamed down Floyd's face. He couldn't be the last Hoffman. What kind of God would take his son? A jealous God. Perhaps he was being punished for seeking comfort in science instead of the church.

Right on cue, the clouds opened up, and torrents of rain dropped from the sky.

Floyd rushed to the wrought-iron gates. He'd expected them to be closed, but instead they were wide open. The sight of two Lincoln Continentals parked on the circular drive caused his pace to slow. "No . . ." He exhaled the word and deflated like a spent balloon. A sharp flash of lightning prompted him to dash between the cars to the shelter of the portico.

Nothing was happening as Floyd had planned. Rainwater dribbled across his glasses. His shirt was sopping wet. And Mrs. Brookman was entertaining rich friends.

The latch clicked, and the front door opened slightly. A melee of male voices spilled outside. The sleeve of a beige overcoat appeared, then the gleam of leather shoes. Laughter flared, and three men stepped out of the house. The first man raised a briefcase above his head and jogged to his car. The second blinked at Floyd with curiosity, then stepped towards the edge of the portico and wrestled his umbrella open. The overhead light reflected off the yawning bald spot amid the curls circling the crown of his head.

"Len," the first man called from the car window.

The second man cast a last look at Floyd and set off into the downpour.

They were followed by a portly man who pulled the door closed behind them. Floyd recognized R.J. McLelland all too well.

"Nice weather, if you're a duck," R.J. called after the other men in a deep whiskey voice. When they ignored his remark, he scowled and pulled a cigar from his suit pocket. "An engineer and a lawyer. Not a sense of humour between 'em," he muttered, searching his pockets. "You going in there?" he asked without looking in Floyd's direction.

"Yup," Floyd replied, trying his best to appear calm.

"Good goddamned luck." The man clicked a lighter and held it to end of the cigar while he drew a series of short puffs. "She'll hand you your ass on a platter if you rub her the wrong way today." He blew a stream of smoke and watched the first Lincoln ease through the gate and onto the street.

Floyd stood smoldering in his wet clothing.

R.J. wheeled towards him, thrusting forward a meaty right hand. "Hey, I'm—"

"R.J. McLelland, Chief Executive Officer of McLelland Pulp and Paper and lapdog to the omnipotent part-owner, Rose Brookman," Floyd said, enjoying the startled look on his face.

R.J. removed the cigar from his mouth. "You cocky son of a bitch!"

"It's unusual to see you outside of the courtroom."

"If you mess with the bull, you're gonna get the horns. Think about that before you stir up more trouble. You'll never win this thing." He jabbed a stubby finger at Floyd, then stepped off the edge of the portico and proceeded to his vehicle without a care for the rain.

"That depends on how you define *win*," Floyd replied.

The moment R.J. McLelland's car pulled out of sight, Floyd's knees turned to rubber.

It took three taps of the brass knocker before the front door swung open to reveal Mrs. Brookman's maid, Marian Smythe, and that much time again for her to recognize him. Her grey-blue eyes were every bit as kind as Floyd remembered. Aside from the silver strands streaking her blond hair, she'd barely changed since he'd last seen her.

"Oh my Lord!" Marian's hands flew to her face.

"I should have called first, but . . ."

"Don't be silly. Let me look at you." Marian was holding Floyd's shoulders before he could fend her off. "You're drenched!"

"Is she here?" Floyd looked over her head.

Marian stepped away, her smile less bright. "Of course. She's a bit laid up though."

"Sick?"

Marian nodded. "A stroke about eight months ago."

Floyd feared all was lost. "How bad?"

"Her left arm doesn't work so well, but she's fierce as ever. Mind like a steel trap and a mouth to match." Marian's eyes softened. "Well, you'd know all about that, wouldn't you?"

Floyd said nothing.

"I'd love to drop by one day. Maybe I could make shepherd's pie for you and Dean. He always loved that when he visited."

"I don't think so, Marian," Floyd said.

She opened her mouth as if to speak but closed it again and motioned Floyd inside. The foyer was designed to intimidate, from the white marble flooring to the vaulted ceiling two stories above his head.

"I'll let her know you're here." Marian smoothed the front of her uniform and climbed the sweeping staircase. She followed the filigree banister across the landing on the second floor, then disappeared from view.

Floyd considered enduring Mrs. Brookman's grand entrance from the vantage point of the foyer bench, as he'd done slavishly in the past. Instead, he walked around the sprawling vase table to a set of French doors and leaned into the parlour. Everything was as he'd remembered. The room was cavernous, its furnishings cringing in corners. Floyd looked across the white carpeting, then down at his shoes, spattered with mud and grass clippings. He removed them and examined his wet socks with skepticism.

He wondered if she would mark the changes time had stamped on his face—the lines deepening at the corners of his mouth or the sparseness of his hairline. Surely, time had changed them both.

Thirty minutes ticked by, and Floyd was still waiting for Mrs. Brookman. His shirt resembled a crumpled newspaper. Pacing the room increased his anxiety, so he turned his attention to specific artifacts in the room and inventoried their minute details.

From a life-sized portrait hanging next to the fireplace, Gene Brookman stared down at Floyd with an expression of mirth. Bonnie's mother had commissioned the painting of her husband following his CEO appointment at McLelland Pulp and Paper. "It's a pretentious business, sitting for this portrait," he'd told Floyd, "but the wife insists." He was born rich, and the trappings failed to impress him. Mrs. Brookman was a different matter altogether. "Money covers up the stink of where she came from," Bonnie had often said. "She wields Father's bank book like a shield."

Silver-framed photographs of Bonnie lined the mantel. It was impossible not to miss her. Dean's face was a constant reminder of her absence. His photos sat mingled among his mother's. None of the pictures Floyd had mailed to Mrs. Brookman over the years were on display. Dean was frozen in time at eight years old.

Floyd's stomach suddenly tensed. Mrs. Brookman's heels struck an uneven beat as she crossed the marble foyer. Her signature gait had lost its staccato rhythm. He dried his palms on the front of his shirt and held his breath. Mrs. Brookman's image appeared in the mirror above the mantel as she stepped through the French doors and into the parlour. She crossed the carpet in halting steps.

They studied each other's reflection for a few seconds before Floyd turned away from the mirror to face her. Mrs. Brookman was thinner than he remembered, and she'd let her hair go white. Her left arm was cradled in a sling fashioned from a silk scarf, and her wedding rings had slid forward to rest against her knuckle.

"Well, if it isn't the prodigal son-in-law."

"Mrs. Brookman."

"If you've come to feast on the fatted calf, you're too late. My advisors tell me your campaign against the mill has sent my stock value plummeting."

"That wasn't my intent."

"You cut me down with the sword of public opinion one day, then come begging the next."

"I haven't come to—"

"Did you think the mill could be drawn under the microscope without consequence?"

"People are dying because of the mill's negligence," Floyd began.

"Both my daughter and husband are dead. You're responsible for that, not the mill." She reached inside the sling and drew out a lace-edged handkerchief, which she then touched to the corner of each eye.

"If I could just explain—"

"If you weren't so soft, Bonnie would have been medicated. She'd still be alive."

"Her mental state was irrelevant to her death. I can directly link her cancer to the dioxins and furans pumping out of that mill."

"Gene wasn't the same man after you filled his head with those lies. He couldn't bear to think that his company played a role in Bonnie dying. You caused his heart attack!"

Floyd's frustration mounted. He couldn't possibly broach the topic of Dean until her anger had run its course.

"I'm glad Gene isn't here to see his legacy being destroyed," she continued. "He poured his heart into that mill and this . . ." Mrs. Brookman's eyelids fluttered, and she swayed to the right.

Floyd rushed towards her and slid one hand beneath her elbow and the other around her waist. A whiff of dried urine reached his nose. "Maybe we should sit." Floyd nodded sheepishly towards the grouping of velvet parlour chairs in the centre of the carpet.

"I'll stand." She glowered up at him from the corner of her eye.

"I do need your help, Mrs. Brookman."

"Ha," she crowed triumphantly.

"Not your money, your influence."

"When the heat turns up, things circle back to money every time."

"It's Dean."

"Of course. You can't manage Dean. You've bungled it all, just like you did with Bonnie."

Floyd wanted to tell her that he'd done his best by Dean. That he loved his son. That despite outward appearances, he'd go to the ends of the earth to save him. Instead, grief expanded inside Floyd's chest and erupted in the back of his throat. A choked sob shot from his mouth when his lips parted. All Floyd could do was reach into his pocket for a handkerchief. As he swiped at his tears, Mrs. Brookman lowered herself into one of the parlour chairs.

"Ohhh." She made the drawn-out sound as if she'd just come to some grand realization. "Is he showing signs?" She tapped a finger against her temple. Her bottom lip trembled, and her brows rose until creases lined her forehead.

"No, Rose. Not *that*."

Mrs. Brookman's right hand flew to her mouth. Her eyes grew round as she whispered through her fingers, "Not . . ."

"Yes. It's in his lungs."

Mrs. Brookman clutched at the armrest to steady herself.

Floyd sagged into the adjacent chair.

"How much time?" she asked.

He shrugged. "We need a second opinion. That's why I've come. You have connections in Toronto. If you just made some calls, someone could help Dean. Maybe the first doctor overlooked something. Maybe a lab worker made an error."

Mrs. Brookman regarded her husband's portrait while Floyd waited for her answer, then she lifted a porcelain bell from the table that separated her chair from his. Her hands shook, and the bell made a sound like silverware tapping against the edge of a china plate. The French doors swung open, and Marian appeared.

"Bring a cup of tea to the study," Mrs. Brookman ordered.

"And Mr. Hoffman?" Marian asked.

"He's fine," Mrs. Brookman snapped. She pushed out of her chair and turned towards Floyd. "Don't move."

When Marian finally returned to inform Floyd that he'd been summoned, his heart raced inside his chest. This was it; renewed hope for Dean's recovery. He followed Marian to the study, where Mrs. Brookman waited behind her husband's desk. The leather office chair dwarfed her slight frame. She positioned her lame arm on the desk at an angle to mirror her right and clasped her hands. A stoic expression replaced the frailty she'd shown earlier.

"Sit."

Floyd settled in the guest chair.

"It's done. He'll be seen Thursday afternoon."

"Oh, thank God!" Floyd's eyes widened. "Which hospital?"

The corner of Mrs. Brookman's lips twitched.

"The doctor's name?" Floyd asked, this time a little more loudly.

Mrs. Brookman sipped her tea and returned the cup to its saucer.

Floyd tried again. "I'll need to know so I can take Dean to the appointment."

"Well, that's just it. You're not taking him. I am."

"But I'm his father."

"Are you?" Her eyes gleamed as she steepled her fingers.

Floyd's back stiffened. "I don't know what kind of game you're playing—"

"He's not yours."

"What?"

"Dean is not your son. You've been cuckolded all these years." The twinkle in Mrs. Brookman's eyes increased with Floyd's discomfort.

"That's ridiculous."

"Is it really?"

"I'm not going to sit back and allow you to—"

"Here's what you'll do. You'll bring Dean here Wednesday morning at 8:00 a.m. sharp. You will sign papers awarding full guardianship of Dean to me. Otherwise, I'll be compelled to tell Dean the truth—that you are not his father."

"This is utter nonsense. I'm not signing anything! What proof do you have that Dean is not my son?"

"Bonnie's word. She told me."

"I don't believe you. Even if I did, she wasn't well, and you should have questioned a story like that."

"Are you calling my daughter a liar?"

"Are you calling my wife a tramp?" Floyd shot back.

Mrs. Brookman's face came alive. "I'm saying you ruin everything you touch. Bonnie was unhappy. If she had a dalliance—or two or three—you drove her to it.

"Then who was it?" Floyd shouted and struck his fist against the desk. "How long did it go on for?"

Mrs. Brookman stared at him levelly.

"I don't need your permission to be my son's father. I won't let you stand in my way."

"I won't need to. You'll get in your own way," she said.

"Hold on a minute—"

"Dean doesn't have a minute. He might have had a minute, a month ago. But you weren't watching. You were licking your wounds at a bar."

Floyd stood slack-jawed, arms dangling at his sides.

"That's right. I know things," Mrs. Brookman said ominously. "By Thursday, I can provide Dean with the best help money can buy. You, on the other hand, can take him to some small-town quack who might be able to arrange an appointment in two weeks or a month. Are you willing to take that gamble with your son? Pardon me—another man's son?"

"Bonnie wouldn't stand for this!"

"I'm slipping a noose around your neck, Floyd Hoffman. You are going to choke, one way or the other. The only question is, will you have the guts to hang yourself, or will I need to kick the chair out from under you?"

Floyd's hands tingled. His breathing grew shallow.

"I think we both know how this will end," said Mrs. Brookman. When Floyd didn't budge, she added, "Get out of my house. Now."

11.

Rain thrummed against the kitchen window throughout the King family's Sunday night dinner. Except for asking his wife to pass the potatoes, Tammy's father had—so far— refrained from any form of communication. Her mother chewed each forkful of roast beef to smithereens and tapped her fingers against the table in a steady tattoo.

"Reverend Findlay is a fine man," she said, "always looking out for the welfare of his flock."

A clump of mashed potatoes rolled around the inside of Tammy's mouth like a ball of wet paper. She stared at her plate and pretended to eat.

"You were in his office for nearly forty minutes. Is there something you'd like to share with your father?" Anger crackled beneath the sugary veneer of her mother's voice.

"Aunt Eva visited Grandma today," Tammy mumbled.

"Swooped in like a vulture is more like it," Mirabelle said. "When your grandmother dies, she'll get everything, you know. Eva's always been the favourite."

Tammy's father shrugged and sopped up some gravy with a torn slice of bread.

"Lawrence," his wife scolded, "must you do that?"

When he ignored her, she set her sights on Tammy again. "You've nothing else to report from your talk with Reverend Findlay?"

Tammy pushed away from the table.

"And where are you going?" her mother demanded.

"To study for my English exam. I write it first thing in the morning."

As Tammy climbed the stairs to her room, her mother called out, "Grandma is the fortunate one. I'd enjoy a mild case of dementia right about now."

Tammy flopped back on the bed and hung her head over the edge of the mattress. With the reverend's advice weighing on her mind, studying was impossible. The maternity home was a more immediate concern than the textbooks and binders strewn across the foot of her bed.

Back in the tenth grade, a girl in school was rumoured to have been pregnant. She'd disappeared during first semester and returned the following September, looking thin and displaced. People said she'd been staying at the Beatrix Home in Hattersburg—the same place Reverend Findlay had recommended.

The maternity home must charge money like a hotel, Tammy supposed. She'd discovered a less obvious cost—her father's respect. If Tammy boarded at the maternity home and gave the baby up, her family would be spared from financial hardship. She could get a job and pay them back. In time, maybe they could love her again. But then, what about Dean's expectation that she keep the baby? Everyone else's wishes clouded her ability to single out what she wanted to do. She might not have what it took to be a mother, but giving up a child couldn't be easy either.

Before long, people would start guessing her secret, and for the rest of her life she'd be "that girl who got knocked up in high school." Her mother had warned, "Scoundrels will circle you like sharks once they know you're willing to lift your skirt. The right kind of boy won't have a thing to do with you."

One thing Tammy knew for sure, she'd need to make a decision soon.

"Pencils down. Papers over."

All around Tammy, students either sighed in resignation or continued to write furiously. She doodled on the sticker affixed to the upper right corner of her desk: D18, to signify her row and column in the exam maze of the high school gymnasium. Adjudicators paced the aisles like sheriffs while she obsessed over the time and thought about seeing Dean.

Tammy pressed her shoulders against the back of her chair and chewed the inside of her lip. She'd completed the short answer section and mangled one of three essay questions. It hadn't helped that the Beatrix Home girl, Leslie Benton, was sitting in the adjacent column at C19. The heel of her army boot was bouncing rapidly above the floor, as it had for the past two hours. When she'd caught Tammy staring at her during the exam, she'd thrust her head forward and mouthed, "What?"

The English teacher's thigh bumped against Tammy's desk as he walked down her row. "Exam?" Tammy passed her test paper into his waiting hand, then she grabbed her purse from the floor.

The sound of scraping chairs legs and the rising conversations volleyed around the room as students began sifting into the aisles. Tammy squeezed into a space among the bodies now ambling towards the double doors at the rear of the gym. She turned to discover Leslie's bleached hair bobbing along behind the shoulder of a boy from English class. His eyes lit hopefully when he saw Tammy looking his way.

Tammy forced a weak smile and turned back towards the door. As the exodus of students spilled into the hallway, nervous chatter escalated to jostling. Locker doors squawked open and slammed shut. Two girls crossed in front of Tammy, consoling each other. "The exam wasn't fair," one complained.

What did they know about fairness? Tammy was mired in complexities they couldn't imagine. That morning, she couldn't even button her shorts. She'd had to thread a rubber band through the buttonhole and loop it over the post of the metal fastener. Tammy frowned and pulled the bottom of her T-shirt over her waistband. She hated those girls. Wanting to be one of them made her hate them all the more.

She continued to the school entrance and lingered in front of a trophy case near the office. When Leslie's reflection swept across the glass front of the case, Tammy followed her out of the building.

Students sprawled across the lawn, eating their bagged lunches and studying for the afternoon exams. As Leslie passed by a large group assembled near the street, a friend of Dean's yelled out, "I'm in love, boys."

Without stopping, Leslie raised her pistol finger and pulled the imaginary trigger. "Bang. You're dead, Allan."

Guffaws rose up from the crowd as the boy stumbled back in a feigned swoon, hands clasped over his heart.

For the next several blocks, Tammy followed Leslie at a distance. Assuming the stories were true, she was someone's mother, yet here she was walking through town like nothing had ever happened. Reverend Findlay had told Tammy it was possible; seeing was believing.

Leslie stopped suddenly on Griffin Street, a few yards before the phone booth, and began rifling through her shoulder bag. When she spun around to face Tammy, a lit cigarette teetered on her bottom lip.

"You're following me," she said.

"I'm walking to the library."

"Just ask me."

"Ask what?" The pitch of Tammy's voice rose.

"The same thing all the fake virgins want to ask me." Leslie stared flatly.

Tammy squeezed her purse strap. How could she ask Leslie questions about the Beatrix Home without giving away her own condition? "I heard you have a *friend* in Hattersburg."

She looked Tammy over. "You heard right, Keener. Me and Beatrix go way back."

"And you stayed with her—for a while?"

"Yeah. Fun was had by all. I even left a little package behind to say thanks." Leslie took a drag from her cigarette while she scrutinized Tammy. "Are you looking to meet my friend?"

Tammy folded her arms across her stomach and looked up the street.

"Okay, play it cool," Leslie said. "But there was a lot of shit about Beatrix in the news last summer. It's all true too. I saw the whole thing." She tossed the remains of her cigarette on the sidewalk and ground it under her boot heel. "Don't fall for everything they tell you, Keener." Leslie stepped close and leaned her heavily made-up face next to Tammy's. "This conversation never happened. Got it?"

Tammy's chin quivered. Her eyes lowered to the tattooed initials *EB* peeking from beneath the neckline of Leslie's shirt. She nodded. "Got it."

Leslie had crossed Main Street by the time Tammy stepped into the telephone booth. Through the smeary fingerprints covering the glass, she watched as Leslie lifted her right hand and raised her middle finger. After she disappeared from view, Tammy fished a dime out of her pocket and dialed Dean's number. He picked up on the first ring.

"How fast can you be here?"

"What's up?" Tammy fumbled to close the folding door with one hand.

"Not over the phone. I want to see your face when I tell you."

"I can be there in an hour."

"I thought you loved me." Dean's voice grew cold.

"I do, but . . ." Her stomach rumbled.

"See you in half an hour." The line went dead.

Tammy lingered in the booth with the receiver dangling from her hand. Dean left her feeling like a little kid whose dog had just bitten the ice cream off the top of her cone. Leslie's warning bothered her too. Last summer, something happened at that maternity home. She needed to know what before Dean got her head turned around again. Her history teacher had told the class about back copies of the *Sentinel* stored at the library on microfiche. She weighed her curiosity against Dean's demand and made her decision.

At the library, other patrons were absorbed by their own pursuits and paid no attention to Tammy rushing past the circulation desk. She cut to the staircase at the centre of the library and headed straight for the microfiche cabinet on the second floor. Her fingers traced the drawer labels until she found *Narrow Falls Sentinel 1970-1980.* She pulled the microfiche envelopes for June through August 1980 and hurried to the imposing girth of the microfilm reader situated on a corner table.

Tammy hung her purse over the back of a chair and dropped onto the seat. Her hands shook as she centred the June fourth microfiche on the glass plate of the reader. She fine-tuned the focus and began skimming headlines for news of the Beatrix Home. After scanning several microfiches without success, Tammy's hope faded. It wasn't until the July ninth microfiche that her eyes widened. There it was, in the centre of page three. "Beatrix Home Accused of Wrongdoing."

A local home for unwed mothers is under fire due to current policies that restrict the personal freedom of its residents.

Someone sneezed. Tammy jumped and swept the glass plate sideways. An elderly gentleman rounded the corner of a book stack, wiping his bulbous nose with a hankie. He glanced at the magnified print on the reader screen with mild interest as he shuffled behind Tammy's chair and disappeared behind a bookshelf. She drew in a deep breath and recovered the article.

The Beatrix Home in Hattersburg was established in 1920. Originally billed as a safe haven for unwed mothers, its reputation has been called into question by reports of outdated practices harkening back to its Victorian origins. Residents offset the expense of their stay by working in the Beatrix kitchen, laundry, or housekeeping services. The tone of the home is one of a punitive and reformative nature rather than one of social support. Heavy-handed tactics are used to influence residents' decisions regarding adoption. The home also faces allegations of forcing mothers to sign legal documents while under the influence of sedating medications.

Her mind went numb. Surely, Reverend Findlay had been aware of these accusations when he recommended the home. And her mother too.

Tammy grabbed her purse and dashed down the stairs. She hurried through the front doors of the library and into the blinding sunshine. When her stomach growled again, she dug into her pocket and pulled out a rolled-up two dollar bill. Her heart was racing as she set off to the Narrow Falls Diner.

The diner was a hub of downtown activity, a gathering place for people who didn't frequent Tony's Pub. Tammy's heart sank when she saw Mrs. Clark through the diner's plate-glass window. She was sitting with a woman Tammy recognized from church. Mrs. Clark smiled and waggled her fingers. As Tammy was returning the gesture, the diner door opened. Her mother gasped and stopped midstride.

"What are you doing here?" she asked.

"Buying a sandwich."

"Open your purse." Tammy's mother slid a hand into her own handbag and produced two dinner rolls wrapped in a paper napkin from the diner.

"I don't want them." Tammy's face burned with embarrassment as Mrs. Clark craned her neck towards the glass.

"Take it!"

Tammy's eyes flicked to the diner window behind her mother just in time to see Mrs. Clark pull away with a smirk.

"Come with me," her mother said. "We're going to Arlene's."

"I wanted to study this afternoon."

"Remember when you were just a little thing? You'd shimmy up in my lap while Arlene set my hair." Her mother sighed. "You were such a good girl back then."

"Mom . . ."

The diner door swung open abruptly. This time, Reverend Findlay stepped outside.

"Mirabelle, you didn't mention Tammy was coming. I would have insisted that we delay eating had I known."

Tammy's mother laughed nervously. "It's a complete surprise to me." Then a new light shone in her eyes, and her smile spread like icing on a cake. "She's treating me to an afternoon of pampering at Arlene's Beauty Salon. Isn't that right, dear?"

Tammy's head snapped towards her mother.

"How nice," the reverend said, placing a hand on Tammy's shoulder. "It's these difficult times that define a relationship."

Mrs. Clark observed it all. She raised a hand to her throat, then leaned towards her friend. The other woman listened intently.

"Honour thy father and thy mother." He looked pointedly at Tammy with one eyebrow cocked. "Perhaps if you'd followed this tenet earlier . . ." He turned to her mother with an exaggerated look of sympathy. "Mrs. King, I'm available for counsel whenever you require it. Perhaps next time we might all meet together." Reverend Findlay walked off and left the King women facing each other on the street.

Her mother's self-satisfied smirk was a knife of betrayal sawing through Tammy's sternum and plunging into her heart. She would never be that kind of mother.

"Shall we?" her mother said, her command disguised as a question. She started walking and stopped at the corner when she realized Tammy hadn't moved. "Get.

Over. Here. Now," she mouthed.

At that moment, Tammy wished she were Leslie Benton. She'd like to give her mother the middle finger and not worry about the consequences. She'd like to say, "Screw you and your antiquated hairdo. I'm going to see my baby's father."

But instead her tears burned hot, and her voice broke. "Just getting a drink." She pointed at the diner.

One sharp nod and her mother marched off in the direction of the salon.

Tammy closed her eyes. "Get me out of here," she whispered. When she opened them again, Mrs. Clark looked down at her with a pinched look and one hand planted dramatically over her heart.

Cigarette smoke and cheap perfume assaulted Tammy the moment she set foot in Arlene's Beauty Salon.

"Here she is," Arlene crowed, "the soon-to-be graduate."

"Hey, Arlene." Tammy sat on a plastic chair at the front of the salon.

"How are we doing your hair for grad, darlin'? There were girls in and out of here all morning scheduling appointments. You better get your name in the book."

Tammy unscrewed the cap from her juice bottle and regarded Arlene as she took a sip. It was easy to picture her as Mirabelle had once described—newly returned from beauty school with peroxide blond hair, a scandalous hemline, and white go-go boots.

"I heard the ministry trucks were at the gorge again collecting water samples," Mirabelle said.

"Hmm." Arlene teased her own hair and fluffed it with the tail of her comb.

"Lawrence says there'll be more layoffs if the pressure doesn't let up. Damn that Floyd Hoffman. What a hornet's nest he's stirred up with that lawsuit."

"What do you think of this colour?" Arlene held her fingernails up for Tammy to see. Instead of answering, Tammy picked at the top of a dinner roll and deposited crumbs into her mouth.

"Is it new?" Mirabelle looked hopeful.

Arlene leaned in close to the mirror, dabbing at her eye makeup. Mirabelle sat taller in her chair. A smile brightened her face. "I saw Mary Jane Spencer at the grocery store last week."

"Really." Arlene settled back in the chair.

"There's only one reason why a woman wears sunglasses indoors."

"Go on, Mirabelle. Don't hold back," Arlene said, leaning towards her.

"Harland's at it again. Mary Jane's makeup couldn't hide that shiner."

"You know the mill just cut him loose."

"Oh, I hadn't heard that," Mirabelle replied. The smile dissolved from her face.

Her mother was so pathetic, feeding Arlene bits of gossip to gain attention. Every appointment started off the same way. Tammy glanced anxiously at the clock. Dean would be wondering where she was by now.

The telephone rang at the reception desk.

"Tammy, be a sweetie and get that," Arlene said.

Tammy laid the dinner roll on top of her purse and made her way to the phone, but the ringing stopped before she could pick up.

"You gotta be faster than that," Arlene said, studying her up and down.

At that moment, the elastic band snapped across Tammy's belly, and the tension released in the waistband of her shorts. Her eyes widened. Arlene's did too. A string of pink rubber was dangling in plain sight below the hem of her T-shirt.

"You look pale," Arlene purred.

Mirabelle screwed her face into an exaggerated expression of maternal concern. "Go splash water on your face." She turned to Arlene with a shrug. "The poor girl studies around the clock. I tell her it's too much."

Tammy's arms pinned her shorts against her sides as she hurried to the bathroom at the rear of the salon. If only she could keep walking down the hall, into the back alley, and straight to Dean's house.

She ran the tap, cupped her hands under the stream of cold water, then splashed her face. The voices of her mother and Arlene drifted down the corridor and through the open bathroom door.

"Come on, Mirabelle. Let's get you shampooed."

Tammy searched her mind for a lie, some viable excuse to explain her leaving. Arlene was on to her. She'd ask questions and peck away until she discovered a kernel of truth that she could tell everyone. Tammy would be ruined. She lifted the front of her shirt and tied the two ends of the elastic around the post of the fastener again.

"Has Tammy settled on a style for her grad dress? Snug bodice? Loose fitting? I could keep an eye out for bargains if I knew what she wanted." The pitch of Arlene's voice raised an octave.

"Not sure," Mirabelle said in a strained tone.

"Interesting. Graduation is just a few weeks away."

Tammy's mother didn't reply. There was the sound of running water followed by the dull thunk of shampoo bottles.

"How is Tammy feeling these days?"

"Fine."

"Well now, that is a relief."

Tammy could hear water spraying against the inside of the basin. "Vivian Parker was in the other day. She lives next door to Floyd Hoffman, of all people."

"Poor thing," Tammy's mother said.

"Mm-hmm. They haven't exchanged so much as a hello since Vivian moved in. Anyway, it seems there's been a young girl skulking around the Hoffman house at all hours. Hatching up with Floyd's boy, I suspect. Oh, I imagine they're trying to be discreet, but Vivian has seen this girl on several occasions, sneaking into the backyard." Arlene paused, then added coyly, "She swears that girl looks just like your Tammy."

Tammy clamped a hand over her mouth.

"That's impossible," her mother hissed.

"I said the same thing, but Vivian insists she's right."

"I don't believe it."

"Me neither. Tammy would have the good sense not to get involved with a Hoffman. I mean, how would it look if she was cavorting with a boy whose father has single-handedly turned our town upside down without a care? Not to mention, if that boy is anything like his mother . . ."

Like his mother. The words hung in the air.

"Shall we?" Arlene asked sweetly.

Tammy peered down the hallway into the salon. Her mother's head was wrapped in a towel, a plastic cape draped around her shoulders. She and Arlene were walking towards the front of the salon. While their backs were turned, Tammy stole out through the back door of the shop and ran down the alley towards Main Street. She couldn't possibly stay in the salon knowing that her mother had just learned from Arlene that the baby's father was Dean Hoffman.

She skirted along a network of side streets that carried her west to the older section of town. After six blocks, a stitch in her side reduced her pace to a brisk walk. Tammy thought of the pain Dean must be experiencing. "Cancer's a bitch," a friend had said when her grandma was dying. "Nanna isn't Nanna anymore." Tammy wondered how she would cope with Dean's last days.

Tammy understood why the baby was important to Dean. He called it a legacy, evidence that he'd existed. But having a baby alone would ruin her. College would be out of the question. If she went to the maternity home, she could have the baby and postpone college until the spring semester. No one in town would be the wiser. Just as Dean wished, his father would never know a baby existed. But if she told Dean about Reverend Findlay's plan, he'd say the church was brainwashing her.

"Giving the baby away to a better home." The reverend used this phrase repeatedly. It made sense to Tammy. The baby *would* go to a better home—with two living parents—situated in a manner appropriate for raising a child. If she planned to give the baby up anyway, she couldn't allow Leslie's warning against the Beatrix Home to affect her decision.

There were lots of variables to work around, but she could manage them. She'd tell Dean what he needed to hear, then when the time was right, she head off to Hattersburg. What Dean didn't know couldn't hurt him—or her, for that matter.

• • •

When Tammy arrived at the Hoffmans' house, she cut to the backyard and let herself in the back door. Dean stood in the hallway, talking on the telephone.

"My dad can't come to the phone right now." He extended his free arm towards Tammy and motioned her to come closer. "Not sure."

She dropped her purse by the door and went to him. He folded an arm around her neck and pulled her face into his right shoulder. She leaned away and tilted her face to peer up at him.

Dean rolled his eyes. "Yup. I'll tell him you called."

He hung up the phone and started walking her towards the bedroom.

"Who was that?"

"My dad's boss is on his case." Dean mimicked the caller. "'Tell your father he must inform me when he is ill so I can arrange for a suitable replacement worker.' Blah, blah, blah. Asshole." He closed the door and scooped her up in both arms.

"Where *is* your dad?" she asked, squirming in his grip.

"Out." Dean buried his face in her neck once she'd stopped struggling. His hands travelled along her back, and his voice grew husky. "Where have you been?" A hand squeezed Tammy's breast.

"Dean, you can't . . ."

"Oh, I think I *can.*" When he reached for the zipper of her cutoffs, his face drew back in confusion. "What's this?" His fingers traced the elastic band and unlooped it from the button on her shorts.

"I don't think we should do this."

"You're getting bigger," he declared with an incredulous expression. "This kid is growing." His right hand rubbed the tiny bulge of her belly, then deftly slid down the front of her shorts.

Tammy twisted away from him. "Dean, this is not a good idea." His free hand pressed into her lower back.

"It's a great idea," he moaned.

"What if I . . . hurt you?"

"I might like it." He mashed his mouth against hers until her teeth bruised the inside of her lip. Her shorts slid to the floor, and he pushed her back on the bed.

Tammy's stomach tightened. She looked at the dried blood on the pillowcase, then back at him.

"Come on," he whispered, "we're celebrating." He pulled his shirt off over his head and tossed it aside.

"What about before, on the phone," she said. "You were so—"

"Oh, I was just messing with you. I've got news."

"Really?"

"Babe, I'm going to Toronto for a miracle cure," Dean said. "I'm going to live forever."

"Oh my God!"

"I knew you'd be happy. We're going to raise this kid together." He grinned and pulled her panties around her ankles.

Tammy lay beneath him, dumbfounded. *Now what?* This news changed everything.

12.

At Brewster's Gorge, a hawk descended from the clouds and soared towards the pines upriver from the waterfalls. Floyd stood at the top of a cliff and watched it dip below the tree line. The toe of his leather shoes hung over the edge of the drop-off. Twenty feet below, water surged at 479 cubic yards per minute, carrying with it McLelland's carcinogenic cocktail of dioxins and furans. When his weight shifted, chunks of loose shale broke away from the cliff and tumbled into the current below.

A bottle of Wild Turkey swung from one hand, and from the other, a clump of wildflowers he'd torn from the shoulder of the road. He held the flowers at arm's length and loosened his fingers from around the stems. The flowers dropped into the gorge, pirouetting sideways on the breeze until they disappeared from sight.

"Bonnie, I promised to keep your secret from our boy. I've never told him a thing about it, just like you asked. But things are changing. He needs to know."

For a split second, he imagined himself stepping over the edge and swimming crazily through the air. His hands had been trembling intermittently since he backed out of Mrs. Brookman's office the day before. Her venomous words hammered at the back of his head.

Dean is not your son.

Bonnie's mother had devolved into a caricature, a wealthy widow deluded by her own bitterness. It was the only possible explanation for the heinous lie she'd manufactured.

Mrs. Brookman had toyed with Floyd, then released a trapdoor beneath his feet. He was still free falling, having miscalculated the depth of her animosity. The night before, he'd lain awake churning out strategies to deflect her scheme. But in the end, he realized she'd have her way no matter what he decided.

If he brought Dean to the estate on Wednesday morning and signed the papers transferring guardianship to Mrs. Brookman, she would exert immediate control over the boy's life. She'd done it before. Dean had fought her meddling, even as a young boy, and when she'd refused to relent, he'd withdrawn from her. Her attempt to control his music choices had been the last straw. At twelve years of age, he'd proclaimed, "I hate Chopin, and I hate her. I'm not going back. You can't make me."

In the future, Dean was bound to find out what Floyd had done. He'd surely conclude his grandmother had been right all along. His father didn't care about him. She'd tell Dean about the paternity question and drive a wedge so deep there'd be no repairing the damage. There'd be no winning Dean over after that.

Then there was the Brookman fortune Dean stood to inherit. Floyd lived frugally and taught him the value of things. Money would come easily through Mrs. Brookman, she'd see to that. She'd purchase Dean's favour with whatever cars, travel, and clothing he fancied. She could provide him with opportunities that Floyd never could—Ivy League schools, career connections, the right friends. The best girl. He'd stand a better chance of surviving to enjoy these things with more immediate treatment.

If Floyd refused to sign over guardianship to Mrs. Brookman, she'd tell Dean her version of the truth. The moment Dean learned that Floyd may not be his father, the goodwill that had taken root would disintegrate. Floyd would be just *some guy.*

Dean's time was short, according to the North Bay doctors. Six months. Floyd could try pressuring Doc Gillespie into arranging new referrals, but he expected the same answer as the first time he'd asked at the end of May. "Floyd, I'm doing my best." Doc Gillespie had said, with eyes closed and fingers pinching the bridge of his nose. "You'll know when I know." Dean couldn't afford to wait, but they'd get nowhere without a proper referral.

Only the mill had ever evoked the same burning hatred Floyd felt for Mrs. Brookman. She had him right where she'd always wanted him—between a rock and a hard place.

Floyd's hand squeezed the neck of the Wild Turkey bottle. He relaxed his grip and squeezed again before wrenching the cork free. He raised the bottle to his lips and tipped it high. The burn rolled down the back of his throat, and the effects of the bourbon spread through him like a ripple on a still pond.

The moment was soon pierced by a shrill whistle and the barking of a dog. Time to move on. It wouldn't do to be caught looking the way he did, especially since he hadn't called his boss that morning to say he was taking the day off. The town had eyes and ears everywhere. Floyd needed a place where no one would find him. He had the perfect place in mind.

On a knoll half a mile from the gorge, Floyd sat in the shade of a jack pine, both legs sprawled before him. Brewster's Brickworks stood vacant in the flats below. The last brick had rolled off the line a few years after his father's departure from Narrow Falls. Kids used to come down here to drink late at night. They smashed out the windows and spray-painted graffiti across the sun-bleached walls. From his vantage point, Floyd had a clear view of the gravel parking lot, now reclaimed by tall grass and goldenrod. The charred remnants of a picnic table jutted from the ground near what used to be the staff entrance.

Floyd drew another swig and rested the bottle on the top of his thigh.

An affair.

His chest burned at the thought of another man's hands grabbing at Bonnie's breasts, hungrily breathing in her smell, or pinning her against a mattress.

Floyd's mind leapfrogged from one question to the next. Whose mattress? Had she met him in a murky hotel room? Bonnie never had a driver's license. The affair must have happened somewhere nearby with a local. Somewhere in Narrow Falls, there was an arrogant son of a bitch with carnal knowledge of *his* wife. Maybe someone he'd seen walking down the street or held a door open for. Maybe someone he saw every day.

"Oh Jesus," Floyd whispered. His eyes cut to the horizon, and his mouth dropped open. A sense of knowing struck him like a bullet. She'd been with another man in their bed, on the sheets he slept on at night.

Think. Think. Think.

Who could it be? Floyd pressed a hand against his forehead, clamping his temples between his thumb and middle finger. Dean was born on December 2, 1964. He must have been conceived in March. Bonnie had told Floyd she was expecting on May sixth, his mother's birthday. He could remember thinking how lucky that he'd just been promoted to a higher paying position at the post office.

Floyd downed a mouthful of Wild Turkey and slouched against the tree. When his eyes drifted, he forced them wide open and willed himself to stay awake.

His mind soon yielded another memory that returned in hazy flickers, as if it were a defective reel of film. The pictures from his childhood soon strung themselves together, and he remembered the woman he'd dubbed "the lipstick lady."

He'd first seen her the summer he'd saved enough money to buy a red Schwinn Spitfire. At eleven years old, the bicycle had extended the edges of his world to new frontiers.

Floyd had been pedaling along the back roads to the gorge when he heard the rumble of an approaching car. Heat and vibration radiated from the vehicle as it eased close to his bicycle. He could see her through the passenger side window, waving her gloved fingers. She wore bright pink lipstick and movie star sunglasses. A pale chiffon scarf was knotted under her chin. Its tails fluttered against her throat. Floyd pedaled madly to keep pace with her, but the car accelerated, and she was lost to him. Only puffs of dust rising from the road affirmed that she'd been real and not a figment of his vivid imagination.

Days later, Floyd had returned to the gorge. He'd climbed to the top of the falls, then cut through the woods to a knoll overlooking the brickworks. Like a scout, he wriggled across the hard-packed ground on his belly and lay still, his chin resting on the back of his wrists. Workers spilled out of the west entrance at twelve o'clock sharp. His father was among them, carrying the aluminum lunchbox Floyd's mother packed for him each morning. Smiling, nodding, and laughing. This version of his father confused Floyd.

Lunch was nearly over when the side door of the brickworks swung open again.

The lipstick lady emerged. She carried a mug to the end of his father's picnic table and took a seat. Moments later, a buzzer sounded and workers filed inside with empty lunchboxes swinging from their hands like pendulums.

Floyd's father and the lipstick lady stayed behind. She slid across the bench and rested her head on his shoulder. His left hand slid across her narrow waist, then trailed lazily to where her bottom curved over the seat, as if it had found its way there a hundred times before. Then, in a profound show of affection, he lightly kissed the top of her head.

A thousand resentments ignited in Floyd's heart as his father's mouth lingered there.

The same mouth that chastised him and withheld stories. The same mouth that ate his mother's mashed potatoes and tightened in a stern line.

Later that night, Floyd's father stood over the bathroom sink, scrubbing his shirt collar with a bar of soap. When he spied Floyd's reflection in the bathroom mirror, his face turned hard and menacing. Floyd lowered his eyes and backed away from the door.

The betrayal still burrowed under Floyd's skin all these years later. He raised the bottle of Wild Turkey to his lips; a liquid flame of bourbon washed down his throat.

Liars never win, and cheaters never prosper. His mother's wisdom.

"Bullshit," he yelled into the open sky. Spittle flew from his mouth. Liars and cheaters walked across the backs of rule-bound people. "They always win, Mutter."

Floyd rose to his feet, swaying at first, then regaining his balance. His mother never swayed from her refusal to acknowledge the evidence of the affair. She must have smelled perfume on his father's neck or felt the damp shirt collar when she reached into the laundry basket or seen the phantom smear of lipstick. Even when his father sauntered through the kitchen whistling strains of "The Blue Danube" waltz, her icy blue stare had warned Floyd to say nothing. For days, he wrestled with the guilt of not reporting what he'd seen at the brickworks. In the end, he decided to tell her nothing. Her humiliation was too high a price to pay for relieving his conscience.

Gossip had surely spread around town. Lipstick lady would have told a friend about her married lover. Other workers must have read signs of familiarity in their interactions. Narrow Falls was a sleepy but watchful town. Someone must have smirked at his mother or whispered to a friend as she passed on the street.

Had his mother known the identity of her adversary? They may have brushed past one another in an aisle at Harding's Family Clothiers or reached for the same brand of laundry soap at Wilson's Market.

Floyd scowled and dug his heels into the ground. She'd earned her unhappiness by allowing the humiliation to go unchecked. He swigged another gulp of liquor and shoved the cork into the bottle. His eyes closed as the Wild Turkey did its work. His hand squeezed the glass neck and pushed the cork upwards until it popped free with a satisfying baritone sound. His thumb pressed the cork back into place.

Push. Press. Push. Press.

A feeling bore down on him, an awareness at the periphery of his memory—there was something he forgot he knew. His eyes narrowed at the ruins of the brickworks.

Bonnie had warned him, "I will disappoint you."

Floyd could recall kneeling, talking in comforting tones. "You couldn't possibly."

"Things happen around me. I will disappoint you. Eventually." She'd looped her arms around his neck and held tight. "I just want you to be happy."

Think. Think. Think.

Had that conversation taken place before or after he'd applied for the mail sorter position? Floyd could only recall his loathing for the department supervisor who'd hired him. Carl Spivey. Scummy son of a bitch with his Brylcreem-slicked hair and creased neckties. No matter the time of day, he could be found with a pen shoved behind one ear, a clipboard full of furled papers in one hand, and a gas station mug clutched in the other. The earmarks of a man trying to look busy. Floyd had always felt lucky that the promotion had come so easily to him. But in the sixteen years since the occasion, his feelings towards Carl Spivey hadn't changed.

The sun shone directly overhead now. Floyd undid his buttons and stretched the bottom of his ribbed undershirt over his face, wiping the sweat from his forehead. Then he popped the cork and took a lengthy swig.

Something else was returning to him. Bonnie's reaction to his promotion to the sorter job. She'd been so excited for him. An *indoor man*, she'd called him. He could still hear her carrying on about dressing him for the part. "I suppose you'll need a briefcase," she'd added, "although that can wait until you take over at the end of June."

His eyes cut to the horizon, and his nerves snapped. That's what she'd said. "Until the end of June."

Floyd couldn't have told her that Bernie was leaving at the end of June. In fact, he hadn't known until the afternoon he accepted the job. Carl had told him. How had Bonnie been privy to that detail so early on?

Carl! It was Carl!

He scrambled to his feet and paced frantically, the bottle of Wild Turkey bouncing against his leg.

"No, not Carl. Anyone but him."

Floyd's eyes darted to the abandoned brickworks, then he drew back the bottle and launched it. He hinged forward, gasping as he watched the bottle careen end over end. Glass shards fanned through the air after it smashed against a pile of tumbled brick.

Images flashed in his mind—of Carl Spivey at Bonnie's funeral. Standing in front of her casket. Touching Mrs. Brookman's arm. Kneeling to shake Dean's hand.

"This isn't happening," Floyd howled. He began a frantic accounting of his wife's pattern of mania and despondency. If she'd been manic that spring when Dean was conceived . . .

Another drink, that's what he needed. He cast a withering look at the abandoned brickyard and turned towards the tree line. When the ground beneath his feet tilted, Floyd leaned against the trunk of a birch until the horizon righted itself again. Then he set off through the woods in search of his car.

March 1964

A rumour circulated the post office that spring. Bernie, a longstanding mail sorter, was planning to retire. Floyd was optimistic about being selected to fill the older man's vacant position.

"This is wonderful news, darling!" Bonnie clapped her hands together. "And won't your parents be impressed," she added, falling back into her armchair.

The same thought had occurred to Floyd. A promotion might raise the Brookmans' opinion of him as well.

Bonnie leaned towards Floyd. "You'll have regular office hours now! We can meet downtown at the diner for lunches, and I'll get you some new trousers. They'll expect you to dress like an indoor man now. When do you start?"

"The sorter's job hasn't been posted yet. Even if I get the job, I've no idea when I start."

Bonnie slumped against the back of her chair. She pursed her lips and fiddled with a button at the neck of her morning jacket.

"I'm sure it'll be released soon," Floyd said, hoping to resume the forward momentum of their optimism.

"What if he changes his mind?" Her hands gripped the armrests now.

"I don't follow."

"Suppose Bernie decides to continue working. Circumstances can change. His wife might bore him. He could need more money. Then there'd be no job to get promoted to."

"Bonnie, that's not going to happen."

"If he doesn't leave, you'll be stuck outside in bad weather lugging that mailbag." Bonnie's voice sped up, and her eyes glistened. "I can't bear the thought of it. You'll be crushed."

Floyd knelt and took her hands in his. He found himself curiously torn between bewilderment over Bonnie's logic and the excitement of being loved so intensely.

"Everything will be fine," he promised.

"I don't want to disappoint you."

"How could you possibly disappoint me, Bonnie? You have no influence over the situation."

"Things happen around me. I'll disappoint you. Eventually." She looped her arms around his neck and held tight. "I just want you to be happy."

A sideways rain soaked Floyd to the skin on the afternoon he sought Carl Spivey out to discuss the job vacancy. Instead of going home for a dry change of clothing, he headed straight for the post office. Bonnie's mood had plummeted since they discussed the job days earlier, and he hoped to return home with some cause for optimism. Floyd sloshed through the employee's entrance and followed the hallway directly to Carl's office. Through the open door, Floyd could see him leaning back in his swivel chair, feet crossed on the desk, poring over his clipboard. The pen was stuck behind his ear.

"Did you fall overboard?" Carl asked with a deadpan expression. He burst into peals of laughter. "You should see your face," he crowed, wiping his eyes. "Paddle in and take a seat, Hoffman." He motioned towards two chairs facing his desk.

Floyd slouched in the closest one and set the mailbag at his feet. Water seeped from the canvas seams and pooled on the floor.

"What can I do you for?" Carl swung his feet under the desk and tossed the clipboard onto the top of a low file cabinet.

"I'd like to be considered for the sorter's position when Bernie retires," Floyd said.

"Right, right. He's been sorting mail here since Jesus wore short pants." Carl cut his chuckle short when he saw the serious expression on Floyd's face. "Yeah, well,

I've got the job write-up here somewhere." He pushed his coffee mug to the forefront of his desk and leafed through a pile of papers. The mug handle was shaped like the arched torso of a naked woman but it was the smear of pink lipstick along the rim of the cup that caught Floyd's attention.

"She's a beauty, right?" Carl cast a salacious grin at the mug as he flattened a creased onionskin sheet on his blotter. "Not half as sweet as the gal who left her lipstick on there." He waited for Floyd's full attention and winked. In a hushed tone, he added, "I was washing her lipstick off lots of places. You know what I'm sayin'?"

"I'm here to talk about the job," Floyd said flatly.

Carl snorted and lifted the document copy, studying it at arm's length. "Uh-huh. Yup." He nodded his head as he read. "Couple of questions, Hoffman." He looked up at Floyd. "Are you a focused kind of guy?"

Floyd nodded.

"Is your mind sharp? Do you comply with operational guidelines, and can you work independently in isolation?"

"Yes."

"Congratulations. The job is yours."

Floyd's head jerked back. "Do I need to submit a written application?"

"You verbally applied, and I just interviewed you. I'm in a giving mood. Say 'I accept,' and it's a done deal."

"I accept."

Carl met Floyd on the other side of the desk and shook his hand. "One of the girls upstairs will be in touch. After Bernie goes, the job's yours. He plans to stay on to the end of June."

Floyd expected Bonnie to share his elation. She congratulated him halfheartedly over dinner. "I suppose you'll need a briefcase. Although that can wait until you take over at the end of June." She broke into tears. "I don't know what's gotten into me," she said, dabbing her eyes. "I'm not myself."

Everything about her was crumpled—her clothing, her demeanor, her mouth, her eyes. Tears streamed down her cheeks. When she ran out of tissues, he offered her a tea towel from the kitchen counter. She laughed hysterically and then cried twice as hard when he laid it across her knee.

"How about a soak in the tub?" Floyd asked.

Bonnie smiled feebly. "Will you read to me?"

Floyd took her by the hand and led the way upstairs. While the tub filled with water, he picked up his Whitman poetry book from the bedside table and collected Bonnie's rose-coloured negligee from the closet, thinking the luxurious silk on her skin might lift her spirits.

Bonnie was untying her hair when he returned to the bathroom. He helped her undress and cradled her elbow while she stepped into the bath. She slid beneath the water and resurfaced slowly. While Floyd read verses of Walt Whitman aloud, she rested her head against the tiled wall and ran a toe around the mouth of the faucet.

After a passage about the beauty of the natural world, she lifted her left hand from the water and placed it above Floyd's heart and held it there. When she pulled away, a wet handprint remained on his shirt.

"'Fast-anchor'd eternal O love! O woman I love!'" Floyd read from the pages. His heart drummed inside his chest. "'O bride! O wife! More resistless than I can tell, the thought of you!'"

In the middle of the night, Floyd jolted awake with a sense of unease. He slid a hand across the cool sheets. The blankets had been flung back and Bonnie's side of the bed was empty.

He spotted her staring through the maple tree branches drowsily brushing against their window screen. Light from a streetlamp filtered through the leaves and through the diaphanous fabric of Bonnie's nightgown. Floyd's eyes traced the contours of her body—the slenderness of her waist, the curve of her hips.

"Can't sleep?" he finally asked.

"'But in my soul I plainly heard. Murmuring out of its myriad leaves,'" Bonnie said in a quiet voice. She pressed her hand against the window screen as if to divine a message from the leaves brushing against the wire mesh. The book of Whitman's poetry lay open on the sill.

"Bonnie, it's late. Come back to bed."

"He's right, you know. We are charged with taking care of the creatures that cannot fend for themselves. Trees too." Bonnie's voice grew louder. "Every day, people slaughter them to feed the mill. No one cares." She paused to rub her forehead.

Floyd wanted to hold his wife and rescue her from herself, but he was afraid to break the spell she was under. After a night's sleep, things would be better tomorrow. His Bonnie would return. He was sure of it.

"I'm going downstairs," she said. Floyd stood to follow, but Bonnie shook her head. "By myself."

Floyd lay back on the mattress and clasped his hands behind his head. His ears grasped at every sound to track Bonnie's movements through the house. When a loud thud set his heart to racing, he resisted going downstairs to investigate. Bonnie had requested solitude, and he'd honour her wishes.

In the soft light of morning, Floyd opened his eyes to find Bonnie curled up on her side and sleeping next to him. But when he draped an arm over her hip, she cast him off. He squirmed back to his side of the bed like a spurned puppy.

He dressed and went downstairs to make tea. The pelting sound of water being poured inside the brass kettle was somehow comforting as was the crackle of the glowing stove element. The underside of his sock grabbed at the floor when he lifted his right foot. Sticky spots dotted the linoleum in a trail that stretched into the hallway. He dampened a cloth and inched his way along the spill, scrubbing as he went.

When Floyd reached the end of the tacky splotches, he looked into the living room and sucked in his breath. He rose slowly to his feet, gaping at the scene before him.

Books he'd collected since boyhood, and so lovingly cared for, lay strewn across the living room like soldiers fallen on the battlefield. His prized editions were now cast about, some facedown and their pages undoubtedly creased or torn. And in the centre of the coffee table, a partially consumed glass of orange juice sat on the open pages of a book Vic had given him. Notes were newly scrawled across its margins in blue ink.

Fury roiled in his belly and pulsed through his clenched fists. The disbelief of it all made his eyes water. He pitched the wet cloth at the fireplace and dragged a sleeve across his teary eyes. Something was horribly wrong. She was affected by a force beyond her control. The Bonnie he married would never ruin the things he so highly valued.

Nothing in his stoic upbringing had prepared him to love someone through turbulence. But he did love her with all his heart—and his intellect. *No such thing as a problem, only solutions not yet discovered.* So he bundled his emotions and compacted them into a tiny pebble, small enough to swallow, and climbed the stairs to the bedroom.

The engineered smile slid from his face when he saw that Bonnie still lay facing the wall. When he patted her arm and spoke her name, she didn't budge. Her gaze remained fixed at some distant place he couldn't reach. Floyd stood at the foot of the bed wondering what to do next.

He recalled the advice he'd received soon after his parents moved away. He'd been anxious about assuming the mantle of adulthood, and Vic shared a Churchill quote. "It is not enough that we do our best; sometimes we must do what is required."

With that in mind, Floyd turned and headed for the telephone.

The Brookmans' Mercedes pulled up in front of the Hoffman house soon after Floyd telephoned them. For ten minutes, he rested his elbows on the tablecloth and watched them through the kitchen window, trying to imagine the conversation they might be having. Finally, Bonnie's father emerged from the car and walked a tight circle to the passenger side to open the door for his wife.

Mrs. Brookman strode up the walk with an intimidating directness that made Floyd sweat. She'd have made a fine military man. Her steel-grey suit and pillbox hat lent to the effect, as did the gunfire strike of her heels against the porch floor.

She stepped into his house and assumed an imperial stance. While her eyes scanned the room, she removed her white gloves one finger at a time. Her nose curled as if she'd smelled something unpleasant, and she scowled at the braided rug beneath her feet. Mrs. Brookman turned her back to Floyd and took in the disarrayed layers of splayed books. When her right arm dropped to her side, the tendons of her wrist flexed as she crushed the gloves in her fist. She pivoted towards him, raising a penciled brow.

Floyd said, "Bonnie is—"

Mrs. Brookman had taken to the stairs before he finished speaking. Floyd wiped both hands on his thighs and counted her footsteps: twelve up the stairs, a turn left at the landing, eight more steps along the banister, and then silence. She'd found Bonnie.

Mr. Brookman watched him through the screen door. The top button of his father-in-law's shirt was undone, and his tie hung loose under the collar. Floyd pushed away from the table to join him on the porch. "Hello, Mr. Brookman," he said in a somber tone.

Bonnie's father nodded a greeting. He looked thoughtfully into the distance, opened his mouth as if to speak, then closed it again. Instead, he drew on his pipe and stared out at the street. Perhaps there was no need for talking. There was enough of that upstairs.

Both men leaned against the porch rail, grasping at the bits of their wives' conversation. The words escaping through the second-story window were indiscernible, but the tone was clearly one of frustration. Bonnie's impassioned monologue preceded her mother's stern voice. For ten minutes, they battered each other with a volley of angry speech. A door slammed in the upper hallway and then silence. It was over.

Floyd flung the screen door open and rushed to the bottom of the stairs, anxious for any news from Mrs. Brookman. His damp palms gripped either side of the newel post as he listened to the report of her heels advancing towards the landing.

Bonnie's mother descended the staircase with measured and deliberate steps. One gloved hand slid along the banister while the other clutched a handkerchief.

"Is Bonnie coming down?" Floyd asked.

Mrs. Brookman regarded him with undisguised contempt. "How could you let her sink into this state?"

"I don't understand."

"Don't play dumb with me. You know exactly what I'm talking about."

"I've no idea."

"Grow a spine. *Make* her take the medication."

He blinked and followed her to the entranceway. "Mrs. Brookman, what medication?"

"Still can't keep up, I see."

Floyd bristled. "I don't think it's a matter of—"

"I'll send her doctor's name," she snapped, "and some pills leftover at the house."

Mr. Brookman fell in next to his wife when she stepped outside. He held her elbow to steady her as they descended the porch steps and made their way to the car. They seemed older somehow than when they'd arrived. While Mrs. Brookman settled in the front seat, Bonnie's father raised a hand to wave apologetically at Floyd.

Alone again, Floyd wiped away the last of the sugary smears and reshelved his books. Just before the dinner hour, he sagged into an armchair. Perhaps it was best that his repeated appeals hadn't coaxed Bonnie from her room. He needed time to think. How could he possibly report for work the next morning and leave Bonnie alone? Perhaps if he intellectualized the situation, he could arrive at some previously unseen solution. Somewhere between decoding Mrs. Brookman's behaviour and determining the next course of action, Floyd drifted into a deep sleep.

It was dark outside when he opened his eyes again. A reading lamp had been switched on, and Bonnie was sitting in the armchair next to his with her legs drawn beneath her.

"About time you woke up, sleepyhead," she said. A spark had returned to her eyes. Her hair hung in damp ringlets, and she smelled of lavender.

"Heyyy," he said, reaching out a hand to touch her cheek.

"I've been watching you sleep," she said with a giggle.

"You're feeling—better?"

"Darling, I feel wonderful!" Bonnie pounced into his lap and whispered coyly. "I've been keeping a little secret. Would you like to know what it is?"

Floyd nodded warily.

"You're going to be a daddy!" Bonnie threw her arms around Floyd's neck and hugged him so tightly he couldn't breathe.

Marian visited Floyd at the post office a few days later to deliver a package prepared by Mrs. Brookman. He brought the sealed box home and showed it to Bonnie.

"I know what's in there," she said. "I won't take them. Those pills make me feel grey. It's no way to live."

Floyd dropped the box into the trash. "Whatever you want, Bonnie. The decision is yours to make."

They made love slowly that night and with such tenderness that Floyd's heart ached. And when they finished, he stroked Bonnie's hair until she fell asleep against his shoulder. Whatever had a hold of her, Bonnie could beat it. They'd find the answers together. Floyd would show Mrs. Brookman that his love was enough.

13.

After parking the Volkswagen perpendicular to the sidewalk in an angled parking space, Floyd pushed the driver's door open and spilled out of the car. He braced both hands against the top of the doorframe and blinked until Tony's Pub came into focus. When his head dropped between his elbows, he noticed that burdock spurs had attached themselves to his trailing shoelaces in a strange juxtaposition.

Arlene Howard stood outside her salon next door to the pub, lighting a cigarette. She leaned back into the salon, and a second later Eva Larkin joined her on the sidewalk. Not nearly as sour as her sister, Mirabelle, but the likeness was unmistakable. The women whispered to each other and shook their heads.

"Heyyy," Floyd called out as he stepped from behind the car door. He doffed an imaginary cap and bowed deeply.

Eva's jaw dropped, and she stormed back into the salon. Arlene smirked and casually raised her middle finger at him before going inside.

Gawkers pushed close to the plate-glass window of Tony's Pub for a look at what was happening outside. Floyd recognized several men from the mill.

"Have a good look, fellas." Floyd swept his arms wide and thrust his chest forward. When new faces appeared, he batted a dismissive hand at the lot of them and reached into the car for his wallet.

"Mindless drones," he muttered. "You're feeding the machine that's poisoning all of us." His teeth ground together as he slammed the car door.

Floyd swept the hair from his forehead. "Shit," he groused. Either his thumbs had doubled in size or the buttons had shrunk, he wasn't sure which. The shirt remained open.

"One drink to assuage the nerves," he said loudly, "then home." He crossed the sidewalk and reached for the brass door handle and pushed. The door didn't budge so he gripped the handle with two hands and tried again. On the third attempt, he remembered to depress the thumb piece and pull.

Floyd shuffled inside and paused while his eyes adjusted to the gloom. Country music played behind the bar, and cigarette smoke filled the air with a blue haze. A few men swiveled their stools towards him and rested their elbows behind them on the edge of the bar.

Tony stood behind the beer taps, drying his hands on a towel. "How's it going?"

"Never better," Floyd replied

A wave of laughter rippled behind him as he headed towards his preferred seat at the far end of the bar.

"Go ahead and laugh," Floyd muttered, "I don't give a . . ." He slid onto the barstool and cracked his neck to the right, then the left. He scrunched his brows together and leaned towards the man occupying the seat next to his. "Hey, I know you."

"Really," came the sullen reply.

Reaching back into his memory bank was like feeling around in the dark for a light switch he couldn't find.

"You look like shit. Did you sleep in those clothes?" Tony leaned against the bar. He had hands the size of bear paws and muscular forearms to match. Floyd wondered how he'd never noticed this before.

"I'll have a whiskey, neat."

"A drink is the last thing you need." Tony slid a bowl of peanuts towards Floyd. "Have you eaten today?"

"Whiskey, neat," Floyd repeated, "and a telephone."

Tony lifted the rotary phone from the back counter and set it on the bar. Behind Floyd, someone tapped a glass against their table. "Be right with you," Tony called out. He leaned towards Floyd, his hand resting possessively on the receiver. "Who you calling?"

"My son."

Tony pushed the telephone closer to Floyd.

"You are a scholar and a gentleman, sir." Floyd saluted and watched Tony top off the coffee mug for the man on the neighbouring stool.

"I do know you." Floyd narrowed his eyes and jabbed an index finger in the man's direction, as if that gesture could somehow levy a name.

"Bugger off, Hoffman." The man gripped his mug and glowered.

"You tell him, Lawrence," a voice called from farther down the bar.

"Ahhh." Floyd slowly lowered his finger. Lawrence King, Mirabelle's husband. "Okay, calling Dean now." He clumsily raised the receiver to his ear and misdialed on his first attempt. All of his focus was required to dial each number in its turn.

The volume of laughter behind him escalated. "Gotta love a good German joke," a voice shouted. Glass clinked against glass. The corner of Floyd's eye pulsed. He lost track of the phone number, so he pressed down on the two buttons in the cradle repeatedly and tried again.

Tony set a mug of coffee next to the telephone and shook his head.

Floyd tried again, this time saying each number aloud as he dialed. He hinged forward over the bar, resting his forehead in his left hand, while his right pressed the receiver to his ear. The line hummed like locusts on a hot day. Then the ringing began. "Pick up. Pick up." He was about to give up hope, but then the line crackled. Dean answered.

"Hey, I've been waiting for your call."

"I love you, Dean."

"Dad?"

"I'm your father."

"Yeah?"

"I'm downtown, but I'm coming home. Soon."

"You're supposed to call Mr. Spivey. He's left three messages."

"Don't listen to him. He's a goddamned liar."

"Are you wasted?" Dean laughed on the other end of the line.

"I'm your dad."

"Let's order pizza later."

"Pizza," Floyd repeated. More laughter, then the line went dead.

Tony took the phone from his hand and returned it to the back counter. He jerked his head towards the men eyeing him from across the room.

"You gotta get out of here. McLelland's announced rotating layoffs starting in two weeks. Everyone's on edge, including all of them." He gestured across the room to a group of pool players made up of loggers and men from the sawmill.

Floyd whistled through his teeth.

"It was in Monday's paper. I figured you knew," Tony said. "If the mill doesn't meet the federal guidelines, the ministry is going to shut them down. Rumour is there's no cash."

"I had no idea . . ." Floyd thought back to the men leaving the Brookman estate on Sunday afternoon and his encounter with R.J. McLelland.

"You should listen to him," Lawrence said with a sneer.

"Yeah, Hoffman," a younger man taunted from farther down the bar. He slid from his stool and stood behind Lawrence. "I can't believe you'd show your face in here."

"Get him, Kenny," a voice yelled from the other end of the bar. A cheer went up, and someone whistled.

"Leave him be. He's not worth it," said Lawrence.

Kenny stepped closer to Floyd. "I'm on the first line of layoffs. No pay for two weeks. I got a mortgage and a baby on the way. What am I supposed to tell my wife?"

"Tell her how good it will feel to go two weeks without systematically poisoning the people of this town."

Kenny bared his teeth. "Why you son of a—"

Floyd tensed as the fist travelled towards his face. Then everything went black.

14.

Tammy stood in the hallway outside of Floyd's bedroom with her arms folded across her chest. Dean studied her profile while he rested a shoulder against the doorframe. His breath remained laboured and ragged after climbing the stairs.

"I can't go in there," Tammy said.

"Come on. We've been over this already. Besides, you promised."

"But rifling through his personal things . . ."

"Hey, we're in this together." Dean pressed a hand against Tammy's belly until she rolled her eyes in defeat. "That's my girl."

"Suppose your dad *does* come home soon, like he said on the phone," she mumbled.

"Hide in my old room," Dean pointed down the hall. "And sneak out while he's sleeping it off. Piece of cake." He held Tammy's upper arm and pulled her inside.

"I need dirt on Floyd. Something to hold over him so he'll leave us be when we take off together. My grandmother hates him." Dean snickered. "She'll be putty in my hands if I find something good."

"Sooner or later, he's going to find out about me—and the baby. Maybe we should just tell him."

"Yeah, right." Dean looked past her to the dresser standing against the exterior wall. "Check the drawers."

"Something happened this morning. I think my mom knows about us." Tammy braced herself for Dean's reaction.

"How?" He stepped towards her.

"Mrs. Parker saw me coming to your house." Tammy shrugged and looked to the window. A lump rose in her throat, and her eyes burned.

"Dust in the wind, babe. Pop that kid out of the oven and we're gone from this dump of a town. Still, no more slip-ups." He wagged a finger. "The less Floyd knows, the better. I don't want him anywhere near my kid. Ever."

"Dean . . ." In this moment, guilt compelled her to atone for her carelessness. He deserved to know about Reverend Findlay and the Beatrix Home. He looked at her with such impatience that she lost courage.

"Spit it out."

"This room—it's not what I expected. Pink satin bedspread? Roses on the wallpaper?"

"Nothing has changed since Mom died." Dean opened a closet door opposite the foot of the bed and tugged the chain to switch on the overhead light. He searched the upper shelf.

"What are you looking for?"

"Ahhh." Dean hunched over. His eyes squeezed together as his hand clamped over the crown of his head. His knuckles whitened.

Tammy rushed to his side, but before she could touch him, his hand raised.

"I'll be fine. It just takes a minute." He shuffled to the foot of the bed and lowered himself onto the edge of the mattress.

"What do you want from the closet?" There must have been a more pertinent question, but Tammy had no idea what else to ask. "The box of photos from 1965," he replied. His lips pursed as he muffled a rumbling cough.

"Are you okay?"

Dean waved his hand at the closet and bowed his head.

Mrs. Hoffman's dresses were pushed to the left of the closet. Their burst of colour contrasted with the pale blue work shirts and dark trousers hanging next to them. Shoeboxes filled the upper closet from shelf to ceiling, each one bearing a label that read: MANZ, black, men's size nine. On the bottom right corner of each box, Mr. Hoffman had marked the year, from 1964 through 1980.

"Your dad has bought the same brand of shoe," her eyes swept the shelf, "since

1964?”

“He orders them through the mail. From Germany,” Dean rasped. “I told you he’s nuts.”

“Hmm.” Tammy pressed into the closet and reached for the shelf with both hands. As she wiggled the 1965 box free, a musty smell wafted through the air, and she thought of the newspaper bundles her father stored in the garage.

“It’s like a museum in here,” Tammy said as she set the box on Dean’s lap. He tore the lid off and tossed it on the bed.

“Mom’s things are just as she left them,” Dean replied as he began leafing through photos packed inside the box. “I like to move things around the top of the dresser while Floyd’s at work. He never says anything, but I can tell it bugs the shit out of him.”

The dresser was covered by a rectangular doily, the crocheted kind she’d seen in her grandmother’s room at the nursing home. Tubes of lipstick lay at odd angles next to a perfume atomizer, a tortoiseshell comb, and a silver hairbrush and matching hand mirror. In the midst of it all, a black-and-white baby picture of Dean stared out from a cut-crystal frame.

Their baby may have Dean’s dark curly hair, brown eyes, and Cupid’s bow lips. She imagined her little boy standing in a crowd, clinging to his adoptive mother’s hand, and her heart sank.

“Tammy, what are you waiting for? Find the dirt.”

A line of women’s underwear fanned across the centre of the drawer—not the robust underwear with wide elastic bands that Tammy’s mother pinned to their clothesline. These size small delicates were lavender coloured, trimmed with lace and bows. At the back of the drawer, half a dozen brassieres lay one behind the other. Tammy reached a hand into the drawer and traced a cluster of pearls stitched between the cups.

“Front left corner,” said Dean. “Check out the pink silk number.”

Tammy rubbed the fabric between a thumb and middle finger, then glanced over her shoulder at Dean.

“Take it out of the drawer,” he said.

She shook her head. "I could never refold the exact same way. Your dad would notice that."

"Let me handle Floyd."

Tammy drew a deep breath and lifted the lingerie from the drawer. She held the straps against her shoulders as she turned to face Dean. The silk hem fluttered towards the floor and rested across the tops of her bare feet.

"Try it on."

"That's weird," Tammy protested.

Dean stared her down with a determination that caused something to shrivel inside her chest. She gripped the lingerie in one fist while she unfastened the elastic band from the buttonhole. Once her shorts dropped to the floor, she pulled the t-shirt over her head and wormed her body into the casing of silk. A muddle of emotions blurred one into the other—daring, confusion, humiliation.

Dean leaned back on his hands. "Bra."

With a sigh, she unhooked the band, slid both arms out of the straps, and tossed the brassiere on top of her discarded shorts. The coolness of the silk lay against her skin.

"You. Are. So. Beautiful." Dean wiped the corners of his eyes. "I love you."

Her misgivings melted away, and her bottom lip trembled. "Me too." She moved to take the lingerie off, but Dean's voice stopped her.

"Not yet," he begged.

"Your dad is going to be home any minute."

"Keep it, then."

"Oh, Dean . . ."

"Consider it an early wedding gift." He held up a photo of his mother. "She'd want you to have it."

"Are you asking me to marry you?" Tammy's excitement quickly turned to trepidation.

"Yeah, I guess I am," Dean laughed.

"We're so young."

"If we're old enough to have a kid . . ."

"Neither one of us has a job."

"We'll never have to worry about money. It's a cakewalk. All I have to do is convince my grandmother that I'm on her side. Until our kid arrives, I'm the last living heir to the Brookman millions. How long can the old bag last? Plus, I'll be able to cut Floyd out of the picture for good. But first, you need to uncover something shady about Floyd. Something not even my grandmother knows about." When she hesitated, he added, "We're in this together, for the kid's future. Remember that."

Tammy closed the top drawer and rested against the dresser. Dean's plan set her teeth on edge; it hinged on other people's misfortune. He'd caught her up in something, and now she must move ahead with him. She'd never been good at saying no to anyone, least of all Dean.

She knelt in front of the dresser. The bottom drawer contained nothing out of the ordinary, just some white T-shirts and blue cotton pajamas. The drawer above yielded pressed boxer shorts and a multitude of black dress socks, paired and stacked like cords of firewood.

"Anything?" Dean asked.

"Not yet."

When she passed a hand under the socks, her fingers touched upon a hard corner of a book. She withdrew a red leather-bound notebook. Tammy blinked. She hadn't made her mind up about Dean's plan. Everything was happening too fast, pushing her this way and that. Time to think was what she needed. Should she hand the book over, or pretend she'd seen nothing?

"You're awfully quiet, babe. Everything okay?"

Tammy made a split moment decision. She felt lost and needed to trust someone. Dean was it.

"This might be what you're looking for." She faced Dean and handed him the notebook.

"You passed."

"Passed? What do you mean?"

Dean coughed into his cupped hands, then smirked. "I was testing you." He continued, not seeming to care about Tammy's wounded expression. "Floyd's been hiding that book under his socks for months. I've read it a hundred times. It contains a list of shrinks and head doctors complete with phone numbers and addresses. Listen to this," he said. "*Peter Grodzinski.* Classic shrink name. There are notes written in code too."

"What does this mean?"

"It means Floyd is a certifiable nutcase, like I always said. Give me the book."

"Have you done this before? Test me, I mean?"

"Often."

"And what if I'd failed?" Her eyes searched his face. Perhaps she wasn't on as firm a footing with Dean as she'd thought. Maybe he didn't love her. Maybe he was using her as a crutch to escape his father. "What do you love about me, Dean?"

"If you don't know, I'm not going to tell you."

"I gotta go." Tammy bent down and began scooping her clothes from the floor.

"Don't be that way." When she barrelled towards the door, Dean reached out and caught a handful of silk. He pulled her close to him and held her hips. She could feel his strength waning, but she didn't wrench away. Part of her wanted to be convinced that he loved her properly.

"I'm sorry. I won't do it again. I promise."

She hugged her clothes against her chest.

"You know I love you, Tammy." He kissed her belly.

Bang! Bang! Bang!

Tammy jumped. Someone was at the front door.

"Floyd must have forgotten his key again." Dean's arms circled around her waist. "He can wait."

The spring on the screen door groaned. A key scrabbled inside the lock, and the front door squeaked on its hinges. Shoes stomped through the kitchen.

"I don't like this one bit," said a male voice. "Let's dump him on the couch and get out of here."

Tammy's eyes widened. "That's my dad," she mouthed.

"Oh shit," Dean muttered, then followed after her into the hallway.

She fled to his old bedroom and eased the door shut. Her hands shook while she fumbled with her clothing. Dean was coughing his way down the stairs as she kicked the lingerie under the foot of his bed. When Tammy finished dressing, she stood motionless and strained to hear conversation from the kitchen.

"Hey there," a new voice called out.

"Is he all right?" Dean asked.

"No. But he will be," her father said. "You're the son?"

Sour bile rose in back of Tammy's throat. *One Mississippi. Two Mississippi.*

"Yes, sir."

Three Mississippi.

"Your father met up with some trouble at Tony's."

It was quiet for a moment. "I'll be in the cab," the other voice said. The screen door slammed.

"Will you be all right—with all of this?" The twinge of concern in her father's voice surprised her.

"Yes, sir, just fine," Dean's voice rasped.

"My old man was a drunk. Can't pick your family, can you?"

"No, sir."

The interior door clicked. Silence filled the house again.

Tammy ventured out of the room and peered cautiously over the banister. Dean stood at the bottom of the stairs, motioning for her to come down. She tiptoed to the kitchen and continued through the hallway to the back of the house, Dean following close behind.

"This is so perfect." Dean struggled to suppress his laughter. "Floyd's been in a fight. Big shiner." He pointed to the ridge of bone beneath his own right eye. "He's passed out drunk. A whole bar full of witnesses plus your dad and the cab driver. The universe is smiling on us, babe. Didn't I tell you this would be easy?"

Tammy tried to look pleased.

"You're coming back tomorrow, right?"

"Sure."

"You better. Day after tomorrow I'm off to Toronto for my miracle cure."

"For how long?"

"Too long." He kissed her and patted her bottom.

The evening news was playing on the kitchen radio when Tammy slipped into the King house. She paused inside the front door to get the lay of the land. Her father must be home. His shoes sat pigeon-toed by the closet door. A pot lid clanked and water poured against the bottom of the stainless-steel sink. Mashing the potatoes would preoccupy her mother for a moment. Tammy kicked off her sandals, tucked them under her arm, and padded across the dining room carpet. She hoped to sneak into her room and avoid her parents altogether.

Tammy sprinted to the second-floor landing and came face-to-face with her father. He stood there doing up shirt buttons, his hair still damp and his cheeks flushed from a hot shower. They both stared at the floor, each waiting for the other to move. The floor squeaked when her father shifted his weight.

"Tammy, is that you?" Mirabelle shouted from the kitchen. Tammy pictured her mother's eyes combing the air, waiting for a response.

"It's just me," her father hollered back as he brushed past, taking care not to graze her arm.

"Well, hurry up. Dinner's on."

Tammy noticed that her mother had removed the telephone stand from the hallway. She liked to make these overt shows of authority, as if Tammy could ever forget who was boss. *Mirabelle.* From today, she would think of her mother by her first name, much as Dean with his father. It made her mother seem farther away.

Once in her bedroom, Tammy dressed in a pair of baby-doll pajamas she'd pulled from under her pillow. She twisted her hair into a topknot and held it in place with a pencil she found on the nightstand. A package of saltines lay open at the foot of her bed next to her bookbag. Tammy broke a cracker into bits and melted them on her tongue.

Downstairs, chairs dragged across the floor. Silverware clattered against dishes.

"Well, what happened?" Mirabelle's voice rose through the air vent.

"I stopped at Tony's after work. The boys needed to blow off steam. Everyone's worried about the layoffs. It's all hush-hush."

Tammy inched closer to the vent.

"Go on," Mirabelle urged.

"Floyd Hoffman showed up, drunk as a skunk."

"Mm-hmm. Arlene called about an hour ago. She couldn't wait to tell me about *that*."

"Why would she feel the need?"

"That's for me to know and you to wonder."

No one spoke.

"Apparently, Floyd put on quite a show before you saw him. Eva was with Arlene. She knows *everything*." Tammy understood. Her mother must have known all along that she'd been hiding upstairs. That comment was directed at her.

"Right . . ." Her father's voice held back a question.

"Why, it's a miracle he didn't kill someone, driving in that condition."

"He pretty much kept to himself. Things didn't get out of hand until the logging crew showed up. The layoffs affect them too. They started talking trash about Floyd, and things took off from there."

"Well, he asked for it."

"Hoffman lipped off, then before you know it, Kenny socked him in the face, and down he went like a sack of potatoes. Tony called a cab and told me to take him home."

Her mother huffed. "Why are you taking orders from Tony? Floyd is no friend of yours."

"Is there more butter?"

The refrigerator door opened and closed.

"It took two of us to get him into the house."

"Did you see the boy?"

"Funny thing. The kid was home—Hoffman called him from the bar." Tammy held her breath when her father's voice paused. "But he didn't answer the door when we knocked. I had to fish through Hoffman's pockets for a key. The kid came walking down the stairs after we'd already dumped his father on the couch."

It grew quiet again.

"I don't know what's wrong with that boy, but he is not long for this world," he added.

"Really?"

"Something is eating him from the inside out. He's skinny as a rail, and there are dark circles under his eyes. There's a bit of wildness about him, something off-putting. Looks like death warmed over."

Tammy slumped forward and clamped a hand over her mouth. Tears rushed to her eyes.

"And the house?"

"It looks like someone just moved out."

"Not as nice as ours, eh?" Mirabelle gloated.

"It needs a woman's touch."

"Hmm. Makes you wonder where all his money goes."

"Just goes to show—everybody's got something."

"You should be as concerned about your daughter, given her condition and the fact that she's not here."

Lawrence mumbled something low.

"Louder. I can barely hear you."

"I said that it's good to have a break from . . . that. Frankly, she's hard to look at. It will be worse as she . . . you know."

"I know."

"The only time I've been more disappointed is when my old man ran off and left Mom and us boys. I promised myself I'd never be the kind of father who'd let a child down. Never gave a thought to it working the other way around. For a smart girl, she sure is stupid."

"We did all we could, Lawrence. A good Christian upbringing. A firm hand."

"What's going to come of it all?"

"I'll see to it that things are taken care of."

"You mean—an operation?"

"Absolutely not. We're already going to hell in a handbasket. No sense in hastening the journey."

Someone sniffled and blew their nose.

"Heard a joke today," her father said. "What do you call a pregnant virgin? A liar."

No one spoke again for a very long time.

Tammy lay in her bed, unable to sleep. It was only seven o'clock. It would be three hours before Mirabelle and Lawrence performed the bedtime ritual of locking up and turning the lights out. Her stomach growled, and she needed the bathroom, but until her parents were asleep, she wouldn't risk leaving the room.

The thought of facing Mirabelle's wrath left her mortified. She'd want to know if Vivian Parker was right. Then she'd be furious that she'd been outsmarted. "At the library. Huh!" Tammy could hear it now. The only thing her mother hated more than being bested was other people *knowing* she'd been bested. Tammy chewed at a hangnail. Bolting from the salon that morning had been like an admission. She may as well have told Arlene it was all true and that she was nearly three months pregnant.

The only thing more devastating may be her father's disappointment when he learned that, out of all the boys in town, she'd chosen Floyd Hoffman's son. What would he say to that?

It seemed like weeks ago that she'd written the English exam, but it had been just that morning. She'd memorized a quote from *The Red Badge of Courage*. She could relate to the character, Henry, questioning his preparedness for battle. She too was in a battle of sorts. "'He felt that in this crisis his laws of life were useless. Whatever he had learned of himself was here of no avail. He was an unknown quantity.'"

Tammy was an unknown quantity, even to herself. She buckled under the pressure, allowing her opinions to be swayed by other people's agendas: her mother, Reverend Findlay, Dean. Her body was changing. Now she speculated that her own parents held little hope for her ability to rise above this situation. How would she cope with the prying eyes and whispers behind her back when gossip started travelling through town?

Time stuttered along in fifteen-minute increments as the room darkened. At ten o'clock, the streetlights turned on. Their faint glow filtered through the curtains. Tammy lay on her side, facing the wall, and listened to her parents' muffled voices as they prepared for bed. The harried tone of their exchange ended abruptly, and a light switch clicked off. In half an hour, she should be able to make it to the bathroom and the kitchen without rousing attention.

Tammy squeezed her toes together and tried to think of anything but her full bladder. She conjured Dean's face on that first time they'd met behind the library. He was so sweet then. He compared their unlikely romance to Romeo and Juliet. The bond between them only tightened with her parents' harsh judgment of Mr. Hoffman. Then she thought of last summer and the stolen moments at Brewster's Gorge. Her mind sifted through information she'd read about the Beatrix Home. The term *outdated practices* turned over in her mind. What did that mean?

Something pricked Tammy's awareness. It may have been the barely perceptible sound of the door brushing across the shag carpet or the scent of cold cream. But she knew Mirabelle was in her room.

"I know you're still awake."

Tammy willed herself to not move.

"You can't sleep," Mirabelle continued, "because you're lying here thinking about how you've messed up your life, and now that boy is dying. You should be scared. Children shouldn't have babies."

The side of the bed sank under her mother's weight.

"Remember your place," she warned. "You own nothing. Everything you have, your father and I gave you. Until you're a breadwinner, your body and everything in it falls under our jurisdiction.

"You are going to spare us the humiliation of a baby that forever ties us to Floyd Hoffman. It's all arranged. The Beatrix Home in Hattersburg is holding a bed for you. They'll handle the details of the birth and adoption. All you have to do is incubate and sign on the dotted line.

"Your father will draw money out of his retirement savings to fund your stay at the home. Consider it a loan. You are going to repay every red cent."

The edge of Mirabelle's voice sharpened.

"While you're away, I'll mop up the mess you've left. Arlene suspects something, and Aunt Eva called this afternoon asking questions about you. I'll tell them you're away working for the summer to help pay for college tuition. The admissions office has agreed to defer your acceptance. You'll go from Hattersburg directly to spring semester."

Tammy's eyes shot open when a hand stroked her hair.

"Tread carefully, Tammy. Your father is under a lot of stress with all of the uncertainty at the mill. You're adding to it. If he has a heart attack and dies, I will never forgive you."

Tammy rolled towards her mother's voice. "I'm so sorry, Mom," she sobbed.

"If you breathe a word to anyone about being knocked up by that boy—you'll be dead to me."

Tammy wanted to close her eyes and never wake up.

15.

Guitar music roused Floyd from a deep sleep just before noon. He sprawled on the living room sofa with a forearm draped across his eyes, wondering if he'd stumbled into the wrong house the night before. Dean hadn't played for weeks. But the vibrato executed in a familiar melody told Floyd he was home. His smile ended in a wince.

Floyd's left hand travelled over his face, taking inventory of his injuries. The skin had pulled taut over his right cheekbone, and the flesh beneath it was swollen and tender. His fingers continued along the orbital bone beneath his eye, pressing lightly as he went. Pain there too. He ran a hand over the back of his head and discovered another tender spot, one that had made contact with the floor after Kenneth cold-cocked him.

A headache pulsed above his brow and at the base of his skull. When he dropped his legs over the edge of the sofa cushions to sit upright, a streak of pain bolted through his head. He clamped his temples between both hands.

A few bars of "Sweet Home Alabama" played from the back of the house, followed by quiet strumming. Floyd focused on Dean's playing until no room existed for his own physical pain or worries. For now, his attention held his son and a guitar.

This could become the normal rhythm of their every day—and why not? Dean could outlive him and continue filling the house with music. Miracles did happen. They both had the right to expect it.

He and Dean could start fresh today. Right now.

Floyd pushed off the couch and crossed to the kitchen. He bent over the sink to splash his face and swill a glass of cold water from the tap. A hopeful feeling ballooned inside his chest as he dried off on a tea towel. After passing a hand over his hair, he set off towards the guitar music.

He stopped short in the doorway of Dean's bedroom.

"Oh!" His head jerked back.

A teenaged boy smiled up at him from the floor below Dean's window. A guitar balanced on his right thigh, and a thumb rested on the upper string. It took Floyd a moment after the music had stopped to recognize Allan, the boy he'd spoken to on Main Street a few days previous.

Allan smiled at him. He raised a finger to his lips and gestured to where Dean slept against propped-up pillows on the bed. In one fluid motion, Allan rocked forward and rose to his feet. He walked towards Floyd with one hand gripping the neck of his guitar and the other extended. "Hey, man. How you feeling?"

"Okay," Floyd replied, shaking the boy's hand.

"Want a coffee?"

"Uh, sure. I can get—"

"No worries. I'm on it," Allan said. He skirted past Floyd and disappeared into the kitchen.

"The coffee is in the—"

Allan leaned into the hallway and flashed a thumbs-up.

Floyd lingered at the bedroom door before going in. When Dean twitched in his sleep, Floyd covered him with a blanket. The corners of the boy's mouth curled upwards when Floyd tucked the edges under his chin.

Dean's curly hair, his colouring, even the shape of his face—all Bonnie. No resemblance to Carl Spivey—or himself, for that matter. Mrs. Brookman's ultimatum marched through Floyd's mind again. How could he choose a course of action by eight o'clock tomorrow morning?

By the time Floyd slumped into the kitchen, coffee was bubbling in the percolator. Two mugs sat on the counter next to a pitcher of milk and a loaf of bread.

"Rough night, eh?" Allan said.

"Yeah, I suppose so." Floyd sat in a chair and crossed his arms over his chest.

"Oh well, shit happens." Allan dropped two slices of bread into the toaster and pushed down on the lever. "Toast?"

"Yes, thank you," Floyd replied, grateful that Allan had let the matter drop so easily. The boy navigated the kitchen with disarming familiarity. "You seem to be finding your way around all right."

"Should be able to. I've been here enough times," Allan replied, wiping his hand on a dish towel. "Not so much lately though."

"Of course." Floyd covered his embarrassment with a thin smile.

"Oh, I almost forgot." Allan slipped into the living room and returned with one hand fishing around inside the bottom of a rucksack. He pulled out a fistful of jam packets and scattered them on the table. "Here you go."

Floyd laughed. It started as a low chuckle, a cold engine in need of warming up. He couldn't decide if it was the sudden and unexpectedness of the gesture or its likeness to a magician pulling a rabbit from a hat, but he laughed until tears streamed down his face. When he caught his breath, one look at Allan's confusion launched him into a new round.

"Oh, my head," Floyd exclaimed, dabbing his eyes with the front of his shirt. "Do you always carry jam?"

"Always be prepared; that's the Boy Scouts motto." Allan winked, then pointed at Floyd's shirt. "Hey, you're bleeding."

Floyd touched the bridge of his nose and grimaced. "It's nothing," he said, examining his fingers. "So you're a scout?"

"Nah. My mom nicks jam from the diner downtown. She works there." Allan wrapped a tea towel around the handle of the percolator and poured coffee into one mug.

"I'll take that—"

"Black? I thought so." Allan set the mug in front of Floyd. When the bread popped up in the toaster, he buttered the slice at the counter, then slid the plate across the table and sat facing Floyd.

Hacking coughs transmitted from Dean's room in a Morse code series of quick barks and drawn-out wheezes. Allan stacked the jam packets in a pyramid, which he then tumbled by flicking quarters at it, one after the other. When the coughing subsided, his eyes cut to Floyd's face.

"Dean's really sick, isn't he?"

Floyd lifted the coffee cup halfway to his mouth and paused. "He hasn't told you anything?"

"I know he's going to Toronto. He's pumped about it." Allan's brows lifted. "Really, he is."

"Pumped about what?" Dean stepped out of the hallway and into the kitchen.

"Well, look who decided to get up," Allan said.

"Tough to sleep with all the laughter going on." Dean's mouth smiled, but his voice carried a plastic quality that silenced Allan.

"I'll put the tea on," Floyd said.

"Don't bother, Slugger." Dean pulled a pack of cigarettes from Allan's rucksack. "You mind?"

Allan shook his head and passed a lighter across the table.

Dean dragged a kitchen chair next to the screen door and raised a cigarette to his mouth. He balanced it on his bottom lip and stared pointedly at Floyd.

Floyd could think of a hundred reasons to protest. But Dean deserved a rite of passage, an act that made him feel he'd crossed a threshold before setting off to Toronto for the fight for his life. Floyd pushed away from the table. He opened the pantry door, then reached into the back of the middle shelf and pulled out a ceramic ashtray, small enough to fit the palm of a hand. He set it on the table corner nearest to Dean and returned to his chair.

"Where'd this come from?" Dean picked up the ashtray and turned it over.

"A shop downtown."

"Do you smoke?" Allan asked.

"No. I had a friend who did and Dean's mother too, on occasion," Floyd replied.

"Something else I didn't know," Dean said and lit the cigarette. He struggled to smother a cough deep in his throat. With determination, he thrust his chin forward and began blowing smoke in Floyd's direction. But then his eyes watered, and he loosened a stream of coughing that drew Floyd and Allan to the edges of their chairs.

Dean extended his arms so his palms rested on the table. His face dropped between his elbows until his sputtering abated. When he lifted his head, a string of bloody drool stretched across his chin.

"You've got a . . ." Allan said, pointing at his bottom lip.

Dean swiped his face with the back of a hand.

"Do you need to lie down?" Floyd said, attempting to strip the worry from his voice.

Dean waved him off and launched from the chair. He pushed through the screen door and let it slam shut behind him.

"I should probably . . ." Allan tipped out of his seat to follow after Dean.

"Of course." Floyd rested his forehead against his steepled fingers. Through the kitchen window, he could hear the creaking of the porch steps, then Allan's voice.

"What's up, Dean?"

"He's such a jerk."

"At least he stuck around, which is more than I can say for my old man," Allan said.

"I'm sick of that what-did-I-do face he gets when I'm upset. Like he doesn't know. And for Chrissake," the volume of his voice climbed until he was yelling, "it smells like someone lit a stink bomb out here. McLelland's sucks!"

"Are you crying?"

"No."

"Maybe you'll get along better in Toronto," Allan said. "How long you going for?

"Depends."

"On what?"

"A lot of things," Dean said.

The boys' voices quieted so Floyd could no longer overhear their conversation. He'd wait for Dean to sort himself out, then try again. People often misdirected their anger. This Floyd had learned as a young boy after someone had painted ugly words on the sidewalk in front of the Hoffman house. His father had left for work, red-faced and cursing, but his mother had hummed as she scrubbed the paint away. "This is the work of someone who fears the world and all the things in it that can't be controlled. That fear grows until it has nowhere to go except to anger." She'd paused to watch his father's car turn at the end of the block and disappear around the corner. "They are to be pitied."

Dean must be terrified.

Floyd drained his coffee cup. He deposited it on the counter and noticed two phone messages from Carl Spivey tucked under the sugar bowl. Floyd grimaced and headed for the telephone. He pressed the receiver to his ear, then paused to watch the boys conversing on the porch steps. Allan sat crossways on a step below Dean, his back pressed against the banister. Thank goodness for Allan.

No sooner had Floyd dialed the telephone number than Carl Spivey picked up the call.

"Yyyello."

"Hello, Carl. I need more time."

"Hoffman, you slippery son of a bitch. I've been trying to reach you."

"I may need an extended leave."

"We'll see about that. There are rules, you know. Papers to fill out."

"Go to hell, Carl, and take the paperwork with you. I have a family matter, and my son comes first. I'll be in next Wednesday. Or the day after."

"Don't bother."

"Tread lightly, Carl. I know some young ladies from the second floor who are disappointed by your ungentlemanly conduct. With very little encouragement, they could become interested in filing a grievance with the union."

"You're bluffing."

"Seems you have a worrisome habit of touching things that aren't yours. I think you know what I'm talking about."

"I've never touched anything that wasn't offered to me first," Carl said in a provocative tone.

A direct hit! Heat rose in Floyd's face. He imagined Carl pressed against Bonnie, breathing hard in her ear. Had Carl ever wondered if he might be Dean's father?

Floyd drew his shoulders back. "I'm a father first and an employee second. See you next week." He hung up the receiver. His hands dropped to his sides. He clenched and unclenched his fists, then he grabbed the receiver and hammered it against the telephone until the earpiece cracked and a sliver of plastic ricocheted against the opposite wall. He stared at the smashed remains of the casing and gripped the receiver until his breathing slowed.

The screen door squeaked opened. Dean stepped into the kitchen, eyes wide and mouth agape. Allan trailed a step behind, peeking over Dean's shoulder.

"Sorry, fellas," said Floyd. "I'm just . . ."

"I heard everything." Dean stared at the floor, and his chin began to quiver. He trudged across the linoleum, then slipped his arms under his father's and embraced him. His head rested against Floyd's chest.

Floyd's arms circled Dean's shoulders. Allan winked and stepped into the living room.

"Dad?"

Floyd let go.

"No offense, but you smell like a hobo," Dean said, wiping his eyes.

"None taken," Floyd said with a smile.

The day had so far been a roller-coaster ride of emotions on too short of a track. He climbed the stairs thinking of the next morning and the horrible choice he'd have to make. His heart would be ripped out either way.

From the top step, Floyd overheard an exchange between the boys.

"It's like I told you, man. You just gotta hug it out."

"Quit reading your mother's magazines, Allan."

"Your dad's all right."

"He has his moments."

Floyd smiled and slipped into his room.

A Neil Young album was playing on the turntable when Floyd came downstairs a half hour later. The boys were sprawled on the sofa, eating grilled cheese sandwiches with ketchup.

"I wanna hear all about last night," Dean said.

"What does the other guy look like?" Allan asked.

"Don't leave anything out, Dad."

Floyd sat in his armchair and rubbed the back of his neck, unsure of how to begin. He couldn't remember what happened after Kenneth decked him.

"You can't wiggle out of this one. Your face is a mess. It took two guys to carry you into the house," Dean said.

"Two guys?" Floyd said.

"Yeah. The cabby and another guy from the bar."

Something in Dean's attempt to sound casual snagged Floyd's attention.

"Remember calling from Tony's, mouthing off about Carl Spivey?" Dean said.

Panic ebbed from Floyd's belly directly to his chest. He lowered his face to his hands.

"What's he doing?" Allan whispered.

"Beats me," Dean said.

Floyd turned his chair towards Dean. "Maybe we should speak alone." He looked apologetically at Allan.

"Don't go," Dean said when Allan stood to leave. He looked at Floyd. "Anything you need to say to me, you can say in front of him."

"All right." Floyd drew in his breath. "I'm not proud of it, but I took a bottle into the woods to take the edge off. There are so many edges lately. One sip, then another—and no food . . ."

"By 'edges,' do you mean me? So now it's my fault?" Dean spoke in an animated voice. "Dear Abby, my son, Dean, has always been a difficult child, and now he's developed the most inconvenient condition. I've tried everything: sending him to Grandma's, spending more time away from home—"

"It's not like that at all," Floyd said.

"Well, what *is* it like?"

"It's complicated to explain."

"I understand *complicated*." Dean glared.

"The ministry is running tests that will connect the mill's pollution to the growing occurrence of cancer and respiratory illness in town. McLelland's is feeling the heat. It's going to get worse. A lot of people will be affected if the mill doesn't do the right thing."

"You mean if Grandmother Brookman doesn't do the right thing."

"Yes, her and the board of directors. Doing the right thing takes a lot of money."

"Will she have money left—after?"

Floyd shrugged. "The mill's discomfort is trickling down to the workers. My initiating the inquiry has made me a target for people's frustrations. Last night, one of the young guys affected by the rotating layoffs came after me."

"Dean can relate," Allan said. "He's been roughed up a few times by—"

"Hey!" Dean shot a warning glance at Allan.

"—knuckleheads at school," Allan continued. "Their big ambition is to become a lifer at the mill. Now they're screwed."

"Dean, I had no idea," Floyd said.

"How could you? You're never around."

Floyd searched his mind for a response.

"You're always sorry. What do you do about it?" Dean's voice rasped. "You don't even know me. I'm just something that reminds you of mom, of all the things you did to ruin her life."

"Dean, you were so young then. You're seeing it all from a child's perspective."

"You've fooled Allan into thinking you're a swell guy. He said I should try to work things out with you." Dean cleared his throat. "I wish you were dead, not Mom."

Floyd's heart squeezed into a hard nugget.

"I acted like a little kid earlier," Dean said. "Of course you're going to let me down again. What's it going to be this time, huh? A disappearing act? Are you going to forget that we're going to Toronto tomorrow?"

"Being upset isn't good for you," Floyd said.

"I should probably go," Allan said, gathering his rucksack.

"I'll never be the kind of father you are. I'll tell my kid the truth, no secrets, and I'll never run away."

"I promised your mother—" Floyd stopped.

"Later, man." Allan patted Dean's shoulder as he passed behind the sofa.

"Promised her what? Just tell me."

The screen door opened and closed.

"Later, once you're feeling better," Floyd said.

"Incredible. She's been gone for years, and you still won't tell me?" Dean rocked out of his chair.

"Where are you going?"

"To get away from you." Dean hollered over his shoulder, "What did she ever see in you?"

Floyd touched his shirt pocket where he carried Bonnie's scribbled bit of Whitman poetry. The scratching of paper against fabric comforted him. *Only themselves understand themselves and the like of themselves.*

Peaceful weeks preceding the baby's arrival convinced Floyd that motherhood would be the balm that saved his wife from slipping into dark moods. Bonnie painted the bedroom next to theirs an orangey red and sewed bedding for the crib they'd bought from a store in Hattersburg. The busyness of it all distracted her from herself. Surely, the daily tasks of caring for their child could do the same.

Dean Randall Hoffman, with shocks of dark hair and the eyes of his mother, was born in the first week of December. The moment they carried him across the porch and into the Hoffman house was one of the happiest in Floyd's life. At long last, he had a family. Floyd pulled a chair alongside the bed and watched while Bonnie slept that afternoon with the baby nestled in the sheets next to her. He made a silent vow.

I will love and care for you both until my dying breath.

Bonnie delighted in costuming Dean each day in the succession of new outfits her mother sent to the house. The baby was spotless, but his mildly soiled clothing mounded in a corner of his room next to the diaper pail. She worried about everything and left Floyd telephone messages at the post office. *Dean's crying again. He refuses to nap.* Floyd would leaf through them at the end of his mail delivery, then rush home to start dinner and launder baby things to ease her burden.

"Have you been out of the house recently?" Floyd asked her one evening.

"Of course not," she answered. "Dean can't be left alone."

"I mean *with* Dean. Take him for walk."

"Don't be ridiculous," she scoffed. "It's February. There's snow and ice everywhere!"

"He won't break," Floyd said. "Dress him warmly and bundle him in blankets. I see other mothers do it all the time."

With a voice tart as vinegar, she replied, "I'm not *other mothers.*"

Over the next several weeks, Dean's crying escalated until his face consistently resembled a crinkled beet. In the night, he loosed piercing screams that drove Bonnie to despair. The gripe water Doc Gillespie had recommended to relieve colic did little to ease the baby's pain.

"I'm a horrible mother," Bonnie told Floyd as she bounced Dean on her lap. "The baby hates me. I know it."

Old worries returned to Floyd. Her eyes were dull with fatigue, and she'd resumed staring listlessly into the distance. From that night onward, he attended to the nocturnal cries in order to stem the tide of Bonnie's low spirit. She embraced the gesture and soon slept through the howling altogether. Some nights, he'd take the baby for a drive along country roads to lull him with the rocking motion of the car.

Dean was nearly six months old when Bonnie sank into a deep state of melancholy. Mrs. Brookman chastised Floyd for his ineffective handling of her daughter. She sent Marian to help Bonnie with the baby for a few hours each day while he was at work.

"Every woman needs personal time, unencumbered by motherhood and wifedom," Mrs. Brookman told Floyd. "It will do Bonnie good to have a little peace, even if it's in that hovel you call a house."

Floyd resented Mrs. Brookman's interference; however, he'd little choice but to accept it. His candle burned at both ends—up early for work and to bed late after meeting family obligations—with little chance for rest in between. Besides, Marian was a good friend to Bonnie, and Dean was being well cared for in his own home.

On occasion, Mrs. Brookman sent her driver to pick the baby up after lunch and deliver him to the estate. Shortly after Floyd's return from work at four o'clock, the driver would reappear on the doorstep to pass Dean into Bonnie's arms.

Something about the entire arrangement felt wrong to Floyd. "I don't like our son being picked up by a driver, as if he's a bunch of shirts from the dry cleaner."

"You know how Mother is. She's determined to help," Bonnie said.

"Our son belongs in his own home. Why can't she come visit here?"

Bonnie sighed. "I repeat: you know how Mother is."

"Yes," Floyd said. "I do."

As the weeks progressed, Dean's visits to the estate increased in both frequency and duration. Bonnie's resignation to the arrangement piqued Floyd's impatience. Where had his wife's fire gone? He missed the Bonnie who resisted her mother's will. "Dean is not your mother's son," he told her. "He's ours!"

"You talk like she's plotting a takeover," Bonnie said defensively.

"Isn't she?"

Bonnie sighed heavily and quirked one brow. "Please, Floyd. I don't have the energy to fight both of you."

The situation worsened a few weeks later. Mrs. Brookman's driver had picked up Dean at the usual time, but by six o'clock had yet to return him. Bonnie watched anxiously through the kitchen window.

"Call the estate again," Floyd said.

"Be patient," she replied, pausing to nibble at a hangnail. "Mother took Dean on an outing. I'm sure they'll be along any minute."

"You need to fix this," Floyd said. "Call the estate."

Bonnie trudged to the telephone and placed the call. "Marian!" she said, her eyes brightening. "So glad to have finally reached someone. Dean should've been brought home by now, so naturally I was wondering . . ." Bonnie stared at the floor, and her mouth stiffened into a straight line. There followed a lengthy silence. "All right, then. Someone will call the minute they return?"

The receiver clunked into place when Bonnie hung up. Her eyes brimmed with tears when she looked up at Floyd. "Mother and her driver took Dean to see a pediatrician in Hattersburg this afternoon. They're expected any minute."

Floyd clapped a hand to his forehead and rolled his eyes as he wheeled away from Bonnie. "A medical appointment without our permission? She's gone too far!"

"I know. I know," Bonnie said. Her countenance hardened. "Fetch your car keys. We're going to get our son."

She's back! Floyd regarded his wife with pride as he followed her out of the house.

They drove to the estate in silence. Floyd got lost in a mental rehearsal of the tirade he wished he could release on his mother-in-law. Bonnie must have been doing the same. He parked the Volkswagen in front of the portico and held his wife's hand briefly. When at last they stormed into the front hall, Marian greeted them with a look of apology.

"Dean. Where is he?" Bonnie asked. "Is he upstairs? Where is Mother?"

From the corner of his eye, Floyd noticed Mrs. Brookman emerging through the parlour doors.

"Darling," she said, smiling coolly. "Lower your voice. You'll wake the baby."

"Where *is* he?" Bonnie asked.

"Dean's sound asleep. It's getting late. You should leave him here overnight."

"Absolutely not," Floyd snapped.

"I see no harm in my keeping him here," she said innocently. "Tomorrow, I'm hosting a luncheon for the wives of the McLelland board members. They're all dying to see him."

"You took our son to a pediatrician without so much as a word to us?" Bonnie asked. "Does Father know about this?"

A cry of protest squeaked from the back of Mrs. Brookman's throat.

Floyd squeezed Bonnie's hand until she piped up and asked, "Where *is* our son?"

"He's in the nursery," her mother answered haughtily. "Next to the guestroom with the tulip wallpaper."

Together, Floyd and Bonnie climbed the curved staircase to the second floor and followed the hallway to the nursery. The sight of it stopped them in their tracks. The room was four times the size of their own bedroom and stocked with a bounty of toys, the likes of which they could not afford. The setting sun shone through the window blinds, laying stripes of light across a chest of drawers and a towering open shelf stacked with concisely folded baby clothing. Next to it was a rocking chair and a low set of shelves stocked with storybooks.

"I had no idea," Bonnie whispered.

They crossed to the far side of the dim room where a crib sat beneath a tall window. Dean was sleeping soundly in a cotton jumper Floyd had never seen before. He in no way resembled a child in need of rescue. To the contrary, he appeared content. His lips pursed and relaxed as if he were nursing in his sleep.

Floyd glanced at Bonnie. Her trembling expression confirmed that she realized the road her mother was leading her down. Mrs. Brookman was endeavouring to insinuate herself into their son's life under the guise of being supportive.

Bonnie wrapped Dean in a blanket and, with her chin thrust forward, carried him to the main floor. Floyd followed closely behind, allowing Bonnie her moment of defiance. At the bottom of the staircase, she stalked past her mother without so much as a word and continued through the front door. Mrs. Brookman's face went blood red.

On the drive home, Bonnie hugged Dean to her chest and kissed the crown of his head as she stared out through the spotty windshield.

"That's the end of that," she said.

The next few months of parenthood were everything Floyd had hoped for. In the mornings, Bonnie would sit across the breakfast table from him with Dean cradled in her arms. They'd marvel at the baby and discuss the day ahead while Floyd drank his morning coffee. Then he'd kiss them both good-bye at the door. Bonnie would scoot to the living room window, and when Floyd took a last look back at the house before setting off down the sidewalk, she'd wave Dean's hand at him.

Floyd had it all—a wife who adored him in spite of his awkwardness and a son to nurture and watch grow up.

Since reclaiming their son from his mother-in-law, Bonnie had taken up a new interest that delighted Floyd to no end. She'd begun to crave order. It started upstairs, with Dean's closet. She'd fold his tiny outfits and place them in neat piles according to their colour. A day or so later, she'd restack items according to their size. His shirts snuggled next to his balled-up socks one day, then the next they'd shift to a different drawer, where they'd be wedged between pajamas and pants.

Soon, the arrangement of the contents inside their own dresser and closet underwent periodic changes of a similar nature. Upon arriving home from work, he'd be whisked upstairs for Bonnie's tour of the latest reconfiguration. Her newfound interest in regime sparked a new proficiency in the kitchen. Her discipline for eating regular meals increased, largely owing, Floyd thought, to her interest in setting a good example for Dean. "Children learn from their parents. We're mentors, really," she'd say. The aroma of roasting meat greeted Floyd most evenings, and potatoes seldom burned on the stovetop as they had in the earlier days of their marriage.

With all the extra hours Bonnie spent in the kitchen, it seemed only natural that her recent passion for organizing might spread there too. She'd classify and regroup the contents of the kitchen cupboards to her liking, then a day later she'd frown and shuffle things around again. A new mother putting her stamp on things. Floyd thought it was sweet. He didn't worry when he came home from work one day and found her sitting at the kitchen table amidst a muddle of utensils, canned goods, and mounded pots and pans. His wife was meticulous. How could that be a bad thing?

In the small hours of one morning, he awoke to the blare of music coming from downstairs and Dean's distressed wailing. Floyd sat bolt upright. When he realized Bonnie's side of the bed was deserted, he darted to the baby's room. The crib was empty too.

Floyd raced downstairs to find Bonnie—dressed in panties and a nursing bra—sitting cross-legged in front of the open pantry. The floor around her was covered in dried goods, canned vegetables, and an assortment of flower vases left behind by his mother. Dean lay on his back across one end of a sofa cushion Bonnie had put down on the linoleum directly beneath the overhead light. On the floor mere inches from the baby's head sat the radio—its speaker crackling and music distorted by volume. Dean's knees drew up to his belly, and his fists flailed with each fresh yowl. With her back towards him, Bonnie continued sorting spice jars and bobbing her head in time to the beat.

Floyd lunged at the radio and pounded the *off* button.

Her head cranked towards him. "You're awake!" she said with a wide smile as he scooped Dean from the cushion.

Floyd wheeled away from Bonnie and stormed into the living room to gather his thoughts in the semidarkness. She'd been doing so well. What the hell was going on? He kissed the baby's fiery cheek and cupped a hand around the back of Dean's head. "Shh. Everything's okay," he whispered. He undid the snaps of Dean's pajamas and began pulling his sweaty arms from the sleeves. The reek of a soiled diaper wafted up to Floyd's nostrils.

"Hey!" Bonnie said.

Floyd turned to find her standing behind him with a soup ladle in one hand. She reached out and brushed a thumb along the baby's cheek.

"Why all the tears, mister?" She smiled at Dean as if nothing were out of the ordinary.

Floyd was gobsmacked. "What are you doing?"

"I'm fixing the kitchen," she said excitedly. "The spices are now grouped by season. Not salt and pepper though. They fall under the category of *daily* spices. Sage is a *winter* spice. We'll use it in winter. And thyme too. Nice in soups. But who will make soup in summer? Not me. Then there's your mother's big soup pots. Winter pots. So I set up a winter cupboard way up high. They need to be out of the way." Bonnie started for the kitchen. "Come see what I've done. It's brilliant!"

"No I'm not coming to see anything."

She spun around to face him.

Floyd rocked side to side, and rubbed circles on Dean's back. "He was screaming. Right behind you." Exasperation leaked into his words as the baby fussed next to his ear.

Her eyes welled up with tears. "I was letting Dean cry himself to sleep."

"Why is he even downstairs? It must be close to three o'clock in the morning."

"I missed him," she said.

There was no sense to be made of his wife's reasoning.

"The radio station was playing Motown music." Bonnie's chin thrust forward. Her voice was losing its apologetic tone. "Dean likes 'My Girl.' I bet you didn't know that."

"Babies need to be kept on a schedule of regular sleep," he told her.

"Oh, here we go with *the schedule*," she said, rolling her eyes.

"We need routines for our son."

"You mean we need to program him to be a predictable bore? Who made that rule?"

Floyd inhaled slowly. "Predictability is necessary in order for the child to flourish."

"Schedule equals monotonous, bland, and joyless. No one really wants to live that way."

"*Some* people find an ordered life reassuring. It anchors them," he replied.

Bonnie's eyes smoldered as she stepped closer to him. "Nothing great ever happened in the world because someone stuck to a boring old schedule. Schedules create dull civil servants with no sense of adventure."

"You're calling me dull, then?"

"Yes. If it weren't for me, you'd be a friendless twenty-eight-year-old virgin."

"I have a friend," Floyd protested.

"Vic Patterson?" Bonnie scoffed. "He's a hundred years old!"

The conversation had leapt the fence, and she was leading it further astray. Although stung by her words, Floyd saw no point in fighting back. He hated conflict. It would only escalate her to a level of agitation she couldn't return from.

"All I'm saying is that Dean should be awake during the day and asleep at night."

"I can make him laugh better than you can." Bonnie tickled Dean under the chin. He turned his head towards Floyd's ear and balked.

Bonnie tried again. "Come on, you. Look over here." When she poked an index finger into his ribs, Dean began to bawl in earnest.

Floyd shifted the baby to his opposite hip. "He's had enough. I'm taking him upstairs." Just as Floyd stepped past Bonnie, her right hand shot out and grabbed his arm, upon which Dean's weight rested.

"Stop! You're not listening to me."

"I've been listening, but now I need to help Dean." Floyd said, his voice low and even. "Why don't you get a cold drink or relax on the couch? I'll be right back."

He'd climbed halfway up the stairs when he heard the crash of shattering glass and the dull *thunk* of something heavy striking wood. He sped downstairs to find Bonnie standing to one side of their dinner table clutching a can of tomatoes in one hand. Glass shards fanned across the table and circled her bare feet on the linoleum flooring.

Her nostrils flared, and her chest heaved with each new breath. She'd smashed the kitchen window.

"Schedule that!"

Words would not leave Floyd's gaping mouth. This physical manifestation of Bonnie's anger was new. What was he supposed to do now? Tend to his son, then leave him alone and distraught in his crib? Or clean up the glass so his wife wouldn't injure herself?

Second only to her mother's campaign to medicate her was Bonnie's disdain of her interference and attempts at control. Floyd wasn't going to follow in those footsteps. With the most placid façade he could conjure, he crossed to the front door and picked up his work shoes with one hand. He leaned over the spray of glass and passed them to Bonnie.

When she looked at him with an expression of bewilderment, he calmly stated, "You're going to need these. I'll see you in the morning." Then he withdrew from the kitchen with his heart pounding in his ears and carried their son upstairs. A choice had to be made. He only hoped he'd made the right one.

He bathed Dean in the bathroom sink. By the time he'd pinned Dean's fresh diaper, he could hear his shoes clomping across the kitchen floor, then the scratch of the straw broom and the clinking of glass inside the metal dustpan. He smiled as they crossed the hall to his and Bonnie's room, and he kissed the top of Dean's head. He settled on the bed with the baby lying on his chest and drifted off to sleep counting his son's breaths.

Floyd roused a few minutes before his alarm was set to buzz. He instinctively swept an arm across the sheets and felt for Dean. Nothing. His head lifted from the pillow, and his eyes cut to the mattress.

"He's fine. I carried Dean back to his crib earlier," Bonnie said. She was sitting at the foot of their bed. Her hair was damp from a shower, and she was already dressed. "I'm going to get him up when you're eating breakfast." Her eyes grew watery, and she wiped them with the heel of her hand.

Floyd fell back on his pillow and stretched a forearm across his forehead. He regarded her for a moment, then asked, "Are you okay?"

She shrugged. "Everything from the cupboards is put away. I swept up the glass in the kitchen and on the porch."

"That's not what I meant."

"I don't know what came over me," she sobbed. "You were talking about scheduling, and it's so different from me. My anger was like a fast-moving train. I couldn't stop it. I'm so sorry."

"I know." Floyd stretched his arms out. "Come here."

Bonnie crawled the length of the bed and lay next to him. She nestled her cheek against his shoulder. "I'm going to try really hard to wake Dean and put him down for naps at regular times. I can do better at meals too."

Floyd hugged her tightly. "I'm proud of you." He was more than proud. He'd been jotting observations about what sparked her changes in mood. Lack of sleep and poor eating habits were the main culprits. Her scheduling of Dean meant scheduling herself as well."

"I called a repair man after you went to bed," she said.

"At four o'clock in the morning?"

"That's what he said, but he's coming this morning to measure up the window and make repairs." She sniffled softly. "I'm so sorry."

"What's done is done."

"The neighbours are going to be curious when they see the window smashed out. I don't know what I'll say if they ask how it happened."

"Tell them your husband broke it. I was fixing something and my ladder fell against it."

"Really?"

"Sure."

Bonnie pressed a lengthy kiss to his cheek. "Nothing like this will ever happen again. I promise."

"I believe you."

16.

The mood was sombre as father and son prepared for the trip to Toronto. Dean didn't speak except to ask what time they were leaving. He waited in the car with his faced turned towards the window.

"You can't leave this behind," Floyd said, laying Dean's guitar case cross the backseat. He eased behind the wheel and smiled weakly.

No response.

"How are you feeling about all this hospital business? A bit nervous?"

Dean jammed a finger against the radio button and turned the volume up. Floyd switched the radio off.

"I'm not sure how things will unfold this morning. Your grandmother—"

Dean's hand shot out again. Floyd sighed heavily and backed the car onto the street, music blaring.

Dean extended his right arm through the open window as Floyd drove to the Brookman estate. His fingers moved as if he were practicing scales on a piano. Patterns of light moved across his face, and the wind tousled his hair.

"Warm enough?"

Dean nodded and drew his arm inside the car.

Minutes later, Floyd pulled into the estate driveway and paused in front of the looming gates.

"Why are we stopping?" Dean asked.

"We Hoffmans have survived decades of hardship through world wars. Life wasn't easy for your Oma and Opa despite leaving Germany. Your mother was a fighter." Floyd's voice wavered. "Your grandmother and I don't see eye to eye. We had different visions of how to care for your mother. But Rose is a dog with a bone once she gets an idea in her head. She knows what she believes is right, and she'll fight to the end to make it happen. That's the kind of stock you come from, Dean. This thing invading your body is the enemy. It doesn't fight fair. But you have smarts," Floyd tapped his temple, "you and your army of experts. You can beat this thing."

The angry expression lifted from Dean's face.

"I haven't always shown up like I should have. But I'm here now, and I'm not leaving, no matter what she says." Floyd looked up at the house, then at Dean. "No matter how much you push me away."

"What about work? Are you worried about being fired?"

"Doesn't matter." Floyd shook his head and reached for his handkerchief. "When you come home, we'll go on a road trip, an adventure. Just you and me."

"I'm going to be fine," Dean said. "This really is my big chance."

"I know." Floyd wiped his eyes.

"Are you staying at Grandma's place in Toronto?"

"No. Why?"

"No reason." The glimmer of satisfaction surfaced in Dean's eyes as he turned his face away.

A florist truck appeared in the rearview mirror, prompting Floyd to continue along the circular drive to the portico. He parked behind a black sedan with tinted windows and checked his reflection in the rearview mirror. A dark purple crescent had formed under his eye, but his glasses concealed the cut on the bridge of his nose.

The truck rolled by and turned onto a separate branch of the driveway that led to the back of the house.

"I'll follow your grandmother's driver to the appointment, but first there are matters I must attend to inside." Floyd got out of the car. He tucked his shirt in and adjusted the waistband of his pants while Dean retrieved his duffel bag from the backseat.

"I'm not going to let her boss me around," Dean said, looking up at house.

"You sound like your mother."

They crossed the portico to the front door. Floyd steeled himself to knock, but Dean stepped past him and pushed the door open.

Mrs. Brookman stood in a shaft of sunlight at the centre of the foyer with Marian at her side. "You're late," she said, pushing her hands into a pair of white gloves.

Dean set his duffel bag on the vase table and kissed her cheek lightly. "Hello, Grandmother."

"Marian, let the driver know we're ready," Mrs. Brookman said, casting an evaluative look at Dean. "And bring our friend out."

"Yes, missus." Marian hastily departed from the foyer.

"Which hospital am I going to?" Dean asked.

"I'll explain on the way." Mrs. Brookman's eyes darted to Floyd. "Postal work has turned violent?"

"The world is an unpredictable place," Floyd said.

"So it is," she replied with a wry grin.

A high-pitched bark echoed through the hall. Marian reappeared with a squirming puppy in her arms.

"Wow!" Dean took the puppy from Marian and nuzzled it against his cheek. "Thanks, Grandmother. I've always wanted a dog."

A golden retriever. Floyd began to perspire, and his face reddened.

"Dean, take the dog and wait out front by my car. I need a word with—Floyd."

Marian clipped a red-and-white-checkered leash on the puppy's collar and escorted Dean outdoors. When she closed the door, all pretenses of civility slid from Mrs. Brookman's face.

"The paperwork is in the study. My lawyer will show you where to sign."

"I'm following you to the hospital. I am Dean's father." Floyd's hands shook. "Your car better still be here when I'm finished."

"Or what?" Mrs. Brookman laughed with a dismissive wave of her hand. "That car won't move until you're done."

Floyd strode to the study. Mrs. Brookman's lawyer stood next to the desk. His sombre expression suggested misgivings about his involvement in this exercise. He gestured towards the overstuffed chair behind the desk. The florist truck passed by the study window as Floyd settled into the chair, its roof just visible above the sill. A second vehicle crunched over the gravel behind it.

Nausea stirred in Floyd's stomach upon seeing the legal papers stacked at the centre of the blotter. The choice he made funneled down to a cost benefit analysis. Dean must be the clear winner.

"God, forgive me." Floyd picked up the pen that had been laid out for him and signed the top sheet.

"Wouldn't you like to read it over?" the lawyer said, looking down his hawkish nose.

"There's no time for that."

The lawyer flipped the pages and pointed to each new signature line. He scanned the document thoroughly after Floyd laid the pen on the desk.

"Are we done here?" Floyd asked. When the lawyer nodded, Floyd left the study and walked briskly through the foyer. Dean's duffel bag had disappeared from the vase table. Mrs. Brookman had vanished too. Floyd rushed to the front door and flung it open. To his relief, the sedan waited just as Mrs. Brookman had said it would.

Floyd crossed the portico, fishing his car keys from his pocket. He slid behind the wheel and started the car, then lowered his window to wave the sedan onward. Thirty seconds later, the sedan hadn't moved. Panic descended on Floyd.

Mrs. Brookman's lawyer stepped out of the house with a leather valise tucked under his arm. He reached inside his suit jacket and pulled out a set of car keys.

Floyd leaned over his steering wheel. His eyes widened. "No! No! No!"

The lawyer walked to the driver's side of the sedan and unlocked the door. He tossed the valise inside, then walked towards Floyd.

"Mr. Hoffman, I have been asked to inform you that Mrs. Brookman and your son are currently en route to a medical facility in the city of Toronto, where he will receive first-rate care."

"How? I've been here the entire time."

"Should it become necessary, in-home care will be provided around the clock. You will receive updates of significant improvement or decline."

"Oh my God. Was there a second car? She planned this whole thing!"

"If you attempt to follow Mrs. Brookman, arrive at the Brookmans' Toronto residence unbidden, or participate in unsolicited communications with Dean, Mrs. Brookman will find herself compelled to share the question of Dean's paternity in addition to filing a cease-and-desist order against you."

"She can't do this."

"With all due respect—"

"Respect?" Floyd cried.

"Mrs. Brookman can do whatever she likes—now."

17.

On the morning of Dean's departure, Tammy awoke with his football jersey wadded beneath her cheek. The solace of his scent had long disappeared. Dean smelled of fabric softener and fried onions. Or was it deodorant mixed with something peppery? That she could forget so easily frightened her.

Tammy reached under the bed to retrieve Dean's book of Whitman poetry. She kicked her laundry against the bottom edge of the bedroom door, then turned on her lamp and flipped the pages until she arrived at a passage underlined in pencil.

> *This is thy hour O Soul, thy free flight into the wordless,*
> *Away from books, away from art, the day erased, the lesson done,*
> *Thee fully forth emerging, silent, gazing, pondering the themes thou*
> *lovest best.*
> *Night, sleep, death and the stars.*

She read the lines over and over until her tears blurred the print. After she turned off the light, Tammy spread Dean's football jersey flat on the mattress and lay her head on one of its shoulders. Then she hugged the poetry book to her chest and tried again to make sense of their botched liaison of the previous day.

They'd arranged a last rendezvous at his house. Everything needed to be perfect. She'd dressed in a T-shirt and the tie-dyed skirt Dean liked. He'd given her a necklace last Valentine's Day, which she'd tucked into her purse along with some cherry lip gloss, then set off downstairs.

"I'm going to school. Grades should be posted on the gym doors by now," she'd said.

Mirabelle had looked up from her lunch with a doleful expression that made Tammy's insides knot up. Although she'd lied many times since becoming Dean's girlfriend, she'd never acquired his level of ease with bending the truth.

On her way to the Hoffman house, she'd slipped a bracelet over her wrist and fastened the clasp of the gold-plated chain behind her neck. The heart-shaped locket lay just below her collar. A generous application of lip gloss was the final touch.

She'd spotted him waiting on a porch step and was about to cross the street when the screen door swung open. Allan Robinson came outside and sat on the step below Dean.

The scene stung like a betrayal. She'd gone to such lengths to see Dean, only to find him hanging out with a school friend he rarely mentioned. How had Allan outranked her? As if he'd read her thoughts, Allan had looked across the street and waved to her, but Dean's head had turned slowly side to side, warning her away. Tammy had continued along the sidewalk, confused and tearful.

Replaying the exchange kept her awake for most of the night. Why hadn't Dean made an effort to contact her? He claimed to love her, after all. *Have my baby.* Easy for him to say. It wasn't living inside him, making him fat or stopping him from attending college. Her breath caught in her throat. *What a heartless thought.*

An hour after her father had left for work, Tammy slumped downstairs for breakfast. Mirabelle was thumbing through her dictionary when she walked into the kitchen.

"A short curved sword?" she said without looking up. "Begins with a *C.* Fifth letter is *A* . . ."

"Is there any cereal?" Tammy asked.

"Cornflakes—middle shelf. Milk's on the table."

Tammy pulled the cereal and a bowl from the cupboard, then she turned towards her mother.

"The word is *cutlass,*" Tammy said.

Mirabelle closed the dictionary with a sour look.

"Pirates carried them in *Treasure Island*." Tammy allowed herself to smirk as she filled her bowl.

Upon hearing a car pull in the driveway, Mirabelle left the kitchen table and rushed to the living room, pen in hand, to peer through the sheers.

"Huh! It's your father. He's sitting there staring into space with the engine running." The doorknob turned, then Mirabelle called, "Lawrence! Turn that car off and come inside." Her voice grew more distant. "Gas doesn't grow on trees." She'd gone outside.

Tammy dropped her spoon and reached for the telephone. She dialed Dean's number and listened anxiously for her parents' return. The phone rang several times before anguish set in. He'd left for Toronto, and she hadn't told him good-bye.

"Hang up your keys and come into the kitchen," Mirabelle said.

Bowl in hand, Tammy scurried to the table. No sooner had she dumped milk over her cereal than Mirabelle stormed into the room. She banged Lawrence's lunchbox onto the counter where Tammy had stood a moment earlier.

"Lawrence!"

Tammy's father ambled into the kitchen still wearing his McLelland's-issued coveralls. Confusion glazed his eyes, much like it did her grandmother's when she'd misplaced a word or an object.

"You're scaring me, Lawrence. For heaven's sake, have a seat and tell me what's going on," Mirabelle said.

"They sacked me."

"Ohhh." Mirabelle's eyes grew round.

"Laid off. Not performance related, they said."

The kitchen grew quiet except for the ticking of the oven clock. Tammy waited with her hands clasped in her lap.

Mirabelle's fist thumped the table. "Unbelievable."

"I thought I'd be all right," Lawrence said. "I thought the younger guys would go if it came to that."

"Rightfully so. You've been there twenty-seven years."

"The young fellas are being put on rotating layoffs. About thirty of us older guys got called in first thing this morning. It's us that got the boot."

"Those pups could have started over easy enough. Who will hire a man your age?" Mirabelle huffed.

Lawrence's chin dropped toward the front of his shirt.

"What about your pension?" she asked.

He patted a crumpled envelope tilting from his breast pocket. "It's all in here." His eyes cut to Tammy. "We can discuss that later."

"Did they offer an explanation at least?"

"Cost-cutting measures. The mill hopes to recoup the cost of repairing the scrubbers through rotating layoffs. There's talk that the ministry may want a full replacement."

Mirabelle pulled a hardened ball of tissue from the pocket of her robe and dabbed her eyes. "I guess we know who to thank for opening that can of worms."

Tammy understood the implication.

"Is there a severance package?" Mirabelle asked.

Lawrence's chin quavered. "It's the only job I've ever had."

"A golden handshake. Is there one?"

He nodded and wiped his eyes.

"One door closes and another opens." Mirabelle leaned slightly towards Tammy. "No sense in putting off a call to the Beatrix Home now that there's a lump sum of money falling into our lap. We can finalize the arrangements for the end of July, right after graduation."

Tammy's mind reeled at the possibility of five months' separation from Dean. She'd no idea how to contact him, and even if she did, she couldn't risk his grandmother picking up. He'd remained adamant about secrecy. How would he feel towards her when he began to suspect she was considering adoption?

She no longer knew what she wanted. If only she could gather the courage to defy her mother and turn the world on its ear. *It's good that graduation is a month away*, she wanted to say. *It will give me time to decide if I want to stay at the Beatrix Home.*

Who was having this baby, anyway?

In the early afternoon, Mirabelle announced that she and Lawrence would be going out for a few hours. Tammy seized the opportunity to embark on her own expedition to see Leslie Benton. She remembered the address from a school friend who'd complained about being Leslie's backyard neighbour.

Leslie Benton lived on what most people referred to as the wrong side of town in a neighbourhood of simple homes with peeling paint and missing shingles. Their proximity to the mill meant the families who lived there endured the bleach and rotten-egg odours escaping from the mill, regardless of wind direction.

The moment Tammy stepped into the yard, a German Shepherd leapt to its feet inside the screen door and began barking. She approached the house with caution and deliberated for a moment at the edge of a crumbling cement pad below the door. Dog slobber and paw prints clouded the glass panel at the top of the storm door. When she leaned over a toppled tricycle and rapped on the aluminum door frame, the dog's ears laid back and his lips curled away from his teeth in a snarl. Tammy pressed the doorbell, then yanked her arm back and waited on the grass. Scotch tape affixed some children's colouring pages inside the window, and plastic flowers jutted out of a clay pot on the ledge.

"Bruno!"

Leslie appeared at the door wearing cutoff shorts and a tube top that showed off her *EB* tattoo. Tammy stared at it until Leslie pushed the dog aside with her knee.

"What do you want?" she said.

"I was hoping we could talk."

"Yeah, what about?"

"The Beatrix Home," Tammy replied.

"Yessie?" A little girl scooted through the kitchen. "Up, up," she said, prancing on tiptoes, her arms raised above her head. Another girl, slightly older than the first, hung back and picked at a sticker on the refrigerator door.

"Why should I tell you anything?"

Tammy shrugged.

"Come get the kids," Leslie called over her shoulder. A pimple-faced boy trudged belligerently into the kitchen to collect the girls and then disappeared around a corner.

"Meet me out back." Leslie opened the screen door and raised a leg to bar Bruno's escape. "Use the gate over there." She pointed to a stretch of chain-link fencing at one corner of the house and shut the door.

Tammy wriggled the gate open. She shimmied around a pair of rusted garbage cans and an old lawnmower sandwiched between the house and the fence, then followed a grassy strip to the rear of the house.

Bruno's plywood doghouse hunkered down at the back of the yard. A shredded blanket hung out through its door, and a dog chain stretched from a metal stake in the ground. Sun-bleached toys lay strewn across the centre of the yard—a plastic pony on wheels, tangled-up skipping ropes, and a naked doll.

Two lawn chairs waited under a maple tree shading the yard closest to the rear of the house. Tammy swept a film of grey dust from one, then sat and bounced her knees while she waited.

"Hey," Leslie called through a window. "Wanna pop?"

"No thanks," Tammy answered.

Seconds later, Leslie pushed the back door open with her hip and sauntered barefoot towards Tammy, soda can in hand. She plopped into the empty chair and stretched out her pale legs. "What's up, Keener?" Leslie popped the tab and sipped from the can.

Tammy looked up at the house. The little girls watched from behind the screen door, licking Popsicles.

"Not that it's any of your business, but they're my half sisters. Mom died, and a couple months later my dad met someone else." Leslie nodded her head as she toyed with her ankle bracelet. "Guys, right?"

Tammy's toes scrunched inside her sandals.

Leslie flicked the pop can tab with a thumbnail. "So you wanna talk? Talk."

Tammy wished she'd accepted the offer for a drink. Her mouth had grown dry. "I wanted to talk about the Beatrix Home. You saw something. I want to know what."

After a moment, Leslie responded. "I'll tell you. But for every question, you're gonna answer one of mine first. Deal?"

"Deal."

A smile lifted the corners of Leslie's mouth. "Are you pregnant?"

"Yes," Tammy said in a breathy voice. She gripped the arm of the chair and posed her question. "The newspaper accused the home of using outdated practices. What does that mean?"

Leslie set the pop can under her chair and picked at her nails. "The girls aren't allowed phone privileges. Once they've got you, there's no calling your boyfriend, your girlfriends, your parents. Their goal is adopting out, so from the day a girl arrives she's brainwashed into giving up her kid." Leslie scrunched her nose. "They spout the standard religious bullshit about righteous living." She exhaled and looked Tammy in the eye. "My turn. How pregnant are you?"

"Three months and a bit. What's the terrible thing that happened? You said you saw the *whole thing.*"

"In the room next to mine, there was this girl," Leslie said, "always going on about how she and her boyfriend were going to get married and take care of the kid. While she was in Hattersburg, he was saving to set them up in an apartment. She went into labour, and a few hours later the Beatrix people drove her to the hospital." Leslie leaned forward in the lawn chair and stared into the distance. "She came back to the home two days later screaming, 'Where's my baby? They stole my baby.' The Beatrix people wouldn't let any of us girls talk to her. But I could hear *them* through the wall. 'You signed the adoption papers. It was all legal,' they said. She cried until late into the night. The next morning, they found her in the bathroom." Leslie raised her eyebrows and made a slicing motion across her left wrist.

Tammy's heart sank.

"She signed the papers while they were knocking her out. Someone took the baby before she woke up. Me again," Leslie said. "Are you going to give it up?"

Tammy nodded, then shrugged. Her face crumpled, and she began to weep. "Is it expensive to stay there?"

"My dad drives a logging truck, and he could swing it," Leslie said. "Who's the lucky boy that knocked you up?"

Tammy remembered her mother's warning. "You're out of luck," she said. "There's nothing else I want to know."

Throughout the neighbourhood, Tammy wandered, munching on a couple of oatmeal cookies and an apple she'd stuffed into her purse before leaving home. Beyond the foresight of packing food, she felt unequipped to plan a future. Just another tick mark against becoming a parent. How could she lead by example when she could barely manage herself?

Her mind was a frenzied rabbit, leaping from one worry to the next. Reflections on her relationship with Dean led her to worry about the ordeal of giving birth. Her uncertainty about Beatrix Home morphed into questions about names in Mr. Hoffman's red journal. When she agonized over her parents' disappointment, the likelihood of Dean's survival inserted itself. And then there were the conversations with Reverend Findlay.

She needed to sort herself out and make decisions. If only she had a confidante who would offer a smile and listen without judgment. Who could she speak to without risk of becoming the stuff of gossip? Like dandelion fluff riding the breeze, an idea touched down so lightly she nearly missed it. Suddenly, Tammy knew where to turn.

Nanna Larkin.

Pineview Home for the Aged was a twenty-minute walk from the library. The building sprawled along the riverbank behind a fringe of gnarled shrubbery and evergreens. When Aunt Eva had insisted Nanna be installed in a private room there overlooking the water, Mirabelle had protested the expense. She'd won a small victory when Aunt Eva agreed to cover the extra cost. Eva and Uncle Cyril's grocery business had grown to seven stores, and Nanna deserved the best they could afford.

"A fool and his money are soon parted," Mirabelle had responded. "Mother doesn't know luxury from squalor anymore."

It had been Christmas since Tammy last saw her grandmother. She'd never visited Pineview alone. Mirabelle included her in a couple of Sunday afternoons each year. Lawrence preferred to wait in the car. On sunny days, he might offer to wheel Nanna onto the terrace to stare at the river and take in some fresh air.

Tammy paused on the sidewalk in front of Pineview and bit the inside of her cheek. She dismissed her nervousness and went inside. A secretary glanced up with disinterest as Tammy slunk by the glass window separating the reception office from the main hallway. She continued past a painting of the queen and turned left at a row of framed portraits documenting important people in Pineview's history. Two nurses hustled ahead of her, their rubber-soled shoes squeaking against the institutional flooring. The corridors smelled of disinfectant cleaners and tomato soup. The low hum of television voices alerted her to the commons room up ahead. Another right turn and she'd be there.

Tammy discovered a frail man shuffling his slippered feet across the doorway of Nanna's room. One of his hands reached behind to pull an oxygen tank on wheels while the other gripped the handrail that ran the length of the hall.

"Hello," she said, trying not to stare at the plastic tubes running from the tank and disappearing up his nose.

A bathroom located immediately inside the entranceway blocked Tammy's view into the room. She could only glimpse the foot of Nanna's bed and a set of deep windows overlooking the river. After the man passed by, she walked haltingly through the narrow passage and peered around the corner.

"Helen," a voice boomed, "you have a visitor!" A rosy-faced woman dressed in nursing scrubs finished tucking the edges of a quilt between Nanna and the arm of her wheelchair.

"Hi, Nanna. It's me," Tammy said.

Her grandmother flinched, and her eyes widened. She gave off the impression of a child wrapped inside a body whose age surprised her.

"You know who this is, don't you, Helen?" the woman said with relentless enthusiasm.

Nanna's mouth struggled to form language. "Jessica," she said.

"Not Jessica. That's Aunt Eva's daughter." Tammy said, her neck craning forward. "I'm Tammy."

"Ohh," Nanna moaned.

"I'm just going to wheel this jalopy over to the window so you two girls can have a nice talk," the woman said in a raised voice. She pushed the chair to the windows and stepped on the footbrake to lock the wheels in place. "She's having a good day, hun," the woman said quietly as she draped a sweater across Nanna's shoulders.

"Will she understand what I'm saying?" Tammy asked.

"Hard to say. She doesn't communicate much these days."

Tammy snuffled.

The woman looked at her warmly. "You're going to be fine. If you need anything, just buzz." She gathered a bundle of soiled sheets from the foot of Nanna's bed and left the room.

Tammy dragged a chair from the corner and sat next to her grandmother. Nanna's cheeks were more drawn than Tammy remembered. Her hair had been brushed straight back and held in place by an elastic at the nape of her neck. White strands stuck out from her temples like down escaping from a pillow. The corners of Nanna's mouth lifted into a gentle smile when Tammy laid a hand over hers.

"I'm in trouble, Nanna," she whispered.

Her grandmother blinked slowly.

"I fell in love with a boy." Grief welled at the back of Tammy's throat. "He's very sick, and now I don't know where he is." She pulled a tissue from the pocket of her shorts and wiped her nose.

Nanna's lips pursed.

"I'm having a baby, Nanna." Tammy searched her grandmother's eyes. "The boy wants me to keep it. Mom is furious. Dad barely looks at me. They told me to put it up for adoption. Even Reverend Findlay says it's the right thing to do. But I just don't know."

"Hello, Mother. Tammy, what a nice surprise!" Aunt Eva sailed into the room, light as a breeze, with a pot of azaleas cradled in her arms.

Tammy forced a smile and slumped in her chair.

"I thought you'd enjoy some flowers," Aunt Eva said as she kissed her mother's cheek. "And I brought more pudding from the store, the butterscotch kind you like."

Nanna's eyes moistened, and her mouth struggled to shape words.

"What is it, Mother?" Aunt Eva rested a hand on the back of the wheelchair and leaned forward with concern.

"Jes-s-sca."

"Tammy's here." Aunt Eva patted her arm.

"B . . . bay."

"Sorry, Mother, I—"

"Bay . . . be," Nanna blurted.

"Baby?" Aunt Eva frowned.

Tammy dissolved into tears and dropped her face into her hands.

"Oh, my poor dear," Aunt Eva said. She waited a moment, then, in a honeyed voice, asked, "How can I help?"

18.

Floyd was pacing the hallway outside Dean's room when the metal flap snapped shut against the mail slot. He wheeled towards the sound but restrained himself from rushing towards it. In the three weeks since Dean had left, Floyd's dash to the front door had been punishing. Instead of letters from his son, he'd found utility bills and late notices scattered on the floor. Mrs. Brookman's lawyer had promised medical updates, but Floyd had yet to receive one, by mail or telephone.

In the bedroom doorway, Floyd rocked back and forth, rubbing his grizzled jaw. He'd left the sheets where Dean had pushed them to the foot of the bed. The pillow still bore the imprint of his head, a shadow of his last night in the house. His fear of Dean's presence fleeing the room in rebellion stopped him from going inside.

When Floyd tried to conjure a vision of Dean's return, he only managed to raise an empty house. The thread connecting them wore thinner each day. Floyd closed the bedroom door and trudged down the hall.

Alive or not, Dean isn't coming back. The admission pushed Floyd into a pool of despair and pulled him under. For months, he'd done everything possible to escape Dean and the gloom of things left unsaid. Now he wanted to seal the windows to trap every skin cell and memory inside the house.

A shiver rippled along his spine.

Mrs. Brookman had flexed her legal might and excised him from Dean's life. *She's castrated me. And I opened myself up to it by asking for help.*

"Witch!" Floyd yelled. His fists drove into the wall—left, right, left, right—until his knuckles bled on the plaster.

He sank to his knees, ribs heaving. The numbness that had swallowed his emotion over these past weeks now spewed sobs between his gasps for breath. Ropes of mucus stretched to his upper lip, and tears dripped from his chin. Everything he'd sacrificed for had been smashed and stripped away by Rose Brookman. How could he recover from that?

He dragged a sleeve across his face and rose to his feet. Something caught his eye at the front door—a white business envelope hanging by one corner from the mail slot. He plucked the letter from the door and turned it over. The post office had written again. The return address included *Personnel Department* in bold letters. He dropped the envelope on the table with the others from last week and the week before. The letters remained sealed, but he could guess their gist. Carl Spivey had indulged the first week of absence, and now, after twenty-three consecutive days of Floyd's failure to report for work, he was seeking his pound of flesh.

Floyd squeezed behind the kitchen table and dropped into his chair. The situation must be dealt with, but not today.

Bonnie's ashtray sat on the corner of the table. It cradled the remains of Dean's cigarette, the filter and a tumbled column of ash resembling a Pompeii ruin. Floyd gingerly pinched the cigarette between a thumb and index finger and raised it to his mouth. The gesture discomfited and consoled in equal measure. He drew air through the filter, then removed the stub from his mouth and blew a stream of make-believe smoke towards the ceiling.

He returned the cigarette butt to the ashtray, taking care not to disturb it, then examined his knuckles. Pain travelled along the back of both hands. He should ice them, but what the hell? It wasn't as if he planned to leave the house. Besides, the escalating throb served as penance.

Tap tap tap.

Oh no. Floyd glanced over his shoulder at the kitchen window, where Allan's forehead pressed against the glass. The boy smiled, transmitting an optimism that vexed Floyd.

"Go home, kid," Floyd muttered, hunching over the ashtray.

Tap tap tap.

Floyd slowly lifted his gaze. Allan ducked below the sill and reappeared with a brown bag raised in one hand and a carton holding three coffees in the other. He wore an imploring expression that, under different circumstances, Floyd may have found amusing.

"I'm coming," Floyd said on his way to the front hall. He rested a hand on the doorknob and counted to ten before pulling the door open.

"Thank goodness you're here. My arm's falling off," Allan said.

Floyd stood inside the screen door and blinked.

"My hands are kind of full here . . ." Allan tilted his head towards the latch.

"Oh," Floyd said, pressing the lever downward.

When the door flung open, the smile dropped from Allan's face. "Whoa."

Floyd realized how he must appear. He'd neither showered nor washed his hair in over a week. To his credit, he had brushed his teeth a few times since Dean left, but dental hygiene remained low on his list of priorities. He'd slept on the couch wearing the same shirt and pants for the past three evenings. Laundry was another of those items that ranked low for the time being. Fresh boxers and clean socks were among the first depleted items. He'd been moping around barefooted and in the same underwear for days.

Allan recovered his sunny disposition and loped into the kitchen. "When did you and Dean get back?"

"A few days ago." The lie jumped from Floyd's mouth before he had time to think.

"I bring the breakfast of champions: some fresh-brewed java and apple danishes delivered to the diner this morning." He set the coffees on the table along with the bag of pastries and shoved some used mugs aside to make room for his rucksack.

"I'm kind of busy . . ." Floyd said quietly, concealing his hands behind his back.

Allan stepped towards the counter. "Holy shi—" He chuffed in disbelief. "Did ya have a party and forget to call me?" Dirty dishes littered the countertop and both frying pans sat on the stovetop; one crusted with egg yolk and the other coated in congealed fat.

Floyd grimaced on his way to the counter. "I'll wash a couple plates." The paper bag rustled on the table behind him.

"Won't Dean want a danish?" Allan asked.

"What?" Floyd gritted his teeth as tap water trailed over his injured hands.

"You said 'a couple of plates.' Won't we *each* need one?"

Floyd considered telling the truth about Dean being in Toronto. But Allan would surely question why *he* hadn't stayed in the city as well. Floyd couldn't bear the scrutiny.

"Dean's sleeping." He turned the faucet on and scrubbed a patch of dried egg on the edge of a plate.

"Cool. I recorded some Rush and a few Dylan tunes." Allan pulled a cassette tape from his shirt pocket and made for the hallway. "I'll leave it on his dresser."

"Now's not a good time," Floyd called after him.

Allan stopped short.

"Dean's a light sleeper." In a parental tone Floyd added, "He *really* needs his sleep."

"Look, man, no problem," Allan said, propping the tape against a used cup on the table. "I'll leave it here."

Floyd rinsed and dried the plates. He took a deep breath, then turned to face Allan's concerned expression. After an awkward silence, they sat across from one another at the table.

"Is he doing okay?"

"Not bad," Floyd replied. The lie had been set in motion. There was no stopping now.

When Allan's eyes lit up, a tsunami of guilt washed over Floyd.

"That's great." Allan helped himself to a danish and pushed the bag towards Floyd.

"Maybe later." Floyd peeled the plastic lid from one of the Styrofoam cups.

"This tastes so good," Allan said through a mouthful of pastry. He licked a blob of fruit filling from the corner of his mouth. "Did they say how long before Dean's all better?"

Floyd shook his head. "We just have to wait."

Allan added two sugar packets to his coffee and swirled a stir stick inside the cup. He looked at the three envelopes stacked to the left of his plate. "Personnel," he said slowly. "There could be something important in there, you know."

"It'll wait," said Floyd, fiddling with the coffee cup lid.

Allan picked up the most recent letter from the top of the pile. "See this?" He held the envelope at eye level. "It's thick. Probably a four-pager." Allan's brows pinched together. "Aren't you even curious?"

Floyd took the letter from Allan. A band of worry tightened around his chest. He held one end of the envelope in either hand and willed himself to remain calm.

"Just open it," Allan said.

"Don't rush me," Floyd replied with a twinge of annoyance. Who was this boy to address him in such a familiar manner?

"It can't be that bad."

"Don't count on it. I've dug a hole for myself," Floyd said as he tore open the letter. "They're not mailing me a prize."

"Well, maybe this glass is half-full. Good guys don't always finish last. Etcetera, etcetera." Allan popped the last bite of danish into his mouth. While Floyd read the letter, Allan added more sugar to his coffee and drained the cup.

A moment later, Floyd refolded the letter and pushed it back into the envelope.

With elbows resting on the edge of the table, Allan raised his eyebrows. "Well?"

"There's a form to fill out," Floyd said with a shrug. "I have to get a doctor's note too."

Allan threw his hands in the air. "What'd I tell ya? Half-full."

The boy's sense of ease made Floyd's skin itch. He resented the I-told-you-so on the heels of being pressured into doing something he wasn't ready for.

"Well, Dean's going to be sleeping for a while, and I'm sure you've got plans . . ." Floyd said.

"Actually, I'm wide open all day."

"You'll be bored."

"No, I brought a book. Lemme show ya." Allan reached across the table and pulled the rucksack towards his lap. The shoulder strap looped around Bonnie's ashtray, like a slingshot around a stone, and flung it to the ground. Ashes of Dean's cigarette scattered across the linoleum amid chunks of the broken ashtray.

"Jeez, I'm sorry, man."

Floyd squeezed his eyes shut and opened them again when he heard the floor squeaking in the hallway.

"Is this the broom closet?" Allan stood outside the closed room behind the kitchen and reached for the doorknob.

"That's private!" Floyd's hands clutched his knees.

Allan jumped and yanked his hand back. "Just trying to help out."

Floyd sighed and in a gentler voice said, "You need to go."

On his way past the kitchen, Allan gathered his rucksack from the chair and slung it over his shoulder. "Please tell Dean I stopped by. And don't forget the tape, okay?" He paused at the door and looked back at Floyd.

The boy expected something from him. *What would Bonnie have said in this awkward circumstance?*

"Thanks for the danish. Very thoughtful of you."

"Right on." A slow smile rose to Allan's eyes. Then he left.

Two days later, Floyd found himself sitting across the desk from Doc Gillespie. Floyd hated this office with its dark wood paneling. With the curtains drawn, it was nothing more than a damned box—a coffin with a desk.

Doc Gillespie removed his glasses and laid them on the blank pad of paper next to his pen. He released a deep sigh without shifting his gaze from Floyd's unshaven face. Finally, he clasped his hands and rested his elbows on the desk. Leaning forward slightly, he asked, "How is Dean?"

"Good."

Floyd's response came too fast, he realized. But it was too late to take it back now. What else could he have said? That he didn't know? That three weeks ago he'd signed his son over like a used car without reading the paperwork? That he'd done nothing but wander room to room, waiting for the telephone to ring?

"Hmm." The doctor nodded, and his upper lip rolled in against his teeth. "It's been too long since I last saw Dean. Why don't you bring him by later this afternoon?" he said, checking his appointment book. "I could slide him in at two o'clock."

"Sure." Floyd looked away to the marble penholder sitting empty in the centre of the desk. He rolled his shirttail under to hide a coffee stain.

"What can I do for you, Floyd?"

"I need a letter." Floyd removed a folded letter from his shirt pocket and slid it across the desk.

Doc Gillespie put his glasses on and smoothed the paper flat against the blotter. "Mr. Hoffman," he read aloud, "due to the recent series of unexplained absences . . . requires a written doctor's note confirming illness on the aforementioned dates . . . disciplinary steps." The doctor's eyes cut to Floyd. "Sounds serious."

"I suppose."

"Carl Spivey's involved as well, I see. The man is a pure menace," Doc Gillespie said, rolling his chair away from the desk. "Well, let's have a look at you."

Floyd followed him into the adjoining room and hoisted himself onto the examination table. The paper sheet crinkled each time his weight shifted. His hands grew clammy, and nausea rolled through his stomach.

"Unbutton your shirt." Doc Gillespie warmed his stethoscope against the palm of his right hand. "When did you last eat?"

Floyd looked at the ceiling while he fumbled with his buttons. "Yesterday. In the morning."

"How are you sleeping?"

"About four hours a night, on average."

The doctor frowned. He pressed the stethoscope to Floyd's chest and deftly repositioned it along his ribs, then between his shoulder blades. "Breathe in," he said, "and again."

Floyd filled his lungs and exhaled on cue. The doctor smelled of aftershave and hand soap as he checked Floyd's blood pressure and reflexes with neatly boxed instruments. Doc Gillespie's white coat waffled against his legs as he strode from the examination room to his desk. He returned seconds later to lean against the edge of a low cabinet and write notes in a folder.

"You appear to be in good health. Heart's strong as ever. Blood pressure is a bit low, but that's not a bad thing." He closed the folder and looked at Floyd. "Some things medicine can't measure—a broken heart, grief, or the pressure of caring for a sick child, alone." He paused before asking, "Would you like medication to help you relax?"

"No."

"Okay," Doc Gillespie replied. "I'm going to draft a letter that confirms illness on the dates listed in the correspondence. I'll include a medical request that you be excused from work for an additional four weeks, at the end of which we will review the need for an extension."

A rush of air escaped the back of Floyd's throat. His hands gripped the edge of the table. "Thank you," he said, dropping his head forward.

"The specialist in North Bay can take Dean on July twenty-fourth. It's an early morning appointment. We can go over the details when you and Dean come in later."

Floyd slid from the table and hurried towards the office door.

"Take proper care of yourself," Doc Gillespie called after him. "Your son's lost one parent. He may not survive losing a second."

Floyd heeded the doctor's advice and picked up some food at the diner—tomato soup and a ham on rye. Again, the waitress called him by name. Her eye shape and hair colour reminded him of Allan's, but he refrained from asking if they were related on the grounds that she might tell the boy about the conversation. Allan struck him as the type who might continue to visit at the slightest provocation, and Floyd didn't need that.

At twelve thirty, he arrived home and scooped the newspaper from the front walk before going inside. Despite the presence of a cooling breeze, he closed the oak door behind him and turned the lock. He stepped into the kitchen and tossed the day's paper into the corner next to the pantry. It rolled off the mounting pile of unread newspapers and came to rest against the table leg.

He rinsed a spoon under the tap and dried it on his shirt, then sat at his usual spot and opened the Styrofoam container. The soup had grown cold, but it would do. He bit into the sandwich and glanced at Dean's empty chair. It sat at an angle to the table, as if Dean might at any moment step from around the corner to join him. The bread lost its flavour and became repugnant to his tongue. He dropped the remains of the sandwich into the wrapper and emptied his mouth into the takeout bag.

When Floyd pushed his chair away from the table, his gaze fell on the rolled-up newspaper. The front-page photograph leered up at him.

Mrs. Brookman.

Floyd's breath caught in the back of his throat. He snatched the newspaper and ripped off the elastic. Then he snapped the paper open. His eyes raced back and forth across the column.

Narrow Falls Sentinel

Local Philanthropist Donates Property

NARROW FALLS – Last night's town council buzzed with excitement upon learning about Mrs. Rose Brookman's plan to donate her estate home and property to the town of Narrow Falls.

Arrangements will be made to prepare the house and vast gardens for community use. "It's an ideal setting for nuptials, galas, and community festivities," R.J. McLelland said after making the announcement on Mrs. Brookman's behalf.

In a prerecorded statement, Mrs. Brookman said, "It's time to share the immeasurable happiness my own family has enjoyed here. People are everything to me."

Her giving away the Narrow Falls estate could only mean one thing. *Dean's stay in Toronto isn't temporary. Rose means to keep him there.* Floyd dropped the newspaper on the table. "She can't do this!" The kitchen chair toppled with a crash when he bolted towards the door.

The drive to the Brookman estate lasted a few minutes, but it seemed like the longest drive of his life. Floyd sped through the gates and passed a piano mover's truck parked in front of the portico. Its doors sprawled open, and a ramp leaned against the bumper. He could see the piano sitting in the foyer as he passed the front of the house.

Oh Lord, it's really happening.

Floyd followed the driveway to the rear of the house and parked at the service entrance. He leapt from the car, ran to the kitchen door, and pushed the buzzer. When no one answered, he banged on the door. "Marian!" he called. "Marian!" He listened for a few seconds, then hammered at the door again

"Coming," she called from inside the house.

Through the glass, he saw Marian hastening towards him. She opened the door and regarded him with empathy.

"Marian, what's happening? Is she bringing Dean back? Is he all right?"

"You saw the article," she said, nodding slowly. Her eyes were red-rimmed, as if she'd been crying.

"It's true, then?" Floyd's eyes widened.

"The first I knew of it was this morning when the paper arrived," Marian said. She waved Floyd into the kitchen and closed the door. "Pull up a stool." She motioned to the cook's island standing at the centre of the room.

The absence of bustle in the kitchen raised the hairs on the back of Floyd's neck. Although the dinner hour approached, no produce, utensils, or bowls appeared on the countertops; no pots simmered on the stove. The appliances gleamed. The room was too perfect, as if it existed in a vacuum. Where was the smell of baking loaves and cookies?

Marian stood on tiptoe and reached into an upper cabinet. She returned to Floyd with two aperitif glasses and a crystal decanter.

"I don't know what's going on anymore. Sherry?" Marian lifted the stopper and set it on the counter. "Rose has lost her damned mind."

"Have you heard anything about Dean?" Floyd asked.

Marian poured the first glass and slid it next to Floyd's elbow. "That was an awful business that was, making off with Dean. If I'd known what Rose had planned, I'd have warned you." Marian filled her glass halfway and set the decanter between them.

"She stole my boy, Marian." Floyd began to cry. "He's all I have in the world."

"I know, my dear. I know how you love that boy—and Bonnie. I can see it, plain as day."

"I loved her."

"And she loved you too. There's never been a woman so happy. Bonnie had her problems, God knows. But you were good for her."

"Am I being punished? How can I go on living? My son . . ."

"There'll be no more of that talk, Floyd Hoffman. Into every life, rain must fall. But one day, the storm will clear away, and then you'll make sense of it all."

"I'm sorry," Floyd said, wiping his face.

"Sorry for what? Raise your glass, and let's toast to Dean's health and the sun coming up tomorrow."

"Prost," Floyd said. He lifted his glass and returned it to the counter, untouched.

The sun would come up tomorrow. This would be his final day of aimless pacing. Rose Brookman had built a fortress with her money and influence. But everyone had an Achilles tendon, and hers was the mill. Truth and science were on Floyd's side, and he would use them to smite her down. R.J. McLelland would fall with her. Floyd would make sure of it.

August 1966

On a steamy Saturday afternoon, Floyd and Bonnie brought Dean for a swim at Brewster's Gorge. They chose a spot on the river some distance away from the falls, where the water was knee-deep along the banks and the current ran slow. Bonnie stripped down to her bathing suit while Dean explored insects crawling between the sun-warmed river rocks that lined the shore.

Floyd lifted his camera gingerly from its leather case. It had cost him a full day of travel back and forth to Toronto and nearly one week's pay, but the sacrifice had been worth it. He'd spent weeks reviewing consumer reports and researching different models before settling on the Nikkorex F. Bonnie had poked fun at his doggedness, but he'd stayed the course. Now she was grateful for his shoebox filled with images that documented the minutiae of their life together. Thumbing through the photographs on low days afforded her a modicum of relief from her gloom.

He snapped a few photographs of Bonnie and Dean, then wandered along the riverbank towards the distant roar of the waterfalls. He paused to aim his lens across the river at a stand of pines and squinted into the eyepiece. After taking several photos, he loaded a fresh roll of film and tinkered with the aperture setting. Floyd had been distracted for some time when the breeze carried Bonnie's voice along the water. He turned to find her wading along the centre of the river with Dean balanced on one hip. She was chattering at him in an animated fashion while scooping up water in her free hand to splash his shoulders and legs. Dean giggled and pointed at a pair of mallards flying overhead.

A smile spread across Floyd's face. He squatted on the shore and trained the camera on their faces, then, just as he was about to snap the photo, Bonnie sidestepped the frame. When he lowered his camera, the water level had reached her waist. Dean's bottom was submersed, and the current trailed around his pudgy knees. With her free arm scissoring back and forth above the river's surface, she leaned against the strengthening current and pushed onward.

"What are you doing?" Floyd asked, trying to sound nonchalant. Any hint of concern in his tone would be construed as mistrust of her judgment, and the harmony of their day would be ruined.

Without answering, Bonnie pressed determinedly towards two boulders huddling against the shore. When she reached a hand into the crevice between them, Floyd rose to his feet and walked towards her. In case she dropped the baby, he'd be ready to plunge in for the rescue.

"Oh my gosh," Bonnie hollered. "It's a monster!" Like a victor celebrating the spoils of war, she hoisted a dead trout above her head.

Floyd took a picture.

"Me see, me see," Dean chanted.

When Bonnie held the fish within the boy's reach, he grasped it with both hands and tilted the face towards his. "Big fiss!" he said.

The trout's eyes were filmy disks. Its fins were intact, but scales flaked from its sides where chunks of flesh had been nibbled away. A peculiar growth ballooned from its side and another sprouted from its head.

"Dean shouldn't touch that fish," Floyd said. "It looks diseased."

"You worry too much," Bonnie protested. "It won't kill him."

"Swim," Dean said.

Bonnie laughed. "The fish doesn't want to swim, baby. He's napping." She laid the trout at Floyd's feet. As she waded back to the centre of the river, Dean cried and reached his arms around her neck. His fingers opened and closed in a repeated clutching motion directed at his lost treasure.

Floyd hung back to photograph the trout. Its deformities were oddly compelling, a gelatinous lump bulging from above one eye. He used a stick to roll it over, then took a second picture.

Bonnie looked back at Floyd and shouted, "Why are you wasting film on that?"

Floyd shrugged. He just had a feeling this could mean something.

The heat maintained its stranglehold for the duration of the week. That Thursday after he'd finished work, Floyd met Bonnie and Dean at the beach at Riverside Park. Earlier in the afternoon, Bonnie had pulled Dean all the way to the beach in his red wagon. When Floyd arrived, she was sitting shoulder-deep in the shallows. Dean was circling her and pushing a toy boat through a drift of pale yellow foam floating on the surface of the water. He lost his balance and splashed face first into the river, then recovered himself quickly and continued his game unfazed.

"Like mother, like son," she called out happily. "Our boy's a little tadpole!"

Floyd unlaced his shoes and rolled off his socks. The chill of the water lapped around his ankles when he eased into the river.

Bonnie shielded her eyes from the sun. "Come in farther than that," she said.

"I'm fine here."

"Chicken," she taunted.

Something shimmery caught Floyd's attention from among the reeds clustered against the shoreline next to the swimming area. When he moved closer to investigate, he found two dead fish floating belly up between the stalks. Like the fish he'd seen days earlier at Brewster's Gorge, lumps pushed like volcanoes against the underside of their scales. Everybody in town knew that McLelland's was responsible for the ever-present stench in the air, but no one ever questioned the composition of the yellow foam floating along the banks of the river. Was it possible that the mill was leaking harmful chemicals into the river? It was all he could think of as he watched his child wading through the froth. He needed to concoct a ruse to pull his family from the water without vexing his wife.

Floyd eased towards the beach. "I'm starving," he said loudly.

"There are a few crackers left. The box is in the wagon," Bonnie said.

"Dean, are you hungry?" Floyd asked, praying his son would take the bait.

The boy looked up from his boat. "Time for supper?"

"I think so," Floyd said. "We should go."

Bonnie rolled her eyes. "Killjoy."

In the middle of the night, Floyd woke up to the sound of Dean calling out for Bonnie. By the third cry, she hadn't budged, so Floyd got up and padded down the hall to their son's room. The boy, his damp hair plastered against his forehead, was sitting cross-legged in the middle of his bed.

"Did you have a bad dream?" Floyd asked as he sat on the edge of the mattress.

"I want Mommy."

"She's sleeping," Floyd said with a sigh and laid a hand above Dean's furrowed brow. His skin burned with fever. Floyd ducked his head and peered into the boy's face. "You feeling okay?"

Dean tugged at the front of his pajama shirt. "I want Mommy," he repeated and flung himself back on the pillow in frustration.

"Let's have a look at you." Floyd pulled the chain on Dean's bedside lamp. When Dean's fists balled up to rub the sudden light from his eyes, Floyd eyes widened at the red spots dotting the underside of his forearms.

"Are you itchy?" Floyd asked.

Dean nodded his head, looking to Floyd as though suddenly realizing it was his father who held the solution to his dilemma.

Floyd unbuttoned Dean's pajama shirt and frowned. The child's torso was peppered with red dots. "Wait here." Floyd returned a moment later with two baby aspirin and a bottle of calamine lotion. He sat Dean upright to remove his pajama shirt, then slathered his belly and the underside of his arms until the boy resembled a frosted cake. Dean chewed the aspirins and flopped back on the bed. First thing tomorrow morning, they'd see Doctor Gillespie.

After switching off the light, Floyd dragged a pillow from his bed and dropped it on the floor next to Dean's. He lay on his back, listening to the even pattern of Dean's breathing and staring up at his son's hand draped over the top edge of the mattress. He gently pressed an index finger against Dean's palm. Despite his worry, Floyd couldn't help smiling when Dean's fingers wrapped around his.

Friday morning, Floyd held Dean on his lap while Doctor Gillespie examined the rash. The boy wriggled and fussed until the doctor finished.

"Did he eat anything different yesterday?" the doctor asked.

"Not to my knowledge," Floyd answered, watching as the man tucked a thermometer into Dean's mouth.

"Has he been exposed to any new products? Gone anywhere out of the ordinary?"

"He and Bonnie swam at the beach yesterday, but that's nothing new," Floyd said.

The doctor stood at the corner of his desk and nodded thoughtfully. "At Riverside Park?"

"Yes," Floyd replied. An uneasy feeling pinched at him, like he'd just supplied the wrong answer to an important question.

"Anywhere else?" the doctor asked.

"Brewster's Gorge last Saturday," Floyd answered as he nudged Dean's hands away from the thermometer.

"Did he develop a rash afterward?"

Floyd shook his head and jangled his car keys to distract Dean. "No. But the following afternoon, he did have a headache, and he napped twice as long as usual."

"Any fever?"

"His cheeks were red. We blamed the heat," Floyd said.

Doc Gillespie removed the thermometer from Dean's mouth and held it up to a window. "He still has a low fever. Looks to me like an allergic reaction. To *what* is he reacting? That is the question." He paused to rub his chin. "Have either you or Bonnie experienced headache, fever, nausea, or rash after swimming at the gorge or at the beach?"

"No, nothing." Floyd's anxiety escalated. *Is something seriously wrong?*

"Are your swims frequent?"

"I'm not much of a swimmer. It's Bonnie who takes him. Since early June, they play in the water whenever the weather permits. When it's too cool, she brings him to the park to walk the footpath along the river at least three times a week."

"I'd like to see Dean again once his symptoms have cleared up. For now, let's keep him out of the river."

Alarm rose in Floyd. He thought of the grotesque lumps sprouting from dead fish. "So you think there's something in the water causing this reaction?"

"I've no idea," the doctor said. His eyes lowered to his desk.

Floyd sensed he was holding something back. "I've recently seen fish floating dead in the river. They've all been covered in strange growths."

"Tumours?"

Floyd's head jerked back. The word *tumour* hit him like a hammer. The fish were dying of cancer? "Doctor Gillespie, has anyone else visited you with similar complaints after spending time in the water?" Floyd asked.

"Enough to raise my interest, but too few to draw any conclusions." The doctor quirked one brow.

The car keys dropped to the floor with a clatter. Floyd held Dean snugly with one arm and leaned sideways in his chair to retrieve them.

"Where is Bonnie today?" the doctor asked suddenly.

"She preferred to wait outside." Floyd shrugged apologetically. "My wife has a fear of doctors."

"Ahhh," Doctor Gillespie said slowly. "You know, we could arrange to meet at the diner one day, or I could come around to your house. Meeting outside my office can be helpful in such cases."

"That's very generous, Doctor."

"Call me Doc," he said. "Everyone else does."

When Floyd left the office and carried Dean outside, Bonnie was pacing next to the baby stroller and biting at a hangnail. Floyd set the boy in the stroller and recounted his conversation with the doctor as they all walked towards the post office.

"Something in the water?" she said.

"Dean's been sick twice in the past week, both times after swimming in the river," Floyd said.

"That doesn't mean anything," she replied. "It's just a coincidence."

"What about the dead fish?" Floyd asked.

"Fish die. You've only seen three," she replied flatly. "Don't turn it into a federal case."

"Still," he said, "Dean must be kept out of the water. And you too."

"No," she said loudly, "absolutely not! The day I left my parents' house was the day I stopped letting people tell me what to do."

"This is different," Floyd pleaded. "There might be something dangerous in the water, capable of killing fish and making our son ill. Until we know it's safe, you both need to stay out."

Her eyes narrowed at Floyd. "And what do you think this *something dangerous* might be?"

"Chemicals," he answered.

"From?"

"The paper mill."

Bonnie stopped pushing the stroller. "Oh, come on!" she howled.

"It stands to reason," Floyd said. "We know the mill pollutes the air. Is it such a big stretch to think they might be releasing something into the water too?"

"The *they* you speak of is my father. Are you suggesting that he would condone dumping chemicals into the river? You think that he would knowingly hurt his daughter and grandson?" Bonnie laughed bitterly. "And I thought *I* was crazy!"

The conversation wasn't going at all how Floyd had hoped. He needed to deescalate her temper lest she become upset to the point of no return. "I'm just trying to protect our family," he said. "It's not my intent to vilify your father."

"I would never put Dean at risk. But my father is a good man. He would never bring harm to this town or to his family. I'd stake my life on it!"

19.

On the afternoon of her graduation, Tammy endured her mother's fits of impatience out of necessity. It was too hot to argue. She sat at the kitchen table and said nothing when Mirabelle tugged a fine-toothed comb through the knots in her hair. Even though Tammy flinched, Mirabelle continued twisting the curlers tightly.

"Last one." Mirabelle stooped behind the chair and pushed a plastic pin through the curler at the nape of Tammy's neck.

Tammy drew a sharp breath, and her nose wrinkled. "That hurts." She scratched at the strands pulled taut at her hairline.

Mirabelle cuffed her hand away. "Should have been under the dryer an hour ago. At this rate, you'll never be ready."

Fine by me, Tammy thought to herself. Her attendance was a charade, part of her mother's plan for keeping up appearances. Tammy dreaded the entire affair. She could only think of the trip she'd make to Hattersburg the next day.

Lawrence leaned into the kitchen with a newspaper tucked under his arm. "When's lunch? I'm starving."

"Can you think of nothing but your stomach?" Mirabelle replied.

He shrugged and looked at the curlers strewn over the kitchen table. "What time's this shindig happening?"

"At seven," Tammy said. She stood and dragged her chair closer to the kitchen cabinet and dropped onto the seat.

"I laid your blue suit on the bed," Mirabelle said. She unwound the electrical cord from the portable hairdryer sitting on the counter behind Tammy's head.

"It's the end of July. I'll sweat to death in that damned thing," Lawrence replied.

"You need to pick up two white carnations from the florist's downtown," Mirabelle told him.

"What for?"

"So I can make Tammy's corsage," she answered with a sigh. "Don't know how I'll find the time, but a penny saved is a penny earned. God knows we need it."

Lawrence's gaze lowered to the floor while she wrestled the plastic bonnet over Tammy's curlers and attached the air hose. He backed out of the doorway and headed towards the living room before she finished.

A knock sounded at the front door.

"Who in the devil is that?" Mirabelle said, examining her faded housedress.

The caller rapped again.

"Lawrence!" she hollered. There was no response. "Oh for Pete's sake, I'll get it." She turned the dryer on and left the room.

Tammy's bonnet inflated in seconds, and the hum of circulating air filled her ears. She rolled her shoulders back and eyed the kitchen clock. Could she stand this for an hour? Her scalp already throbbed, and the torrent of heat was burning the tops of her ears. She slid a finger under the gathered edge of the cap and stretched it away from her face for relief.

Aunt Eva appeared at the kitchen door with the arms of her chiffon blouse outstretched. Her head tilted to one side, and a smile lit her face.

Tammy's eyes widened. Her aunt seldom stopped by—and never unannounced.

Mirabelle followed close behind wearing a sour look. She hung back in the doorway and rubbed her throat. Tammy worried that her mother may guess what prompted the visit. That wouldn't be good for anyone, Tammy least of all.

Aunt Eva let her purse drop onto the kitchen table and passed Tammy a paper bag stamped *Gilmour's Flower Shop.* She flapped her hands and gestured for Tammy to open the gift.

Tammy removed a handful of tissue paper and lifted a clear plastic carton tied with pink ribbon. She stole a look at Mirabelle, whose eyes were trained on her sister. Her mother's lips twitched as though she'd been stumped by one of her crossword puzzles.

Eva untied the bow, then waited while Tammy opened the carton. Inside was a corsage the size of a saucer—five orchids with greenery, bound with a band of lace. It outshone what her mother had planned. Tammy's mouth dropped open; Eva glowed victorious.

"Thank you," Tammy said loudly above the roar of the dryer.

Aunt Eva pressed her bejeweled hands against Tammy's cheeks and leaned forward to kiss her forehead. Then she pulled away and executed a forlorn expression. "It will be okay," she mouthed, nodding her head.

Aunt Eva turned to waggle her pink-lacquered nails at Mirabelle. "I just had them done. Would you be a peach and get my keys?"

Tammy's mother rolled her eyes, then unclasped her sister's purse and rummaged inside. She took out a key chain crusted in rhinestones and dropped it into her sister's palm.

"Ta ta," Aunt Eva said, delivering air kisses to Mirabelle's cheeks before jetting off.

With arms folded across her waist, Mirabelle stared at the orchid corsage and smoldered like kindling. Red blotches climbed her neck. Her chin began to quiver, then she turned away and stomped up the stairs, wiping her eyes with the back of her hand.

Of all the people to confide in, Tammy thought, why had she chosen Aunt Eva? They'd never been especially close. In fact, Eva had humiliated her plenty of times, implying that her achievements were paltry in comparison to her cousin Jessica's. Tammy cursed herself for trusting in Eva's discretion. The kiss, the hands on her cheeks—all clues that Eva knew more than she should. Maybe she'd already told Arlene about their frank discussion at the nursing home. In time, Mirabelle would know Tammy had blathered.

What if Eva told Mirabelle directly? She'd never missed an opportunity to needle her sister. But maybe that was the point. Perhaps in some strange way, Tammy had found an ally, one who could best her mother. In the months ahead, she may need to exert herself against her mother. She hadn't the will to do it right now, but she couldn't be a pushover forever. There was strength in numbers.

Tammy extracted a pin from the curler at the nape of her neck. She removed two more from her temples and another from the back of her head. The air hose burned her right shoulder, and her head was beginning to pound. Twenty minutes left on the clock. Close enough. Tammy pulled the cap off and let it drop to the floor. When she plucked the remaining pins, the weight of her hair tumbled the curlers to her shoulders.

Tammy exhaled and savoured her small victory. A slow tingle swept through her belly, like bubbles rising along the inside of a soda bottle. Tammy looked down at the swell beneath her T-shirt and smiled.

Later that afternoon, Tammy stood in front of the full-length mirror, examining her graduation dress. She'd be the laughingstock of the evening. The high neckline and low hem were better suited to a chaperone than a teenage girl.

Mirabelle leaned into the room. "That'll do the job nicely."

"This colour reminds me of canned salmon." Tammy frowned.

"Quit being melodramatic."

"Mom, I'm not wearing this." Tammy said, shaking her head. "It's a grandma dress."

"Beggars can't be choosers. And besides, the first dress I bought for you is out of the question. You'd never squeeze into it now."

Tammy bit the inside of her cheek. "Look at how the polyester clings. Everyone will know."

"Just a little static. A splash of water will remedy that."

"How can I cross the stage looking like this?" Tammy threw her hands in the air. "And these sleeves are ridiculous."

Mirabelle's fingers dug into Tammy shoulders. "That's enough!"

"I'm not going." Tammy dipped her head and glared.

"Oh, you're going," Mirabelle said. "You *will* wear this dress, and you *will* cross that stage because if you don't, everyone *will* know." She released her grip and let the words sink in. "We'll all be ruined by the shame of what you've done."

Disapproval hung in the air long after Mirabelle left the room.

At seven o'clock that evening, Tammy waited for the last of the graduates to be seated. Students on either side of her whispered during the final bars of "Pomp and Circumstance." She stared at the banner strung across the rear wall of the stage: *Congratulations Graduating Class of 1981.* The weight of Aunt Eva's corsage pulled the bodice of her dress askew. Each time she had repositioned it, the dress had sagged in a new direction.

She looked down the row to where Dean should have been sitting. Someone else occupied his spot. Leslie sat near the centre of the front row. A few seats to her right, Allan Robinson was laughing it up with a girl from Tammy's homeroom. How could Dean have squandered their last afternoon on him? Allan certainly didn't appear upset over Dean's absence. *Some friend he turned out to be.*

The music ended, and the principal stepped forward to the podium. Behind him, a row of teachers looked into the audience while they fanned themselves with printed programs and loosened their neckties.

By the end of the opening address, a few boys had shed their jackets and unbuttoned their collars. The girl seated in front of Tammy patted her neck with a tissue. Tammy's dress clung to the places where perspiration slicked her skin beneath the polyester.

"And now, the academic achievement awards." Subdued applause rippled through the gymnasium after the principal's announcement. "For attaining the highest overall average, this year's English award goes to . . ."

Tammy's gaze drifted to the fire exit at the side of the gym. While the crowd cheered behind her, she daydreamed about escaping through the door and hopping a bus to Toronto. Dean needed her. She'd find his grandmother's address in the phonebook and go to her—

"It's you! They called your name." The girl in the next seat urged Tammy to her feet.

"There she is," the principal said. "Tammy King, recipient of the English award."

The dress clung to the front of Tammy's legs when she stood, and by the time she'd sideways shuffled to the end of the row, it had moulded itself around her belly in a telling manner. She discreetly adjusted the fabric away from her body only to hear the crackle of static electricity that drew the dress around her like cellophane over Sunday leftovers. On the long walk across the stage, her knees shook. It was going all wrong. She sensed the scrutiny of all those pairs of eyes, measuring her and putting things together. *Just keep walking. Don't faint,* she told herself. *Don't faint.*

She accepted the award from the principal and shook his hand, but when she paused to face the audience, no one came forward to snap her picture. Mirabelle and Lawrence had refused to claim her. Somewhere beyond the blinding stage lights, they'd made the deliberate choice to remain seated. The principal leaned towards the microphone. "Congratulations, Tammy," he said quietly. Her face burned with humiliation as she left the stage and scurried to her seat. A pair of girls in the front row gawked at her belly. One of the boys sitting behind them called out, "Shit! She's knocked up."

Water rushed to Tammy's eyes. She flopped onto her chair and pulled both hands inside the embroidered cuffs of her dress. A snowstorm of white speckles materialized in front of her eyes. She dug her nails into her palms to fend off a sense of panic. The room began to spin, then everything went dark. She woke to find herself being lifted from the floor by students who shared looks of genuine concern edged with curiosity.

"Low blood sugar or something." Tammy smiled weakly at the boy holding her elbow.

Somewhere in the darkness, a female voice added, "Yeah—or *something.*"

The next boy to cross the stage waved to the crowd and broke out in a tap dance. "This is for you, Mom!" While the crowd applauded his antics, Tammy slid from her seat and squeezed through the side exit into the cool night air.

She didn't have a plan; she let her feet do the thinking. They carried her to a bench at Riverside Park, where she kicked off her shoes and watched the current flow. Just as the sky darkened and stars began to shimmer, a car horn blasted from the street behind her. Tammy looked over her shoulder at the white Ford Galaxy flashing its lights. She reached for her shoes and wept.

The next morning, Tammy stepped around the open car door and onto the lawn. The morning dew left a pattern of dark speckles on the canvas of her sneakers. She lifted her suitcase and propped a corner on the edge of the backseat.

"Trunk's open," Lawrence said.

She loaded the suitcase along with her backpack and climbed into the car.

"Got everything you need?" he said, tapping his fingers on the steering wheel.

"Yeah." Tammy stared at the back of her father's neck. Deep lines crosshatched his skin, and grey hairs bristled over the collar of his shirt.

Mirabelle came through the front door, dabbing her eyes with a handkerchief. She slid into the passenger seat and closed the air vent, as she always did, to preserve her hair. The shoulders of her church dress rose slightly on either side of the headrest.

"A bit dressed up, don't you think?" Lawrence said as he started the car.

"Just drive," she replied.

Lawrence reversed out of the driveway as a light mist began to fall and proceeded to the town limits. A dense fog swallowed the car once they reached the gravel roads. There was no view past the reach of the headlights and no sound except for the repeating swish and click of the wipers across the windshield. Temporary reprieves came when the car climbed out of the lowlands and gullies to where the morning sun had burned the fog away.

Tammy rested her head against the vinyl upholstery and closed her eyes. Her wet ponytail lay down the centre of her back. Although it dampened her T-shirt and chilled her, she refused to rub her arms for warmth in case her mother noticed. Mirabelle had instructed her to wear a sweater, but she'd refused. Instead, she'd packed it between precious cargo inside her suitcase: the book of Whitman poetry, Dean's photo, his football jersey—and the red journal from Mr. Hoffman's dresser. She didn't fully grasp its significance, but she couldn't leave it behind for her mother to discover.

She pretended to be asleep for the hour-and-a-half drive, through which her parents barely conversed. At one point, her father turned the car radio on. The news played for a moment before Mirabelle leaned forward and switched it off.

Tammy opened her eyes as the *Welcome to Hattersburg* sign flashed past the car window. She'd been here once before when she was very young. Lawrence and Mirabelle had taken her to the Santa Claus parade, an event more spectacular than anything Narrow Falls could hope to produce. After the last float, they'd joined the queue on Main Street so Tammy could visit Santa in the Woolworth's store.

Have you been a good girl this year?

The King family car rumbled through the downtown area, its loud muffler drawing unwanted attention. Tammy slouched in the backseat. Shops and professional buildings lined the streets with a sophistication not seen in Narrow Falls—extravagant store windows, bank fronts with stonework and brass plaques. She counted two hospital signs and three stoplights before they chugged onto the two-lane highway leading away from Hattersburg.

"Not much longer now," Mirabelle said.

Five minutes outside town, Lawrence turned right onto a side road. A half mile in, the pavement narrowed and transitioned to gravel. Stones pinged against the undercarriage of the car, and a dull roar filled the inside.

Beyond the smattering of trees that flanked the road, a farmer's field lay lush and green. A laneway cut through rows of corn to a house and barn. Tammy pictured the family gathered around a table, drizzling syrup on pancakes. They smiled and told stories. She envied them.

Lawrence slowed the car as they approached a woman standing next to a rusted mailbox at the side of the road. She put something inside, then closed the door and raised the metal flag. When he eased into the driveway behind her, she turned and gave a curt nod. Tammy looked through the rear window of the car. The woman followed behind with her chin held high.

The Beatrix Home stood inside a shroud of trees hemmed in on three sides by cornfields. It was a brick building, two stories high, with an open veranda stretched parallel to the driveway. A small barn sagged apologetically at the rear of the house. Parked next to it was a white minibus.

The car stopped next to a cement birdbath, and Lawrence cut the motor. He looked over at Mirabelle as she rifled through her purse.

"What did you bring a Bible for?" He gaped.

"Just you never mind." Mirabelle sniffled.

"Jesus Christ," he muttered and got out of the car.

Mirabelle's door creaked open, and she swiveled in her seat to look at Tammy. "Well, what are you waiting for?" The leather spine of her Bible jutted from her purse when she stood to smooth her dress.

Lawrence rested his weight against the car and stared down the laneway as if something across the road had captured his interest.

"Bye, Dad." Tammy hugged him tightly and pressed her cheek against his arm.

"You be good." Lawrence's voice broke. He patted the top of her head with one hand.

She nodded and wiped her eyes.

"That's enough fiddle-faddle," Mirabelle said, motioning to the open trunk. "The office is waiting for us to sign in."

Tammy threaded her arms through the straps of her backpack, then pulled the suitcase over the edge of the trunk.

"Lift! Don't drag." Mirabelle scowled. "That's *my* suitcase. If you scratch it, I'll be saddled with that mark for the rest of my life." With a tilt of her chin, she strode towards the side door marked *Office.*

Lawrence stepped next to Tammy and hefted the suitcase to the ground. He shrugged at Tammy before looking away. She sighed and wrestled the luggage across the veranda, following her mother into the home.

The side door introduced them to a sterile hallway. Except for the squeak of floorboards as they walked, the house remained eerily quiet. They peered into a simply furnished room with bookcases along one wall. Tammy stopped at the sight of two girls sitting there under a picture of Christ. The first, dressed in a robe and slippers, sat hunched over, hugging her ribs. Another girl leaned her pregnant belly against the armrest of the chair and patted a consoling hand on her friend's shoulder. Tammy's breath caught in her throat.

"Tammy!" Mirabelle called from a doorway down the hall.

Both girls raised their eyes to meet Tammy's. Red-faced, she hoisted the suitcase and joined her mother.

"Leave your bags in the hall and come in," a voice instructed from the other side of the wall.

"I'll do the talking," Mirabelle whispered to Tammy over her left shoulder. She smoothed her face into a smile and paraded into the room.

The woman they'd encountered at the mailbox sat behind her desk, reviewing a stack of forms. Without looking up, she added, "Have a seat."

Mirabelle discreetly shimmied the contents of her purse to show off the golden lettering on her Bible. "My name is—"

The woman raised an index finger to hush Mirabelle and continued reading. Tammy's mother huffed and settled back in the chair.

The austerity of the office did little to assuage Tammy's anxiety. She'd expected cheery posters on the wall, like the ones in the high school guidance office, or perhaps photos of happy babies and mothers. Instead, a calendar and a framed copy of the Ten Commandments hung on the wall behind the woman's head. A plaque displayed on top of a file cabinet showed a name: *25 Years of Service, Marjorie Peel.*

Mrs. Peel laid the papers inside a red file folder. She regarded Mirabelle's frown with indifference before settling her attention on Tammy.

"So, you are Tammy King: grade A student; only child; in very good health; referred to us by Reverend Findlay of the Narrow Falls United Church; periodic churchgoer." Then raising her brows, she added "Baby's father—unnamed."

This distilled summation caught Tammy off guard. She looked away from Mrs. Peel's sharp gaze and pulled a tissue from her pocket.

"You've arrived early, Miss King."

"We were asked to arrive at this time," Mirabelle said.

"That's not what I'm referring to," Mrs. Peel said. "You're four months gone. We don't usually see girls until their last trimester. Why so soon?"

Tammy stole a glance at her mother's indignant expression.

"I see," Mrs. Peel said. She leaned forward in her chair and rolled a pen between her fingers.

"We've done our best, but—" Mirabelle replied.

"A parent's *best* isn't always good enough, is it, Mrs. King?"

Mirabelle sucked in her breath.

"That's where the Beatrix Home comes in. We don't mollycoddle our girls. Reality is the key to reform. They perform assigned housekeeping and kitchen duties—a sampling of the unwed mother's burden, one might say."

"Cooking?" Tammy said in disbelief.

"And tidying up after meals," Mrs. Peel answered proudly. "This isn't Toronto. We do things a bit differently here."

"That's refreshing," Mirabelle said.

"It's not all work, of course. We schedule leisure activities, and our bus takes the girls into Hattersburg for church services on Sunday mornings. Wednesday evening is reserved for prayer meetings, but we run those in our dining room."

Mirabelle smiled as if she'd discovered a gold coin in her pocket. "Sounds lovely. I've filled out the paperwork you sent to the house." She laid the Bible on the desk and opened it to a white envelope that she handed across the desk.

"The cheques are inside?" Mrs. Peel asked.

"Oh yes, they're all there."

"Grand. There's one last order of business." Mrs. Peel slid the red file folder across the desk and passed Tammy a pen. "We'll need your signature, dear, next to the Xs."

Tammy held her breath and opened the folder. *Adoption papers.* She needed more time. Too many voices competed in her head: Dean, her mother, Reverend Findlay, and now Mrs. Peel. How could she be sure what she wanted?

"Tammy, we've discussed this," Mirabelle said. She rested a hand on her Bible and smiled nervously at Mrs. Peel. "Go ahead and sign."

Tammy squeezed the pen and stared at the paper.

"Right there and there." Mirabelle reached in front of her and pointed at the signature lines. Her voice was no longer coaxing; it had become harsh and commanding.

Panic worked its way through Tammy's body. Her hands tingled, and her lips had grown numb. Even her knees felt like jellied masses that would surely buckle if she tried to leave the room.

"Tammy, be reasonable and sign the papers," Mrs. Peel said.

The words sparked resentment in Tammy. All her life, she'd been reasonable. Must she always bend to meet other people's expectations?

A whisper passed across the inside of her stomach, like the soft stroke of a paintbrush. The sensation was so fleeting she barely noticed it. But when it happened a second time, she understood the significance.

Tammy made her choice. She laid the pen on the desk and braced herself for the fallout.

20.

Floyd realized the need to venture beyond the walls of his house in order to escape his own mind. After breakfast one morning, he pulled Dean's favourite baseball cap low over his forehead and set off walking to nowhere in particular. It was late September, too early for frost, but it would soon come. A red tinge had begun creeping along the edges of the maple leaves. In another month, leaf piles would line the streets, and families would gather for Thanksgiving dinners. With any luck, Dean would be home. It could happen.

No, it couldn't. Not the way Rose had things sewn up.

There'd been no further word from her. Floyd despaired over the reasons why Dean hadn't phoned him either. *Has Rose broken her promise and told him I'm not his father? Is he too angry? God forbid he's too ill.* Floyd, in hope of news, telephoned Marian regularly, but she was as much in the dark as he was. No member of Rose's Toronto house staff would tell her anything.

Floyd's walk brought him to the Brookman estate. The wrought-iron gates lolled open. Three vehicles were parked in the circular drive—a pair of municipal vehicles and a green pickup truck with gold lettering on the door. *Belford Estates, Home Builders and Renovators.* A pair of men stood at the front bumper and studied a broad sheet of paper they'd spread across the hood. One rolled the paper under his arm, and then they both went inside.

The initiation of Rose's plan to pass the estate into the town's hands confirmed the bitter truth that Floyd had long feared—she would never bring Dean home to

Narrow Falls. Instead, she'd isolate the boy at the Toronto estate and turn him so that he loathed Floyd more than he did already.

Something inside Floyd snapped. With both hands, he grasped the rungs of the gate, and gritted his teeth together. A low growl swelled in the back of his throat. Tendons in his neck strained, and the corner of his right eye pulsed. He shook the gate so that every loose bit of metal thundered. And when he stopped, the vibration of its clatter travelled through his hands and along his arms.

Floyd's chest heaved as his eyes raked the face of the looming house. He couldn't locate his son right now, but he had to believe that sooner or later Dean would call him or come home. Floyd needed to accomplish something of worth to show his son that the events had changed him as a father. The demonstration must be significant enough to impress Dean no matter how angry he was.

Floyd needed to move the lawsuit forward to a triumphant close.

At that moment, Floyd's determination burned like hot coals. His crusade against McLelland Pulp and Paper was the key to regaining his son's respect. Dean would come to see that during the period of his grandmother's part ownership, the mill had made decisions—ones she must have known about—that resulted in his mother's death and his own illness. Rose's spell over Dean would be broken. He'd come home to be nearer to friends, if not his father. It was a long shot, but it was all Floyd had.

When a brisk wind lifted from the east, Floyd zipped his jacket under his chin and headed home. He'd organize his thoughts into a succinct plan and set up a meeting with Clive and Gerald. He strode towards home, fueled with renewed vigour for his cause.

Fighting the mill was fighting Rose.

"You want to *what?*" Gerald said.

"To reduce the dollar amount of the lawsuit," Floyd repeated.

"How much of a drop are we talking about?" Clive asked calmly.

"By half."

"Ha!" Gerald wheeled away from Floyd and raked his fingers through his hair. The jangling warble of an unanswered telephone reverberated from the outer office. "Carol, would you pick that up?" he hollered through his office door.

Clive regarded Floyd thoughtfully. "Half a million dollars is a lot to give up," he said calmly.

"It sure as hell is! A lot is riding on this case, for you and for us," Gerald said, casting a glance at his partner.

Floyd understood Gerald's inference. He and Clive could be losing out on fifty percent of their take on potential damages and the notoriety of a court win.

With a slow shrug, Clive settled back in his chair. "Well, it's a kick in the pants, but McLelland's keep finding new ways to stretch this thing out," he said. "A bird in the hand *is* worth two in the bush,"

"R.J.'s an opportunist, and I'm giving him an opportunity," Floyd said. "I'll step away from half the money if the mill installs a new scrubber *and* cuts the amount of toxins pissing into our river."

Clive's eyes narrowed. "Something's changed. What's got you riled up?"

How could Floyd face the humiliation of admitting that he'd signed away all rights to his child without consulting them? To do so would require explaining Rose's leverage—that Dean may be the result of Bonnie's affair. Floyd's eyes watered. He needed to tell them something.

"Dean is sick," he admitted. "Same thing Bonnie had."

"Jeez, Floyd, you should have told us!" Gerald said.

"So sorry. We had no idea," Clive added. "Do you want a coffee, a water or something?"

Floyd wanted to tell them that Rose Brookman had whisked Dean away in the middle of June. But that would be facing their questions and making painful admissions. That he'd no idea of his son's whereabouts. That he'd signed over guardianship of his son to a proprietor of McLelland's Pulp and Paper without legal consultation. And he'd done so to avoid the painful revelation of his wife's affair.

He couldn't say the words out loud, *Dean may not be my son.*

Like a fox picking up the scent of its quarry, Gerald's attention locked on Floyd's hesitation. "You're sure about offering to settle out of court?" he said. "It might mean losing out on a chance at vindication with folks in town."

Floyd nodded. Regret was a worm twisting in his stomach, but Dean came first.

Gerald looked down at the desk and rolled a pen between his fingers and his thumb. He lifted his gaze to Clive after a moment and unpursed his lips. "You're the client. At the end of the day, it's up to you."

The meeting with R.J. McLelland and his lawyer was set for the following Tuesday. Soon after sunrise that morning, Floyd spent a few hours at the gorge. He skipped rocks across the stream and talked to Bonnie and Dean. Then he continued to Narrow Falls and parked his car along the curb on Main Street, a few doors south of the law office. He glanced at his wristwatch. *Eight forty-five. Plenty of time.* Sitting on the front seat next to him was his cardboard carton filled with documents and photos. Better to be battle ready than underprepared. Gerald had asked him to come in at nine o'clock to go over the game plan for the meeting one more time. "Stick to the facts," he'd said. "The first side to show emotion loses." Floyd stretched his fingers wide and raised his hands to examine their steadiness.

Shaking like a leaf.

He gripped the top of the steering wheel and breathed deeply. This would be the closest formal interaction he'd had with R.J. McLelland. In the courtroom, they'd always been separated by the breadth of an aisle and the lawyers seated between them. Today's encounter would be different, more personal. They'd face each other from across a table and talk without the constraints of protocol required when Justice Reynolds presided. No tricks or fancy wrangling. Just a good, honest conversation.

Floyd got out of the car and circled to the passenger door. He lifted the document box and bumped the door shut with a hip. Farther along the sidewalk, two of the diner's waitresses approached quickly. The first woman carried a tray jammed with takeout coffee cups, and the second, two plates of pastries covered loosely in plastic wrap. He reached the law office doors just ahead of them. The moment Carol spotted him through the glass, she sprang from her steno chair and ran to open the door.

"Mr. Hoffman, I've been calling you for the past hour." She waited for the two waitresses to slip past, en route to the narrow hallway leading to the conference room at the rear of the office.

"What's going on?" Floyd asked, his eyes trained on Carol's face.

"The McLelland's team bumped the meeting up. They'll be here in fifteen minutes."

"Damn it!" Floyd repositioned his fingers along the bottom edge of the heavy carton.

"Clive and Gerald are ready for them. They've been here since seven," she said, leaning over the carton to reach for Floyd's necktie. "This is all wrong."

Floyd lifted his chin and rolled his eyes towards the ceiling while she untied the knot.

"I'd like to be a fly on the wall this morning when you have a go at R.J. McLelland," Carol said. "I imagine you've thought a lot about what you're going to say." The lift of her voice turned the statement into a question.

"Not really. I'll leave the talking to Clive and Gerald." Floyd's face grew hot. In truth, he'd been up half the night imagining himself addressing the room with the calm authority of Gregory Peck playing Atticus Finch. The other half of the night, Floyd was Al Pacino. *You're out of order. This whole trial is out of order.* In either version, R.J.'s bloated face quivered with worry until he agreed to the settlement and to honour Floyd's demands.

Carol squared up the new knot at Floyd's throat. From the corridor behind her, the floor strained beneath the weight of someone's rapid approach.

"Hey, Floyd," Clive said. "You've been brought up to speed?" Without waiting for a response, he continued towards Carol. "They'll be here soon. You remember everything we discussed?"

"Yes," Carol answered, preparing to count the steps off on her fingers. "I welcome them. Ask for their jackets. 'Please be seated.' I buzz you. Wait a few minutes. Yada yada yada. I say, 'They'll see you now,' then I walk them down the hallway and knock at the door."

"Good, good." Clive led the way to the conference room. "We'll control the momentum of this thing, show McLelland and his people who's boss."

"How many people are you expecting?" Floyd asked. He stole a glance at Gerald, who sat steely eyed at the far side of the conference table

"R.J. and a couple of lawyers." Clive stepped into the room first and directed Floyd to the seat at Gerald's right.

Floyd set his carton on the floor directly behind his spot at the table. When he pulled his chair away from the table, the back legs banged against the box.

"What is *that*?" Gerald asked, gawking at Floyd's canvas windbreaker.

Floyd blinked at Gerald. He'd worn the jacket for years. No one had ever complained about it before. He didn't own a suit. After Bonnie's funeral, he'd burned his in the bottom of a metal trash can.

"He looks fine," Clive said, taking the seat at Gerald's left.

"Fine's not good enough." Gerald stood and called out to Carol. "Bring the navy blazer hanging on the back of my office door."

The muscles across Floyd's shoulders tightened like winches. This wasn't at all how he'd envisioned the lead up to R.J. McLelland's arrival. He needed more time to adjust, get comfortable.

"Floyd, you're pale as a sheet," Clive said. "Relax, man. We're ready." He tapped his pen against the file folder lying on the table in front of him. "It's all a big game of chicken."

"Say nothing unless Clive or I prompt you to speak," Gerald added. "Today is about drawing the mill into agreement, but R.J.'s lawyer will needle you to find your soft spot, just like in court. If you explode, he'll know exactly how to pry you open and wear you down. So we can't let that happen."

Carol appeared with a navy pinstriped jacket draped over one arm. She passed it to Floyd from across the table. "Five minutes," she said and closed the door behind her.

Gerald lifted a black rotary telephone from the window ledge behind his chair and set it on the table corner to his left. Gerald sat down again and smoothed his tie. His steepled fingers pressed against his lips as he stared into the distance.

Floyd pushed his arms through the jacket sleeves and tugged the cuffs over his wrists. Wearing someone else's clothing unsettled him, as if he were an imposter in costume. But then something took hold. The square shoulders and sleek lapels became his armour. He sat tall and positioned his chair closer to the table.

In a matter of minutes, there'd be nothing separating him and R.J. but a tray of paper coffee cups and plates of iced doughnuts. Previous appeals had failed to puncture the man's capitalist veneer, but today would be different. Floyd's future with Dean depended on it.

A hum of voices arose from the outer office.

Gerald leaned back in his seat and blew a stream of air through his pursed lips. His gaze never left the closed door. Clive rested a hand next to the telephone. His fingers drummed against the table while he waited for Carol's call.

"Sirs? Excuse me!" Carol called out from the other side of the door. "If you'd like to wait just a moment . . ." The trample of feet drew closer to the conference room.

Clive's fingers stilled. "So much for planning."

A knock sounded at the door before it swung open. Phillip Dixon, a lawyer Floyd recognized from court, stepped into the conference room. He immediately laid claim to the chair at the head of the table nearest to Clive. Five more people filed into the room behind him. R.J. McLelland was not among them. Floyd's ears strained above the clatter of people settling into chairs, hoping to hear R.J.'s bluster in the hallway.

"Good morning, Mr. Smith, Mr. Harper," Dixon said, acknowledging Floyd with a quick nod.

Three of the arrivals choosing seats directly across from Floyd and his lawyers had been present at the McLelland table during the last court session. A younger man now organizing himself at the end of the table nearest Floyd was a stranger to him, as was the thin, stooped woman blocking Carol from the doorway.

Where in the hell is R.J.?

"Carol," Clive called out, pointing to the corner just inside the door. "We're going to need two extra chairs."

"Sure," Carol said. She lifted her brow and shrugged apologetically before setting off to the outer office.

Dixon stood and rested both hands on the back of his chair. "My personal secretary will be taking notes today," he said. "I'd prefer she sat here, on my right, rather than being wedged into the corner."

For a few seconds, Gerald and Clive held their ground. But when Dixon shoved his chair around the corner of the table towards Clive, his meaning became clear. He wanted the men to shift their chairs to make room for his secretary.

"Okay," Clive said. His voice snapped like a dry twig.

After inching their chairs farther right to accommodate the woman, Floyd and his allies found themselves sandwiched together with their shoulders mere inches apart. The room felt claustrophobic. The secretary positioned her pad of paper and collection of pens on the table while Clive twisted awkwardly in his seat to return the telephone to the windowsill.

Carol dragged two chairs to the doorway and offered one to Dixon. He mumbled something to her. She cast a stricken look at Clive and Gerald, then retreated from the room with the second chair.

What was that about?

"Thank you for coming today," Clive began. A tone of courtroom formality had replaced his usual small-town warmth. "Mr. Hoffman, Mr. Smith, and myself look forward to some critical dialogue. Perhaps you'd enjoy a refreshment while we wait for Mr. McLelland to join us. The coffee's hot, and the doughnuts are fresh."

No one reached for a cup. Dixon wore an expression of superiority. His colleagues stared gravely across the table, as if waiting for Floyd and his lawyers to catch on to what they already knew.

Gerald rested his elbows on the table and glared at Dixon. "When *will* Mr. McLelland be arriving?"

"Mr. McLelland sends his apologies. Important matters require his attention today."

Gerald dropped his pen onto the table. "So you're a well-compensated *messenger*, then, paid to relay the details of our conversation to your client?" he said, then added flatly, "No offense intended."

"None taken," Dixon countered with a wry smile. "I'm more than a messenger. I am Mr. McLelland's eyes and ears. He won't make a move without my say so."

"Let's get down to it, then," Clive interjected. "Our client's case is backed by science and the sympathies of Justice Reynolds. If this case is fought in the courts, the mill *will* lose, and Mr. McLelland could potentially be ordered to pay millions of dollars in damages."

Floyd clenched his hands in his lap. He barely drew a breath.

"Mr. Hoffman would offer new terms in the hope that the matter can be resolved. Here."

"Would he?" Dixon shared a knowing smirk with his colleagues. "Precisely what does Mr. Hoffman propose?"

"He will accept five hundred thousand *if* McLelland's will commit to replacing the scrubber within six months, and *if* the level of effluents released daily into the river meets government guidelines within one year."

The McLelland's team remained pokerfaced, each member scribbling their own notes or casting glances at Dixon from the corners of their eyes.

"If my client were to acquiescence to these terms, that would be tantamount to an admission of guilt. And yet," Dixon said with an incredulous expression and his palms raised to the ceiling, "Mr. McLelland hasn't broken any laws. There are none to break. Only guidelines, to which the mill strictly adheres."

Arrogant son of a . . .

"With all due respect, Mr. Dixon, Enviro Consultants' report indicates that the concentration of tetrachloroethylene and trichloroethylene present in the river is much higher than your client reported to the ministry," Clive said.

"And the mill's test results over the same four-month period show that Enviro was wrong." Wearing an expression of disinterest, Dixon began clicking his pen and looked out the window.

"I would remind you, sir, that Justice Reynolds was impacted by their results," Gerald said. "As a matter of—"

Dixon interrupted and waved a dismissive hand. "Your impact on Reynolds is temporary."

Bastard! Floyd imagined lunging the length of the table and shaking him by the collar.

Dixon's pen stopped clicking. "We could fill this room four times over with boxes of data compiled by water and air quality testers far more experienced than Enviro's expert. They all say he's wrong."

Lies! McLelland's stack vomited carcinogens into the sky nonstop. Children were inhaling fly ash daily at Riverside Park. The playground equipment was coated in the stuff.

"I'm sure your client can appreciate Mr. Hoffman's pain and suffering upon the loss of his wife," Clive said. "Now he finds his son is afflicted with the same type of cancer. At the end of the day, all of you will return to Toronto. But Mr. Hoffman and his son, along with their friends and neighbours, will continue to live in the shadow of the mill. The resolution of this case is about more than the damages in question. It's about ensuring the long-term prosperity of his community. And for your client, the sustainability of his company and the goodwill of Narrow Falls."

Dixon flicked a glance at his secretary and raised a palm. She promptly stopped writing and laid her pen across the pad of paper. When he finally spoke, it was to the young lawyer sitting at the end of the table next to Floyd. "Explain to these gentlemen why you would recommend Mr. McLelland *against* accepting Mr. Hoffman's terms."

Floyd's mouth gaped.

"Well, sirs, if Mr. McLelland accepted your offer," the man began his explanation, "he would stand to lose more money than the half million he would save after paying reduced damages to Mr. Hoffman. Based on weaknesses in the plaintiff's arguments, I would recommend that Mr. McLelland wait out the trial for his assured win. Mill business would continue uninterrupted, and," he looked apologetically at Floyd, "he could avoid an unnecessary payout to Mr. Hoffman."

Gerald's head bowed forward. He raised his glasses and pinched the bridge of his nose between a thumb and an index finger

"This from a first-year junior associate," Dixon said. "I'm surprised your lawyers advised you to pursue this tact, Mr. Hoffman."

Floyd glared him. *You heartless son of a bitch.*

"The terms are laughable," Dixon said. "Do you really expect my client to assume the unnecessary capital investments of a new scrubber? You failed to mention the related consequences—lost revenues during retooling, cancelled contracts. Not to mention the impact of negative publicity on new business opportunities."

My wife and son are more than dollars and cents on a spreadsheet. Clive and Gerald were being far too cordial in light of Dixon's aggression. No progress would be made today. *What will I have to show Dean?*

Floyd could be silent no longer. He tried to push away from the table, but a corner of the carton obstructed the movement of the left rear chair leg. Floyd attempted to stand but instead found himself wedged awkwardly between the chair and the edge of the table.

"By all means, Mr. Hoffman. Did you have something to share?" Dixon asked coyly.

Gerald laid a hand on Floyd's left forearm and looked up at him with a raised brow. Floyd sank to his seat.

"It's just a matter of time before the ministry catches up with Mr. McLelland," Gerald said. "Our client is offering him a chance to get ahead of this thing. Mr. Hoffman will accept half the original amount in addition to the conditions we outlined earlier. Your client can tell the newspapers a story of remorse that includes plans to replace the out-of-date scrubber with modern technology, thus ensuring community safety. Spin your public relations, and Mr. McLelland will be a hero."

"I'm not in the hero-making business, Mr. Smith. I'm in the winner-making business. It's why I'm rich," Dixon said. He sniffed and cast a critical glance around the crowded conference room.

"Finance and ethics needn't be mutually exclusive," Clive said. "Swiss pulp and paper mills have installed purification technologies to fix the same problems that McLelland's is experiencing. The incidence of disease dropped significantly in the workforce and surrounding communities without long-term fiscal sacrifice of the industry. We would ask Mr. McLelland to consider carefully."

The man whom Floyd had mentally dubbed *Professor* on account of his wire-rimmed eyewear, piped up from across the table. "If I may, I'd like to circle back to Mr. Dixon's assertion that the mill has consistently adhered to the guidelines. Bonnie Hoffman died in 1973. Referring back to court testimony, forestry students from Wainright College drew test samples from the river in 1969 through 1979. They corroborated the mill's findings that levels present in the river did not pose a threat to human health."

"No threat? Along the riverbanks, fish are washing up with growths springing out of their bodies. Tumours! You've seen the photographs in court," Gerald said.

"Spare us," Dixon said in disgust. "Your pictures could have been taken anywhere."

"My point is," Professor continued, "that Mrs. Hoffman could not have been mortally affected by exposure to the river."

"What did you mean earlier by 'weakness of our case'?" Clive said, thrusting his chin at the young lawyer. "Our expert countered Wainright's data with the fact that test samples were drawn during peak flow seasons in March and April. Their findings are invalid."

"Let's assume your numbers are accurate," Professor continued. "Even at higher effluent concentrations, the mill's waste management practices can't possibly be linked to Mrs. Hoffman's death. You cannot reconcile that a short dip taken a few times each week in July and August could end in death."

Gerald ground his elbows into the table and leaned towards his antagonist. "Actually, we can. *Bioaccumulation.* You'd know what that meant if you'd paid attention to our expert's testimony at the last court date."

"Yes," Dixon chimed in. "And I believe he also plied Justice Reynolds with facts about dioxins—trichloroethylene and tetrachloroethylene—becoming airborne as wastewater evaporates, similar to what transpired in Love Canal." He paused for a moment. "I tipped my hat to your Enviro expert. A nice piece of drama that was, comparing McLelland Pulp and Paper to a toxic landfill in New York State."

"Well, if the environmental disaster *fits* . . ." Gerald said sarcastically.

"Bioaccumulation is a myth. If toxicity in the body truly builds over time with repeated exposure, what about the people who have lived in this town all their lives?" Professor said. "Or families like mine? We've vacationed in Narrow Falls since I was a child. None of us have cancer."

"Not that you know of," Floyd said. *"Yet."*

Professor's face turned ashen.

"But if your loved ones are ever afflicted, let us know," Clive piped in. "We'll gladly help you sue the mill."

Dixon stood and began buttoning his suit jacket. "That's enough theatre for today."

"Agreed," Gerald said sternly. "We'll finish this in court."

Clive stood as well. "I'll see you out," he said.

"No need. I'm unlikely to get lost on the short walk to your front door." Dixon strode out of the room with his entourage falling in behind him. "Come to Toronto sometime," he called over his shoulder. "I'll show you what a *real* office looks like."

"Prick," Gerald muttered.

Clive dropped back into his chair once the last of McLelland's team had left the outer office. "Well, that was interesting." He reached for a doughnut and a cup of cold coffee.

Floyd squirmed out of the jacket and whipped it inside out onto the table. He clamped his hands over the top of his head and paced the length of the room.

"You did a great job," Clive said to Floyd. "It's not easy to keep cool during meetings like that one."

"Being quiet didn't change anything," Floyd said. "Nothing happened."

"Not true. This is the beginning of the end. Dixon will never disprove the science behind bioaccumulation," Gerald said. "Nor does he think he needs to. This fight isn't over yet. R.J. McLelland's pride will be his undoing,

"That's right," Clive agreed. "All we have to do is wait."

Waiting. That was a luxury that Floyd couldn't afford.

$$21.$$

At the beginning of October, Floyd returned to work. No further communications had arrived detailing Dean's progress, so he dared to hope that no news was good news. Maybe Mrs. Brookman planned to hoard Dean's recovery for a final reveal, a dramatic unveiling to confirm her superior capabilities. At Floyd's request, Dr. Gillespie made enquiries at Princess Margaret, Sunnybrook, and St. Michael's, but without the necessary hospital privileges, no one would tell him anything about Dean's progress.

But then came the November afternoon when a man dressed in a beige uniform knocked at the front door. The badge on his pocket read, *Speedy Time Courier.*

"Sign here," he said, holding out a clipboard and a pen.

Floyd eyed the courier's gelled hair. "What am I signing for?"

"These," he said, pointing at two boxes sitting on the porch—one smaller box measuring roughly twelve by twelve inches and a second, double that size. "And this fella too." The courier stepped aside, giving Floyd a view of the golden retriever waiting at the bottom of the stairs. The dog stood tethered to the banister by a red-and-white-checkered leash.

Floyd steadied himself against the doorframe.

"You okay, mister?"

He nodded and scribbled his name on the paper.

"This must be one special dog," the courier said. "The dispatcher told me to pick him up this morning at the sender's house in Toronto and drive him straight here."

"The boxes too?" Floyd asked.

"Yes, sir, boxes too."

"Do you know what's in them?"

"Nope. They just said to keep the smaller box upright."

Floyd's knees began to shake. "Is there a letter?"

"Don't think so." Then the courier's face lit as if he'd just remembered something. He ran to his truck and returned with a pet carrier and dog food bag. "This is yours too."

"Right . . ." Floyd said. He knelt and passed a hand slowly over the cardboard surface of the smaller box.

"G'day, sir."

Floyd waited until the courier's truck backed out of the driveway, then he pressed his palms against the box. "Please, God, no," he whispered. He took a penknife from his pants pocket and, with trembling hands, ran the blade along the taped seam between the top flaps. A lump of anguish expanded in the back of his throat as he laid open the box.

The inside was filled level with Styrofoam chips. Floyd blew a stream of air between his lips as he swept the top layer onto the porch. A brass dome the size of an elbow appeared. He dug more white chips from the box; they scattered like ashes across the porch.

Floyd fell back on the plank floor and pulled the box between his knees. "Oh, no."

A brass urn.

A delicate inscription on the lid read, *Dean Hoffman*, and directly below this, *In the world too briefly*. A sob caught in his throat. Floyd pushed his hands deeper into the box, sliding his palms along the curve of the urn until his fingers slid under the bottom edge. He lifted it from the box tenderly and pulled it to his chest as if it were Dean as a small boy. One hand cradled the bottom of the vessel and the other folded over the lid, just as it had folded over the crown of Dean's head.

The dog whined and climbed the stairs as far as his tether would permit. He barked and pawed at the air with uncertainty. This show of compassion, albeit from a dog, unlocked Floyd's grief. It splashed from him in moans and sobs.

So this was it. There would be no opportunity to apologize for not being the father Dean wanted, no road trip to Kitchener, no one to carry the Hoffman name forward. No more of Dean's voice in the house. No guitar music. No hope of patching things up.

"Floyd. Oh, Floyd," a woman's voice called.

Marian fumbled with the latch and burst through the front gate. Her overcoat flapped away from her body as she hurried up the cement walk with a hand pressed over her mouth.

"Jesus, Mary, and Joseph—it shouldn't have happened like this." Marian climbed past the dog and bent over Floyd. She held his shoulders and kissed his forehead. "Bring Dean inside, and I'll put the kettle on. You must be freezing."

Floyd allowed himself to be led into the house. He sat in the kitchen chair Marian pulled out for him before she tended to the kettle. He restrained his emotions until she turned up the collar of her coat and went outside to retrieve the dog. Then he pulled a handkerchief from his pocket and dried his eyes before she came through the kitchen door with the dog in tow.

Freed of the leash, the dog sniffed around the kitchen, his tail wagging frantically. He looped around and sat next to Floyd's chair, staring up as if to ask, *What now?*

Marian returned to the porch and wrestled the larger box inside. "Where is Dean's room?"

"End of the hallway," Floyd replied flatly.

With the box cradled in her arms, Marian disappeared down the hall, then rushed back into the kitchen a moment later. "I'm so sorry. What an unimaginable shock."

"He's gone." Floyd hugged the urn tightly. "Just like that, he's gone."

"I only found out half an hour ago that they were sending him home today. I came as quickly as I could."

"Rose had him cremated. She didn't even ask me."

"He was a beautiful boy." Marian dabbed the corner of her eye with a tissue.

"I never got to say good-bye," Floyd said. "Even the day she took him away, I never got to hold him, tell him I loved him."

"My heart breaks for you."

"I don't even know if he died alone."

Marian blew her nose and shook her head. When the kettle whistled, she rocked out of her chair and prepared the tea. She put her hand to her heart when the dog eased onto the floor and laid his muzzle across the top of Floyd's left foot.

"That dog must have been such a comfort to Dean," Marian said. "He certainly likes you."

Floyd's face turned stony. "Rose Brookman."

The lid clanked on the teapot, and Marian leaned her back against the counter.

"Dean must have been dead for days, and she kept it from me." His eyes grew wide. "I don't even know when it happened."

Marian folded her arms across her waist and stared at the floor. After a lengthy silence, she brought the teapot and two mugs to the table.

"I'm calling Rose."

"Not now. Give it a few days." She slid into her chair without looking him in the eye.

"How could she hurt me now? There's nothing left." His voice shook. "There were things I needed to tell him."

"Floyd—"

"All my life I've been waiting for the beginning or the ending of something. I've sat by while people left me or were taken from me. I've been faithful in word and deed, but I've been punished for it. Loyalty has always been a gun that turns and points at me."

"Please reconsider." Marian toyed nervously with a button on her coat.

Floyd studied her for a moment. "What aren't you telling me?"

Marian sighed. "I called the Toronto house this morning. No one answered. So I tried again about an hour ago. Rose has had a second stroke."

"Seems fitting," Floyd said sharply.

"The housekeeper explained that Rose's lawyer has been visiting the estate to go through her mail. She took it upon herself to contact the hospital, thinking that at least she could visit Dean. But when she did, the nurses' station informed her of his passing."

Floyd's hand covered his eyes, and his jaw tensed.

"He'd been gone for two days before Rose's stroke, but she told no one," Marian said. "And since the stroke, she can't communicate. Blackmore's Funeral Home called a week ago to ask when she planned to pick up the remains."

The hand slid from Floyd's face and rested on the urn.

"Mrs. Brookman's driver made the pickup and took the urn back to her house." Marian's eyes watered. "When I heard about the courier bringing Dean home, I came right over."

Floyd watched her mouth.

"There should be a memorial," Marian said.

Her lips continued to move, but caught inside the vacuum of his mind, Floyd ceased to hear the words.

For five nights following Dean's return, the gravity of loss consumed Floyd. The volume of silence grew. Except for the dog sleeping on the floor outside the closed bedroom door, Floyd suffered alone. The quality of aloneness differed from the one he'd experienced after his parents left Narrow Falls. Then the expectation of life's offerings had stretched before him—love, marriage, and children. This was a deeper kind of alone than the one that followed Bonnie's passing. He still had his son then. Now his existence seemed pointless.

He folded the covers back, taking care not to disturb Bonnie's side of the bed, and stepped into his slippers. Floorboards creaked under his weight as he crossed the room, and when he opened the door to the hallway, the dog scrabbled to his feet with the cockeyed grin of an eager sentry. Floyd paused to stare at the dog for a moment before squeezing past on his way to the stairs. One hand slid along the banister as he made his way down to the moonlit kitchen and rounded the corner to Dean's room with the dog at his heels.

The bedside lamp remained lit, as Floyd had left it. He hadn't known the protocol, what to do with the urn. He wanted Dean to be comfortable, as odd as he knew that must be, so he'd constructed a platform of hard-covered books butted against the pillows and set the urn on top. He imagined Dean reading before lights out, which of course, he could not. He was dead. Floyd knew that.

The first night Floyd visited Dean's room, he explained Mrs. Brookman's deception and how he and Dean had been surreptitiously excised from each other's lives. The next night, he told Dean everything he'd ever wanted to know about his mother. The third night, he talked about his own childhood by way of explanation for his lackluster countenance. On the fourth night, he leaned the guitar against the bed and cried, then apologized for his outward demonstration of grief.

While the dog watched from the doorway, on this, the fifth night, Floyd stood next to the bed, hands clasped in front of his pajamas. Marian had planned a memorial gathering at the house for the following afternoon. How would he face those people in his living room when he only wanted to crawl inside the urn with his son and disappear?

The larger box delivered by the courier sat on a chair in the corner of the room. Floyd couldn't tolerate sifting through its contents. His grief was already a sharp knife. For the past four evenings, he'd averted his gaze, but his desire to be nearer to Dean compelled him to acknowledge it. He lifted it in his arms—nothing but an address sticker on the upper right corner and two-inch packing tape down the centre.

Floyd lowered himself onto the chair before setting the box on the floor between his feet. The dog's nails clicked across the hardwood. He sniffed at the box and sat on his haunches while Floyd's fingers traced the cardboard edges. Floyd breathed in deeply, then pried a corner of tape away from the cardboard and tore away the strip that held the top flaps in place.

The first item inside the box—a letter addressed to him.

Mr. Hoffman,

Please accept my condolences at the passing of your son. Dean was a lovely boy and is already sorely missed by the staff here. As one might, when living in the close proximity of servitude, I've been privy to certain details of you and your son's situation as it relates to Mrs. Brookman.

I've managed the estate households for twelve years. While I hold Mrs. Brookman in the highest esteem, and will continue to do so, I have not been entirely comfortable with her reasoning. I believe, as do others in this household, that her recent decline in health may have contributed to her choices.

It is only proper that Dean's remains and belongings be returned to you. Mrs. Brookman is gravely ill, and I fear the mishandling of these items should she succumb. I would ask that you share this letter with no one as I have written to you at great personal risk.

Sincerely,

Helen Curtis

Thank God for Helen, Floyd thought as he returned the letter to its envelope. Beneath a layer of white tissue paper, he found Dean's clothing, pressed and neatly folded. Floyd lifted a T-shirt from the pile, closed his eyes, and held it to his face. Dean's scent had been replaced by the smell of fabric softener. He thrust his hand into the box and grabbed a different shirt, a pair of jeans, pajamas, and socks, then flung them each aside. Grief tightened inside Floyd's chest; they'd all been laundered.

With his tail wagging, the dog pushed his snout into each successive item of clothing as it landed on the floor. He finished quickly and lay down, resting his muzzle on top of his paws. He couldn't find Dean either.

A miscellany of smaller items remained at the bottom of the box, among them guitar picks, a wallet, a cassette player, and a few tapes. A denim-covered book at the bottom of the box attracted Floyd's attention. He reached inside to retrieve it. He turned the book over to examine the back, the pages opened at a spot bookmarked by a photo of Bonnie. A diary. Floyd steeled himself and read the entry.

Note to Self   June 18, 1981

Lost a dad. Gained a dog. All in all, a pretty good day.

P.S. Named him Strum. Wagged his tail like crazy when I tried out the new guitar Rose bought me.

Tears rolled down Floyd's face. He'd expected Dean might feel this way, but still, to see it in writing wrenched his heart. He flipped through the diary to earlier pages. *Miserable piss tank.* Floyd's shoulders heaved as he sobbed. Strum raised his head and whined.

Floyd wiped a pajama sleeve across his face, then closed the book and pushed the box aside with one foot. "Come on, Strum. That's enough for now."

They climbed the stairs together and stopped at the guest bedroom. Floyd switched on the closet light, then stood on tiptoe and pushed the journal onto some boxes high up on the shelf.

He'd just finished when Strum barked behind him. The dog pounced towards the foot of the bed, along the bottom edge of the bedding, and barked again.

"Shush, shush," Floyd whispered. "What's the matter?" He knelt and raised the bed skirt away from the floor to have a look. Floyd's head jerked back.

Rose-coloured silk. How did Bonnie's lingerie wind up here?

Just after eleven o'clock on Saturday morning, the crunch of gravel alerted Floyd to a car pulling into the driveway. He drew the kitchen curtains back. Marian had arrived. She tied a flowered scarf over her hair and gathered the collar of her overcoat beneath her chin before opening the door. The sky had been overcast, and a light drizzle had been falling off and on since breakfast. No sooner had she stood up than a passenger emerged from the other side of the car. She'd brought Allan.

Marian opened the car trunk and handed Allan a large serving tray. She then gathered shopping bags in her arms and walked briskly towards the house with Allan in tow.

"I can take these," Floyd said when they reached the front door. He relieved Marian of the heaviest bags, and she continued to the kitchen counter with the remaining groceries. Floyd held the door open for Allan before taking the bags into the kitchen. "How did you two meet?"

"At the diner when I ordered the platters," Marian explained as she draped her coat over the back of a chair. "I mentioned your name. Allan said he and Dean were friends, and he wanted to lend a hand. Didn't you, Allan?"

Allan waited on the hall mat, cradling a tray of cold cuts and cheeses covered in plastic wrap. "I tried to call a bunch of times, but . . ." He sighed and hung his head.

"I haven't felt much like talking," Floyd replied. He took the tray from the boy's arms and set it next to the shopping bags, the contents of which Marian now sorted on the counter.

Allan froze in the centre of the kitchen and gawked at the urn. "Is that him?" he finally asked.

"Yes," Floyd replied. The crinkle of shopping bags ceased, and Marian slipped in beside him.

"I can't believe that's it," Allan said, his eyes brimming with tears. "And he's in there. I mean, shit." His head dropped forward, and his shoulders heaved up and down.

The gentle press of Marian's hand between Floyd's shoulder blades nudged him to step towards to Allan. He stretched an arm across the back of Allan's damp jacket and patted the boy's right shoulder. Floyd closed the lid on his own grief and buckled it down tight. Allan's emotions ran high enough without his weepiness added in.

"It's raining," Floyd said.

"A bit," Allan replied.

Floyd sensed Allan studying him. He ignored the feeling for several seconds, thinking that surely the boy would look away. But he didn't, and Floyd was forced to return his gaze.

"It's okay to cry," Allan said. "I mean, if you wanna, you should just do it—seriously."

But Floyd wouldn't cry, not in front of Allan and certainly not in front of Marian. To show such unabashed emotion in the presence of others was tantamount to standing naked under a spotlight. He could no longer play the role of husband or father, but he was still a man. It fell to him to be the stalwart caretaker of this grieving trio, the balancing keel of their overwhelmed ship. He refused to roll over and expose his vulnerable underbelly.

Floyd let his hand slide from Allan's shoulder. "Dean should be moved into the living room, I suppose."

Allan looked away.

"I've left some photos and an album on the sofa," Floyd said. "Maybe you could put them here and there."

"I'm on it." Allan set off to the living room with the dog following closely at his side.

Marian stood next to the counter, tying apron strings behind her back. "You're a good man, Floyd Hoffman."

Floyd stared at her. "The jury's out on that."

Guests began to trickle in by one o'clock in the afternoon. Marian welcomed them, and Allan heaped their jackets over the banister. Floyd twisted his wedding ring around his finger or gripped the armrest of his chair as, one by one, people came to offer their condolences.

Marian's cousin, Phyllis, arrived first. She worked at Arlene's Beauty Salon. Floyd often saw her smoking cigarettes out front when he visited the pub. They'd known each other since grade school, long before he'd known Marian. Tony showed up with Eloise Donaldson from the library. "I remember Dean sitting cross-legged in the carrel while you read and took notes," she said. "Such a darling little boy."

"He is." Floyd replied, then corrected himself. "Was."

While Tony offered his condolences, Eloise joined Phyllis on the sofa. They flipped through a photo album, stopping to point at the pages and shake their heads.

"How are you holding up?" Tony asked.

Floyd shrugged. "I'm the last Hoffman. The end of the line."

From behind the sofa, Allan stared at him with a peculiar expression Floyd couldn't quite put a label on. When their eyes met, Allan turned away.

"You haven't been around lately," Tony said cautiously. "Laying off the drink for a while?"

Floyd glanced up at the urn looming on the mantel. "For good," he replied.

"Hats off to you," Tony said, leaning back in the chair.

From the corner of his eye, Floyd noticed Vivian Parker stepping inside with a casserole dish in her hands. Her presence surprised him. They'd barely exchanged a word in the past ten years. When Allan offered to take her coat, she waved him off and made a beeline for Floyd. She set her casserole dish on the coffee table and took Tony's chair when he offered it.

"It's nice of you to come, Miss Parker," Floyd offered.

"Vivian, please." She smiled nervously. "I'm so sorry for your loss. There's nothing to take the sting away. I know." She looked around the room. "Is Tammy here?"

Carl Spivey appeared in the living room entrance.

Floyd's stomach lurched. "Who?"

"Dean's girlfriend," Vivian said.

Floyd squeezed the armrest. Had there been a girlfriend? Nothing would make him happier. He'd play along and see what he could find out. "She's not here."

"Poor dear, too distraught, I suppose."

"You know her?"

"Yes. She comes into the salon with her mother. She visited your house every few days over the summer." Vivian paused. "I should call Mirabelle to see how she's doing."

Mirabelle King? Floyd had to know. "The Kings are a fine family," he ventured.

"Truly." Vivian sighed. "I shouldn't keep you from your guests."

Last summer, he'd suspected Dean had a girl, and now he knew for sure. Floyd could certainly guess the chain of events that led to his discovery of Bonnie's negligee the previous evening. It pleased Floyd. He thought of the fragile and forlorn girl he'd seen downtown with Mirabelle. It made sense. She'd known Dean was ill.

"Thank you, Vivian."

He watched her carry the casserole into the kitchen, then he cast a wary look at Carl standing to the left of the fireplace with Allan, telling some bullshit story, Floyd thought. After seventeen years of working with Carl, he recognized all the signs— the animated hand gestures, the elbow nudging, the jolts of laughter.

It was Bonnie's funeral all over again. But this time, Floyd knew what had existed between them. His gut curdled like sour milk at the sight of Carl Spivey. And now he stood in Floyd's home, as if they were friends. As if he'd arrived to stake his claim on Dean.

Marian crisscrossed the room, offering guests a plate of snacks. She laid a napkin on the end table next to Floyd's armchair. "Here," she said, presenting a few crackers and a slice of cheddar. "I won't let up until you've eaten a little something." She rested a hand on his shoulder.

Beyond her sympathetic smile, Floyd could see evidence of the young woman he'd first met on one of the few occasions he'd called on Bonnie at the Brookman home.

Floyd patted the back of her hand. A kind of weak promise that he would try. But he doubted it.

"It will benefit no one if you starve." Marian shook her head. Just as she turned towards the kitchen, Carl stepped into her path. "Oh!" she said with a start.

"I'll take a couple of those off your hands," Carl said. He cupped one hand and filled it with crackers and the last of the cheese slices. "I'm Carl," he said with a wink. "And you are?"

"Marian."

"Nice to meet you M-a-a-rian." Carl's chin dipped.

"I should refill this plate." Her gaze shifted to the floor as she headed to the kitchen.

Carl dropped into the chair next to Floyd's. "Jeez, what can I say? I'm just so damned sorry for you. First Bonnie and now this . . ."

Floyd glowered at Carl. A surge of molten emotion bubbled at the base of his throat.

"And don't worry about work. Take all the time you need. It's the least I can do." Carl pushed the two-bite cracker into his mouth all at once. Crumbs fell onto his lap each time his jaw hinged open to reposition the chewed-up food.

"Yes. It is the *least* you can do. Why not do less than the least you can do? Why not—nothing?" Floyd rose to his feet. "In fact, you should leave. Now!"

The room quieted.

Carl raised his palms in mock surrender as he lifted slowly from the chair. "Floyd, I'm here to express my condolences on your loss." His eyes swept around the room with an incredulous expression. "I'll just pay my respects and go." He stepped towards the mantel.

Floyd's nostrils flared, and his jaw clenched.

Then Carl laid a hand against the brass surface of the urn.

Floyd lunged forward and grabbed the back of Carl's collar, yanking him away from the mantel. When their legs slammed against the coffee table, a collective gasp rose from the sofa. Floyd spun Carl around and clutched his lapels. "Don't touch my son," he shrieked.

Carl jerked free of Floyd's grip. Colour burned high in his cheeks as he looked around the room. He opened his mouth as if to speak but then he closed it again without uttering a word. Carl stormed from the room and snatched his coat from the banister. Seconds later, the front door slammed.

Decorum required Floyd to apologize for the kerfuffle. But he didn't plan to. He sat in his armchair and ate cheese and crackers instead.

November 1966

In the earlier days of their marriage, Floyd could not decipher the language of Bonnie's sadness, but he'd learned the significance of a smile that ended too quickly or a shrug given in lieu of words. He'd also come to recognize that the expectations of holiday cheeriness caused her no end of worry. With Dean's birthday fast approaching and the Christmas season soon to follow, Bonnie lapsed into woe. In the days before depression swallowed her, she'd bemoaned the inescapable social obligations she'd need to meet in order to please her mother.

The slide began slowly at the beginning of the month. It was the little things that gave it away. Laundry unattended. A thickening layer of dust that covered the furniture. Eventually, she stopped getting out of bed to see Floyd off to work. He'd fix Dean's breakfast and then rouse Bonnie before he left the house. She'd wipe the sleep from her eyes and smile weakly at Dean when he stood at her bedside and gazed expectantly into her eyes. Floyd trusted her assurances that she could care for their son. All the same, Floyd came home each day over the noon hour to relieve her of making Dean's lunch.

One day midmonth, Floyd returned home after work to find Bonnie sound asleep on the sofa. Breakfast cereal had been dumped from the box and mounded in the centre of the coffee table. Toy cars and trucks were scattered over the floor. Bonnie's favourite Motown record was skipping on his father's turntable.

I've got su—

I've got su—

I've got su—

He lifted the needle from the album and set off looking for Dean. When he didn't find the boy in the kitchen, he climbed the stairs, calling his name. He searched behind doors, under beds, in closets, and even behind the shower curtain. In the most playful voice he could muster, he sang out, "Dean, come out, come out wherever you are!" When the child didn't appear, Floyd's alarm grew. He flew downstairs and unlocked the empty room behind the kitchen. No Dean. It wasn't until Floyd ran to check the spare room at the rear of the house that he noticed a sliver of daylight through the back door. He flung the door open and discovered Dean, a spot of colour in the centre of the dying lawn.

The boy—dressed in a red toque, flannel pajamas, and corduroy slippers—had gone outside to pet a cat that had wandered into the backyard. When he saw his father striding towards him, he said, "Kitty!"

Relief coursed through Floyd as he knelt to hug Dean. "Are you all right?"

"I'm petting Kitty," Dean answered excitedly.

"Yes, a nice cat," Floyd said. He warmed the boy's hands in his own, all the while thinking that something had to change. He could not ask it of Bonnie. The change needed to come from him.

If only he could be in two places at once so he could both earn a living and be assured of his son's safety. He needed help. Today's event had driven the point home. But who could he trust enough to ask their assistance? He could pay a local woman to take care of Dean while he was at work, but considering the velocity of gossip, Bonnie's condition would become public knowledge in no time. She'd be devastated and spiral even deeper. He'd nowhere to turn but to family, and the only family he had was Bonnie's.

The next morning, Floyd combed the boy's hair neatly to one side and dressed him in a new outfit Bonnie had ordered from the Sears catalogue. He and Dean both kissed Bonnie good-bye and went downstairs to bundle up warmly before trundling into the car.

On the drive across town, Dean sat quietly in the passenger seat. Too small for a view out the window, he occupied himself by playing with a stuffed yellow rabbit Bonnie had named *Sunny Bunny*. He held the blue ribbon circling its neck and jumped the rabbit across his knees and onto the car seat.

"You're going to have fun at Grandma and Grandpa's house today," Floyd said, trying to draw him out.

"Mommy there?" Dean asked, hugging the rabbit to his chest.

"No, Mommy is resting at home, remember?"

"She gaw tummache."

"Yes, a tummy ache," Floyd replied halfheartedly with a manufactured smile. "But she'll be better soon."

Dean regarded him skeptically.

Marian answered the Brookmans' door after Floyd's first knock. She bowed forward and plucked the hat from Dean's head. "Well, here's the little man!" He plunged forward and wrapped both arms around her legs.

Mrs. Brookman stepped out of the parlour. "Gene," she called. "They're here."

"Hi, Gamma!"

"Grandmother," she corrected him.

"Hey, champ!" Mr. Brookman strode out of his office and scooped Dean up in his arms. "I delayed going to the office just so I could see you."

"Mommy gaw tummache," Dean said.

Bonnie's mother raised a brow at Floyd. "A tummy ache?"

"But we're sure she'll be better soon," Floyd said levelly without blinking. "Incidentally, I'll be here at four o'clock to pick him up." He was sending his mother-in-law a message. *We're not sliding into old habits. You're not calling the shots.*

"Marian will have him ready," Mr. Brookman said. His wife fumed in silence.

Floyd knelt and laid a hand on his son's left shoulder. "What did you want to ask Grandmother and Grandfather?

"We gaw 'ave cake!" Dean said.

"And?" Floyd prompted.

"You come t'my birfdee pardy?"

"Your birthday party? We'd love to!" Mr. Brookman responded.

"For dinner on Sunday," Floyd added. "Just a simple affair."

"I'd expect no less," Mrs. Brookman replied. Then she held out a hand to Dean and escorted him to the kitchen.

The party was an awkward affair. Bonnie slouched at the kitchen table to the right of Dean, who was sitting on his new booster seat. Her gaze seldom left him. She'd found the energy to put on a clean dress, but her hair hung in oily tresses, and a faint tang of dried sweat lifted from her body throughout dinner.

From across the table, Mrs. Brookman sat with her hands folded in her lap and studied Bonnie. She reminded Floyd of a museum patron leaning over velvet ropes to view a new exhibit. Her silence spoke volumes. A cold dollop of macaroni and cheese sat marooned in the middle of her plate. Earlier on, she'd scowled at the balloons Floyd had taped to the cupboard doors and the blue crepe streamers he'd draped over the curtain rods.

"I believe I'll have another frankfurter," Mr. Brookman said, reaching into the centre of the table for a second hotdog. A happy birthday napkin was tucked into his shirt collar, and his sleeves were rolled above his elbows.

Floyd nudged the ketchup and relish bottles across the table and cast a sideways glance at Mrs. Brookman. Eager to relieve Bonnie from her mother's scrutiny, he racked his mind for avenues of conversation to distract Mrs. Brookman. Finally, he asked, "How are preparations coming along for this year's Christmas party?"

She appeared not to hear him. Instead, she gazed at Dean with concern. His half-eaten hotdog lay mangled on the tablecloth. With his chin inches above the table, Dean happily licked his fingers after having dragged them through the remains of condiment puddles dripped on his plate.

"He's a mess," Mrs. Brookman told Bonnie in disgust. "Won't you at least clean the child's hands?"

Bonnie slowly wiped Dean's hands on a napkin. Until Mr. Brookman broke the spell by reaching for the mustard jar, they all watched her deliberate movements as if hypnotized.

"Mrs. Brookman," Floyd said, "the Christmas party?"

The index finger of her right hand absently traced the edge of her plate.

"Rose," Mr. Brookman said around a mouthful of hotdog.

Her head jerked towards him as if she'd just woken up.

"Floyd's asking about the Christmas party. How's it going?"

She turned to Floyd. "It's going well," she answered with a slight tremor in her voice.

Her vulnerability softened his heart towards her. Now that he was a parent, he could better imagine her heartbreak over Bonnie's predicament. He smiled at her softly and asked, "Will most of your Toronto friends be joining you this year?"

"I believe so," she said in a voice thin as air. "It's difficult to get everyone up in the winter once the weather has begun turning foul. They dread the unpredictable snow squalls." Her bottom lip trembled. "Bonnie, do you remember the parties at Uncle Bart's summer house in the Muskokas?"

A corner of Bonnie's mouth twitched. "Yes," she mumbled. "He took me to the zoo once. I liked the elephants."

Mr. Brookman struggled to empty his mouth of food. "She's talking about the Toronto Zoo," he told Floyd.

"I recall the grand birthday parties we used to have at Uncle Bart's like they were yesterday. All of you children swimming in the lake each summer," her mother said. "Those were wonderful times. We must take Dean there, a little summer vacation away from this." She scowled at the dish-strewn counter on the other side of the kitchen.

"That might be nice," Bonnie said. Tears chased each other down her cheeks. "But Floyd disapproves of Dean swimming outdoors. I don't think he'll allow it." She bowed her head forward and wiped her eyes.

"What's this about, Floyd?" Mr. Brookman asked, his previously congenial expression now replaced by sharp concern. His head craned forward, and both fists rested against the table on either side of his dinner plate.

"It's nothing. Just a little misunderstanding," Floyd said. "I think we're ready for dessert." He pushed away from the table and unboxed the vanilla cake he'd picked up from the bakery that morning. He struggled to open the clear tape stuck along the edge of the lid, all the while hoping the Brookmans wouldn't question him further. Bonnie's father had been friendly so far, but that would end if he knew Floyd suspected his mill of spewing toxins.

"Is that what it is, Bonnie?" her mother asked. "A misunderstanding?"

Bonnie lowered her gaze.

Before she could respond, Floyd said, "It's all right to swim in your uncle's lake, Bonnie." He stuck a pair of candles in the cake and lit them with a match.

"So it's all right to swim at the summer house, but not *here*?" her mother asked in a voice tinged with suspicion. She eyed Floyd with mistrust as he set the cake on the table in front of Dean.

"Happy birthday to you," Floyd sang haltingly. Bonnie and her parents joined in. Dean looked from the cake to his family and back again. Before the song had ended, he stood on the front edge of his chair and bent over the cake. When he blew out the last candle, they all clapped.

"What a set of lungs on you, Dean!" Mr. Brookman said and ruffled the boy's curly hair.

"I de birfdee boy!" he said emphatically.

Floyd busied himself with slicing the cake and scooping ice cream. When he passed the plates to the Brookmans, he detected a preoccupation in their eyes. They wouldn't allow the swimming issue to drop so easily.

Mrs. Brookman sampled a nibble of cake and laid her fork on the tablecloth. "Much too sweet," she said with a shudder, then set her sights on Bonnie. "Our conversation was left unfinished. Why can't Dean swim here?"

Bonnie laid a hand on Dean's arm. "Floyd thinks there's something wrong with the water."

Floyd's brows raised. Intentional or not, she'd hung him out to dry. He hadn't wanted to discuss water quality with his father-in-law, not on his son's birthday and not in Mrs. Brookman's presence. Now everyone was looking at him. He felt cornered.

"What's this all about?" Mr. Brookman asked.

"In the middle of the summer, during the hot stretch, the three of us went swimming a lot to get relief from the heat," Floyd began. Relaying the events was tantamount to playing hopscotch in a minefield. He slowed his telling to be sure he got the words just right.

"Get on with it," Mrs. Brookman said.

"Dean developed a fever and a rash, so we took him to see Doctor Gillespie."

"I remember. What does that have to do with anything?" she sniped.

"Well," Floyd began, "the doctor seems to think Dean had a reaction to something in the water." He watched their faces to measure their response. "He recommended we keep him out of the river."

"A reaction to what? An insect? A plant?" Mr. Brookman asked with a puzzled look.

"No," Bonnie blurted. "The doctor thinks there are chemicals in the water making people sick. So does Floyd. Tell him he's wrong!"

"Chemicals . . ." Mr. Brookman repeated.

Floyd shrugged. "Dean's not the only one to get sick from contact with the river. There've been others," he said. "I've been photographing a lot of dead fish along the riverbank, from Riverside Park—across from the mill—to the gorge. They're covered in tumours. If something in the water does that to fish, what's it doing to people over an extended period of time?"

"You're pointing a finger at McLelland's!" Mrs. Brookman said.

"There is no connection to my mill!" Mr. Brookman said. "McLelland's conscientiously monitors water returned to the river. We are diligent on that point."

"That you would suggest otherwise is repugnant," Mrs. Brookman added loudly.

"Gamma mad!" Dean said, his brows furrowed. Melted ice cream dripped from his chin and cake crumbs stuck to his cheeks.

Bonnie leaned her elbows on the table and started to cry. Her parents both glowered at Floyd as though it were all his fault. Her shoulders shook, and she sniffled. "I'm sorry," she said between sobs. "I just can't seem to stop." She pushed away from the table and plodded out of the kitchen.

"I come too," Dean said. He climbed down from his chair to follow her upstairs.

Until they trailed out of sight, Floyd stared after them. He pressed his eyes shut briefly and steeled himself before turning to face Bonnie's parents again. Her father had clamped his head between his palms and leaned back in his chair. With his gaze lowered to the table, he blew a stream of air through his pursed lips.

"How could you let her slide into this condition?" Mrs. Brookman said. "For God's sake, take a stand and insist she take medication!"

"She needs help," Bonnie's father said sternly. "I know she doesn't want it, but she needs it. It's time, with a little one."

Floyd squared his shoulders. He'd made a commitment to Bonnie. No medication. He planned to stand by it.

"Think of Dean," Mrs. Brookman implored. "This roller coaster of emotion and her erratic behavior is going to affect the child. Do it for him."

"We're teaching Dean tolerance and acceptance. He'll be the better for it," Floyd answered.

"And what if you're wrong? What then?" Mr. Brookman said. "Picture him as an angry young man, poisoned by all of this."

Mrs. Brookman leaned across the corner of the table towards Floyd and in a raised voice said, "Get her the help she needs, and get it now."

Floyd was about to respond when the Brookmans' eyes cut to the kitchen door. He turned around and found Bonnie standing there with Dean's stuffed rabbit hanging at her side. "Dean wanted Sunny Bunny . . ." Her face slowly contorted into an expression of rage. "You're all talking about me. I heard you!"

"Nothing, darling. We're just talking," her mother said in a soothing tone.

"Lies! Lies! Lies!" Bonnie shouted. "You're all conspiring against me."

Bonnie's father stood with his arms open wide.

"Don't even think about it," Bonnie said. She looked into Floyd's eyes like a wounded animal. "And you, you're in on this too!"

"No," Floyd said. "I never said—"

Bonnie turned and pounded up the stairs.

"Take me home, Gene," Mrs. Brookman said. She dabbed her eyes with an embroidered handkerchief. "I can't take any more of this."

Mr. Brookman looked to Floyd with empathy. "Maybe we should stay, just until we know she's calmed down."

"No. I want to leave now," she said. "And we're taking Dean with us. This is no place for him, not with Bonnie in a state and this one so ineffective at managing the situation."

"Our son stays here," Floyd said.

Mrs. Brookman slid from her chair and stood behind the table. "You'll be the ruination of Bonnie and that boy."

No sooner had she said the words than a door slammed upstairs to punctuate her point.

The coffee percolator was rattling on the stovetop as Floyd made his way down the stairs for breakfast the next morning. He rounded into the kitchen with a pensive but hopeful smile. He'd given Bonnie a wide berth the previous evening so she could sort herself out. But when he'd climbed into bed, she'd rolled away from him and refused to speak. There was no telling what mood he'd be greeted with this morning.

Bonnie was standing in front of the stove, melting butter in a skillet. "I thought you'd like eggs this morning," she said, smiling a little too brightly. "Sit, and I'll pour your coffee. Your newspaper is on the table."

He stared back at her with a look of surprise that made her laugh. Her shift to cheeriness should have relieved him, but the sing-song cadence of her voice only stirred his wariness.

Bonnie set a mug of coffee on the table and said, "Enjoy!"

He swallowed a few tentative sips and pretended to read the first section of the newspaper while Bonnie fried the eggs and then buttered his toast. Her hair had been brushed smooth and clipped in place at the nape of her neck by a barrette. She'd dressed in a matching sweater set and a tweed skirt. He chided himself for being pessimistic. Surely, the care she'd taken with her appearance indicated that her equilibrium had returned.

Dean suddenly appeared at the kitchen door with Sunny Bunny trapped in the crook of one arm. His cheeks were rosy with sleep, and the corners of his mouth curled downward in a frown.

"Well, good morning," Floyd said.

The boy rubbed his eyes with a balled-up fist. The vinyl soles of his flannel pajamaed feet scraped against the floor as he scurried towards his mother.

Bonnie lifted him into the air and planted kisses on his face. "Remember what you were going to tell Daddy today?" When he whined and nuzzled into her neck, she told Floyd, "Sunny Bunny doesn't want to visit his grandparents today. He wants to stay here—with me."

"Dean, you want to stay with Mom?" Floyd asked.

The boy nodded and clung tightly to his mother.

"Will you be all right?" Floyd asked Bonnie.

"Of course," she replied. "Nothing would make me happier."

The decision lifted Floyd's spirits too. Notifying Mrs. Brookman that Dean wouldn't be spending the day with her had been unexpectedly satisfying. He passed the morning at the post office with a smile on his face. He found himself whistling a happy tune on more than one occasion. In spite of his confidence in Bonnie's turnaround, he decided to telephone her at the start of his lunch hour to make sure things were going smoothly at home. She didn't answer. Perhaps she'd taken Dean for a walk to play at the park. A light snow had been falling since midmorning. He doubted they'd gone far.

Floyd called her twice more before recommencing work. Still no answer. A grain of worry niggled at the back of his mind, but he brushed it away. After all, Bonnie had been fine that morning when he'd left the house.

At the close of his work day, he thought of calling her again. When he last called, she could have been home feeling agitated at being checked up on and refused to pick up. He set the receiver down and hurried outside. The snow was falling heavier, and the wind was picking up. He regretted not having driven the car to work. He shouldn't like to be traveling any great distance, however, as visibility would be diminished, and without snow tires, the car had never handled well in poor weather.

He'd light the fireplace once he'd returned home. He and Bonnie could spend the evening in front of the warm glow and read storybooks to Dean. A hot cocoa might be nice too. Bonnie always liked that.

As he approached the house, his gait slowed. Where was the car? He squinted to see past the driving snow to where the Volkswagen should have been parked. It was gone. His eyes cut to the house. The windows of their house were all dark. Floyd rushed to the end of the driveway, hoping to see tire marks in the snow, some indication as to which direction the car had been taken. But the snowfall had filled in the tracks, and so he could only speculate.

Stay calm and think. It made no sense that Bonnie would take the car. She didn't have a driver's license.

Floyd strode across the front yard and up the porch steps, fishing house keys from his pocket as he went. He burst through the front door and kicked off his boots. "Bonnie? Dean?" He jogged up the stairs shouting, "Anybody home?" No one answered. The beds were made and the rooms tidied. He looked in his and Bonnie's closet and their dresser drawers. Nothing appeared to be missing.

He returned downstairs to check for Bonnie's purse. It was absent from its usual spot next to the kitchen door. Hers and Dean's coats had been taken from their hooks as well. Their boots were still lined up against the wall, Dean's mittens stuffed into the tops of the smaller pair. Floyd's son was out there somewhere and dressed inadequately for the bitter weather.

Where could they have gone? Floyd despaired over calling the Brookmans' home to see if Bonnie and their son were there. It seemed unlikely that she would visit her parents after the previous day's blowup. She might have arranged to meet Marian somewhere—away from the estate—but she'd have left a note for him if that were the case.

"Damn it," Floyd shouted in frustration. The last thing he wanted to do was call his in-laws with news that Bonnie had run off to parts unknown with Dean. The car heater had been acting up. If his wife and son were stranded somewhere, they'd be cold and scared. Maybe Mrs. Brookman had been right. He would be the cause of Bonnie's and Dean's ruination. He'd wait just a little bit longer, and then he'd have to place the call.

He paced the house, stopping every few minutes to look out the window and search the street. When the telephone rang, he raced to pick it up. Wrong number. He slouched against the wall and tapped the receiver against his forehead. *Think,*

think, think. Where would Bonnie go?

Outside, the snow had stopped, but darkness was beginning to fall. He couldn't wait around doing nothing. Floyd needed to get out there to search for his family, but he'd need a vehicle to do it. Vivian Parker's lights were on next door. She might lend her car if he promised to return it with a fresh tank of gas. He threw on a jacket and was about to run next door when the telephone rang again.

Floyd wrapped a wool scarf around his neck as he hustled towards the telephone. "Hello!" he said. The line was silent. "Hello?" he said again with more urgency.

"Did you lose anything today?"

It was Rose Brookman.

"What?" Floyd said.

"Has anything gone missing from your house—perhaps my daughter and her son?"

Floyd closed his eyes briefly and clamped his temples with his free hand. "You know where they are."

"I do," she said.

"Well?"

"They're here with me."

"Are they all right?" Floyd blurted.

"They are now," she answered sharply.

Floyd leaned his forehead against the wall and closed his eyes tightly. "What do you mean—*now*?"

"Now that they've been warmed up and given a square meal," she snapped.

His eyes shot open. "Warmed up! What happened?"

"They were stranded on the side of the road halfway between Hattersburg and Narrow Falls," Mrs. Brookman said in a steely voice. "Bonnie turned off on a side road and slid the car into a ditch. She and Dean sat in the freezing cold for nearly two hours before some stranger spotted them."

Floyd clenched his fist. He should have never let this happen. "Where was she going?"

The line went quiet for a moment. "To the zoo," Mrs. Brookman finally said.

"Bonnie wanted to show Dean the elephants."

Floyd groaned.

"A logging foreman picked them up and drove them to the nearest gas station," she explained. "Gene left a meeting to drive out there and picked them up. How could you so carelessly leave a spare car key lying around? She doesn't even have a license to drive. They could have both been killed." The accusation leapt through the receiver. "Bonnie was hysterical when she arrived, and the poor baby was frightened out of his wits."

"She could have called me," Floyd said.

"But she didn't. She called her family," Mrs. Brookman said. "When Gene picked them up, Bonnie and Dean were wearing sneakers. She hadn't brought hats or mittens. There wasn't a crumb to eat."

"I'm coming over," Floyd said.

"No. They're both sleeping. Leave them be."

"Then, tomorrow," he relented.

"You're going to be busy begging a ride to retrieve your car tomorrow. It will need to be shoveled out before you can hire someone to drag it from the ditch. And who will watch Bonnie and Dean then?" she said in a sarcastic tone.

At that moment, Floyd hated her more than anyone else in the world. "Tomorrow, and that's it."

"What about the next day and the day after that? You can't guarantee that her misjudgment won't risk her safety and Dean's in the future. If the child stayed with us, he'd be properly protected."

"Never!" Floyd said. His chest was heaving with every breath. "And Rose?"

"Yes?"

"Wake my wife and son. Now. I'm bringing them home even if I have to carry them."

A soft *click* and then the dial tone began to drone in Floyd's ear. He hung up the receiver and slid his back down the wall until he rested on the floor. Then he covered his face with his hands and wept until his shoulders shook.

22.

Tomorrow would mark the one hundred and third day of Tammy's stay at the Beatrix Home. According to the calendar, she'd been pregnant for two hundred and twenty-one days. She sat on the edge of her mattress while she stared out the bedroom window and stretched her achy back. She barely recognized her own body. That a miniature human being resided inside her bulging stomach still surprised her. Yet in approximately fifty-nine days, she'd hold the baby for the first time, and her parents would be forced to accept her firm intent to keep it. Until then, she'd feign indecision and cocoon herself in the refuge of the home.

The stretch of property in front of the Beatrix Home resembled tufts of pewter beneath the light of the November moon. A windbreak of pine trees flanked the far side of the laneway. Wind shifted their silhouettes against the charcoal cast of the night sky.

On the distant horizon, a point of yellow light shone each night. Tammy guessed it came from the farm she'd ridden past with her parents that first day. She'd seen the house and outbuildings on one other occasion from her seat on the Beatrix Home bus. Mrs. Peel drove the white minibus to the United Church service in Hattersburg each Sunday. Tammy couldn't forget the curious looks of parishioners as she and the other residents filed into the church.

"Who's that?" a little girl had said loudly, pointing at Tammy.

"A Beatrix girl," her mother had answered softly. "Don't be like her, darling."

Tammy refused to return after the first week. She'd experienced enough shaming to last a lifetime—no need to go looking for it.

From beneath her pillow, she slid the Walt Whitman poetry book and opened it to a poem whose page number someone had circled in blue ink.

*For the one I love most lay sleeping by me under the same cover in
the cool night,
In the stillness in the autumn moonbeams his face was inclined
towards me . . .*

Guilt pricked Tammy's conscience. When her mind summoned Dean's image, the edges of his face blurred, and his features drifted away. The harder she fought to construct him, the more diluted he became. His photo lay in the drawer of her nightstand, but since being separated from one another, she'd become less compelled to look at it. An accidental glimpse left her unsettled, as if her mother had dropped by for a surprise visit. She wanted to miss him more, but the desperate yearning of the early days had cooled. When she saw Dean in the future, with their baby, the feeling would spark up again. Tammy wanted it to. He'd be so proud of how she'd stood her ground to keep the baby. She needed someone to be proud. And Dean had a plan, not one she completely supported, but a plan nonetheless. How could his grandmother not be thrilled with a great-grandchild? Surely, she'd help them get on their feet. They could pay her back in a few years.

"Knock, knock," called a chirpy voice from the hallway. The bedroom door creaked open wide enough for one of the girls to crane her head into the room. "Watcha doin'?"

"Getting ready to turn in for the night." Tammy said.

"Oh, come on. It's only quarter to nine, and there's a card game starting."

"Too tired," Tammy shrugged. "Sorry."

"Okay, but you're French braiding my hair tomorrow, right?"

"Sure. In the commons area after breakfast."

"Bring your basket along. There'll be a lineup when everyone sees how good I look." The girl grinned and pulled the door shut.

One evening after kitchen duty, Tammy had found the basket on her nightstand, brimming with silk flowers, hair elastics, bobby pins, a pink comb, and half a can of hairspray. The other girls had each contributed a few items as a gift. "You've got a knack for hair styling," they'd told her. Maybe beauty school was in her future.

Her stay at the Beatrix House was the best bad thing that had ever happened to her. She flourished away from her mother's attention and her father's inattention. Here, she acted with confidence and discovered talents never exercised at home. She'd made new friends—people who didn't judge her, people who listened without silencing her, people who didn't smother her under a blanket of their own agenda. She never felt like an add-on to someone else's life. Her value stood on its own.

Laughter from the card game drifted into Tammy's room. She lay under the covers and wondered what Dean might be doing. When her eyes grew heavy, she returned the poetry book to the nightstand and switched off the light. Soon after drifting to sleep, she dreamt of panties caught around her ankles.

Midmorning the next day, Tammy and Jill, a recently arrived girl, worked together in the laundry, folding the towels and facecloths they'd later deliver to the rooms upstairs. They stood on opposite sides of a wooden table working in silent tandem until the last dryer shut off.

"Do you ever get letters?" Jill asked.

"My mother writes. Sometimes."

Jill sighed and laid a hand over her heart. "I mean from your boyfriend."

"Boyfriend?"

"Yeah. You didn't get in this condition on your own."

Tammy considered explaining, then dismissed the idea. "It's complicated," she mumbled.

"It's always complicated. What's his story?"

"I can't talk about it." Tammy reached for a new towel.

"Is he okay with you keeping the baby?"

"Yup. He wants me to."

"If you're keeping it, what are you doing here?"

Tammy circled to Jill's side of the table and spoke in a hushed voice. "I don't want to go home, so I let my parents hold on to the hope that I'll go along with giving the baby up."

Jill leaned towards her. "Be careful."

"What do you mean?"

"You must have heard the story about the girl who . . . you know."

"I heard about her." Tammy tried to look unaffected, as if Leslie Benton's story concerning the baby's removal and the mother's bad ending didn't revisit her daily.

"Mrs. Peel must be after you. She's big on adoption."

Tammy nodded.

"That other girl didn't sign either." Jill raised a brow. "I heard she was nice. Like you. They say nice guys finish last for a reason, you know."

Mrs. Peel appeared in the doorway as if she'd materialized out of thin air. She surveyed the laundry room, then pushed her shoulders back. "There's a phone call for Tammy," she said.

Tammy's eyes cut to Jill.

"It's long-distance," Mrs. Peel said, "so be quick about it." Then she pivoted sharply and set off to the stairwell across from the laundry room.

Tammy hastened towards the hallway.

"Maybe it's your guy!" Jill called after her.

A flush of hope propelled Tammy towards the office. But then she realized it couldn't be Dean. He knew nothing of her stay at the Beatrix Home. Mirabelle must be calling, but why?

Tammy picked at a ragged fingernail as she stepped through the office door. Her eyes locked on the receiver lying in the centre of the desk blotter. She picked it up as though it were a snake set to strike.

"Hello?"

"It's your mother."

"Is everything all right?"

"Funny, I was about to ask you the same thing."

Tammy hesitated. "What do you mean?"

"Floyd Hoffman knocked on our front door this morning."

Tammy's free hand flew to her belly.

"Your father was in the shower, thank the Lord. Don't know how I would have explained things if he'd come down the stairs."

"What did Mr. Hoffman want?"

"He wanted to speak with you—urgently."

Oh no.

"I told him you were away at school, not that it was any of his damned business."

"Did he believe you?"

"You'd better hope so."

"Why did he want to talk to me?"

"He wouldn't say, but I think we both know." Mirabelle breathed heavily into the phone. "Care to explain how he made the connection between you and his boy?"

"I've no idea."

"Have you been feeding Floyd Hoffman hints about your situation?"

"No." Tammy's brow furrowed, and her mouth gaped. "I haven't told a soul except Dean."

The line went quiet for a moment.

"Mrs. Peel tells me you aren't listening to reason."

Tammy stiffened. "I haven't signed the papers, if that's what you mean."

Mirabelle's voice softened. "Do you intend to?"

The change in her mother's tone opened a gate she needed to walk through. "I'm still thinking," she lied. "My decision will be based on what I think is best for me and my baby."

"Tammy, I know you think you're in love with this boy—"

"I *am* in love with this *man*," Tammy said, gaining courage. "And he loves me too."

"Reverend Findlay is coming to Hattersburg tomorrow especially to see you."

Tammy leaned against the desk, fighting to maintain her composure. "I won't talk to him. I'm not a child. I won't be strong-armed into signing anything."

Silence.

"Dean is dead," Mirabelle said. "The memorial service was yesterday."

"Dead?" Tammy's knees buckled. She thought she might vomit. *He can't be. What about our life together? The baby?*

"It's hard for me to tell you this."

Tammy began to weep. "You're wrong about that, Mother." She stifled a sob, and her voice shook. "I don't believe it's hard for you at all."

She laid the receiver on the desk and left the office. The tinny sound of Mirabelle's voice shouting her name grew fainter as she walked down the hallway.

For the rest of the day, Tammy curled up on her bed and cried. Jill came to check on her when she didn't return to the laundry and again when she didn't come down for lunch. Each time, she sent her friend away. When she skipped dinner, Jill climbed upstairs a third time and sat on the end of the bed. "It has something to do with that phone call, doesn't it? The reason why you're upset."

"Yup." Tammy's bottom lip trembled. She pulled herself upright and leaned her back against the wall. "My boyfriend died."

"Whoa." Jill's head craned forward. "Does Mrs. Peel know?"

"I don't think so. They want to take my baby, but it's all I have. I can't give it up."

"What are you going to do?"

Tammy shrugged, and tears rolled down her face.

Jill patted Tammy's leg. "Come to the prayer meeting tonight. It'll help you feel better. I promise."

That night, most of the girls filed downstairs for Mrs. Peel's weekly prayer meeting. They bunched around the dining room tables and joked about pocketing extra cookies from the snack tray while copies of the Holy Bible were being distributed. Tammy dropped into the seat next to Jill, who gave her an empathetic smile.

The wife of a United Church minister in Hattersburg stood at the front of the room, hoping, no doubt, to strengthen the girls' bonds to God. "It's Remembrance Day, so I've come to speak about the strength of women during wartime and the testing of our faith." She spoke about sacrifice for the greater good. "I commend the courage of young mothers who give their children up to parents equipped to provide a home full of love and possibility."

Mrs. Peel managed to interject, for the umpteenth time, a sidebar about the importance of abstinence.

The minister's wife read aloud from her Bible. "'Do not fear, for I am with you: do not be dismayed, for I am your God. I will strengthen you and help you: I will uphold you with my righteous right hand.'"

Is God with me? Tammy couldn't be certain, given that the adults in her life—her parents, Mrs. Peel, and Reverend Findlay—all expressed such confidence that He favoured their side. And there she was, Tammy King, an army of one. She couldn't count on Dean's grandmother to help her. She'd probably suspect Tammy of being a gold digger.

The possibility of being forced into signing adoption papers had Tammy vibrating like a tuning fork. She couldn't cope with Reverend Findlay. If she spent a second pinned down by the reverend's commanding gaze, he'd make her question her reasoning. Before an hour had gone by, he'd be passing her signed adoption papers to Mrs. Peel, she was sure of it.

The reverend couldn't manipulate her if she wasn't here.

Tammy's eyes cut to the dining room windows. Although the grandfather clock in the commons area had just chimed seven thirty and darkness had fallen, she could still make out the moonlit fencerow on the far side of the road. When would conditions be more perfect?

"Let us bow our heads," the minister's wife said. "Lord we ask that you . . ."

Tammy sent up her own prayer. *God, I need to leave this place. Tonight. Is it the right thing to do? I need a sign.* No sooner had she thought the words than her baby moved, sending a distinct ripple across her belly. The corners of Tammy's mouth lifted. "Thank you," she whispered.

Three hours after Mrs. Peel had walked the hall, calling each girl's name in turn, Tammy stood at the foot of her bed and wrung her hands. Her terry bathrobe hung like drapes on either side of her belly, and the outline of her navel protruded through the thin cotton nightgown. She'd wear her nightclothes out of the building to avoid suspicion in case Mrs. Peel stopped her on the way out. Tammy's mind buzzed with the possibility of all that could go wrong with her plan. "It's going to all work out," she whispered to herself. "One step at a time."

The clock downstairs chimed once. Mrs. Peel must be asleep by now. Tammy pulled her backpack from under the edge of her bed and sprawled it open one last time. She'd packed the Whitman poetry book, Dean's photo, his football jersey, Mr. Hoffman's journal, one change of clothing, her ski jacket, and running shoes. Everything else she'd leave behind.

Tammy closed the zipper and opened her window to a gust of cold air. She hung the backpack over the sill, held her breath, and let go. She watched it land on the ground next to the foundation of the building, then closed the window. Her ears strained for signs that the faint thud may have awakened someone. No one stirred.

She tiptoed into the hallway then closed the bedroom door gently, so as to not make any sound. Her heart raced like a frightened rabbit. She barely allowed herself to breathe on the way past Mrs. Peel's room. *One foot in front of the other.* She looked straight ahead. *Keep going. You can do—*

"Be careful." The signature sharpness of Mrs. Peel's voice jabbed into the dim hallway.

Tammy turned to face Mrs. Peel where she stood inside a shaft of pale light. "Careful?" Tammy repeated. Every nerve in her body crackled.

"You're going downstairs, are you not?"

Tammy's eyes widened.

"Restless?" Mrs. Peel asked.

"Yes. And hungry."

Mrs. Peel pointed at Tammy's stocking feet. "Hold tight to the banister. Those wooden stairs are slippery. A tumble is the last thing we need."

"Right." Tammy gave a curt nod and headed towards the glowing exit sign that marked the stairwell. She allowed herself a glance over her shoulder before rounding onto the first step. The hem of Mrs. Peel's nightgown swooshed back into her room ahead of the closing door.

Tammy's right hand slid along the banister as she hurried to the ground floor. She scooted past the laundry room, then the kitchen and dining room, and through the commons area to the front entrance of the Beatrix Home. She breathed deeply, then turned the lock and let herself outside.

In the lowest crouch she could muster, Tammy scuttled over the frosted grass to where her backpack rested against the house. She pushed her feet into her running shoes and struggled into her jacket.

With the backpack slung over her shoulders, Tammy rushed to the south end of the house. Wind whipped at her face as she crossed the parking area. Everything terrified her at night. Loose boards banged against the carriage house. The white minibus glowed eerily in the moonlight. Dried leaves rattled on tree branches with each new burst of wind.

When her lower belly cramped, Tammy paused in the shadows of the pines to catch her breath. She leaned forward, bracing her hands against her knees, and looked across the neighbouring field. The hardened soil and stubble of dried cornstalks might be treacherous to navigate, but if she crossed the field on a diagonal, she could step onto the road without the risk of being seen from the house. She gathered the edges of her open jacket to her chest and headed off.

Barelegged and shivering, she hurried across the field. The force of the wind increased in the open expanse and numbed her cheeks. Hardened clumps of clay jabbed into the thin rubber soles of her running shoes until she crossed the last furrow.

Tammy's body shook with fear as she looked back in the direction of the Beatrix Home. Her eyes strained to see any flicker of light beyond the stand of pines. There was only darkness. She turned to cross the road but stopped mid-stride.

A female deer scrabbled out of the ditch across from her. They each froze and stared at one another. In the moonlight, the doe appeared otherworldly with its velvety coat and wide, dark eyes. Tammy squinted against the wind and slid a hand beneath her belly. The doe's neck straightened, but instead of bolting, she crossed the road with tender steps and disappeared into the darkness of the empty cornfield.

A feeling of calm swept through Tammy, and she set off down the road towards the yellow point of light.

The pole light in the barnyard bathed Tammy in a yellow cast while she waited in front of the farmhouse. She'd already knocked on the screen door. A dog barked; then a moment later a light came on. The inside door swung open, and a middle-aged woman appeared. A border collie pushed past her legs and pressed its nose against the screen.

"Yes?" Her brow furrowed, and she gathered her sweater across the chest of her nightgown.

"I'm so sorry. It's late . . . but could I use your telephone?" Tammy asked. She wiped her nose on the cuff of her jacket.

"It's after two in the morning," the woman exclaimed, looking Tammy up and down. "Are you alone?" she asked with concern.

"Yes." Tammy's voice cracked. "I really need my mother."

"Well, come in, then." The woman led Tammy into the kitchen and pointed to a telephone mounted on the wall. "My husband's upstairs," she added warily. Then she leaned her back against the edge of the kitchen counter and crossed her arms over her waist. The dog turned in a circle and flopped down on a braided rug at her feet.

Tammy read the phone number sprawled across the palm of her hand and dialed.

"Hello, Mom?" she said in a small voice.

"Who is this?"

"Mom, it's me. Tammy."

"All right," Aunt Eva said slowly.

"Please come and get me." Tammy began to cry. "I know it's a long way from Ashfield . . ."

The farmer's wife took the receiver from her hand and explained the directions to Aunt Eva, then hung up. "She's on her way," the woman said. "I'll put the kettle on."

"I don't want to be a bother," Tammy said.

"No bother at all. I'd have been up in a few hours anyway." She looked at Tammy and shrugged. "A change of life thing, you know. A woman's lot isn't an easy one. It's good that we help each other out."

Tammy pulled a chair away from the table and sat down. The border collie crossed the floor as soon as she sat and leaned against her leg, waiting to be petted.

"Your day's getting better already," the woman said as she lit a burner on the stove. "Whatever your situation may be, dear, it will turn out. Things always do."

Tammy scratched behind the dog's ears and tried to believe it was true.

Thirty minutes later, Aunt Eva appeared at the door wearing a velour track suit and a scarf tied over her hair. She and Tammy thanked the woman for her kindness and trundled out to the car. During the ride home, Tammy explained the events leading up to her call.

"You poor thing," Aunt Eva said. "I'm sorry about the Hoffman boy, but you're certain about keeping the baby?"

"I've made up my mind."

"Your mother's not going to like this," Aunt Eva said with a hint of satisfaction. "But don't worry, Tammy. I can help."

Tammy leaned her forehead against the passenger side window. *One step at a time.*

The rattle and hum of Aunt Eva's automatic garage door opener roused Tammy from her nap. She rubbed the sleep from her eyes as the car eased into one of the two empty bays.

"Will Uncle Cyril mind that I'm here?"

Aunt Eva's eyes welled up. "It'll be fine."

"Are you all right?"

Aunt Eva dipped a hand inside the neck of her jacket to pull a tissue from her brassiere. She dabbed the corners of her eyes. "Let's get you settled, shall we?"

Tammy kicked off her running shoes in the garage and followed Aunt Eva into the house. Pink carpet cushioned her steps. She'd forgotten the opulence of her aunt and uncle's home. The chandeliers, figurines displayed in glass cases, oil paintings in gold frames. Uncle Cyril's grocery stores had always been a source of envy for both her parents.

A shocking sight awaited her on the mirrored wall at the top of the stairs. Tammy stopped to look at her full reflection, a view she hadn't seen since leaving home in July. What a dismal picture she made. Beneath the nightgown, her stomach looked like a balloon trapped under a sheet. The bathrobe hung down the back of her legs, and the cuffs were wadded inside the sleeves of the ski jacket so she could barely bend her arms. Socks drooped around her ankles, and scratches from dried cornstalks in the field crisscrossed her calves.

"You can take Jessica's room," Aunt Eva called from down the hall.

Tammy joined her and let the backpack slide to the floor.

Aunt Eva pulled the curtains open before facing Tammy with a wavy smile. "You must be hungry."

"Not really."

"I suppose we should let your mother know where you are."

Tammy's shoulders dropped. "Please, not yet."

"The Beatrix staff will phone her. She'll be in a state."

"I know," Tammy replied. She imagined her mother's fists pounding against the kitchen counter after receiving the call. "Could you talk to her?"

Aunt Eva smiled softly, and a twinkle returned to her eyes.

Later that morning, Tammy stepped out of the ensuite bathroom, rubbing the ends of her hair with a towel. After a fitful nap and picking at morsels from Aunt Eva's breakfast tray, she'd decided a shower might distract from the dread of facing what lay ahead.

She'd just tugged her maternity pants over her hips when the banging started at the front door.

"Coming," Aunt Eva called. The heels of her sandals clacked across the foyer.

Tammy slipped a T-shirt over her head, then rushed to the bedroom door and opened it slightly.

"Tammy!" Mirabelle shouted.

Tammy sucked in her breath.

"Settle down now," Aunt Eva said. "The child's scared enough as it is."

"I knew the two of you were in cahoots. It's not enough that you've taken from me all these years, now you want my daughter too?"

"I've not taken anything from you."

"Of course you have," Mirabelle said. "Mother never had time for me. It was always *Eva* this and *Eva* that."

"You're a broken record," Eva laughed.

"Ever since we were kids, you've gotten your way. Not this time. Tammy's mine."

"You're a nasty piece of business," Aunt Eva said. "That's why she came to me."

"Thou shalt not covet thy neighbour's house." Mirabelle's voice rose.

"You're very handy with a verse when your back is against the wall. *Love is patient; love is kind.* How about that, huh?"

" *You* should tend to your own family," Mirabelle replied in a sly tone.

The room went quiet.

"Struck a nerve, did I?" Mirabelle continued.

"We're discussing Tammy," Aunt Eva's voice grew strained.

"That's just it. I've been hearing things at Arlene's salon that lead me to believe you're in no position to give advice to anyone. How long were you going to wait to tell me that Cyril's left you?"

"I don't wish to discuss it," Eva sniffled.

"Was it you who put the fool notion into Tammy's head about keeping this baby?"

"No."

"Can you afford to put her up? Maybe Cyril will move his fling in here, and you'll be out on your ear. How long will you be able to sustain your little game of chicken then?”

"My niece will stay here as long as she likes," Aunt Eva said in a shaky voice.

"Tammy!" Mirabelle shouted again. "I know you can hear me. Children shouldn't have children. You're a selfish girl. When you're ready to apologize and act like an adult, come home."

Tammy's insides quivered like jelly. The front door slammed shut, then footsteps crossed the foyer. Seconds later, Aunt Eva's bedroom door closed. Tammy waited a moment, then padded down the hallway and knocked softly. When no answer came, she went downstairs to Uncle Cyril's den. She found a telephone book in the desk drawer and looked up the number for *Robinson* in Narrow Falls. There were three listed, so she dialed the first number and waited for someone to pick up.

"Hello?" a woman answered.

"Is Allan there?" Tammy asked.

"Who may I say is calling?"

"A school friend."

"One minute." A muffled voice called for Allan. The sound of static followed as the receiver changed hands.

"Allan here."

"It's Tammy King. Dean's girlfriend."

"I know who you are. Oh my gosh—"

"Is it true? Is he really gone?" Tammy cried softly into the telephone.

"Yeah. There was a thing at his dad's house. I thought for sure I'd see you there."

"I've been away."

"You should tell Dean's dad about the baby."

The pitch of Tammy's voice shot upwards. "How did you know?"

"Dean. He told me everything," Allan replied.

"Everything?" Tammy leaned into the phone.

"Yes, and Mr. Hoffman is really busted up about Dean. It would really help if he knew there was a kid."

"I promised Dean I wouldn't let his dad near the baby. I can't go back on my word."

"In a town this small, you don't think he'll find out?"

"Allan, swear you won't tell him."

"Not my story to tell."

"I've got to go. Bye, Allan."

"Tammy, you've really got to—"

Tammy hung up the receiver. The last thing she needed was one more person telling her what to do.

23.

"Come on, come on," Floyd muttered. Just as he raised a hand to knock again, the King family's front door jerked open.

Mirabelle stood before him, red-eyed and clutching a ball of spent tissue in one hand. Her vulnerability dissolved the moment she recognized him. "Go to hell!" She retreated into the house and began to shut the door.

Floyd lunged onto the threshold and wedged his right shoe between the edge of the door and the outer frame. "Please, Mirabelle. One minute, I'm begging you."

"Remove your foot before I dial the police." She bounced her weight against the door. "If Lawrence comes down here, you'll be sorry," she hissed. "Because of you, he lost his job."

"My boy's dead," Floyd blurted in desperation. "Where's your compassion?"

The door opened, and Mirabelle sighed heavily. "It's 8:00 a.m.," she scolded.

"I apologize for the hour, but if we could talk for a moment," he replied shakily, "I won't return uninvited. You have my word."

She thrust an index finger at him. "One minute."

"I believe your daughter and my son were spending time together over the spring and summer months."

"That's not possible." The corner of her mouth twitched. "I would have known."

Floyd thought a moment. "Perhaps I could speak with Tammy."

"Like I told you yesterday, she's away at school." Mirabelle began to ease the door closed again.

"Then give me her phone number," he said quickly. "I can—"

The latch clicked shut.

Floyd knocked again and shouted, "I just want to ask her about Dean." The door whammed open, and he jumped back. "Lawrence!"

"You've got some nerve showing your face around here."

"I should have come later in the day, but—"

"They sacked me, you know." Lawrence glared at him. "Only five years away from a full pension."

"Please ask Tammy to contact me."

"What connection does my daughter have to you?"

"Actually, it's more to do with my son."

"Your son?" Lawrence's head craned forward.

Mirabelle stood behind his elbow. A look of panic had returned to her eyes.

"Dean passed away . . ."

"Jesus, Floyd." Lawrence's brows pinched together.

"Someone in the neighbourhood saw Tammy visiting frequently while I was at work." Floyd noted the birth of an idea in Lawrence's softening expression. "It seems our children were *very* close."

When Lawrence cast an incredulous look at Mirabelle, she turned away, shamefaced, and retreated deeper into the house. He exhaled slowly before responding. "I'm sorry for your loss, but I can't help you. Tammy wasn't involved with your son."

"But you haven't asked her."

Lawrence folded his arms across his chest and regarded Floyd with a steely countenance. "You need to leave."

Floyd's hands shook as he backed down the stairs. He paused next to the garage after the front door slammed, then strode towards the street. A woman walked slowly past the front yard and paused at the end of the driveway.

"Trouble with the Kings?" she asked, falling into step beside him as he continued along the sidewalk.

Floyd wiped a handkerchief across his eyes and cast a look at her. "A misunderstanding," he replied.

"They're a quirky lot."

"You know them?"

"I live next door," she said. "Lots of strangeness going on in that house."

Floyd's eyes cut to her face. "Really?"

"I'm not one to gossip, but they zipped that daughter out of town at the end of July," she said, leaning towards Floyd and snapping her fingers, "just like that."

"Tammy's gone off to school," he replied.

"Not with one suitcase she hasn't," the woman said with an air of knowing. "I saw Lawrence loading the trunk the morning she left. Not a single box *plus* she hasn't been home once for a visit."

"That is odd."

"Aren't you going to ask me what school she's *supposed* to be attending?"

"You know?"

"Wainright College over in Crompton. A letter meant for Tammy made its way to my postbox by mistake." She winked. "I'm Blanche Clark, by the way. And you are . . . ?"

"Floyd Hoffman."

"Ohhh." Her mouth drew into a tight circle. "You're not a very popular fellow these days. What business do you have with the Kings?"

"If you see Tammy, would you tell her to contact me?"

Creases deepened at the corners of Blanche's eyes, and her lips stretched across her teeth. "I'd be delighted to."

On the walk home, Floyd tried to make sense of everything he'd heard that morning. A strange moment had passed between Lawrence and his wife. Floyd could tell by her expression she'd been caught at something, although he'd no idea what. Their vehement denial convinced him that Vivian's assertion was correct: Tammy had been Dean's girlfriend.

Had Dean been in love? Puppy love, at least? The lingerie he'd discovered pointed towards intimacy. Nothing could make Floyd happier, not that he could ask the King girl about such a personal detail.

Blanche Clark could be a tremendous help. He suspected she and Mirabelle got along like oil and water. Blanche impressed him as being someone who might be gratified by aiding the enemy, as it were. But what if it took weeks before Blanche saw Tammy? He couldn't wait that long. There must be another way to reach her without breaking his promise to stay clear of the house.

He'd begin with Allan.

First thing after returning home, Floyd rummaged through the odds-and-ends drawer for a takeout flyer from the Narrow Falls Diner. He dialed their phone number, then paced the hallway with the receiver pressed hard against his ear.

"Good morning, Narrow Falls Diner."

"Is this Mrs. Robinson? Allan's mother?" Floyd asked.

"Yes. Is something wrong?"

"No. It's Floyd Hoffman calling."

"Oh yes, Allan told me about Dean," she said. "So sorry for your loss."

"Could Allan come by? I'd like him to have something of Dean's. I'm here all day, so anytime . . ."

"I'll let him know."

For the rest of the morning, Floyd's thoughts swirled like an eddy. Every few minutes, he looked out to the street in frustration. What was keeping Allan? Floyd tried distracting himself by reviewing the box of research he'd collected on the mill, but his thoughts kept turning to Tammy King. What could she tell him about Dean?

Documents and file folders carpeted the bedroom floor by the time end-of-day sun filtered through the curtains. Floyd tipped his head back and waited for the last drops of his morning coffee to trickle from his cup. He rubbed his eyes, then clumped downstairs to stretch his legs. The plate of leftovers Marian had insisted on leaving after the memorial gathering sat undisturbed on the top shelf in the refrigerator. Food was the last thing on his mind.

Darkness loomed as Floyd parted the curtains and looked outside. Still no Allan. "Damn it!" Floyd turned away and pounded his fists against the table.

Shortly after eight o'clock, Strum whined and nosed his empty water bowl across the linoleum. Floyd picked it up, and as he ran the tap to refresh the water dish, a knock sounded at the door.

Allan greeted him with a bag of day-old pastries. "Hey, Mr. Hoffman. Mom said you called."

It was all Floyd could do to stop himself from launching into an interrogation about Tammy King. "Yes, about a keepsake. I should have thought of it earlier, but . . ."

"No worries."

Floyd led the way to Dean's room and waited at the door. Allan entered tentatively and stood at the foot of the bed with both thumbs hooked through his belt loops. "That's all wrong," he said, eyeing the urn perched on the platform of books. "Dean hated reading."

The viewing of his private farce through someone else's lens left Floyd feeling vulnerable.

"He *would* dig sitting on his guitar case," Allan said.

"Oh," Floyd replied, wishing it had been his idea.

Allan examined the items strewn across the top of Dean's dresser. He chose a pair of sunglasses, the ones Floyd had bought for the day at Brewster's Gorge, and a guitar pick.

"That's all you want?

"Sure," Allan said.

Floyd looked back at the urn.

"Well, I should get going. Some friends are expecting me."

"Wait," Floyd said a little too loudly. "Was Dean seeing Tammy King?"

Allan looked like a kid who'd been caught stealing from his mother's purse.

"My neighbour saw her visiting a lot over the summer."

"I'm not sure," Allan replied, staring at the floor.

"Have you any idea how I could reach her? I just want to ask about her last conversations with Dean."

The boy shook his head.

"Is there something you're not telling me?"

Allan's face wiped itself clean like a blank slate. Too blank, Floyd thought.

"Hellooo," a female voice called from the kitchen.

"Marian?" Floyd leaned into the hallway.

"Yeah, it's me. The door was unlocked, so I let myself in.

"I'll be right there." Floyd glanced at the sunglasses dangling from Allan's right hand. "If you'd like something else of Dean's, let me know."

"Will do."

They returned to the kitchen, where Marian stood holding a plate of cookies. "Allan, this is a pleasant surprise."

"Sorry, I'm in a bit of a rush." Allan looked over his shoulder at Floyd before darting past Marian and out of the house. "See ya."

"What was that all about? The boy couldn't get out of here fast enough."

"He's off to see friends. That's all," Floyd said, stepping closer to look out the screen door.

"If you say so."

Allan raised his collar and leaned into the wind as he walked away from the house. When he disappeared from view, Floyd shut the inside door and tried to conceal his disappointment before dealing with Marian. He wanted to be left alone.

"I brought your favourite—date-filled oatmeal cookies." She smiled and smoothed the plastic wrap over the plate. "I remembered."

Floyd's face reddened. Marian had baked that sort of cookie for his and Bonnie's picnics. They were indeed his favourite. He recalled years ago peeling wax paper away from the sticky filling.

"Thank you, Marian."

"Oh, they're just cookies." She waved him off, her eyes shining.

"I'm talking about everything else. You were so good to Bonnie."

"She was like a sister to me. Now it's just you and I," she said.

"And the memorial too . . ." Floyd's voice broke.

Marian held out the plate of cookies and regarded him expectantly.

"Have you time for tea?" Floyd asked, secretly hoping she'd decline. This emotional business exhausted him.

"I do," she answered brightly.

In short order, they depleted polite conversation about the weather and renovation progress at the Brookman estate. Her reaction to Vivian Parker's story about Tammy King visiting Dean disappointed Floyd; she didn't appear to grasp its significance. When the spotlight finally turned on him, Floyd began shifting uneasily in his seat.

"How are you doing—really?" Marian asked with genuine concern.

"Well . . ." Floyd raised his palms and shrugged.

"Are you sleeping and eating as you should?"

"Yes, to both of the above," he tried to assure her with a lie. "And how are you doing?"

"All right, I suppose. Becoming a jobless nomad has been a step down for me, but I'll survive." She paused to sip her tea. "I didn't hear so much as a 'thanks for your service' from anyone."

"Still living with your cousin, then?"

"Yes. Phyllis has been a dear, but I worry about wearing out my welcome. It's been nearly two months," she said, running a finger along the edge of her saucer. "I should really look for a place of my own. The last thing I want is to become a burden, but I just don't know where to start." She waited a moment before adding, "I've never lived on my own, you see."

Floyd detected the subterranean intent of her statement. She hoped he'd rescue her with an invitation to live at his house. "The wind is kicking up, and it's beginning to rain," he said, looking outdoors at the swaying pines across the street. "I should drive you home now."

"All right," Marian whispered, then left the table to gather her purse and coat from the newel post. While she dressed, Floyd dashed outside to warm the car.

The rhythmic squawk of windshield wipers filled the silence between Floyd and Marian as he reversed out of the driveway. A few blocks away from the house, he voiced the thought that had been gnawing at him all day.

"Mirabelle King is lying."

"Mm-hmm," Marian replied, looking through the passenger side window at the fading daylight.

"The woman's infuriating. She expects me to believe every word that falls from her mouth like it's the gospel truth."

"The weather is letting up. I could have walked home, after all."

"The girl's been in my house. I know it." Floyd said nothing of the silk negligee he'd discovered in the guest bedroom.

"What do you expect to gain by talking to her?"

"I don't know."

"If you are looking for absolution, you're not going to find it from this girl. She's a child."

"I know that," he mumbled.

"This is my corner." Marian tapped a finger against the window.

Floyd tapped the brakes and cranked the wheel sharply to the right.

Marian braced her hands against the dashboard, and her purse slid from her lap. "Oh golly." She righted herself, then pointed at the two-story house ahead. "Stop there."

Floyd parked his car across the mouth of the driveway. He regarded Marian's forlorn expression, then glanced towards a lit window on the upper floor. The sheer curtains parted, and Phyllis's face peered out for a moment, then disappeared.

"I'll get the door for you," Floyd offered, unbuckling his seatbelt.

"Wait." Marian frowned. "It's *possible* that Vivian Parker is wrong and the King girl has never set foot in your house."

"She's the girl," Floyd said, nodding his head emphatically. "I know it."

"Well," Marian continued, "maybe she dropped schoolbooks off for Dean. Perhaps there was no romance at all."

Floyd sank back in his seat and stared over the dashboard. "There's only one reason for letting a girl into your house. Because you like her." His stomach dropped when he looked at Marian again. In the semidarkness, her face had transformed into a schoolgirl's, full of delight and hope. She leaned across the gearshift and pressed her lips to his cheek, just above the right corner of his mouth.

"Marian, I—"

She touched a finger to his lips, then, without waiting for him to get the door, stepped out of the car.

While brushing his teeth that night, Floyd touched his face where Marian's lips had been. What had the kiss meant? What did he want it to mean? If she aspired to romance, her timing stunk. His grief should preclude any thoughts of his own happiness. And yet he couldn't stop thinking of her. He spat in the sink and wiped his mouth. After hanging up the towel, he paused to scrutinize his reflection in the mirror, wondering what Marian might see in him.

"Dean's right," he said aloud. "You are an asshole."

Floyd switched the light off and walked back to his room. He rounded through the door and stopped short at the foot of his bed. "Strum!"

The dog lifted its head from Bonnie's pillow.

"Get down," Floyd shouted, pointing at the floor.

Strum's head sagged forward as he climbed down and skulked into the hallway.

For eight years, Bonnie's side of the bed had been a shrine. Now the covers were mounded in creases like ripples of silt on a shoreline.

After smoothing the sheets and plumping Bonnie's pillow, Floyd rested on his side of the bed. He remembered the warmth of her breath against his skin and how she'd lie tangled in the sheets, unable to sleep after lovemaking.

"Read to me," Bonnie would say.

"More Whitman?" he'd ask, knowing full well that's what she wanted.

"Of course."

He'd heft the book from beneath the edge of the bed and rest it against his knees while Bonnie lay back on her pillow, eyes closed.

"'Perfection,'" Floyd read. "'Only themselves understand themselves and the like of themselves. As only souls understand souls.'"

"If only *themselves* understand *themselves*, they must be difficult for others to understand," Bonnie had commented once.

"It takes one to know one." Floyd's index finger had underlined the words as he repeated the last line. *"As only souls understand souls."*

"I should imagine a soul inside a body is like fireflies bumping against the inside of a jar," she'd mused.

He'd kissed the top of her head. "I think people recognize like souls intuitively."

"What if one person's soul is buried so deeply beneath layers of peculiarity that no one understands them?"

Even now, he could recall his answer. "They should trust there is another soul—one in their life already or soon to come along—that *will* understand their soul, not through a logical process, but through some miracle of the heart."

He would never claim to be a spiritual man, but he couldn't help wondering if the timing of this memory held meaning for the present. Did Marian perceive a likeness between their souls?

Dean must have seen pieces of himself reflected in Tammy King. Maybe by speaking to her, Floyd could regain lost fragments of his son. He reclined and swept his fingers under the bed, where the poetry book should be. He couldn't feel it. Curious, he knelt on the floor and lifted the bed skirt. The book was gone.

Floyd sat on the floor, absently touching the thin cotton of his pajama pocket. Inside was the curl of paper on which Bonnie had scrawled *Themselves.* He looked around the room, trying to think where he might have stashed the book. Tomorrow, he'd search the house. *The book must be here, somewhere.*

Guilt nipped at him when his eyes lit on the cardboard box sitting in a corner of his room. The information he'd collected about the paper mill represented a loose end that needed tying up. He'd spent so many hours clipping newspaper articles, typing letters to the editor in duplicate, and photographing malformed fish bobbing in yellow froth at the river's edge. His correspondence with the Ministry of the Environment had begun to bear fruit in late spring. Their responses alluded to an interest in some chlorine-related research being conducted in Swiss paper mills.

He'd been naïve to think he could go up against McLelland alone. No one else in Narrow Falls seemed to want change. They'd rather disregard toxic odours wafting from the mill or the sulfur stench rising off the river. The obituary notices Floyd had collected for nearly a decade were the canaries in the mineshaft. People needed to see the connection between local deaths and the mill emissions.

His outcry could be the catalyst for change. The lives of someone else's wife or child may be spared in the future. Or he could strive for vengeance. Dean would have endorsed the latter cause. The dog rambled into the room and dropped onto the floor.

"Tomorrow's a new day, eh, Strum? I'm going to finish what I've started, and that includes finding Tammy King."

The next morning, Floyd rose at five o'clock and carried the box of documents downstairs to the dining room table. He unfurled a street map of Narrow Falls next to a second map of the town and surrounding area, then weighed down the corners. After organizing the obituary clippings by date and surname, he assigned a number to each of the deceased and began recording their number at the corresponding home address on each map. If he knew they'd been mill employees, he circled their number with a yellow pencil crayon he'd found in Dean's school things.

Around eight o'clock, Floyd heard the laughter of children on their way to school. His thoughts turned to Tammy King again. What might the Kings tell their daughter about his visit to their house? He worried that Mirabelle and Lawrence might poison the girl against him. He needed to speak to her before that could happen.

An idea overtook Floyd. He carried a pen and paper to the telephone and dialed the operator.

"I'd like the number for Wainright College in Crompton." He jotted the number and dialed.

"Good morning, Office of the Registrar."

"I need to get in touch with a student, Tammy King."

"Please hold." Instrumental music played softly until the voice returned. "I'll need more information, sir. Your relationship to Tammy King?"

Floyd hesitated. "I'm her father."

"Your name and address?"

He closed his eyes and inhaled deeply. "Lawrence King, 12 Chestnut Street, Narrow Falls, Ontario." He remembered the house number from visiting Mirabelle yesterday. Fingers crossed, the clerk wouldn't insist on the postal code as well.

"Mr. King, our records show that Tammy's acceptance has been deferred to September 1982 due to illness. If this is not the—"

Floyd slammed the receiver into the cradle.

Where in the hell was Tammy King?

July 1968

The scorching temperatures drew a crowd to downtown Narrow Falls that day, effectively shredding Floyd's hope for a quiet afternoon with Bonnie and Dean. Several other families lazed beneath the maples of Riverside Park and cooled off in the river.

Floyd removed his glasses briefly and wiped his face with a handkerchief. He backed away from the river's edge and looked over his shoulder to check on Bonnie. There she was, twenty feet away, in a dress he'd never seen before, laying out their lunch of pickled herring, rye bread, and apples. Her gold sandals, with their square two-inch heels, sat neatly on one corner of the picnic blanket.

Two small boys zoomed away from the playground area at the centre of the park and tore past Floyd to the strip of sand along the river. Before they stepped into the tea-coloured water, he noticed the fly ash dusting the back of their swim trunks. They joined two other boys in the water, already engaged in lobbing gobs of the yellow froth that gathered daily along the banks.

"Hey," Floyd called to the boys, waving his arms above his head. "Put that down!"

They looked up at him as if he'd spoken in a foreign language. Foam dripped from their faces and hands.

Floyd shook his head. "Don't touch that stuff. It comes from over there." He pointed east to the paper mill looming on the opposite bank of the river. Its smokestack was bleeding puffs of brown haze into the sky. Twenty-four hours a day, the mill churned out the combined roar of drying fans and pulp refiners along with the jarring racket of wood chippers.

"My daddy works over there," said the smallest boy.

His older friend splashed him. "Everybody's dad works there, stupid."

Next to Floyd, a portly woman appeared wearing a swimsuit and a flowered bathing cap. "Tell you what, mister. You look after your family, and I'll look after mine." Then she turned to the boys. "It's a free country. Throw that foam and let's have some fun." She plowed into the water full tilt, splashing the boys as she went.

A father entered the water with his three children in tow. The mother followed after them. Floyd noticed that she watched him from the corner of her eye as she tiptoed across the sand. He shook his head and slumped towards Bonnie.

She was slicing apples when he reached the corner of their blanket. "The weather is nice. We were supposed to have a *nice* day with a *nice* picnic at the *nice* park," she said. "Quit bitching about the mill!"

"I was only talking," Floyd said.

"About the usual?" she asked, standing to face him.

"Yes. People need to reflect."

Bonnie laid the knife blade across one wrist. "I swear I'll do it if you don't shut up." Her eyes filled with tears. "Your bullshit theories are sucking the life out of me."

"Okay!" Floyd raised his palms to the sky.

Her face puckered, and she tossed the knife onto the blanket.

A few feet away, Dean sat cross-legged in the grass with his hands clamped over his ears. His Johnny West and Geronimo action figures leaned inside the fortress of his legs. He remained a quiet audience until his father remembered him there.

"Dean," Floyd said, reaching a hand towards Bonnie's right shoulder, "your mother is—"

"Don't touch me!" Bonnie jerked away as if she'd been scalded. When she stepped back to escape his touch, her right heel caught on the corner of the cooler. One minute she was standing, the next she was on the ground, staring up at him with a dazed look.

Floyd offered a hand to help Bonnie to her feet, but her eyes widened and she scrambled farther away. His brow lowered. Were people watching? He looked around the park and towards the town library on the western edge of the park where a couple had stopped on the walkway to gawk. His knuckles pressed against the legs of his twill slacks while he considered his next move.

Tears slid down Dean's cheeks, and his bottom lip rolled out, glossy and pink.

"Baby, come here." Bonnie stretched her arms out.

Dean scuttled towards her with Johnny West and Geronimo grasped tightly in either hand. She pulled him against her chest and crushed her cheek against his dark curls. "Deany, I'm so sorry. Daddy's in a bit of a mood today." She held the boy's shoulders and smiled, even as her eyes leaked tears.

Floyd sensed more eyes watching. A pair of young women glared at him from their bench next to the seesaws. "Let's go home," he said.

"I don't want to go home. We haven't had our swim yet, have we, baby?" Bonnie tweaked Dean's chin and plopped him onto the blanket.

"Not today!" Floyd chucked their food, item by item, into the cooler and closed the lid.

The women at the playground were speaking to a brawny mill worker and a boy Floyd had seen around town. They were all looking in Floyd's direction.

"Deany won't be a baby forever, and I want him to have all the fun he can. Next year he starts school." Bonnie stood and wriggled out of her dress. "New bathing suit. I saw Elizabeth Taylor wearing the same one in a magazine. What d'ya think?"

Of course he liked it. So did every other red-blooded male in viewing distance.

From a blanket a few yards away, a man looked Bonnie over from head to toe. When Floyd glared at him, he turned back to his family.

"Don't you like it?" she asked.

"You know how I feel about swimming in the river so close to the mill," Floyd said in a low voice.

He glanced past her towards the playground. Both women still looked on worriedly, but the man lumbered towards him along with the boy, a smaller version of himself. Floyd's stomach dropped.

Bonnie took the action figures from Dean's hands and tossed them on the blanket. "You can't stop me from taking a little dip with my son," she said, yanking Dean's T-shirt over his head.

"*Our* son," Floyd said. Bonnie snatched Dean's hand with a determined look, but Floyd caught her arm as she stalked past on her way to the shore. "Bonnie, listen—"

"Ma'am," the man interjected, "is everything all right here?" He flashed a warning look at Floyd.

"Everything is just fine," Floyd replied, dropping Bonnie's arm.

"I'm asking the lady," the man said. His gaze darted to her cleavage when she lavished him with a provocative smile.

"I'm doing just fine—now." Bonnie's chin dropped slightly, and she peered at him through her lashes. "My son and I are going for a dip."

"Actually, we're leaving," Floyd said. He picked her dress up from the ground and wound it around her shoulders. "Bonnie, let's go."

She flung the dress aside and pouted theatrically. "I just want to have some fun."

Dean scooted around the grown-ups to retrieve his action figures from the blanket, then plunked down on the lid of the cooler. He swung his legs—*left, right, left, right*—banging his heels against the metal.

"Bonnie, listen to me," Floyd began.

Dean kicked faster.

"Cut her some slack," the man said menacingly. "For Chrissake, what's a swim gonna hurt?"

Floyd regarded the well-muscled arms before answering. "This is a matter between my wife and I." He glanced at the boy and added, "You can go back to the park and play with your son."

The boy looked to his father with uncertainty, then back at Floyd. "I'm too big for the park," he said, puffing out his chest.

"Kenny, be quiet." The man stepped forward until mere inches separated him from Floyd. "We don't take orders from you. And neither does she." His hand shot forward and shoved hard against Floyd's chest.

Floyd reeled backwards and landed hard on the ground. Once he'd given his head a shake, he scrambled to his feet and braced himself.

"Bugger off," Bonnie snapped. She lunged between the men to where Dean sat round-eyed and quaking on the cooler.

"My apologies, ma'am." The man recovered from her rebuff and glared at Floyd. "Asshole," he muttered before stalking off with his son.

Bonnie shoved her feet into her gold sandals and stooped to fasten the buckles. "I married a soul-sucking wet blanket." She stood and hoisted Dean onto one hip. "Dean and I are coming back here—without you—and we'll swim any damned time we like!"

Silence was the best response. Floyd knew it well. She'd take it all back tomorrow, and things would be all sugar and spice again.

Dean blinked at Floyd, then buried his face in the cloud of his mother's dark hair.

Smatterings of applause rose up from onlookers as Bonnie tore across the park towards Water Street. Floyd gathered the corners of the blanket into a ball, which he bunched under one arm, then hefted the cooler with the other and tromped in the direction his wife had taken.

Up ahead, Bonnie carried Dean across the pitted asphalt of the street, then continued along Main. Floyd had parked their car on Main Street outside the Narrow Falls Diner. Surely, she'd wait for him there.

Heads turned to follow Bonnie's scantily clad trek through town. Three old men were smoking cigarettes outside Tony Monteiro's pub at the northeast corner of Main and Water. Two of them leaned around the corner of the building to watch her sashay along the sidewalk.

Floyd rushed across the street and hollered after her when she blew past their car. "Bonnie, stop!" Only Dean responded by lifting his face from his mother's shoulder. He issued a stinging look Floyd had often referred to as the "how-could-you" face.

"You giving her grief again, Hoffman?" the first smoker said as Floyd struggled to open his car door.

"If you can't manage her, send her my way," a second voice shouted. The other men chuckled.

Muscles tightened across Floyd's chest. No one understood.

By the time Floyd parceled the cooler and the blanket into the backseat of the car, Bonnie had passed the stationery shop and would soon reach Doc Gillespie's office at the end of the block. He fired the engine of the Volkswagen Beetle and reversed out from between the gas-guzzlers parked on either side of him. Once he'd shifted to first gear, he cranked the driver's side window down and followed slightly behind his wife.

Along the street, the curious leaned through shop doors and halted on the sidewalk to watch her hourglass figure parading past in two-inch heels and a bathing suit that didn't hide any secrets. Bonnie's hair hung down the centre of her back in a dark mass of wild curls. In Floyd's opinion, her beauty outranked that of any other woman in town.

Bonnie cast a look at their car. "Stop following me," she called tearfully over her shoulder. "Go home."

"No. I'm not leaving," he answered.

An air horn blasted behind Floyd. His eyes cut to the rearview mirror, now filled by the grill of a logging truck. He waved his left arm through the window, signaling the driver to pass. The cab rolled by, its engine churning out throaty rumbles while chains clanked against its empty flatbed trailer.

Floyd maintained his plodding pace to the south end of Main, where he waited for Bonnie to cross the street in front of him and press towards their house.

She pretended not to see him. And he pretended not to notice.

A short time later, the Volkswagen sputtered to a stop in front of the narrow carriage house squatting at the top of Floyd's driveway. He squeezed his eyes shut and leaned back against the seat. After several deep breaths, he got out of the car.

On his way to the porch, he saw Bonnie trudging along the sidewalk with a sandal dangling from both hands, and Dean lagging slightly behind, an action figure gripped in either fist. By the time Floyd pulled back the screen door and unlocked the house, Bonnie had unlatched the gate and begun climbing the porch steps.

She paused to regard him with a profound look of sadness that made him uneasy. Then she continued into the house, up the stairs, and out of sight.

Dean stood in the doorway. With his tousled hair and sunburned shoulders, he resembled one of those feral boys from *Lord of the Flies*. "Where's she going?" he asked.

"Up. Like usual."

Dean was looking at Floyd with that face again. "You should be nicer to Mommy."

"I *am* nice to her."

For several seconds, Dean looked at the braided mat beneath his feet. When he raised his eyes to meet his father's, he said, "I don't like you."

"Not right now, perhaps. But tomorrow, you will love me again."

"Tomorrow, I will hate you," Dean replied calmly, then dropped his toys on the floor and scooted soundlessly up the stairs.

No need to chase after him, Floyd thought. If given sufficient time to be alone, Dean would forget what he'd been angry about. Hunger would get the better of him, and the smell of dinner cooking would lure him to the kitchen. After all, the boy couldn't stay angry forever.

24.

From the corner of her eye, Tammy caught the blur of a fuchsia dress swooshing past the kitchen door as Aunt Eva led the real estate agent on a second tour of the living room. She'd been all through the house with him, showing off every cupboard and stretch of crown moulding. The Realtor's business card lay next to Tammy's lunch plate. *Clay Houghton: Real Estate King.* Tammy dreaded what his visit may be signaling. If the house was sold, where would that leave her?

She licked a smear of peanut butter from her thumb and pushed the empty sandwich plate across the white marble counter of the breakfast bar. If things had turned out differently, she might have been at home on Christmas break or maybe walking amid the holiday bustle of Toronto streets with Dean. Instead, Tammy sat on a chrome-legged stool in her aunt's opulent kitchen, looking through French doors at snow accumulating on the pool cover.

In Aunt Eva, she'd found her port in the storm. Things had gone smoothly up until now except for the initial awkwardness of explaining to Cousin Jessica about being pregnant, living in her old bedroom, and dressing in Uncle Cyril's track pants. Her cousin cried foul when she learned her old crib and a box of baby clothes she'd worn would be on loan to Tammy. "So what? She can't figure out how to use a condom, and now she gets my stuff?"

The hard feelings didn't seem to bother Aunt Eva. She'd laid a hand over her heart and said, "It's like you're sisters."

Aunt Eva's liberal take on life contrasted Mirabelle's constant refrain about paternity, expenses, and the future. According to her divorce lawyer, Uncle Cyril's affair had left her in the catbird seat. Aunt Eva aimed to soak him for every last cent she could get, or at least that was the plan. "Never worry about money," she told Tammy. "There's always more when you know where to look."

Tammy tipped forward in her seat to get a better view of the real estate agent. His fancy suit and toothy smile reminded Tammy of one of those motivational speakers from late-night television.

"I'm seeing great bones here, Eva," he said.

"Really?" Aunt Eva's hand touched Clay's shoulder briefly before fluttering to the diamond pendant at her neck. "I worry that the house might be a bit old and dated."

"You're far too modest."

"Not saying I want to sell, but if I did, what do you think is a reasonable asking price?" Aunt Eva's voice tinkled like the crystal drops on one of her chandeliers.

"A lot of new buyers appreciate the craftsmanship found in a mature home." He gave her one of those salesman smiles, then scribbled something on his clipboard and turned it towards her.

Aunt Eva sucked in her breath. "That much?"

"If you were to put it on the market, I suspect you'd attract a lot of interest."

She giggled, and all Tammy could think was how jealous Mirabelle would be that her sister was flirting with a handsome man nearly ten years her junior.

When Aunt Eva noticed Tammy sitting in the next room, she looped her arm through Clay's and escorted him to the foyer. They spoke in hushed voices while Tammy finished her glass of milk. The front door opened and closed, and a car engine revved in the driveway.

"So what did you think of Clay?" Aunt Eva's eyes sparkled as she swept into the kitchen.

"He seems nice. Are you selling the house?"

"Oh, I don't know. Who wants to think of anything so serious?" Aunt Eva opened the refrigerator door and pulled out a half-empty bottle of chardonnay.

"Uhhh!" Tammy's eyes widened, and she clutched the edge of the counter with both hands. Muscles cinched her belly with a suddenness that caught her off guard.

"Everything okay?"

"I'm not sure."

"If it was anything to worry about, you'd *know*. Trust me."

The tension soon released Tammy's stomach, and she sat tall against the backrest of the stool, massaging her sides.

"He's invited me to have dinner with him sometime," Aunt Eva said. "He knows a cute little place where they play jazz music."

"Will you go?"

"Maybe. Sure. Why not?" Aunt Eva poured a glass, then screwed the top back on the bottle. She took a sip and set the glass down. "Your mother phoned again. She wants you to call her when you go into labour."

Of course she does, Tammy thought. Mirabelle hoped to pounce when she was most vulnerable. Given the opportunity, her mother would storm the hospital, outrank Aunt Eva, and design a plan to tear the baby from Tammy's life. In her mother's devious mind, the battle hadn't been lost yet. The more distance Tammy gained from her mother, the easier it became to recognize her agenda. She was her mother's daughter, after all, and capable of countering with her own ploy—rallying the troops.

"That's not happening," Tammy said. "She can ask as many times as she likes. I'm not changing my mind."

"Atta girl. Stick to your guns," Aunt Eva said, right on cue. She could always be counted upon to side against her sister. She'd become something more than Tammy's ally, a cross between a second mother and a best friend.

They sat and watched the snow drifting against the pool fence.

"Pain gone?"

"Almost."

"Didn't I tell you?" Aunt Eva raised her glass and patted Tammy's shoulder. "It's nothing. You're not due for two weeks, kiddo."

"Two weeks . . ." Tammy repeated. She'd never so much as kept a house plant alive, yet soon after the calendar flipped to the new year, she'd be holding a living creature in her arms. A tiny, helpless being that would depend on her for everything—food, a home, guidance. She'd been reading through baby and parenting books. The information overwhelmed her, so she often flipped through the photographs and read what she predicted were the most useful sections. She needed to know so many things, and time was running out.

Aunt Eva leaned across the breakfast bar, the deep valley between her breasts on full display. "Don't look so worried. Ready or not, this kid's coming. You're a smart girl. You'll figure it out as you go."

"I will," Tammy replied with a catch in her voice.

"All the same, be sure to give me a heads-up before the serious labour arrives. Hattersburg is an hour's drive in good weather." Aunt Eva burst into laughter. She picked up the wineglass in one hand while the other waved in front of her as if she were fending off a ridiculous idea. "We don't want to deliver a baby in my car."

"My birthing book says I'll have several hours after the first pain till the actual delivery. There shouldn't be a problem."

"Oh, honey, you're so cute." Aunt Eva set her glass on the counter, then cupped Tammy's face with both hands and patted her cheeks.

The gesture, meant to comfort, left Tammy imagining the worst.

For the next two nights, Tammy's worries kept her awake until the small hours of the morning. She regretted not asking Leslie Benton more questions about the experience of pushing a baby from her body. She was the only person Tammy knew who'd had one recently and the only person she felt remotely comfortable questioning. The process couldn't be as easy as the clinical diagrams in the baby books showed. On the other hand, movies made childbirth look like medieval torture, women hollering and blood everywhere. If it were that bad, the world would be underpopulated by now. Who would go through that a second and third time?

"Birth was a piece of cake. In fact, I slept through the whole thing," Aunt Eva had told her, offering zero insight into natural birth. She'd opted for sedation before the pain became too severe.

"I laboured for over twenty-two hours without medication, and I never uttered a single peep," Mirabelle had told Tammy many times, "even though you nearly tore me in half." A you-owe-me expression always accompanied the telling of this story.

Part of what kept sleep at bay was imagining the dreaded first conversation she'd need to have with her parents. Aunt Eva couldn't hold Mirabelle and Lawrence off forever. They'd spent part of her father's buyout from the mill on her stay at the Beatrix Home only to have her run off. At some point, she'd offer herself up for an obligatory tongue-lashing, but first, she needed an airtight life plan, something to demonstrate she'd thought this all through. Just a couple of months to line things up.

One thing was for sure—she wouldn't be attending university next fall as her parents had hoped. If Tammy was going to be someone's parent, she needed to do it on her own terms, even if it meant sacrifice. She wanted to be self-sufficient—eventually—and that meant getting a job and saving enough money to leave her aunt's house and rent a cute little apartment for herself and the baby. Hopefully, Aunt Eva's hospitality would last until then. She seemed about to embark on a new relationship, and a crying baby upstairs would not make for a romantic evening. It occurred to Tammy, for the first time, that romance may be one of the things she was destined to do without. How many guys would want to date a girl who toted a baby everywhere?

Zero.

Dean would be happy with that status quo. He'd blown up at her after learning that she'd offered to tutor one of his football friends. His teammate was flunking out of calculus, and she'd been looking forward to some pocket money.

"Drop him. You don't know this guy like I do," Dean had said. "One minute you'll be solving for x, and the next he'll have his tongue down your throat."

It had annoyed her to give in to his demand, but she had anyway, as always. He'd schemed about moving her into his grandmother's home with no consideration for what she might have wanted. A slow anger had begun to burn around the edge of her affection for Dean. He'd left her holding the bag. She'd stay true to her promise of raising the baby, no matter the cost. Then there was her promise to not let Dean's father near their child. How she'd accomplish that in a town the size of Narrow

Falls, she'd no idea. Maybe Dean had been right. Maybe she did need to leave town. When her thoughts circled back to missing him, her anger was doused by nostalgia. What a horrible person she'd been to think ill of someone who'd recently died. Remorse plodded through her mind, making sleep even more elusive.

On her third night of fitful sleep, Tammy dreamt of sitting in a small boat set adrift on a river. Her bare feet rested in a skim of dark water spreading across the bottom of the hull. The dream continued in a pleasant manner until she suddenly noticed water lapping around her calves. She began to panic when the lace hem of her skirt floated around her knees like jellyfish. A voice called her name from the stern. Dean reclined in the rear of the boat, resting his elbows behind him. "You shouldn't be here," she said. You're dead."

A searing pain roused Tammy from her sleep. She held her breath until the deep burning sensation ended, then lifted herself upright and ran a hand over her nightgown and the bedding. Both were damp.

"Aunt Eva!" Tammy leaned against the headboard and rubbed her belly. A spasm of pain hit her hard. She cried out at the shock of it. "Eva, come quick," she shouted.

A few minutes passed before the hall light switched on. Her aunt appeared in the doorway wearing a leopard-print negligee. A black satin sleeping mask stretched across her forehead. "What is it?"

"I think my water broke."

"Well, what are you waiting for?" Aunt Eva said, throwing her arms in the air. "It's showtime."

The first half of the journey to the hospital was spent bumping over gravel back roads. Snow zinged at the windshield. Beyond the reach of the headlights lay the darkness of predawn. Tammy hugged her ski jacket against her nightgown and struggled to remain calm as each new contraction took hold.

"Another one's starting." She gripped the armrests and braced her snow boots against the floorboards to keep from sliding off the gently reclined front seat. Aunt Eva had insisted Tammy sit on a folded blanket to protect the white leather upholstery. "Do I *have* to sit on this lumpy thing?"

"Yes!" Aunt Eva glanced anxiously at Tammy, then added, "We're almost at the highway. Just breathe, keep breathing."

"Ahhh!" Tammy's eyes squeezed shut. She leaned forward and huffed shallow breaths through her mouth. As the strength of the contraction subsided, she relaxed against the back of the seat and readied herself for the next barrage.

"It's hard to be precise with this clock," Aunt Eva said, glancing at the dash, "but there were about four and a half minutes between that last set." The fluorescent green numbers glowed in the darkness, twenty-five past three.

"Is that bad?"

"Depends on how quickly I get us to the hospital." Aunt Eva steered the car onto the paved highway, and the thunderous rumble they'd endured over the gravel roads disappeared.

By the time Hattersburg's streetlights flanked the car, Tammy had lost count of her contractions. Her face scrunched each time she weathered a painful spasm to its conclusion.

"You're doing great, honey. Another block and we're there," Aunt Eva said. They passed a hospital sign jutting from a drift of snow, then entered the circular drive and stopped the car outside the emergency room entrance. "Can you make it inside while I park?"

Tammy gauged the distance to the emergency reception desk on the other side of the sliding glass doors. "Yup, if I go right now." She pushed the passenger door open and rocked to her feet. She held both sides of her belly, then, taking a series of short, quick steps, shuffled towards the entrance.

The patient intake desk was dead quiet, not a nurse in sight. Tammy braced her hands against the admissions desk in anticipation of another contraction and waited. *In and out with the breath,* she told herself. *Ignore the smell of floor wax and antiseptic.*

A man walked past, using a mop handle to push a cleaning bucket on squeaky wheels. "She should be right back," he called.

Pain seized Tammy again. She hinged forward and moaned. Her stomach muscles squeezed, and her knees shook. A nurse dressed in pink scrubs hustled towards her with a tall Styrofoam cup in one hand.

"Name and OHIP number?" the nurse asked as she slid behind the desk.

"Tammy King. My aunt has my card. She'll be here any minute."

The woman looked at her skeptically "How many minutes apart?"

"About three." Tammy breathed in sharply and looked over her shoulder for Aunt Eva. She didn't want to do this alone.

The nurse pushed a wheelchair from behind the corner of the desk "Okay, Tammy, hop in and we'll get you to the maternity ward."

Ten minutes later, Tammy was dressed in a hospital gown and lying on a gurney. The night nurse breezed in and drew the privacy curtain closed. "Let's check your dilation."

Tammy stared at the ceiling with her jaw clenched. She spread her legs, and tears leaked from the corners of her eyes.

"You're young to be doing this," the nurse commented with a sigh. "Won't be long now, a few hours at most." She pulled a flannel sheet and blanket over Tammy's legs before tugging the curtain open. "This must be grandma!" she said.

Aunt Eva stood at the foot of the bed with her purse and Tammy's overnight bag in one hand and a vending machine coffee cup in the other. She seemed about to protest when her face melted into a broad smile. "That's right. I'm the grandmother." After the nurse left them, Aunt Eva leaned over Tammy and kissed her forehead. "You're doing wonderfully, brave girl."

Tammy beamed and fiddled with the hospital wrist band. "I'm going to be a mom," she said in disbelief. "Oooh." The mounting pain built towards a crescendo, then slowly receded. "That was a bad one."

Aunt Eva chucked the paper cup into the garbage. "I noticed the Beatrix Home bus in the parking lot. One of their girls must have been admitted tonight."

"Oh my God. Mrs. Peel is here?"

"Probably."

"Ring for the nurse."

"Your eyes are big as saucers. Why the panic?"

How could she explain her terror based on a litany of circumstances which had begun to sound illogical, even to herself? Was it plausible that Mrs. Peel would connive to wait until Tammy was drugged, sneak past hospital staff, then thrust a pen into Tammy's hands and successfully coerce her into signing away the rights to her child? Ridiculous as it sounded, Tammy couldn't let go of the idea. "Please," she insisted.

A few minutes after Aunt Eva buzzed her, the nurse bustled through the door. "How you doing, love?"

"I want to be awake the whole time," Tammy blurted. "Please," she paused as her belly tightened again, "don't put me to sleep."

"Good. We'd prefer it." The nurse laid a hand on Tammy's left arm. "Are you feeling the urge to push?"

"I think so." She inhaled sharply. "Yes!"

"We're off to delivery early, then." The nurse circled the bed, stopping at the corners to lift the brake lever on each wheel. "Grandma, you can wait in the lounge down the hall unless you'd like to be present for the birth?"

Aunt Eva raised a palm to the nurse. "The lounge suits me fine."

"You'll be here after, right?" Tammy looked at her aunt hopefully as the nurse pushed her bed towards the door.

"Of course, I'm not going anywhere." Aunt Eva waggled her fingers, then disappeared from Tammy's peripheral view as the bed rolled into the hallway.

The nurse steered left, swung wide around a corner, and turned right two more times. Bile rose in the back of Tammy's throat with the swooping motion of the advancing bed. To quell the nausea, she turned her head and laid a cheek against the pillow. Through a set of closing elevator doors, Tammy noted an unwelcome figure. Marjorie Peel stared back in surprise, her fingers still buttoning her coat as Tammy whisked by.

Oh my God, no. Guaranteed, Mrs. Peel would squeal to Mirabelle, if not immediately, then in the next few hours. Her mother was going to show up and ruin everything. Tammy wanted something to be hers, just hers alone. She hated her mother.

The bed turned once more, just as a fresh contraction gripped her. The nurse pushed through a set of double doors that opened into the delivery room, then rolled to a stop parallel to a sheeted table. Two new nurses wearing surgical masks assisted her awkward struggle onto the new surface.

"Feet in the stirrups, love," one nurse said.

"That's it," the second said, easing Tammy into place. "Try to relax when you can. Is there anyone with you?"

"My aunt's waiting in the lounge."

"We'll keep her posted."

"No drugs," Tammy said. "I have to be awake."

"That's up to you, barring complications. Then it's up to the doctor's discretion."

"I'm keeping the baby," she said defiantly. "No matter what anyone says."

The nurse rested a hand firmly against Tammy's arm.

"Sweetie, no one is taking this baby. You are the legal parent."

"The legal parent . . ." The words settled over Tammy like a warm blanket.

"You have full rights to your child. No one's told you this before?"

"No. My parents are pressuring me to give it up. Mom especially."

"This is *not* your mother's child." The nurse shook her head. "You're the last word. It's what *you* want that counts."

Me, with the last word. Tammy held tight to the thought.

The door swung open, and in strolled the doctor. "Hello, Tammy. So you're here to have your tonsils removed?"

The nurses both twittered. "He's a ham," one said, "but you couldn't be in better hands."

His dark brown eyes transfixed Tammy from above the top edge of his surgical mask. They were familiar and comforting, as were the ringlets curling from beneath his cap. His resemblance to Dean must be a sign: everything will be okay.

She could almost hear Dean's voice. *See, babe? I'm takin' care of you.*

The doctor stepped to the foot of the table. "The birth is progressing quickly, Tammy. On the next contraction, you'll need to push."

"Okay, okay." Tammy gripped the edges of the gurney. On the next contraction, she bore down with a fierce determination that made the rest of the world disappear.

"Jordan Nathaniel King. He's the most beautiful and perfect thing I've ever seen," Tammy told her aunt. An hour after the birth, she was still high on adrenalin. "I can't believe I made him."

"I saw a mop of dark hair when they moved him into the nursery. Takes after his father, does he?"

"Yeah. Same eyes too."

"Well, he's a cutie all right," Aunt Eva said checking her watch. "I need to head home for some beauty sleep." She hugged Tammy's shoulders and kissed the top of her head. "The nurses will let me know when you need picking up."

"Will you visit before then?" Tammy felt pathetically desperate. She'd been counting on her aunt to buffer Mirabelle's temper over being shut out of the birth.

"No. You'll be far too busy to even notice I'm gone."

Although unconvinced, Tammy mustered a smile.

"That's the spirit. See you in three or four days." Aunt Eva gathered her coat and purse from the chair. "Ciao," she said, then zipped out the door, leaving Tammy to stare after her.

Inside, Tammy felt the kind of panic children experience when they lose sight of their parents in a crowd. Was Aunt Eva brushing her off?

Stop acting like a victim, she told herself. You're someone's mother, for Pete's sake.

From now on, she'd block Mirabelle's banter from playing in her ear and forge a path charted by her own opinions. She imagined herself meeting people for the first time as the new Tammy.

"Hi, I'm Jordan's mother," she said aloud. *No, too formal.* "Jordan's mom." Tammy pictured herself meeting young mothers at a park. "Hi, I'm *Jordy's* mom." She liked the sound of that.

Jordy.

• • •

Tammy awoke from a deep sleep shortly after one o'clock. She devoured a muffin and a fruit cup from the plastic tray left on her bedside table. Another woman now occupied the bed next to hers. Muffled voices and the mewing of a baby filtered through the drawn hospital curtains.

Why hadn't the nurses brought Jordy to her room yet? Tammy's mind flipped through a list of worrisome explanations. She eased out of bed and hobbled towards the hall, her hospital-issued slippers scuffing across the floor. "Everything's okay," she told herself repeatedly as she passed elevators and the nurses' station.

Tammy sidestepped a harried father with three meandering children in tow. Farther down the hall, a linen cart had been parked against the wall, blocking her view of the nursery. She skirted around it, then stopped short.

Mirabelle stood ten feet away from her. The fabric of her best Sunday dress showed below the hem of her winter coat as she stared through the window at the rows of babies. "Don't pretend you haven't seen me," she said without turning her head.

"I'm not pretending anything. You took me by surprise is all." Tammy discreetly searched for Jordy among the newborns.

"Yeah," Mirabelle replied sullenly. "Well, you've been hiding long enough."

A couple chatting a few feet away glanced at Tammy with concern. The wife whispered to her husband, then they moved farther down the hall and continued their conversation.

"Do we really have to do this now?" Tammy gripped the handrail mounted below the window.

"Which one's him?"

"Second row, third basket." Tammy said, hiding her relief. Jordy slept peacefully among the other infants, swaddled in a blue blanket.

"It's not too late. You can sign him over anytime."

Tammy wheeled on her mother. "He's my son. I have rights. No one's taking him away from me."

Mirabelle remained ominously quiet. Tammy measured her, then took a step back.

"One of the nurses told me the baby's *grandmother* stayed during the delivery."

"How did you find out I was here?" Tammy asked. "Did Mrs. Peel tell you?"

"No. Eva called."

Tammy's head jerked back.

"You look surprised," Mirabelle scoffed. "She couldn't wait to tell me everything I'd missed. Jordan Nathaniel King. Eight pounds and seven ounces. She even held him before I did."

"I didn't think you'd care," Tammy said, shifting her weight to the other foot.

"I've known Eva all my life. She has no interest in helping you."

"You underestimate her."

"Mother miscarried twice after she had me. Depression hit her hard. Some days, she could barely get out of bed. Then Eva was born. The sun rose and set on her, as far as my parents were concerned. I could have stood on my head and spit nickels, no one would've noticed."

Tammy thought back to the day she'd told her grandmother about being pregnant. The degree of her excitement made sense now.

"Eva's always gotten her way," Mirabelle continued. "If I treasured something, she found a way to take it for her own. Now she's taking more than a hair ribbon and some trinkets. She's after you and that baby."

Tammy counted the squares of the wire grid embedded inside the nursery window to keep from crying. "That's not how it is. Aunt Eva's being supportive," she protested. Her aunt's motives didn't matter now. There'd be a roof over their head long enough for Tammy to chart her course and ensure Jordy was safe.

Mirabelle blew her nose. "I've tried to be a good daughter, a good wife, a good mother. I volunteer at church. And for what? My mother doesn't recognize me. I have no real friends. My sister undermines me. And my daughter, well . . ."

"You've still got Dad."

"Ha." Mirabelle rolled her eyes and snorted. "You think you're so smart. Eva's using you to spite me. Once she's made her point, you'll be out on the street. Single mother. No job. No education."

Tammy maintained her stoic veneer.

"Life is going to kick you square in the behind. And when it does, you'll need someone to steer you in the right direction. Your *real* mother," Mirabelle said as she tucked her scarf inside the collar of her coat. "And a very merry Christmas to *you*. Jordan's a nice name, biblical even."

"I'm calling him *Jordy*," Tammy replied sharply.

"I'm not," Mirabelle countered. Her shoulder grazed Tammy's when she turned away abruptly and headed towards the elevators.

It took several minutes for Tammy to process her thoughts. She could neither trust her mother nor rely on Aunt Eva. Her father clearly hadn't come around. *This must be the bottom rung*, Tammy thought. *I can't get any lower.*

Tammy raised her palms and pressed them against the glass. "Jordy Nathaniel, I promise to love you without crushing you." She closed her eyes. "I will find a way to keep you safe."

But even as the words passed from her mouth, she wondered how.

25.

On a Thursday afternoon in December, four days before the end of his bereavement leave, Floyd installed himself in front of the living room window to watch for Marian. She wasn't due to arrive for another twenty minutes, but he never knew. Suppose she was early and needed help carrying something up the stairs. He should be there just in case. A gentleman would have offered to pick her up in his car. Next time, he'd do that.

He'd been thinking about her a lot—more often than his dread of Carl Spivey or his regrets concerning Dean. Could he be developing feelings for Marian, something beyond friendship? All those years ago, when he first met her at the Brookman estate, he could have never foreseen this development. He remembered her and Bonnie standing side by side, her hands clasped in front of her uniform while Bonnie's flitted through the air in accordance to the tempo of her chatter.

In the first flushes of love, Bonnie's movie star looks had dazzled him—the flashing eyes and long dark hair. She was unlike anyone he'd ever met, spontaneous and full of fire. Marian, on the other hand, possessed a quieter beauty, one that blossomed with familiarity. Over the years, she'd impressed him as being a fine woman, someone genuine and reliable. In his opinion, the strands of silver now weaving through her blond hair only added to her appeal.

He and Marian had fallen into a pleasing routine. She'd arrive late in the day with groceries for their dinner and cook while Floyd read the newspaper at the kitchen table. Marian was a river of giving, and he floated along in the current, grateful for the easy silences that punctuated their conversations. They discussed happenings in town and the legal case concerning the mill. On occasion, they touched on reminiscences of Bonnie and Dean. No awkward explanations of the past were ever required. Marian knew the history, and what she didn't know, she could well imagine. They ate dinner at six o'clock sharp. He'd help clear the table, and by eight she'd be packed up and ready to return to Phyllis's apartment. It was an agreeable arrangement and a comforting one leading into his first Christmas without Dean. Floyd appreciated Marian's sensibility, the way she'd chosen to edge her way into his insulated world to avoid rattling him.

Voices from across the street drew Floyd's attention. Three neighbourhood boys chased each other along the sidewalk, lobbing snowballs and calling out to one another. The boys were followed moments later by an elderly couple who lived farther down the block. The husband smiled up at the window and nodded as he and his wife tramped by the front gate with their festive shopping bags. Floyd returned the gesture and folded his arms across his chest.

He had taken up the habit of walking the dog at night to avoid the holiday brouhaha. The stillness soothed him as did the biting cold against his cheek and the numbness in the tip of his nose. He often paused in front of cheery homes to imagine the families living beyond the slices of light exposed between pulled curtains. The pictures he conjured filled him with a yearning for the very thing he'd been trying to run away from for so long—companionship.

Marian finally came into view, and a warm lightness filled Floyd's chest. He stepped onto the porch and waited for her. She'd worn a winter coat he recognized, but her shiny scarf was new, and she'd styled her hair differently, he thought. She carried a rectangular dish wrapped in a towel, and from one elbow hung a canvas shopping bag. It wasn't until she neared the bottom step that he noted the puffiness around her eyes and her sorrowful expression.

"Marian, what is it?"

"She's dead."

"Phyllis?"

"No. Rose Brookman."

"Huh!" Floyd's head jerked back. Many times, he'd imagined the pleasure of receiving the news that Rose had died alone in her ivory tower. No one would be genuinely sorry to see her go. It seemed like a fitting end. He noticed the disapproval on Marian's face and tried to stifle his satisfaction. "Come inside." He reached to take the dish from her hands, but she held tight. She avoided looking at him when he held the door open for her.

"I've been asked to attend the reading of the will this Wednesday in Toronto," she said, pushing past him. "Probably some trinket she's left me, don't you think?"

Floyd huffed. "How can you take anything from that woman?"

"There's no excusing what Rose did to you," Marian snapped. "She wronged a lot of people, but she was always good to me." She pulled the towel away from the dish and slid the casserole into the oven.

"How will you get to the city?" Floyd asked.

"Phyllis will drive me." Her tone was subdued.

"She still works at Arlene Howard's beauty shop?"

"Yes, although not happily."

"Well, if she can't get the time off," Floyd said slowly, "I'll take you." The line of Marian's mouth relaxed, and she removed her coat.

"Phyllis and I have all the details worked out." Marian pulled an apron from her bag and faced him squarely as she tied the strings behind her back. "Besides," she said, smoothing the front, "you can't afford to miss work. Not on your first week back."

"Of course," Floyd answered, as if only just realizing it himself. He eased onto a chair and unfolded the front section of that day's newspaper.

Marian tumbled handfuls of potatoes and a bunch of carrots into the sink and covered them with water. "How are things between you and Carl Spivey?" she called over her shoulder.

"What do you mean?" Floyd said, trying to sound nonchalant.

"Well, when he was here for Dean's memorial, you were both so angry with each other." She was facing him now.

"Nothing too serious. It'll work itself out." Floyd feigned interest in a heading on the front page.

"That's underplaying it, don't you think? You nearly took the man's head off."

For a moment, Floyd considered unburdening himself. *My son may not have been, in fact, my son, but rather the product of my wife's affair with Carl Spivey. Dark thoughts return to me each time I share a room with the son of a bitch.* But would he really feel better if he told Marian everything? Perhaps her affection for him would be replaced by sympathy. She'd see him as something less than a man and more of a buffoon. Or would she be hurt by her disappointment in Bonnie? To tell her would be destructive on either count.

So Floyd said nothing.

"You are a man of mystery, Floyd Hoffman. Someday, I'll pry you wide open," Marian sighed. "I'm going to find out what's in the locked room behind this wall while I'm at it."

Floyd wasn't prepared to be pried open yet and even less so to unlock that room. "A man should reserve a little mystery." He grinned nervously.

Marian issued her own smile, the sort reserved for children who've told clever but unconvincing stories to cover their lies. "That sounded like a challenge. I'm like a dog with a bone when there's a mystery to solve." She turned back to washing vegetables. "You've met your match, sir."

To Floyd, her words sounded all at once promising and threatening. Why must life always take one step forward, then two steps back?

Later that night, he sat on his bed, tapping the end of a pen against the notepad on his lap. The letter to Marian was proving more difficult to write than he'd expected. He glanced over the edge of the mattress to where Strum lay on the carpet. The dog cast a worried look upwards, then settled his muzzle against his paws and closed his eyes. Floyd started writing.

> *Marian,*
>
> *I am a simple man who's grown accustomed to his own company. You've helped me over a difficult transition, and for that I am grateful. I feel prepared to move on, to meet whatever the future has*

*in store for me. I must navigate these waters in the only way I know
how. Slowly. I want . . .*

Floyd laid the pen down and clasped his hands behind his head. What did he
want?

He wanted to fall asleep to the sound of someone else's breathing. He wanted
companionship without losing his solitude. He wanted to be known but not fully
revealed. He wanted to turn the clock back and perfect fatherhood. He wanted the
mill to pay for their negligence. He wanted something good in his life and to not be
afraid when it arrived.

After tearing the first letter from the pad, Floyd crumpled it in his fist. He picked
up the pen and tried again.

> *Marian,*
>
> *I want to ask for your patience. It's been some time since I've been
> the focus of female attention, and too much happiness too quickly
> feels self-indulgent. Dean has been gone such a short time. Perhaps
> you and I should call it quits until I can get my bearings. Thank you
> for understanding.*
>
> *Sincerely,*
>
> *Floyd*

He slipped the folded letter into an envelope and laid it on the nightstand.
Tomorrow, he'd be in town to meet with Doc Gillespie at the diner. He'd drop it in
her mailbox on the way by. Maybe.

Floyd bided his time at a corner table in the Narrow Falls Diner and waited for Doc
Gillespie to join him. Excluding the odd trip to the bank or the grocer's, it was the
first time he'd been in such a public place since Dean died. He could have done
without the piped-in Christmas music.

Life had moved on without his son. A trio of high school girls sat on the tall stools at the diner window, tucked in shoulder to shoulder, watching the street. An elderly couple seated nearer to the service counter was placing their order with Allan's mother. Like her son, she was lanky and fair-haired. She'd served Floyd before. He remembered all those silver studs along the outside of her ears. Must be a hippie thing.

The string of bells hanging from the diner door jingled to signal a new arrival. Floyd sat tall against the back of his chair and peered anxiously across the restaurant to the entranceway, hoping to discover Doc Gillespie. Instead, Allan sauntered through the door dressed in white coveralls, the sort a painter might wear. He tossed his coat on a stool and sat at the counter, casting a discreet glance over his shoulder at the girls sitting in the front window. His mother poured him a coffee and thrust her chin towards Floyd's table.

Floyd felt unexpectedly pleased to see Allan swivel his stool and stride towards him, mug in hand.

"Hey, Mr. Hoffman," he said, dropping into the chair across from Floyd. "How's it going?"

"I'm doing all right, I guess."

"Great. And Strum?"

"He's good. Eating me out of house and home."

"Maybe I could come check him out some time."

"He'd like that," Floyd replied. "What have you been up to?"

"Odd jobs mostly—a bit of grunt work, some painting. My uncle's a contractor, so he's showing me the ropes."

"No college?"

"No way, man. I'd prefer what you'd call a 'didactic' experience."

"How did you acquire that word?"

"I read. Same as you." Allan scrunched his nose as if the answer was obvious and Floyd should have known better.

"Sorry, Allan. I just thought . . ."

"I've seen part of your book collection." Allan's elbows rested on the table, and his head tilted to one side. "I expect people are surprised to find out the mailman reads heavy shit like philosophy or Darwin.”

“Touché,” Floyd answered.

“How'd you come by all those books?”

“Years of collecting. Some I inherited from an old friend.”

“The drugstore guy?”

Floyd's eyes widened.

“Dean said he was like your guru or something. Very cool.”

“Yes, Vic Patterson. I bought my first books with money I earned running deliveries for his pharmacy.”

“Last time I was at your place, you said I could have something else of Dean's, that I should think about it and let you know.”

“Yes.”

“I thought about it. What I want is to hang out with you.” Allan pointed his pistol fingers at Floyd simultaneously.

Floyd tensed. *What precisely does that mean?*

“Relax. Just once in a while. We can talk about stuff like philosophy, history, and whatever else is in your library.”

Floyd leaned forward, resting his forearms on his thighs. “There must be someone you'd rather spend time with? A special girl maybe?”

“There might be.”

“Well, then?”

“The situation is kind of messy. It's tough to break in.”

“I had a similar time of it with Dean's mother. I'm going to ask you the same question Vic Patterson asked me when he saw I was dragging *my* heels.”

“Shoot.”

“Do you know a woman named *Ann Wright*?”

“Nope.” Allan shook his head.

“Neither did I and for good reason. She was the only girl Vic ever loved. But she was the fish that got away because he was too slow setting the hook. He remained a bachelor his entire life.”

“So you're saying I should take the plunge?”

"I'm saying, procrastinate and the opportunity maybe lost."

"Uh-huh," Allan said with a smirk. "And how's Marian, by the way?"

"Fine."

"Are you practicing what you preach?"

Floyd gawked across the table and thought of the letter tucked inside his jacket.

"Uh-huh, I figured," Allan said. "What's stopping *you*?"

Just then, the jingle of bells announced Doc Gillespie's arrival. Floyd raised a hand to catch his attention. The doctor stomped the snow from his boots and headed in Floyd's direction.

"By golly, it's cold out there," he said, sliding his arms from his coat. "Allan, this is a surprise. I haven't seen you around for a while."

"I'm working for the man now," Allan replied, rising from his chair. "I should be going."

"Nonsense. Stick around," Floyd said.

The doctor claimed the seat next to Allan and rubbed both hands together. "Did you bring the maps, Floyd?"

"I've got them right here." Floyd lifted the roll of paper from the seat next to his and unfurled it on the tabletop.

The doctor's face clouded as he looked over the markings. "It's quite something to see it all laid out this way."

"What is it?" Allan asked.

"Each of these numbers represents a citizen who's died in the past decade," Floyd said, pointing at the map. "All of these deaths won't be related to dioxins, but the clustering effect along the river and in the vicinity of the mill will raise concern. It all adds up to proof that McLelland's is doing harm."

"There's so many here." Allan pointed to a concentration of numbers recorded on the south side of the river. His brows knit together with worry as he looked up at Floyd. "That's where I live."

"If we combined both our data so your maps also included the incidents of respiratory events I presented in court, the results would knock R.J. McLelland on his ass!" said Doc. "It's just a matter of time until ministry studies begin rolling out. Once the bigger newspapers sink their teeth into this thing, McLelland's will be on the ropes. The pressure for change will force his hand."

"You're gonna save lives," Allan said with disarming seriousness.

"I hope so," Floyd replied. On the inside, he was glowing with pleasure at the comment.

"I gotta get back to work." Allan stood and pushed in his chair.

"Allan, have you heard any recent talk about Tammy King?" Floyd asked.

The doctor's eyes cut to Floyd's face, then to Allan's.

"Nope."

"Nothing about her leaving school or where she's at now?"

"Sorry, can't help you out." Allan scratched at his ear and shrugged. "Well, see you around."

Floyd watched Allan stride to the front of the diner, where his mother was wiping down a counter. They spoke briefly, then he grabbed his coat and headed into the weather.

"What's your interest in the King girl?" Doc asked as he perused the menu.

"Dean was seeing her in secret since last spring, maybe longer. I'm hoping she can tell me something about his time in Toronto. I'd feel better knowing anything."

"Huh." The doctor sank back against the upholstery.

"What is it?"

The doctor stared thoughtfully, then replied. "We should order some lunch, don't you think?"

"You know something you're not telling me," Floyd said firmly.

"If I knew something—and that's a big *if*—I couldn't tell you, Floyd. You know that."

"Oh well, Tammy King will surface eventually. This town is too small to hide in forever."

"I suspect you're right," Doc Gillespie said, then he turned to wave down the waitress.

• • •

On Monday morning, Floyd didn't want to get out of bed. He had to levy every ounce of self-discipline he possessed to reenter life as usual at the post office. Halfway through his walk to work, he wanted to return home and brew a second pot of coffee, finish reading about Russian history, and spend time with Strum. After arriving at the post office, he spent five minutes standing in the snow-filled alley strategizing the walk from the employee entrance to his workstation. By entering through the back of the building, he could avoid interacting with the service clerks— two gossipy women bound to quiz him on every detail of Dean's death. Them, he'd avoid at all cost. He'd come to escape his memory, not to swim in it. Just inside the door, two rural delivery drivers stood drinking takeout coffee from the diner. They nodded politely and made space for him to pass. Floyd didn't know where to direct his gaze as he made his way through the rest of the building. To look directly at people felt too much like fishing for sympathy. Not looking at them didn't seem right either.

One colleague, a woman just a few years older than Floyd, stepped out from behind her counter, eyes tearing and arms spread wide as she barreled towards him. She hugged him and sobbed into the front of his jacket. "God bless you, what you've been through. I'm so sorry. If I can ever do anything to ease your burden . . ."

People were staring at them now—a couple of mail carriers, the maintenance men working nearby, and a driver he recognized from the Toronto depot.

". . . you just say the word."

Floyd looked down at the crown of her head and focused on the grey roots sprouting along the part in her dark hair until she released him moments later. The onlookers turned back to their work and feigned busyness until he moved on.

He walked an indirect path to his area in the hopes of bypassing Carl Spivey, who would undoubtedly enjoy creating further spectacle to increase discomfort. What he wouldn't give to escape this place and drive somewhere far away.

Three envelopes, each addressed to him, laid on the wooden stool at his post. Condolence cards. He slung his coat on top of them and tucked his snow boots under his counter along with his lunchbox. All he had to do, he reminded himself, was make it through one day at a time, hour by hour.

Avoiding Carl Spivey proved to be impossible. By nine o'clock, he'd strode three times back and forth along the front of the counter that hemmed in Floyd's work area. The smell of his cheap aftershave lingered in his wake. On no occasion did he say hello or nod, which both relieved and irked Floyd. Carl was wearing the bright orange necktie Floyd despised, the one with a picture of Mickey Mouse swinging a golf club. What kind of grown man wore such drivel in the middle of December? He didn't even golf. Floyd's gut burned each time he entertained the possibility of this man being Dean's biological father.

Again, Carl passed by, this time to visit his most recent conquest, an attractive dark-haired woman in her late twenties, a temporary hire for the Christmas season. She stopped working and listened to Carl with rapt attention. His disingenuous laughter jabbed at Floyd. Carl executed facial expressions and sweeping hand gestures in such a rehearsed manner Floyd could predict which move would come next.

The new woman threw her head back and laughed, exposing the hollow of her throat. Carl laid a hand on her left shoulder, then cast a superior glance in Floyd's direction and winked. He strolled past Floyd's work area, trailing his pen along the edge of the counter. "Ha! It's so easy," he said over his shoulder, "like shooting fish in a barrel."

"For Chrissake," Floyd said, "she's young enough to be your daughter."

Carl stopped short and rested his forearms on the counter. He leaned forward and looked up at Floyd, grinning through his contempt. "What? You wouldn't like a piece of that? She's got an ass to die for. Don't even get me started on her tits."

Floyd's jaw tensed. All he could see was Carl's orange necktie.

"Mmm. I'd have guessed you'd go for that black wavy hair," Carl continued. "Reminds me of your wife. Now she was a good—"

Floyd's left hand shot out and grabbed Carl's tie. He yanked downward with all his might and swung his right fist forward in a wide arc. His knuckles smashed into the centre of Carl's face with a sickening crunch. Carl reeled left, wrenching his necktie from Floyd's grasp. With the back of his shoulder turned to Floyd, Carl moaned and lifted a hand to his face.

Adrenaline charges imploded inside Floyd's chest. Among the surprised faces of his coworkers he found discreet smiles. Someone in their midst applauded. *Nice to be on the winning side of things for a change.*

Carl turned slowly to face Floyd. Blood flowed from his nostrils and dripped from his chin. "Oh shit." His eyes widened in amazement, and his lips curled back to reveal blood filling the cracks between his teeth. "You little fucker. You busted my nose!"

He began to charge around the end of the counter.

Floyd froze like a kid watching from the middle of a railroad track while a locomotive bore down on him. The impact of Carl's shoulder against his chest knocked him back against a mail bin. Before he'd recovered his balance, Carl's hands clamped around his neck. With eyes bugging, Floyd gripped his wrists to wrestle him away, but his thumbs only dug deeper. After Floyd fired a knee into Carl's groin, the pressure on his neck ceased. Carl folded forward with a groan as Floyd greedily sucked air into his lungs.

"What in the Sam Hill is going on in here?" One of gossips from the service area stepped warily through a side door and took measure of both men. "Oh my Lord!"

Floyd grabbed his coat from the stool, stormed past Carl, and veered right towards the rear exit. Colleagues stepped back to make way as if to make room for a gladiator leaving the Colosseum. "Didn't know you had it in you," one driver said. "Good on ya."

"I'm writing you up, asshole," Carl shouted after Floyd. "You're finished here."

"I quit!" Floyd yelled back without turning around. He pushed the steel door with sufficient force that it swung in a full arc and smashed against the brick exterior of the building. Chest heaving and nostrils flaring, he burst outside and continued walking. The destination was irrelevant as long as his feet kept moving.

His mind spun with images of Carl Spivey's face when he took that punch to the nose. Floyd had never hit another human being before, although he'd been sorely tempted. Hopefully, from somewhere on high, Dean had been watching. He'd have loved that, seeing his old man deck someone. In fact, line them up, Floyd thought. Who's next? Where were all the obnoxious bullies of his youth? R.J. McLelland and the strapping Neanderthals from the mill who'd threatened him over at Tony's? He was ready. Bring on every doctor who'd ever given him bad news or called his judgment into question. He'd show them all.

Floyd plowed along the sidewalk with puffs of snow kicking up in his wake. He reached Marian's apartment before he realized where his feet had carried him. He wanted to tell her what he'd done, to celebrate, rage, be excited or frightened with her. He stopped short and felt inside his pocket for the letter he'd written Marian. The words were still true. It was too soon after Dean. The timing was all wrong. But then he thought of Vic. The timing was never right, was never going to be right. How many chances did he have to be happy? Could he afford for Marian to be his Ann Wright?

He could still remember Vic Patterson telling him the story. He had seemed so old, though he'd been the same age Floyd was now. "She could have been Ann *Patterson*—but I hesitated and lost."

"You loved her?" Floyd had asked.

I love her still, had been Vic's reply.

Floyd stood at the curb with the toes of his shoes overhanging the sidewalk. No more putting life on hold and living with regret. He raised his collar against the wind, blew air into his palms, and kept walking until he reached Marian's apartment. He climbed the exterior staircase to the second floor and knocked on the door.

Marian answered immediately.

"Are you alone?"

"Well, yes," she said with a puzzled look. "Phyllis just left for work."

Floyd closed the gap between them.

"What's happened? Is everything all right?" Her eyes searched his face.

He slipped an arm behind her waist and pulled her close. He stared intensely into her eyes and thought of every word he wanted her to hear. His free hand traced the outline of her cheek.

Marian relaxed in his arms and regarded him steadily. "Something's changed. You're different."

Then he kissed her.

26.

Tammy looked to the forested lot behind Aunt Eva's property as she pushed the baby carriage onto the pool deck. Gone were the last smatterings of ice that had lingered in the shade of the pines. The grey end of winter had given way to spring. After raising the canopy to shield Jordy from the March sun, she settled into in a deck chair with one leg stretched in front of her and a worn paperback cradled in her hands. He slept soundly in his cocoon of blankets while she lost herself in one of Aunt Eva's dime-store romance novels.

"You've been spoiled by this baby's good nature," Aunt Eva had told her more than once. "It's unlikely you'll be so lucky with the next one." The circumstances under which she'd have a second child were unimaginable. That aside, Tammy counted her blessings. Jordy slept through the night, and he was easy to settle on the rare occasions when he fussed.

It hadn't all been straightforward. Taking care of a baby looked easier in the pregnancy books than it was in real life. A nurse in the hospital had to coach her along when she struggled with breast feeding. "There's always the bottle," she suggested once when Tammy had dissolved into tears. The cost of bottles and baby formula had driven Tammy to keep trying. Jordy eventually found reward through his own determination, and Tammy took pride in the knowledge that she was providing for him.

At Christmas, Aunt Eva had given her a fifty-dollar bill. "Treat yourself, girl. Get your hair done," she'd said, "or maybe a manicure. We'll go together." Her exuberance faded when Tammy chose the practicality of cloth diapers over self-indulgence. "You are out of your mind. Do you know how much work it takes to launder those things? Cyril's store gives you disposables for free." But Tammy declined. Nothing was free.

Her aunt had been correct about one thing though. Maintaining a steady supply of clean diapers was demanding given the lengthy drying time and how often Jordy wet himself. The plastic overpants leaked urine onto his clothes and bedding, which only added to her work. Still, she didn't feel right accepting more of Aunt Eva's charity than was necessary. Especially when she worried about wearing out her welcome.

Upon hearing Jordy fuss in the carriage, Tammy laid the novel facedown on the deck and got up from her chair. She swept her long hair behind one ear and bent over the baby. His nose crinkled, and his bottom lip quivered as if preparing to wail. But then he relaxed and continued sleeping. As much as she'd once loved Dean, she loved Jordy all the more. There was nothing she wouldn't do for him.

"The kid's got it made."

Tammy spun around. Clay Houghton stood next to her deck chair with one hand in his pocket and the other one balancing a lit cigarette.

"Napping poolside while the rest of the world takes care of business."

"My aunt's in the house," Tammy said. Her frown reflected back to her in the lenses of Clay's dark sunglasses.

"I know. She's putting on the finishing touches before we head out for the day." He drew on his cigarette and released a slow stream of smoke. "You know how they are at that age. It takes more effort to cover the ravages of time."

"I'm sure she'll be down any minute," Tammy said, crossing her arms over the front of her sweatshirt.

"In the meantime, I'll just enjoy the view," he said, sweeping an arm in front of him.

He and Aunt Eva had been seeing each other a couple times a week since Christmas. She was completely infatuated. The morning after Valentine's Day, Tammy had discovered a vase of long-stemmed roses on the kitchen counter and a toppled wine bottle with two empty glasses on the coffee table. The sofa cushions were askew, and the pillows had been kicked across the floor. On the way back to her and Jordy's room, she'd encountered Clay in the hallway wearing a pair of black briefs that left little to her imagination. From that morning onward, he'd become somewhat of a fixture at the house, one she tried to avoid.

"What's this?" Clay flicked his cigarette butt into a flowerbed and bent to pick up Tammy's book.

"Please give it back." She held her hand out.

"I will. In a minute." He flipped to a new page in the middle of the book and chuckled. "Oh, this is good."

"Give me the book," Tammy demanded with more urgency.

"Her breasts heaved against the lacing of her bodice as he gathered her skirt above her slender waist."

Tammy stepped towards him, on the verge of tears, and made a desperate grab for the novel. His left arm circled her ribs and pulled her against him while his right held the book just beyond her reach.

"She shuddered as his tongue traced the cleft of her—"

"Well, what's all this?" Aunt Eva called out from between the French doors. The pitch of her voice was uncharacteristically high and her smile too bright.

Although the question had been aimed at Tammy, Clay was first to answer. "Just a little kidding around, sweetheart. That's what uncles do."

Aunt Eva sighed with relief, and her head dropped to one side. "Clay Houghton, you are a peach of a man." Her smile faded slightly when she addressed Tammy. "There's someone on the phone for you."

"Is it my mother?" Tammy asked warily.

"No, it's a male voice," Aunt Eva replied in a coy tone.

"Good." Must be Allan, Tammy thought. He'd been calling a few times each week to update her with interesting gossip he'd overheard at the diner. The only downside to their friendship was his insistence that Dean's father was hurting and that she should tell him about the baby. *No damned way.*

She was about to lift Jordy from the carriage and take him inside, but Aunt Eva stopped her.

"Let the baby sleep. We'll keep an eye on him."

"Yeah, I'm great with kids," Clay added.

Aunt Eva waited in the doorway until Tammy brushed past on her way to the phone, then she stepped outside and pulled the French doors closed behind her.

Tammy picked up the receiver from where it lay on the countertop. "Hey, Allan. How's it going?"

A few seconds of silence followed.

"It's Dad."

Tammy's eyes cut to Aunt Eva's face on the other side of the French doors. Her aunt turned away with a satisfied smile. The tail of her chiffon blouse fluttered behind her as she made her way towards Clay.

"Does Mom know you're calling me?"

"No."

More silence.

"You haven't spoken to her for over three months," Lawrence said. "She was nearly fit to be tied when you didn't come home for Christmas. When's this going to end?"

"I dunno."

"Easter's just around corner. For Chrissake, at least come home for the day, then you can go back to Eva's and continue with whatever it is you're trying to prove."

Tammy watched Aunt Eva stand on tiptoes and whisper something in Clay's ear. They laughed together, then his arms reached around her and his hands roamed her back.

"What about the neighbours?" Tammy asked.

"You know how it works here. Aunt Eva told Arlene Howard, Arlene told everyone who came through the salon, including Blanche Clark, and now the whole damned street knows."

"Dad, do you love me?"

"You're my daughter," he answered, as if that's all she needed to know.

Tammy wiped her eyes and tried not to sniffle into the phone.

"Couldn't you just apologize to your mother," he continued, "tell her you're sorry for all this mess? I gotta live with her, you know."

"Dad, I need to go now."

"Will you think about it?"

"We'll see."

She was about to hang up when she heard his voice again. "The baby—does he look like us?"

"Does it matter?"

"Only if he doesn't," Lawrence replied. "It would be best, considering . . ."

"I gotta go now." Tammy hung up the telephone and burst into tears. Between sobs, she looked outside to where Aunt Eva swayed back and forth with dark spikes of Jordy's hair peeking over her right shoulder. Next to her, Clay checked his watch and flicked a look towards the house.

What had she gotten herself into?

Long after she'd gone to bed that night, Tammy's ears strained against the silence of the house. Her aunt and Clay hadn't yet returned from their night out, and she was in the house alone with Jordy. Even the tiniest sound set her on edge. At two in the morning, she heard the soft click of the front door unlocking. Her body relaxed when she next heard the sputter of Aunt Eva's and Clay's laughter as they came into the house.

A sliver of light appeared along the bottom edge of Tammy's bedroom door. The steps began to creak as the pair made their way upstairs.

"Shhh. They're sleeping," her aunt whispered loudly.

Clay's deep voice mumbled something once they'd reached the landing. "Mmm, you are a devil, Mr. Houghton," Aunt Eva responded in a sultry voice. Renewed laughter followed the rustle of fabric. The sliver of light disappeared, and a door closed at the other end of the hallway.

Tammy lay awake staring into the darkness. For how long would she be alone? Odds were against meeting a nice guy, especially one her age who'd want a girlfriend with a kid.

Muted jazz music began playing down the hall. Soon after, low moans of pleasure interjected themselves between soaring guitar and saxophone riffs. Just as the volume of the couple's fervour escalated, Jordy began to bawl.

Sounds of passion ceased.

Tammy rolled back her bedcovers. "Shhh. It's all right. I'm here," she crooned. By the time she reached into the crib, his wailing had reached a fevered pitch. She clucked softly as she carried him to the bed, unbuttoning the front of her nightgown. His cries faded to mild protest as she distracted him with a late-night feeding.

A rhythmic thumping began, slowly at first, then picking up speed. Tammy sang a melody for Jordy in hopes of drowning out the unmistakable sounds of sex coming from her aunt's room. "You are my sunshine, my only sunshine. You make me happy when skies are—" The baby's face rolled away from her breast, and again he howled.

The thumping stopped.

She shushed the baby and rubbed his back. Nothing she tried seemed to work. "What's wrong, Jordy?" Her eyes brimmed with tears of frustration as she switched him to her other breast. After a few attempts, he gave up crying and latched on. Tammy sagged against the pillow with a heavy sigh.

The hall light reappeared under her bedroom door, and it occurred to her that the jazz music was no longer playing. The steps creaked again, this time from the weight of people travelling downstairs. Voices hummed low from the foyer. The front door clicked open and shut. The crunch of gravel from the driveway told her Clay had left. She began to think Aunt Eva had gone with him, but then Tammy heard someone climbing the steps slowly. A shadow stretched across the gap beneath her bedroom door and rested there for several seconds. Tammy braced herself for a knock, but the shadow turned away from the door, and the hallway went dark.

Early the next morning, Tammy nursed Jordy again, then changed his diaper and buttoned him into a clean outfit. She brushed out her own hair and pulled on a pair of acid-wash jeans and a fitted T-shirt Aunt Eva had bought for her. She examined her figure in the full-length mirror. Her waist had returned to its small size, but her hips remained fuller and her breasts heavier. She liked this more womanly version of her old self. She scooped Jordy from the crib and headed downstairs. "What do you want to do today? Maybe a walk?" She kissed his face, and he formed a gummy grin and babbled happily.

Aunt Eva was waiting at the kitchen table, still wearing her terry cloth robe and a cotton nightgown. Her elbows rested on a placemat as she sipped coffee from a large mug. "Morning," she said.

Tammy could sense eyes measuring her as she held open the fridge door with one hip and took out a carton of orange juice. She poured herself a glass one-handed and carried it along with the baby to sit across the table from her aunt.

"Wow, look at you. Seems like you have everything under control," Aunt Eva said.

"We're doing okay." Tammy cradled Jordy in the crook of her left arm and sipped her drink.

"I suppose you'll be out looking for work soon."

"It's been on my mind," Tammy lied.

Aunt Eva set her cup on the table and leaned towards her. "I hope you won't mind, but I spoke with Arlene Howard this morning. She's looking for a girl to wash hair, sweep up, take appointments. When I told her about your natural talent, she said the job's yours."

Tammy gawked at her aunt.

"Play your cards right, "Aunt Eva continued, "and there may be an apprenticeship at the end of this rainbow."

"But the job is in Narrow Falls."

"Beggars can't be choosers. It's a start, right?"

"My mom gets her hair done there. I can't deal with seeing her."

"I've already discussed that with Arlene. Your mother has a standing appointment on Tuesday mornings at nine o'clock. You'll start at eleven on Tuesdays and stay two hours later to wash floors and give the place a good scrubbing."

"But, Aunt Eva, I—"

"It really is time to be on your way, don't you think? I've helped out more than most would have."

"There's no one to watch Jordy. I was hoping to stay until—"

"Clay didn't want me to bring it up, but he explained what really happened yesterday by the pool."

Tammy's stomach dropped.

"Can't say as I blame you. He's handsome and charming."

"It's not like that."

"I had to pry the truth out of him. He knew I'd be crushed to learn that my own niece had made a play for him."

"He's lying!"

Aunt Eva shook her head. "I knew it the minute I saw you glomming on to him yesterday."

"What? He was all over *me*!"

Jordy's arms jerked upwards, and he loosed a startled wail.

"Shhh." Tammy rocked in her chair.

"There are other considerations. This," Aunt Eva said, flicking a glance at Jordy, "is not conducive to my current situation."

"I won't go home to my parents," Tammy said with determination.

"Then don't. No one ever said life was easy, but you're a smart girl. You'll figure it out," Aunt Eva said, snaking a cigarette from an open pack next to her mug. She lit it and blew a trail of smoke from the corner of her mouth.

Tammy scrambled to find the right response in the flurry of thoughts racing through her mind. Her eyes focused on the cigarette hanging loosely between the fingers of her aunt's right hand. So this was it. The Eva her mother had warned her about. Wouldn't Mirabelle enjoy hearing about this?

"Clay's dropping by later this afternoon. You might want to make yourself scarce."

Tammy's eyes cut to Eva's face. "No problem. I doubt I'll be here by then."

"Well, don't let *me* stop you." Aunt Eva swept her arm towards the door in a grand gesture.

Tammy hugged Jordy against her chest and left the table.

"I won't."

Upstairs in her room, Tammy paced the floor, raking her fingers through her hair. *What the hell else could go wrong in my life?* Aunt Eva was supposed to be her ace in the hole. She'd planned to stay on and start looking for a job nearby. If she cleaned houses, she could be paid under the table and bring Jordy along so she didn't need a sitter. Once she'd earned enough money, she could rent a cute little apartment and buy a car. She'd be free. The whole scheme was a bust now that she was being forced out prematurely.

What was it about her that was so intolerable and undeserving that no one could stick around to love her? First Dean, then her parents, and now Aunt Eva. She stood over the crib as Jordy happily gummed his fist. "Stop wallowing and do something parental," she whispered to herself.

She was getting out of here, and she was doing it today. The big question was *how*. What about Allan? He'd be willing to drive the hour to come get her and the baby, plus he already knew the dynamics of her situation, so there'd be no need for explanation. But then she soured on the plan. What if he got the wrong idea? If he fancied himself as her white knight, there may be expectations of payback after the rescue. Why risk another guy's warped sense of entitlement?

Another name came to mind, someone who could help her out of this jam. She wound up the mobile hanging above Jordy's crib, slipped a pacifier into his mouth, and hurried to Uncle Cyril's den. After closing the door, she searched out a telephone book and ran a shaky finger down the listings until she reached the single entry for *Benton*. She dialled and crossed her fingers. The phone rang three times before someone picked up. Tammy didn't wait for them to say hello.

"Is Leslie there?"

"You got her. Who's this?"

"It's Tammy," she sobbed into the receiver. "I'm in such trouble."

"So what's it to me?"

"Leslie, please, I'm begging you. I need a ride back to Narrow Falls."

"No way."

"I'm at my aunt's in Ashfield. She's got this boyfriend . . ."

"Shit."

"I know. It's almost an hour's drive, but I'll pay your gas. I swear."

"This isn't some bullshit kind of emergency, is it? 'Cause if I get there and find out you all had a Kumbaya moment and made up, I'm going to be pissed."

"I need out before he shows up again."

"You should have led with that, Keener. How do I find you?"

"Just follow the highway into town, go right at the four corners, and keep driving for about two miles past Sterling Stables. It's the second driveway on the right. You'll see *C&E Fletcher* on the mailbox."

"I'm on it."

"Leslie, do your parents still have your little sister's car seat?"

"Yeah."

"Can you bring it?"

"Unbelievable. This just gets better and better."

"I hope so," Tammy replied.

It took five minutes for Tammy to gather her belongings. She packed nothing that Aunt Eva had paid for except the clothes she and Jordy were wearing. A sinking feeling weighed on her after taking inventory of the items she planned to leave behind. She'd taken the loan of Jessica's baby items for granted—the clothing, linens, the crib, and even the carriage. The task of replacing those items would fall squarely on her wallet now. She'd counted the last of her money that morning before rolling it tightly and pushing it into her front pocket—fifty-three dollars was all that remained of her childhood savings. With that, she must devise a way to house, feed, and clothe herself and Jordy until receiving her first pay cheque from the salon. Somehow, she'd make it work, but right now she could only think about getting out of this house.

Just before Leslie was due to arrive, Tammy dropped a plastic shopping bag of soiled nappies into the bottom of a garbage bag, which she further stuffed with laundered diapers and knotted tightly.

She sat on the end of the bed and examined the contents of her backpack before zipping it shut. The Whitman poetry book and Mr. Hoffman's red leather journal were inside along with a teddy bear and two storybooks she'd bought for the baby, Dean's football shirt, and a few pairs of underwear.

She hoisted the pack onto her shoulders and hurried into the hallway to toss the bag of diapers over the top step. It rolled end over end down the stairs and came to rest in the foyer. Then she fetched Jordy from the bed and pressed his cheek against hers as she descended the staircase. The front doorbell chimed just as her foot lit on the bottom step. Tammy punted the bag of diapers ahead of her as she scooted across the foyer to open the door.

"Hey, I got here as fast as I could," Leslie said. Behind her, a blue Mustang with a white stripe painted the length of its hood sat in the driveway with its trunk open.

"Oh my God," Tammy said, snatching up the garbage bag with her free hand. "I'm so glad to see you. Let's get out of here."

"Where's the rest of your stuff?" Leslie asked as they hurried towards the back of her car.

"This is it."

"You're kidding!"

Tammy grimaced and flung the garbage bag into the trunk next to a jug of wiper fluid and a cardboard box with *KEEP* scrawled across the top flap in red marker. She rushed to the passenger side door before Leslie had slammed shut the lid of the trunk.

The moment she stooped to fold the front seat forward, Tammy spied the owl-eyed girls in the backseat. They sat on either side of the car seat, one with an opened package of cookies in her lap and the other with a ring of crumbs around her mouth and melted chocolate on her fingers.

"My stepmother is working today, so I had to bring my kid sisters. They promised to be good, right, Dee?" Leslie peered through the driver's side door to level a stern look at the older girl, who nodded and reached into the bag for another cookie.

Tammy maneuvered around Dee's legs to position Jordy in the car seat. He began to cry after she fitted the straps over his chest and buckled the clasp. "Jordy, don't cry. Mommy doesn't have time for that." She ducked her shoulders and squirmed backwards out of the car. The crown of her head struck the edge of the car roof as she stood. The sharp burst of pain brought tears to her eyes.

"Oh shit," Leslie said. "Is that your aunt?"

Tammy spun towards the house, where Aunt Eva was stepping onto the driveway with one hand shading her eyes from the sun and the other waving over her head.

"Wait," Aunt Eva hollered. She wobbled across the gravel in her high-heeled sandals until she reached the hood of the Mustang. "I'm Eva, and you are?" she asked, looking at Leslie.

"A friend," Leslie answered.

"Well, you're a good friend, driving out here and so quickly too." Aunt Eva's sugary voice betrayed no hint of her earlier mood. "You just take Tammy home and get her settled down. She'll be fine."

Tammy wanted to slap her.

Aunt Eva's right hand reached through the neck of her floral chiffon blouse and produced a fifty-dollar bill, which she extended towards Leslie.

"What's this?" Leslie asked, squinting into the sun.

"A little something to cover your expenses."

"I don't think that's going to do it."

Tammy's jaw tightened. The situation left Tammy feeling as if her friend and her aunt had negotiated her removal fee. Leslie had no business taking the money, and her demanding more served only to cheapen them both.

Aunt Eva's smile turned to a grimace. She hesitated, then pulled a second bill from her brassiere. "One hundred dollars."

"That's more like it." Leslie plucked the money from Eva's hand.

"Let's go, Keener. This place is giving me a headache." She slid behind the wheel and started the engine.

Tammy dropped into the passenger seat and slammed the car door.

"That played out nicely. I'm up a hundred bucks," Leslie said.

"Good for you." Tammy glared through a spidery crack in the windshield and watched her aunt return to the house. "And my name is Tammy, not Keener."

"Okay," Leslie said, as if she just realized Tammy had a voice. "Where was that hostility when your aunt was being a b-i-t-c-h?"

Leslie had a point.

Tammy flung the car door open and leapt to her feet. "Hey!" Aunt Eva paused at the front door and turned towards the car. Tammy's mind went blank. She so badly wanted to lash out at her aunt, to say something brilliant that she and Leslie would repeat and laugh about all the way back to Narrow Falls. Informing her of Clay's flirtations might feel good, but only for a minute. The real payback would come when he took her money and dumped her.

"Well?" Aunt Eva called out. A look of superiority appeared on her face, the same look that had vexed Mirabelle over the years.

Words suddenly rushed to Tammy. "You and my mother are opposite sides of the same coin. All the money in the world won't change that." Without waiting for her aunt's response, she dropped back into the car

"That was lame," Leslie said as she reversed the car past the mailbox and onto the road.

"You're wrong. That hit the target."

"If you say so, *Tammy*. Your aunt's a head case. I could see that a mile away."

Tammy turned towards the window and sulked quietly, watching the blur of fence posts whiz by.

"Why'd you get bounced?"

"My aunt's boyfriend is a manipulative perve. And not a kid person. The end."

"That sucks." Leslie's eyes narrowed, and she leaned closer to the steering wheel. "Do you have any money?"

"A few dollars. But I'm starting a job next week at Arlene's Beauty Salon."

"Oh no. The chick who owns that place is such a jerk. I went in to get some split ends trimmed, and she sliced my bangs off up to here, like I was a five-year-old," Leslie said, laying an index finger across her forehead. "That place is for old ladies who want their hair done up in curlers."

"Look, I need a job, and that's the one I've got," Tammy snapped. She stared at a grove of gangly pines crowding the shoulder of the road. Dee waggled a Barbie doll over her right shoulder and giggled.

"Who's watching the kid while you're at work?"

Tammy's eyes cut to Leslie. The questions had begun to feel more like an interrogation than a conversation. Not knowing all the answers raised the all too familiar insecurity she'd experienced living with Mirabelle.

"You know a sitter will run you about eighty bucks a week?" Leslie said.

"Eighty?"

"That's why my parents stick me with rug rats when I'm not at work," Leslie said, rolling her eyes. "What's the salon paying you?"

"I'm not sure," Tammy said quietly. "Aunt Eva got me the job this morning."

"It's impossible to support yourself and a kid on minimum wage, even with full-time hours. You're gonna need help."

Tammy rubbed her temples and began to weep. "Oh shit! What am I going to do?"

"You said *shit*," Dee yelled from the backseat. "I'm telling."

"Not now, Dee," Leslie called over her right shoulder. "Tammy, you don't need to have a perfect plan laid out for your entire life. Focus on today. And tomorrow, do the same thing again. It'll all come together." Leslie stopped the car at the main intersection in Ashfield. Its left turn signal made a dull clinking sound as they waited for a logging truck to pass so they could turn onto the highway.

Groveling at her parents' door was not an option. She refused to allow her mother the satisfaction of an "I told you so." There must be a way she could stand on her own and provide for herself and Jordy.

"If I am really careful, I'll have enough money to buy food until my first pay cheque comes," Tammy said.

"There's a box of baby stuff in the trunk for you, and I can lend you some clothes."

"Thanks, Leslie."

"You should take the hundred bucks your aunt gave me too."

"I don't want her money!"

"There's a thin line between pride and stupidity, you know."

Tammy's shoulders relaxed. "I guess," she conceded. "One week's pay for a babysitter, right?"

Leslie stole a sideways glance. "Are you staying at your parents' tonight?"

Tammy shook her head.

"There's another option. Who's his daddy?"

Fence posts whizzed by the passenger side window while Tammy prepared to speak the name she'd been holding onto all these months. "Dean Hoffman."

"Oh no. I heard about him. That sucks."

"Pretty much."

"What about his place? His old man's still around."

"No way. I promised to steer clear of his dad. Dean told me he's trouble."

"And you trust his opinion?" Leslie scoffed. "Let's be honest, he was a bit of a dick sometimes."

"You said *dick*. I'm telling." Dee giggled in the backseat.

"Hey, do you want me to keep bringing you leftover pie from the diner?" Leslie said, addressing the rearview mirror.

More giggles.

"Sometimes he was," Tammy replied. "But Floyd Hoffman really is bad news. My parents talk about him all the time, especially since Dad lost his job. Mom went to school with him. So did my aunt and Arlene from the salon. They all say the same thing: he's strange."

"You realize three of those people are on your do-not-trust list."

"I know what went on at Dean's house. His father was no father at all. He's got big issues, and I don't want him near my son."

"You know what he's doing for the people in town, right?" Leslie asked.

Tammy jerked her thumb at the backseat. "I know by the time they grow up, there won't be any jobs left thanks to him. Narrow Falls will be a ghost town. Everyone I know says so, even Dean."

"Don't you get it?" Leslie said. "Dean probably died because of the mill."

"I know."

"His dad just wants the mill to stop making people sick. The guy's a hero." Leslie pulled her collar aside to show the tattooed letters *EB* on her chest. "Elizabeth Benton, my mom. She worked in an office at the mill. When I was twelve, she suffocated from an asthma attack," she said, her voice full of anger. "Dee's always getting nosebleeds. We keep our windows on the north side of our house closed so the ashes from the mill stacks don't blow through the screens. There's a grey film coating our house unless it's rained recently."

Tammy couldn't argue with Leslie, not after hearing that sad story. But she'd never buy Floyd Hoffman as a good guy. People could look shiny on the outside, but there was always something ugly buried underneath.

"Dean made me promise to keep his dad out of our baby's life. I have to keep my word now. I mean, he's dead. You don't go back on that kind of promise."

"But you're not," Leslie countered. "Do what you gotta do. You wouldn't have to stay with Hoffman forever. Look at it this way: his son knocked you up, and he owes you. You're just collecting."

Although Tammy hated to admit it, Leslie's argument made sense. So what if she stayed there for a few days or even a week? What harm could it do?

"Let me think about it," she said.

"Think fast. You've got two miles to make up your mind."

27.

A procession of cars streamed past Floyd as he hastened along Main Street towards the river. The sky's colour reminded him of soggy newsprint, and the air was rife with the stink of rotten eggs. Conditions were perfect to stoke the crowd now gathering to hear R.J. McLelland address tensions over the mill's future.

With every stride, an overstuffed valise bumped the outside of Floyd's left knee. A document tube hung against his back, its shoulder strap forming a dark slash across his chest. The rolled-up maps and charts inside would illustrate facts capable of shredding R.J.'s credibility with the audience. Floyd was battle ready. He'd pry the mill wide open until all its dirty secrets rolled out in plain view.

Up ahead, taillights blinked red as drivers turned west onto Water Street, undoubtedly bound for the public meeting at the McLelland Community Centre. The advance of traffic stopped as a grizzled old man stepped off the sidewalk and began shuffling across the turn lane. If R.J. had his way, Floyd would be hunched over a cane himself before the resolution of his lawsuit. No way in hell that was going to happen.

"Floyd!" Tony waved from the centre line of Main Street and hustled towards the sidewalk. "How are you doing, you son of a gun?" He pumped Floyd's right hand in a firm handshake.

"I've been busy," Floyd replied.

"Heard you clocked Spivey. After it happened, he came in for a beer. Two raccoon eyes and tape over his nose."

"No kidding." Floyd pulled his shoulders back with a foreign sense of pride.

"High time someone kicked that braggart's ass. But I gotta say, I was surprised *you* did it."

"It's good to be a little unpredictable," Floyd replied. "Are you attending the McLelland's meeting?"

"Yeah, I'd like to hear firsthand what this clown has to say." Tony whistled and jerked back his head. "Holy Toledo, the smell's wicked bad today."

They waited for a break in traffic and then loped across Water Street. The presentation was set to begin in twenty minutes, but already cars were doubling back from the community centre parking lot in search of open space out front along the curb.

"So why'd you do it?" Tony asked.

Floyd's shoe struck a loose chunk of sidewalk and sent it skittering into the grass. "Do what?"

"Hit Spivey."

Full disclosure was out of the question, so Floyd improvised. "Ungentlemanly conduct."

"I get it," Tony said. "There's more, but you're keeping it under your hat." His chuckle ended abruptly. "Oh shit."

Mill workers had congregated in groups across the community centre lawn. Floyd recognized most of them from his afternoon visits to Tony's Pub. Among their numbers were men who'd been laid off and others waiting to join their ranks. Shoulder to shoulder, they joked casually and smoked the remaining stubs of their cigarettes.

One figure, dressed in a camouflage jacket, flicked his cigarette into the grass and stepped away from the crowd. "Hey, asshole!" Kenny yelled at Floyd. "Where do you think you're going?"

Floyd bristled as Kenny stormed towards him.

Onlookers edged closer to the walkway, their eyes flashing with anticipation.

"I'm talking to you," Kenny said, thrusting his face close enough for Floyd to see the corner of one eye pulsing.

"It's a free country." Floyd inched forward.

"Come on, fellas," Tony said. "There's women and children present."

Kenny directed his glare at Floyd. "Don't buy everything this guy's selling, Tony. He wants to shut us down. No mill—no money. We'd all have to start drinking at home. Capisce?"

"Like the man said," Tony replied flatly, "it's a free country."

With hands raised in mock surrender, Kenny backed onto the lawn. Floyd's expression remained stony as he and Tony continued to the front of the building.

"It'd be a mistake to rile this crowd," Tony said, peering over his shoulder.

Floyd looked straight ahead and kept walking.

The McLelland's Community Centre sign was fixed to the brick face of the historic building. R.J.'s family left its mark on everything, like a dog pissing on a tree.

Floyd hadn't been at the community centre since an end-of-season party for Dean's baseball team nearly five years previous. Inside the foyer, the smell of floor wax and damp plywood distracted from the mill's stench. A column of people stuttered through the single entrance to the meeting hall, impeded by friends and neighbours pausing to greet one another. Baseball and hockey trophies of McLelland-sponsored teams jammed the display cabinets on both sides of the door. Floyd searched the photos wedged among them for a glimpse of Dean's face.

"Big turnout," Tony commented as they squeezed into the hall.

"There must be over two hundred people here," Floyd replied, his mouth slightly agape as he searched for vacant seats.

The hall had been arranged with rows of wooden chairs separated by a centre aisle. McLelland's scarlet company banner stretched across the front wall above a long table that had been draped in matching cloth. Four empty chairs huddled tightly against the back edge of the table. To the right of this arrangement, a podium stood, outfitted with a microphone.

A journalist, one Floyd recognized from a headshot in the *Sentinel*, was leaning against the far wall. Behind him, a photographer squinted into the eyepiece of a camera sporting an impressive zoom lens. Floyd sighed and thought of his own camera, now relegated to the back of a closet. He'd never take pictures with it again.

He'd only bought it to photograph family. There was no one left whose life needed documenting.

The aroma of coffee called out to him from the opposing wall. Below the kitchen service window, a sturdy table had been set up with a percolator and trays lined with cookies and doughnuts. A handful of people lingered there holding Styrofoam cups. They stepped aside to make way for a grey-haired woman carrying a plastic water pitcher and four glasses to the speaker's table. She completed her delivery and hobbled stiffly back to the kitchen door.

"Over there, third row from the back." Floyd pointed out a pair of empty chairs left of the centre aisle. They'd afford a clear view of the podium, plus he'd be positioned to read the room once R.J. got rolling.

"Your lawyer boys are here," Tony said, thrusting his chin towards the front of the room. Clive's head bowed over a clipboard as he flipped through some papers. Next to him, Gerald smoothed his tie and glared at the hall entrance over the top of his glasses. Before he and Tony took their seats, Floyd caught Gerald's attention with the wave of a hand. Gerald motioned for him to come forward to an empty seat he'd saved, but Floyd declined.

"You should be with them, up front," Tony said.

"This spot suits me just fine," Floyd answered. The crowd would better hear him speak from the centre of the room.

He set the valise between his feet and rolled open the leather flap. The portly woman sitting to his left began rifling through her handbag as he touched each file folder tab for good luck. She eyed him with curiosity after she bumped the document tube lying across his lap. Floyd glanced over his shoulder at the pair of senior ladies occupying the chairs directly behind him. One smiled at him through a clear plastic oxygen mask with tubes that ran to somewhere beneath her chair.

"Where the hell is McLelland?" Tony said. "If a man calls a meeting for ten o'clock, he should be here at ten o'clock."

"It's all posturing," Floyd replied with a scowl.

At twenty minutes past ten, the Napoleonic figure of Mayor Bidwell strutted up the aisle with the self-importance of a man about to enjoy his moment in the limelight. Three sombre men dressed in dark suits filed along behind him. The first was Phillip Dixon. He met the audience's curious stares with a confident smile as he paraded to the front of the room. But the second man followed with rigid shoulders and his gaze directed at the floor. Although his curly hair and thinning crown seemed familiar, Floyd couldn't remember where they'd met. Anger roiled in his gut when he recognized the hawkish features of the last man to claim a seat at the head table. What in the hell was Rose Brookman's lawyer doing here?

Bidwell reached over the podium and tilted the mic downward. "Good morning!" Feedback squealed through the speakers. Among the audience, shoulders cringed and hands flew to cover ears. "Return to your seats," Bidwell said. Stragglers sauntered to their chairs or crammed into slivers of space along the back wall. "The ladies will make sure there's hot coffee after the meeting. If Frank sits down, there'll be cookies left over too." Laughter rippled through the crowd as a startled man slunk away from the snack table.

"Narrow Falls—a great town made by three generations of McLellands, all men of vision." Bidwell paused to beam at the crowd. "Put your hands together for a man who needs no introduction around here. R.J. McLelland!"

Applause swelled as R.J. McLelland showboated down the aisle, grasping the hand of his shapely wife dressed in a pale yellow pantsuit. Each time he stopped to shake supporters' hands, she stood by, staring at the floor until he latched on to her again. R.J. spun her towards the crowd once they'd reached the front of the hall. "My wife, everyone," he said with the sweep of an arm. "A yellow rose of Texas right here in Narrow Falls."

She squinted as he crushed a kiss into her left cheek. R.J. milked the last drop of applause from the crowd and nudged his wife towards a vacant chair in the front row.

"My mill employs many of Narrow Falls's sons and daughters. Like any family, we need to convene on occasion to get right with one another. So I'm not gonna stand behind that podium and pontificate from on high. I'm gonna talk with you like the old friends we are. Whatever questions you have, I'm here to answer."

Tony leaned towards Floyd. "This ought to be good."

From the rows ahead of them, a gravelly voice called out, "Is it true that McLelland's is looking into why so many folks living along the river are sick or dying?"

"Hand to God, I would look into it if I believed the operating processes of my mill were to blame for any misfortune in our town."

A sharp whistle cut through the hoots of approval. Floyd's head jerked towards the sound and found Kenny loosing a second round of adulation on the crowd.

Near the kitchen entrance, a middle-aged woman sprang to her feet. "We're all losing friends and neighbours. I worry about my boys and my husband working for you." She shook a finger at R.J. "My brother-in-law's been a welder at McLelland's for nineteen years. Now he's got six months to live, and I wanna know why."

R.J. puffed his cigar and waited for the room to quiet. "We all have our vices," he said, patting his belly. "For years, my doctor's been telling me to watch my diet. But do I listen? No. And I'm smoking these things." He lifted his cigar in jest. "I'm sure they'll be the death of me. When tragedy strikes, we point the finger of blame away from ourselves. It's only natural." He shrugged. "But you mustn't tie the mill to the whipping post. Our operations satisfy the guidelines established by the government. I personally guarantee that McLelland's is the cause of neither ailment nor death."

Blood boiling, Floyd rocketed to his feet. "You are covering up the truth!"

"Sit down, Hoffman," someone hollered. "No one wants to hear from you."

He shook the rolled-up papers from the tube and waved them above his head. "The mill is poisoning us. It's all documented here."

R.J. raised a hand to silence Floyd. "You carry neither the authority nor the expertise to document anything substantive, Mr. Hoffman."

"It is your moral obligation to fund a morbidity study," Floyd said. Booing had risen from the crowd before he finished the statement.

While R.J. acknowledged his supporters with an appreciative nod, the journalist raised his hand. Floyd sank to his chair, undaunted. This wasn't over yet.

"Mike Hornby with the *Sentinel.* Mr. McLelland, I spoke recently with Justice Reynolds on the matter of the morbidity study. If he sides with the plaintiff in the

Hoffman case, he may consider including it as part of the judgment. Have you any comment?"

R.J.'s smile faded. "A study like that would cost nearly two hundred thousand dollars and take four years to complete. And for what? So some city boys can tell us what I already know? That the mill never harmed anyone? Ha! I could put a bunch of you back to work for the same money, and we'd all be a hell of a lot farther ahead."

"I'll take one of those jobs! And so will Hank!" Kenny called out. The room broke into thunderous clapping as he jostled the man next to him.

"What do you say to claims that the mill needs to upgrade the scrubber to reduce the release of chemical vapours and fly ash?" Hornby asked.

"If it's not broke, don't fix it. Our tests prove one hundred percent that the mill satisfies the emission standards recommended by our government."

"Where's the proof?" Floyd yelled from his seat.

A spotted hand grabbed his sleeve from the row behind. "Knock it off," the friend of the oxygen-mask lady said. Her breath smelled like sour milk and peppermint when she spoke next to his ear. "If that mill shuts down, we'll both lose our husband's pensions and their health insurance too."

"Respectfully, madam, I'm not trying to shut anyone down. I just want them to change."

The woman on his left leaned her shiny face next to his. "Same thing," she said emphatically.

A young mother stood with a whimpering toddler straddling one hip. "I live just off Water Street, east of downtown. Two of my kids are on puffers, and now my youngest has a cough that won't go away. Some days, I can't open the windows for the stink. Something's wrong!"

Floyd bounded to his feet before R.J. could formulate a response. "Independent testing confirms your scrubber is releasing airbourne particulate at levels grossly exceeding the guidelines. We're talking fly ash and chemical vapour spewing into the air. The mill is piping a toxic soup into our river. From here to Brewster's Gorge, you can find dead fish sprouting tumours. They're floating belly-up along the shoreline from here to—"

"You've had your moment, Mr. Hoffman," R.J. said. "Sit down."

Floyd trapped the roll of maps under his right arm and gathered the open valise to his chest. The laughter began to subside as he squeezed past Tony in an effort to reach the aisle. "The Swiss have already outlawed the use of chlorine gas in kraft pulping."

"Oh, your beloved Swiss again." R.J. puffed his cigar while his supporters jeered at Floyd.

"Boooo," Kenny and Hank shouted in tandem. Voices throughout the hall joined theirs.

"Let him speak," Tony yelled.

"They've published multiple studies proving chlorine's negative effects on people and the environment. I can show you." Floyd fumbled with the valise as he approached R.J.

Partway to the podium, two men wearing scarlet McLelland jackets left their aisle seats to block Floyd's advance. "Sit. Down. Now," the taller one said.

"You claim to love this town," Floyd pressed forward raising his voice, "yet your mill withholds pollution monitoring results from the community and refuses to perform studies critical to safeguarding public health."

R.J.'s voice boomed, "Mr. Hoffman, please sit down. You are frightening the ladies."

"How many of us have to die before you agree to upgrade the mill's antiquated scrubber?"

"You are out of line, sir," R.J. responded. "Our tests show clearly that our emissions are below the recommended levels, isn't that right, Len?" He looked over his shoulder to the speaker table. The curly haired man bolted to attention and gave a curt nod.

Mike Hornby raised a hand above his head and called out to the man. "Sir, your last name and position, for the record."

Len fidgeted with his necktie and answered, "Rathburn, engineer."

"Come clean, Rathburn," Floyd shouted. "What's really pouring out of that mill?"

Rathburn's eyes darted to R.J.

Floyd turned towards the audience and pointed to a man seated nearby. "Franklin, your house is directly south of the mill. Your Louise is five years gone, and you've been recently diagnosed with a spot on your lung." When he paused to suck in a breath of air, his gaze landed at the back of the hall. "And Kenny! You grew up in the same neighbourhood. Your father worked in the mill, fished the river, and lived along its banks his entire life."

"Leave my old man out of this!" Kenny said, striding away from the back wall with a finger aimed at Floyd.

"Two years ago, the cancer got him." Floyd dropped the valise and maps at his feet.

"Son of a bitch!" Kenny steamed towards him.

"You could be next," Floyd blurted. He raised his fists, but it was too late. Kenny tackled him and bounced his head off the floor. Pain exploded inside Floyd's skull. He blindly pushed his hands against the heaving bulk that had pinned him to the floor. Kenny's mouth screamed insults and spittle just inches from his nose. "I'm trying to help you," Floyd wheezed. The two McLelland men grabbed Kenny's arms and wrenched him off Floyd. While they hustled Kenny out through a side door, Gerald and Clive hauled Floyd to his feet. A light round of applause broke out, followed by excited chatter.

"I can drive you home, if you like," Gerald said.

"Hell no." Floyd adjusted the collar of his jacket and smoothed his hair into place. "I'm just getting warmed up." He gathered his valise and crushed maps, then returned to his original seat next to Tony, head held high.

Mayor Bidwell returned to the podium and tapped a finger against the microphone. "Folks, Mr. McLelland is ready to resume the meeting."

R.J. folded his arms across his pinstriped suit and waited for the crowd to settle. "My father always said that it takes two to tango. Mr. Hoffman, I believe it's clear to everyone here that you aggravated your opponent to the point of fisticuffs. It seems only fair that you excuse yourself from the remainder of this meeting as well."

Even when one of McLelland's henchmen stood glaring at the end of his row, Floyd stared at the podium with his chin thrust forward in defiance.

"Well then, we'll forgive your excesses," R.J. said, "knowing full well that your behaviour is coloured by personal losses, past and present."

Like a playground bully, R.J. was taunting him in full view of everyone.

"As I was about to say, we could make the changes Mr. Hoffman's proposing, but without support from outside sources, we're gonna have some trouble." His hands dropped to his sides, and he paced the width of the hall. "I won't lie to you. Losing our largest American contract last year set us back. That's what comes of Mr. Hoffman airing our dirty laundry in the newspapers." He raised his right palm to subdue the booing at the rear of the hall.

Floyd's jaw clenched.

"What about government funding?" someone called out. "The mill in Reardon got money from the feds."

"My people submitted paperwork months ago. But you know the government." Murmurs travelled along the rows, and R.J. flashed a grin. "Just this week, I got the Minister of the Environment on the telephone. I told him he'd better get his bean counters in line and take care of us because the fine people of Narrow Falls will not put up with his bureaucratic red tape!"

"You tell 'em, R.J.!" Hank delivered an earsplitting whistle.

"What if they don't come through?" someone asked.

"More layoffs, and not just at the mill." R.J. paused to knock cigar ashes into a water glass sitting on the table. "If this thing goes south, a lot of people are gonna feel the pinch— the logging company, sawmill, truck drivers, downtown business owners. Our young people will flee to the cities for work. There'll be a real estate glut when families start leaving. Your home price'll drop like a stone."

Groans sprang up throughout the hall.

Mike Hornby raised his voice above the fray. "Do you foresee a mill closure?"

With the conviction of a Southern evangelist, R.J. McLelland spread his arms wide and stepped closer to the front row. "You all are my family. We're joined at the hip. The man spreading wild claims based on unfortunate coincidences was not born and bred here. Foreigners don't understand that what happens to you, happens to me." He laid a hand over his heart. "I feel your hurt deeply, and I will fight with everything I have to make sure this mill stays open so there are jobs for the generations to come."

Floyd grimaced at the murmurs of ascent. How could people be taken in by R.J.'s theatrics?

"Duty calls, but I leave you in the capable hands of my protégées. They will take down your questions, each and every one of which I promise to address personally." R.J. extended an arm to his wife, and together they hastened down the aisle. The sheen of sweat on his forehead was visible when he steamed past Floyd's row, and a trail of cigar smoke lingered in his wake.

Phillip Dixon positioned himself behind the podium. Before he'd time to clear his throat, a hailstorm of questions rained down on the podium.

Floyd drummed his fingers against his kneecaps. "You sticking around, Tony?"

"For a bit."

"I've seen enough," Floyd said, rising to his feet.

He left the community centre and headed home along Water Street, then onto Main. He was mulling over the wins and losses of the past hour when a black Lincoln Continental pulled alongside him and slowed to match his pace. The back window slid down, and R.J. McLelland's right arm lolled out. "Did you enjoy the show, Mr. Hoffman?"

A couple watched from the steps of the stationery store across the street. "This conversation is *not* happening," Floyd said. He looked straight ahead and continued walking.

"You're tough, I'll give you that. Rose and I thought for sure you'd buckle after signing your boy away, especially with you believing you weren't his real father."

Floyd stopped dead.

"She really had you over a barrel with all that paternity business." R.J. paused to adjust a cuff link. "Carl Spivey's a real son of a bitch. He was tied to the old ball and chain once. It didn't work out. The wife went on to remarry. She had a whole passel of kids with the new fella. Not a one with Carl."

"If you got something to say, McLelland, come out and say it."

"You jumped the gun on signing those guardianship papers for Rose. Should have done a little research into Mr. Spivey's ability to perpetuate the human species."

Son of a bitch! Is he telling the truth or torturing me with another lie? Floyd fought the urge to knock the smug look from R.J.'s face.

"Call off this David-and-Goliath sideshow. You're getting nowhere with it. A peashooter versus a cannon, that's the fight you've started. I can stall this thing until we're both old men and no one remembers why we're fighting in the first place."

"I won't let that happen."

R.J.'s robust laughter left him breathless. "He won't let that happen!" he sputtered. The heel of one hand swiped the tears from his eyes. Upon his order, the Lincoln pulled away from the curb and sped off.

Floyd watched the car disappear from view. If R.J. felt confident of winning the case, he'd have never risked approaching his adversary publicly after the meeting. The uncertain outcome of the ministry's findings and the court ruling must be weighing on him. Four years into this wait-and-see legal game, Floyd sensed a fracture developing in his opponent's armour.

Change was coming. He felt it in the air. But even so, R.J.'s reference to Carl Spivey rankled Floyd like a toothache. What was he missing?

A few blocks from home, Floyd's thoughts turned to Marian. It had been two days since they'd been together. That afternoon, he'd take Strum and drive out to see her. Maybe they'd stay for a few days of fresh country air. He still couldn't believe Marian had received such a generous inheritance from Rose Brookman. Marian splurging on a red Camaro coupe seemed out of character, but he was most troubled that she'd bought a hobby farm twenty minutes' drive outside of town. What did it all mean?

"When winter strikes, you'll never make it out of the laneway," he'd warned her. "The outbuildings need work, and the orchard needs taming."

"Oh, you sweet man. I've always dreamt of a place in the country, a place of my very own," she'd said, laying a hand against his cheek. "I love you. Nothing will change between us."

And it hadn't.

Marian had moved into the farmhouse at the end of February, so they'd not had a chance to fully explore the surrounding sixty acres of wooded lot, nor the creek that ran through it. They'd found pleasure in the discovery of deer tracks at the edge of the barnyard and spreading birdseed for the siskins and nuthatches that frequented the feeder outside the kitchen window. Then, of course, there'd been the lovemaking after which they'd laid back on the pillows, breathless and laughing like teenagers.

Floyd found himself smiling as he rounded onto his street. Daisies would please Marian. He must remember to pick up a bouquet at the florist before heading over.

Half a block from home, an approaching car caught his attention—a blue Mustang with a distinctive white stripe running up the centre of its hood. A little girl leaned her blond head through the back window as the car drew nearer. She hooked her fingers inside the corners of her mouth and made a face as the car zinged past.

The brake lights flickered at the next corner, and the girl disappeared inside the car. Where was she going? Not to a house downwind of the mill, he hoped.

He'd just resumed walking when he glimpsed a female figure sitting on the front steps of his house. A sheath of long hair swept forward when she leaned over her knees to search the opposite end of the street. Floyd breathed in sharply. He hesitated in front of Vivian Parker's house and balanced himself against her picket fence.

She turned to face him, then rose to her feet. Floyd scarcely blinked as he unlatched the gate and closed it behind him. He was all but certain she was Tammy King.

Her face was pale and her eyes red-rimmed, as though she'd been crying. Floyd didn't speak for fear she might bolt. The young woman wiped her palms on the front of her jeans and cautiously descended the steps until she'd stepped onto the walkway in front of him. They stood in mutual silence until he worried that she might leave without telling him anything.

"Can I help you?" he asked softly.

"I was a friend of your son's."

It is *her.*

"We were very close," she added.

"You're Tammy King?"

Her cheeks reddened. "You know my parents, Mirabelle and Lawrence King."

His name must have suffered maligning in the King household. Floyd could sense the girl measuring him for signs confirming her parents' opinion. He must tread carefully here, walking a line between her preconceptions and his overwhelming urge to pepper her with questions. Could she tell him any details about his son's final days? Did Dean forgive him in the end?

"We've met."

"I should have come sooner, but . . ." Tammy's head hung forward, and she traced a crack in the walkway with the toe of her right sneaker.

"We've both suffered a loss." Floyd hesitated before adding, "There was a memorial service for Dean, here at the house."

"Sorry, I couldn't make it." She hugged her arms around her stomach and stared down the street.

The girl's nature troubled Floyd. She was hiding something.

"Did you have contact with Dean," he asked gently, "after he left for Toronto?"

"No," Tammy answered.

"You're not here to deliver a message from him?"

Her head shook slightly.

Floyd clamped his temples between the heels of both hands. So much hope he'd pinned on this girl telling him some bit of news to absolve him from the guilt of failing his son. Did Dean understand how desperately he'd wanted him to come home? There was no guarantee that Rose had kept her end of the bargain. Did his son leave this world convinced that Floyd was not his biological father?

"Mr. Hoffman, I—"

"No formality," he said, wiping his eyes. "Just call me *Floyd*."

"I was hoping to speak to you about a private matter," she said. "Would it be all right if we went inside?"

"Of course."

Partway up the porch steps, he noticed her scant belongings piled to the right of the door. A crumpled T-shirt and some socks had escaped the unzipped backpack lying prone at his feet. A bulging garbage bag leaned against her cardboard box and offered glimpses of white through the tears in its side. He pulled the screen door back and pushed the key into the lock. When he stole a second glance at the heap, he noticed what had previously been shielded from view behind the first of the porch columns and the overgrowth of climbing vines.

A baby!

Floyd's hands dropped away from the door like felled trees. His mouth gaped. No sound came out except for air escaping the back of his throat.

The child was sleeping in an upholstered car seat. Right there on his porch. A baby. He must be seeing things.

Tammy's shaky voice reached his ear. "My son," she said.

The dark hair and lashes. Those delicate fingers with nails like tiny seashells. It was as if he were looking at a snapshot of Dean at that age. It seemed almost too much to hope for. "Is he . . . ?"

"Yes, he's Dean's."

"Ahhh." A swell of joy surged inside Floyd's chest.

Tammy stepped between Floyd and the car seat to unbuckle the shoulder straps. She picked the baby up and cradled him in her arms.

Floyd's voice shook. "Can I touch him?"

"I guess."

Floyd nudged an index finger against the underside of the baby's right fist. When the miniature fingers curled around his, the feeling in his heart topped anything he'd ever experienced. Dean was present in this child—in his blood, his breath, and his features.

"I called him Jordy," she said, twisting away from Floyd slightly.

He let the baby's hand go and studied her face.

She repositioned Jordy and directed her gaze to the door. "Could we . . . ?"

"Of course." Floyd ushered her inside. Women were mysterious creatures. In teenage form, they were even more confounding. Tammy King must have expected his interest in the child, yet that very interest seemed to put her off. If Marian were here, she'd try to feed the girl. Yes, food solved everything.

"Please make yourself comfortable." He gestured towards the living room. "I'll be in directly."

She turned away, and Jordy, with his chin resting on her shoulder, focused his eyes squarely on Floyd. A corner of his mouth lifted slightly.

Buoyed by what he felt sure had been a smile, Floyd determined to win Tammy over. She held the key to his redemption. Without her approval, he'd never get close to his grandson.

He looked inside the refrigerator. Milk or orange juice? He poured a glass of each and then buttered two slabs of Marian's banana bread. He arranged the refreshments and napkins on a silver tray, as Marian often did, and headed towards the living room.

He froze in the doorway. Tammy occupied the armchair next to the fireplace with her left leg tucked beneath her. Jordy rested in the crook of her an arm, cooing happily. So many times, he'd seen Bonnie sit the same way, singing lullabies to Dean.

Tammy let her tucked foot slide to the floor. "Is something wrong?"

"You . . ." His voice caught in his throat. He took a second and tried again. "You reminded me of someone is all." Floyd set the clattering tray on the coffee table and slid the glasses towards her. "Milk or juice?" he asked, his voice thin as a wire. "The banana bread is homemade. I didn't bake it . . ."

She forced a weak smile. "You must be wondering why I'm here."

Floyd settled back against the sofa. "I figured you'd tell me when you were ready."

"I've been out of town for several months. I'm back now, but the situation's not so good with my parents, you know?"

"Do you need a place to live?" Floyd wanted to laugh out loud. Things couldn't be going any better. "Stay here. You and the baby."

Her cool grey eyes narrowed.

He'd shown too much enthusiasm and used too many words. Still, he couldn't stop himself from going on. "There's lot of space. And a dog. He's in the backyard. Kids love dogs."

"Just for a few days," she cautioned. "Once I get on my feet, I can look after us." A glint of determination shone in her eyes.

"My home is your home."

Tammy straightened the baby's socks and smoothed the shirt over his belly. "I'm starting work at Arlene's Beauty Salon on Monday," she said.

"That's good," he said halfheartedly. In a few weeks, Tammy might have enough money to strike out on her own with the baby. But Floyd needed more time. "Have you arranged for someone to look after Jordy while you work?"

"Not yet," Tammy replied, "but I'll figure something out."

"I'll do it. No charge."

"But you have a job."

"My situation has changed."

"Are you good with babies?"

The tone of her voice dredged up Dean's voice in Floyd's mind, as though he'd asked the question. "I took care of my son."

Tammy wore a faraway look, as though she were weighing the pros and cons of Floyd's offer. "All right," she finally answered. "But like I said, it's only temporary."

"It could be longer than you think," Floyd said hopefully. "Arlene won't pay much." When Tammy's chin lowered, he regretted his words.

"I should bring my stuff in from the porch," she said.

"Could I hold him?" Floyd asked.

Tammy hesitated, then passed the baby into his arms.

Awash with adoration, Floyd studied his grandson's face. He glanced at Tammy and noted the concern in her eyes. Or was it agitation? "I've got him. He's all right," Floyd assured her. He touched a finger to the baby's chin. "Isn't that right, Jordy?" The baby produced a joyful squeal. Floyd's gleefulness switched to bewilderment when he heard the screen door bang shut behind Tammy.

He stared after her for a moment before lifting Jordy close to his face. The sweet baby smell of his cheek rolled back the years to when Dean first came home from the hospital, so helpless and vulnerable.

"Thank you, Dean," he whispered. "Thank you for this gift. I promise to love and protect your boy. Whatever he asks me, I will tell him. About you. About your mother. About anything. And Tammy too. You loved her, and I will love her, as a daughter."

Jordy's face grew rosy, and his mouth puckered.

Floyd jounced him lightly, but tears began rolling from the corners of his eyes, and a light whimper followed close behind. "What's taking your mother so long?" Floyd said as he crossed the kitchen. A few feet before the screen door, he stopped abruptly.

Tammy and Allan faced each other on the porch, deep in conversation. They weren't touching, but their closeness belied a level of familiarity. Maybe Allan had known about Tammy and the baby all along.

Floyd stepped forward as Jordy began to balk. Tammy and Allan turned sharply towards the door. Their cheeks burned red.

"Jordy's upset," Floyd said weakly.

"He's hungry," Tammy replied. She opened the screen door and came into the kitchen.

"Can I help?" he said, passing the baby into her arms. "Are there bottles for him in your backpack?"

Tammy mumbled, "No. I just need a room."

"A room? Oh." Floyd realized his gaffe. She wanted privacy to nurse the baby. His face grew hot with embarrassment. "Let me show you to the guest room."

"No need."

Floyd's eyes widened as she marched up the stairs unprompted. Of course! Bonnie's negligee under the guestroom bed. Tammy knew her way around his house.

"How you doing?" Allan said sheepishly.

Floyd looked him in the eye. "Except for Dean being born, I've never been happier."

"That's cool, Gramps."

"You could have told me."

"Nah, I couldn't. Not my news to tell."

Floyd nodded and looked back at the stairs. "I've put my foot in it a little with her, haven't I?"

Allan shrugged. "Honesty and time, man. Keep talking it out. She'll come around."

"That'll work, huh?"

"I'm counting on it," Allan replied.

Floyd's breath lingered in brief white puffs during his walk to work. A light frost had dusted the rooftops overnight, and blades of grass poked up from the earth like brittle swords. Downtown shops had already begun hanging Halloween decorations in their windows. He made a mental note to remind Bonnie of her plans to transform a red skirt into a Superman cape for Dean's costume. The distraction of a project was good for her. Good for Floyd too.

The October chill stayed with Floyd throughout the morning as he sorted bins of envelopes and parcels. Shortly before noon, one of the women from the customer service wicket leaned over the counter that framed his work area.

"Your wife's here," she said with an inflection of annoyance.

Floyd hurried past her towards the lobby.

"Try returning her calls why don't ya?" she hollered after him.

He expected to find Bonnie waiting, wide-eyed and fretting. Instead, there was only an unkempt teenage boy staring out through the bank of windows overlooking the street. Fearful that Bonnie may be pacing the sidewalk in a state of agitation, Floyd headed straight for the window next to him.

For three consecutive nights, he'd slept alone while she buzzed around the house doing who knew what. The dam was due to break, and her lightness would give way to dark emotions. Hopefully, he could redirect the surge back to the privacy of their home. There were eyes everywhere, and in their small town judgment and ridicule trumped empathy and compassion.

"I'm right here," a voice said.

Floyd's head jerked back. It took a few seconds to reconcile that his wife's voice had come from this figure dressed in baggy clothes. But then he saw the familiar doe-like eyes and sensual lips, and he understood.

Bonnie's hair had been hacked close to the scalp. Uneven patches jutted up from her crown, and a jagged fringe lay across her forehead. A few unsevered strands coiled on her shoulders.

"Your hair . . ." Floyd finally said.

"I need money," she said, as though nothing were amiss.

"Use the grocery money," he said slowly. Without the distracting mass of dark hair hugging her temples, Floyd noticed a sharpness that was new to her cheekbones. Her expressive eyes now overwhelmed her face.

"It's gone," she said angrily, "and I can't exactly ask for more at the bank, can I?"

"And you know why," Floyd replied.

"That was months ago. It's not like I bankrupted us."

A mother and two children had just carried a parcel to the first wicket. She turned to eye Bonnie with curiosity.

"We're just being careful, that's all," Floyd said.

"Any photographer worth his salt has a bigger camera than yours and a bunch of lenses. And tripods. I thought new equipment would make you happy. You should have kept the extra sets of tires too. There's plenty of room in the carriage house to store them."

"Your shirt looks familiar," Floyd said, trying to steer the conversation in a new direction. He recognized the red plaid flannel as having once belonged to his father. And the rubber boots had been his mother's.

"I found it in a box of old things in the carriage house. The pants too." When she lifted her shirttails, he saw that the belt he'd just bought from Harding's Family Clothiers was cinched tight around her waist. He groaned inwardly at the fresh nail holes she'd hammered into the leather. Bonnie turned her face towards the windows and coughed into her sleeve. Her cheeks were flushed, but the rest of her face remained pale.

Floyd pulled some folded ten-dollar bills from his wallet. "Have you eaten today?"

"Kind of." Bonnie grabbed the money and counted it. "This should do for today."

"What do you need money for?"

"It's a surprise," she said, smiling broadly.

Floyd hated surprises. She was holding herself together for the benefit of his coworkers and the few patrons trickling through the lobby, but if he vexed her, she'd uncoil like a spring, and there'd be no stopping her. "Does it have anything to do with the fish drawings taped across the kitchen cupboard doors?"

"It might. Ha!" She blew him a kiss and headed for the street.

When he came home that evening, Dean was absorbed by after-school reruns of the *Little Rascals.* A carton of milk sat next to a glass on the coffee table, and an open cookie bag was nestled in his lap.

"Hey," Floyd said. "Don't ruin your dinner." He reached out to ruffle the boy's hair. Without looking away from the television, Dean leaned away to escape his touch. "Where's your mother?"

Dean pointed in the direction of the room behind the kitchen.

Floyd knocked and tested the doorknob. It was locked. "It's me. Open up," he called, but she didn't answer. When he pressed an ear against the door, he heard a rhythmic scraping sound.

"Hold on!" Bonnie said. A moment later, the door eased open wide enough for her to squirm her way into the hall with a wince. "No peeking," she warned, rubbing the small of her back. The circles under her eyes appeared darker than they'd been earlier in the day.

"Have you eaten?" Floyd asked.

"Too busy."

"Bonnie, you know what happens if you don't eat."

"I know, I know. But nothing tastes good." Then she looked past him and called out. "Put your shoes on, kid, and grab your coat. We're outta here."

Dean cheered and dashed for the front door.

"Where are you taking him?" Floyd asked as he followed behind her.

"Out."

"On a school night?"

"A little fun never killed anyone."

"Be back for dinner in an hour."

"Yes, *Mom*." She made a face and then tickled Dean while he laced up his runners. "Your father is a killjoy."

Two hours later, Floyd finished his dinner alone. As the sun began to set, he drove around town searching for Bonnie and Dean. They'd left the house on foot. How far could they get? He found them at Brewster's Gorge, scaling the waterfall rocks in the dying light.

When sadness returned in November, Bonnie took to their bed wearing her father-in-law's pants and grey flannel shirt along with a pair of thick wool socks. By the third day, she'd begun to smell of dried perspiration and unchanged underclothes. She'd cough and rouse slightly, then quickly drift back to sleep. Her refusal to eat had begun to take its toll. Bonnie's hip bones pushed against her skin. Her once full breasts had retired the lower portion of her brassiere cups.

One Saturday, while Dean played at a friend's house, Floyd's curiosity got the better of him. He checked the pantry, where spare keys hung from a nail, but the key to the locked room was not among them. He resorted to climbing a few rungs of a ladder he'd propped against the house and peered through the side window. The aged finish had been sanded from the floor and the wood lay bare as bones.

The following week, Bonnie was out of bed and at it again. He supplied her with a pail of paint in the shade she'd requested. Royal blue speckles smattered the front of her shirt and the knees of her pants. The smell of drying paint eked from the room. The door remained locked. When Floyd peeked through the window from outside, small paint cans lined the windowsill and blocked his view of the floor. Their next-door neighbour, Vivian Parker, paused over the pile of leaves she'd been raking in her yard. It must be strange, Floyd thought, to see a man peeping into his own house.

During the week, he decided to come home for lunch and check on Bonnie. Just as he arrived, Marian stepped out of the house. Her stylish appearance caught him off guard. She'd dressed in a long fitted coat with a real fur collar. Her blond hair fell over her shoulders.

"I'm worried about Bonnie," she said.

"She'll snap out of it, like always," he replied.

"I should warn you, Mrs. Brookman is hell bent to get her on medication. Bonnie's new haircut put her over the top."

"Bonnie will never agree to that."

Marian tipped her head and looked apologetic. "And Mrs. Brookman knows about Dean's trouble at school."

"It was only a minor scuffle," Floyd responded. "These things happen." But that was the tip of the iceberg. A truancy officer had recently surprised Floyd with an enquiry about Dean's spotty attendance record. Bonnie had been keeping their boy home from school, yet each day the two of them had been playing it up like Dean had been in class. Knowing how much the boy's company bolstered his wife, Floyd didn't have the heart to challenge them.

"I should be running along," Marian said. "The longer I'm away, the longer Mrs. Brookman's interrogation when I return to the estate." She looked up at Floyd with concern. "You really are doing a marvelous job of things, Floyd. I have some insight into how difficult it must be for you. If you need help, you'll call on me?"

Floyd shrugged.

"You will, won't you? Bonnie's my friend too."

"Of course," he said.

After Marian drove off, Floyd went inside to find his wife. She was crouched on the floor of the room next to some small paint cans and a fish drawing she must have torn from a cupboard door. Her head bobbed in time with the music blasting from the radio while she applied feathery strokes to the dorsal fin she was painting on the wood. She cleared her throat and coughed twice. Her cheeks puffed out as she attempted to stifle a deeper cough, and then another. She grimaced and loosed a barking round. One hand flew to press against her back while the other pushed against her chest. When Floyd turned off the music, she recovered herself immediately and sat upright.

"Are you okay?" he asked.

"You've ruined my surprise." She gave him a pained smile.

He sat on the floor next to her and draped an arm around her shoulders. "What's all this?"

"I'm making a happy room. *Our* happy room." Her eyes glistened. "The floor is our river, and I'm painting life back into it."

In the week leading up to Halloween, the fish drawings disappeared one by one from the kitchen and came to life in colourful forms on the floor of the happy room. Speckles of orange, yellow, green, and crimson paint layered the tails of Bonnie's shirt. Her tempestuous moods smoothed into a stretch of calm, but her cough grew more persistent. "A stubborn cold," she insisted. "It will pass." Tea and dry toast sustained her. Floyd recognized the signs of her frequent naps—a nest of blankets in a corner of the happy room and rumpled sheets on the bed he'd made that morning. She was free of her mooring and drifting out to sea. It was part of a pattern. Her mood spiked and crashed, and her energy with it. He'd seen it many times. But this time, he sensed something else hiding behind her eyes. A secret, perhaps. One that left her sombre.

"You're sure everything is all right?" he asked. "Maybe you should see Doc Gillespie about that cough. Sometimes when you're coming down with something, it causes emotions to get stirred up."

"You know I hate doctors," she replied.

"I know but—"

"No *buts*," she warned. "Trust me on this."

28.

For the second time in a week, Tammy looked over her shoulder to find Allan coasting towards her on his ten-speed. She was walking Jordy after dinner, as she had been on the first occasion. Allan leaned over the handlebars, and she could see his wrists below the flipped-up cuffs of his jean jacket. A guitar lay against his back, secured by the leather strap slung across his chest. His feathered hair blew back in an Andy Gibb kind of way that left Tammy with the sensation of goldfish swimming inside her stomach.

"Hey, Tammy." He hopped off his bike to push it alongside her. "That's new," he said, looking at the stroller.

"Yeah." Tammy's mouth turned down at the corners. "Floyd and Marian bought Jordy a ton of new stuff."

"You say that like it's a bad thing."

"Floyd drives me crazy the way he stares at Jordy all the time. The minute I've saved enough money, I'm getting my own place."

"It's gotta beat living with your parents, eh?"

"He doesn't ask me a lot of questions. And he says nice things about how I take care of Jordy. That's been bugging me too."

"I don't get it," Allan replied.

"He's hiding something. Everybody can't be wrong about him being a nut job. Dean complained about him all the time. There must have been something to it." The velocity of her words increased, and her pitch climbed one octave higher. "And another thing, Floyd sucked as a father, but he's like the perfect grandpa with Jordy. It freaks me out. My son's not going to be Floyd's do-over."

"You worry too much. Floyd's a cool guy. Dean said a lot of shit, but I didn't always agree with him."

It grieved her to admit that Allan had a point. Still, her instincts pushed her towards caution. Tammy eased the stroller off the curb to cross the street as a pair of girls approached from farther along the sidewalk. She didn't know their names. They were part of the popular set a year behind her in school. Gossip about her wheeling a baby around town was going to spread like wildfire once they'd seen her.

"So did your parents flip out when you told 'em where you're staying?" Allan asked.

"Ha! They don't know." She tried hard not to look at the girls as they drew nearer.

Allan stopped pushing his bike, and his eyes cut to Tammy's face.

"I'm figuring things out," she said. "There are enough voices in my head right now without adding theirs to the mix."

The girls were close now. They looked from Tammy to Jordy and back again. Their faces lit victorious when her cheeks turned deep red. Once they'd brushed past the stroller, there were giggles and hushed chatter. Tammy's eyes squeezed shut for a second.

"The thing between you and Dean, do you think it would have lasted forever?" Allan said.

She'd been thinking of this a lot lately. But still, it felt strange to say out loud, "No."

The smile that flickered across Allan's lips both pleased and worried Tammy.

"New job keeping you busy?" she asked.

"Always. How was your first week?"

"It was okay. Arlene's a piece of work though. Kind of like the puppet master of gossip central. I don't think I'll have any trouble with her as long as I lay low. After I've been at the salon a while, she'll let me do more than wash hair and pass curlers.

I'm going to liven up the joint one day, attract younger clients—maybe even some guys."

"I'll be first in line when you're ready."

Tammy's expression revealed none of the delight that zinged through her heart.

"Well, I'm late for a jam session with the guys. Better split." Allan stretched a leg over his bicycle and began to pedal away. "See ya, little man," he called to Jordy.

Tammy stared after Allan, listing all the reasons why falling for the friend of her son's dead father would be near the top of her stupidest-things-I've-ever-done list. "Let's go home, Jordy."

Home. So much for not getting comfortable.

Monday morning, Tammy arrived at work ahead of schedule to find her new boss lounging with one arm draped over the back of a salon chair. Arlene looked up from her magazine briefly to acknowledge Tammy, then flipped the page and continued smoking her cigarette. Her colleague, Phyllis, waved a hand from the pink sofa in front of the plate-glass window. She smiled at Tammy and said, "Good morning."

Tammy hung her sweater in the laundry room at the rear of the salon, and then, as she did each morning, she emptied the dryer and began folding towels. When she overheard her name arise in the women's conversation, she froze.

"I can't believe Tammy's baby is Floyd and Bonnie Hoffman's grandson," Arlene said.

"And your point is?" Phyllis asked.

"Poor kid," Arlene said. "Ha," she added a moment later, "I wonder how much Tammy knows?"

Knows about what? Tammy strained to hear more. But the conversation cut off when the welcome bells tinkled on the salon door, announcing the day's first customer. For several seconds, she wrestled to sort her feelings. Her instincts had been spot on. Floyd *was* holding something back.

The bells rang a second time, and Tammy returned to the salon to welcome Mrs. Thorne and a newly arrived client named Eloise Donaldson. Tammy shampooed each woman's hair in turn and escorted them to Arlene's and Phyllis's chairs. Then she answered a few telephone calls and recorded a new entry in the appointment book. She turned the page to *Tuesday* and searched her mother's name. As expected, Arlene had written *Mirabelle King* in an early timeslot, three hours before Tammy was scheduled to begin her work day.

The mystery behind Arlene's earlier comment involving the Hoffmans plagued Tammy throughout the morning. Of all the women she'd encountered at the salon, Phyllis was among the most genuine and trustworthy. Before leaving for home that evening, she'd find an opportunity to question her.

Perhaps she was on the verge of discovering Floyd's secret, the very source of Dean's frustration. But how terrible could the secret be? She'd observed Floyd's positive traits firsthand. Which version of him was the real him? It was impossible to know but—

"Tammy!"

She turned sharply towards the sound of her name.

"Three times I've called you," Arlene said over the hum of Phyllis's blow dryer. She shared a mischievous look with Mrs. Thorne. "Whoever he was, he must have been very good." She sighed wistfully as she raised the height of the woman's chair.

Tammy repaid her with a forced smile and wheeled a curler tray next to the salon chair. Arlene extended her right hand, and Tammy laid a blue curler and a plastic pin across her palm.

"So are you going to tell us who he is—your young man?" Arlene asked. With the tail of a comb, she portioned out a new section of hair and presented her hand for another curler.

"There is no one," Tammy answered.

"Really?" Arlene said with exaggerated disbelief. "Hard to believe a beautiful girl like you wouldn't have a beau tucked away somewhere. Are you holding out on us?"

"No."

"When I was your age, I had to beat them off with a stick," Arlene said. "Your mother will tell you it's true." She wrapped a section of Mrs. Thorne's hair around the curler and skewered it with a plastic pin. "You know, Jordy's daddy is gone, and it's not like you were married or anything."

"Arlene," Phyllis snapped, "leave the girl alone."

"Boys your age don't want a kid tagging along. Is that the problem?"

"Miss Howard," Tammy said, "I prefer not to discuss such matters at work, thank you."

"Ooh, *Miss. Howard*," Arlene laughed. "She means business."

The blow dryer switched off. "Leave her be," Phyllis warned. "If she says she's not interested, she's not interested."

"She knows I'm just teasing her. Right, Tammy?"

"Arlene, we haven't heard anything about your love life recently," Miss Donaldson interjected.

"I manage just fine, thank you very much," Arlene said. "You have to go to the Legion dances over in Hattersburg if you want to find an unattached gentleman of some means. Around here, they're either happily married or dying of something."

"Isn't that just the truth," Mrs. Thorne said.

Tammy looked up to see Phyllis's sombre expression reflected in a mirror.

"Yes, it is," Phyllis whispered as she untangled her curling iron.

Arlene bided her time before turning Mrs. Thorne's chair towards the plate-glass window. "You see that couple crossing the park?" she asked loudly. "They remind me of Floyd and Bonnie Hoffman."

Tammy's eyes flashed. A shapely woman was crossing the library lawn with a man whose right arm hugged a stack of books against his side.

"You remember *them*, don't you, Phyllis? Floyd, from the post office—and his wife, Bonnie, that little dish from Toronto?"

Creases deepened at the corners of Phyllis's mouth. She tipped Miss Donaldson's head forward and combed at the nape of her neck.

"Didn't you go through school with Floyd?"

"Yup," Phyllis answered. "And I've always liked Floyd. He used to walk me home when kids were giving me a rough time in grade school."

Tammy organized the curler tray while attempting to glean every detail of their conversation.

"Hoffman's a good-for-nothing," Arlene said with a snort. "Have you forgotten the day last summer when he rolled into Tony's, rip-roaring drunk?"

"Have *you* forgotten what drove him to it?" Phyllis asked. "First his wife, then his son. He's lost more than he's gained from this town, and he still fights for it. He's a man of principle."

Miss Donaldson spoke up. "The *Sentinel* claims that the ministry may be coming through with some money for the mill so they can do those repairs Floyd's been fighting for."

"Well, hallelujah," said Mrs. Thorne. "Maybe we'll be able to leave the windows open this summer. "

"Hmm." Arlene sulked. "Well, Floyd Hoffman's odd, if you ask me. Even as a kid, he was buttoned down too tightly—no friends his own age and spending time with that old man at the pharmacy! What could they possibly have had in common?" she said with a sneer. "He likes books more than people, for all the good it ever did him. He never learned to keep his wife from all her shenanigans."

"What kind of shenanigans?" Tammy said, trying to sound nonchalant.

Phyllis's eyes flicked at the mirror. "Don't pay her any attention. It's all gossip and hearsay."

"Where there's smoke, there's fire," Arlene said. "My God, Bonnie Hoffman was crazier than a loon! Eloise, you worked at the library. Don't you remember that time at the park when she was screaming and bawling? Floyd had to manhandle her to the car and take her home. She was pitching things out the front door of their house that afternoon until he hauled her indoors again. Vivian Parker told me that Bonnie didn't set foot outside for two weeks."

Tammy felt ill.

"That's enough, Arlene!" Phyllis said, glancing at Tammy.

"Didn't he try to help her?" Tammy asked.

"I never saw evidence of it," Arlene replied.

"Well, I certainly did. He devoted himself to Bonnie's care," Miss Donaldson said

"What did he do?" Tammy asked.

Miss Donaldson's gaze shifted between Arlene and Tammy. "Perhaps another time," she said.

"There's a lot of crazies out there," Arlene cautioned. "You think you know a person, and then . . ." She shrugged and arched her brows. "Mark my words, Tammy King. Watch who you trust your child to. I wouldn't want Floyd Hoffman looking after mine."

Phyllis sucked her teeth and shook her head.

Tammy was sweeping the floor around the base of Miss Donaldson's chair when the clamour of a revving engine and scraping metal set off a round of high-pitched screams in the salon.

She looked up just in time to see the grill of the white Ford Galaxy rushing towards the plate-glass window. It bounced to a stop inches from disaster. Mirabelle flung the car door open and stomped around the back of the vehicle.

Mrs. Thorne pressed a hand to her chest. "Well, will you look at that!"

"She's fit to be tied," Arlene said with a smirk.

Mirabelle wrenched the salon door open and stood on the threshold with car keys dangling from her fist. The buttons on her blouse were misaligned, and she'd worn house slippers in the place of shoes. Her lips mashed together in a bloodless line, and her eyes locked on Tammy.

"You *are* here!" she said. "When Blanche Clark told me this morning that she'd seen you working at Arlene's, I told her she must be mistaken. If my daughter was working for my dearest friend, one of them would have told me."

"That's some parking job," Arlene said. "I thought you were coming through the damned window."

Mirabelle glared at her. "Shut your gob, Arlene."

"We're not doing this here, Mom, not where I work."

"You're a grade-A student, and you are going to settle for this? I've told three-quarters of the town you were accepted for computer studies at Wainright."

"I'm not going."

Mirabelle's mouth dropped open. "I don't recognize you anymore. You're not the child I raised."

"That's right. You raised me to be a compliant doormat, to let you make all of my decisions."

"You want to stand on your own two feet?" Mirabelle huffed. "So far, so good, huh? You got pregnant, dropped out of school, and landed a dead-end job—all on your own. Fantastic!"

"Tell her where you're staying." Arlene tapped a comb against her palm.

"Where?" Mirabelle asked.

"With Dean's father," Tammy shouted. Her knees clattered against one another behind the hem of her dress.

Mirabelle gasped. "Since when?"

"Nearly two weeks ago," Arlene said.

"You're a bitter disappointment, Tammy."

"It takes one to know one," Tammy replied.

Mirabelle gasped.

"Yeah, that's right. You're a bitter disappointment to yourself. Stop trying to relive your life through me. It's not my job to be perfect so you can feel better about how you turned out. And my son won't become your next project."

"I demand to see my grandson," Mirabelle said.

"You don't get to call the shots here. You don't own me, and you sure as hell don't own my son. I'm Jordy's mother, and I'll say who does or doesn't see him. For my whole life, you've made me feel small to make yourself feel bigger, and I'm not going to let you do that to my child."

"Vicious lies!"

"That's it. I'm finished with you. You've been so busy trying to mould me into what you think is perfect, you don't really know me at all."

Mirabelle's jaw dropped open. "Please, Tammy, he needs me. What do you know about raising children?"

"From your example, I've learned what *not* to do!"

Mirabelle's chin trembled.

Arlene clapped her hands together. "The apple doesn't fall far from the tree," she laughed.

Tammy turned to face her. "You and Aunt Eva and my mother, you all deserve each other." She thrust a finger at her mother and stared down it as if it were the barrel of a gun. "For as long as I live in this town, you don't know me. If you see me walking down the street with my son, cross the road. Don't speak to me. Don't even look at me. We're done!" She shoved past her mother, then stopped in the doorway. "Oh yeah, I quit!"

Tammy charged across the street and towards the river with Mirabelle's dumbfounded expression etched in her mind. She didn't turn around when the undercarriage of the Galaxy scraped the sidewalk again or when its tires squealed down Main Street. Her eyes remained fixed on the tumble of ice chunks surging along the shore. She hugged her arms and paced back and forth, splattering her white stockings with mud. The act of standing up to her mother had been an out-of-body experience. She laughed in disbelief at her own feistiness.

From the opposite bank and farther upriver, puffs of smoke billowed from a towering stack at the mill. The downshifting of trucks and the hissing release of their hydraulic brakes travelled through the stillness. She rubbed her arms to ward off the cold. Her breath slowed, and her heartbeat returned to its regular rhythm. For all of its flaws, this town was home, and she'd find a way to stay.

No one had contradicted Arlene's story about Floyd's public drunkenness. With the exception of Dean's bedroom and the locked room behind the kitchen, Tammy had checked every corner of the house for alcohol. So far, she'd found none. But still, something didn't add up. Dean had complained about his father stopping off at Tony's every day. "He reeks of the pub when he gets home at night. Floyd's not here for me, just like he wasn't for Mom." She'd known this, yet she trusted Jordy to his care.

"Crazy as a loon," Arlene had said. How did that fit Dean's story? He'd accused Floyd of stealing his mother's joy and draining the life from her. Phyllis and Miss Donaldson had painted Floyd as dedicated and principled. Who was right?

Tammy looked towards Water Street as the shade was raised in the window of Tony's Pub. She jogged back through the wet grass and seconds later pressed her weight against the pub door. It swung open easily, so she stepped inside to look for

Tony Monteiro.

The sound of men's voices drew Tammy to the corridor entrance below the restroom sign at the rear of the pub. Plastic crates propped open a door that revealed the cab of a beer delivery truck parked in the alley. In spite of this ventilation, stale cigarette smoke and the yeasty smell of beer lingered heavily in the air. She dried her eyes and pulled her shoulders back.

Mr. Monteiro struggled through the door, pushing a dolly of beer cases ahead of him. Once inside, he acknowledged Tammy and steered the dolly behind the bar. "If you're looking for a coffee, try the diner around the corner," he said, opening the flap of the first case.

"That's not what I want." Tammy measured him for signs of his willingness to answer questions. She guessed he was about her father's age. His shirtsleeves had been rolled up to his elbows, and a greying tuft of chest hair jutted above the neckline of his undershirt. She noted a whiff of Old Spice as he stocked the beer fridge.

"I shouldn't have unlocked the door so early. We don't open for half an hour, miss."

"I don't want a drink, Mr. Monteiro. I want to ask you a few questions."

"It's Tony," he corrected her. "Sorry, didn't catch your name." He rested both hands against the bar.

"Tammy King." She answered, then quickly added, "Lawrence King's daughter."

"Look, miss, I don't open until eleven, and frankly, I am not sure this is the place for you. Do you know what I am saying? The diner sells coffee and you could get a doughnut . . ."

"I don't want a goddamned doughnut!" Tammy's eyes welled. Her nose had begun running, and she didn't have any tissues. *Shit.*

Tony slowly wiped his hands on a bar towel. "Let's start this conversation fresh," he offered. "What would you like, Miss King? Can I help you in some way?"

"I have questions about Floyd Hoffman."

"Floyd Hoffman," Tony repeated warily. "I'm not much in the habit of telling tales about customers, much less friends."

"You'd be helping him by talking to me."

Tony glanced at his wristwatch. "You've got two minutes."

"I am the mother of Floyd's grandson."

"You—and Dean?" Tony's face lit.

Tammy nodded.

"Well, I'll be damned."

"We're staying at Floyd's place for a while. He seems decent, but this morning at the salon, I heard things that worry me. Is he trouble?"

Tony folded his arms across his chest. "Let me guess, Arlene Howard has been shooting her mouth off again."

"Is he a drunk like she says?"

"Not even close," he replied.

"Please don't bullshit me. You sent him home in a cab last summer. It took two men to carry him into the house. I was there when they dumped him off."

Air whistled through Tony's nose as he rubbed his chin. "Floyd's wife dying was hard enough, but this thing with Dean really busted him up. Yes, he stopped here most days," Tony leaned in and raised his brows, "but he never overdid it except that once. He'd have a beer and a coffee, and when he finished, he'd hit the can to spruce up. A couple of minutes before five, he'd head home. He hasn't darkened my door since Dean, you know . . ."

"He should have quit sooner. Dean needed him."

"Show him a little sympathy, would you? He needed to brace up and put on a good face for the boy. That was no easy task after seeing how Bonnie wasted away. Nobody should have to go through that cancer business twice."

"She died of cancer?"

"Yup, it was a hell of a thing."

Dean, you had it all wrong. She should have known. No one died of a broken heart.

The pub door opened, and Eloise Donaldson walked inside.

"Here comes the most beautiful woman in town." Tony stepped from behind the counter to kiss her.

She laughed and pushed him away. "I just dropped in to say hello." Her expression turned sombre when she looked at Tammy. "How are you doing, love?"

"Not sure yet," Tammy replied.

"I only wish I had half your spunk. If there was another decent shop in town, I'd never darken Arlene Howard's door again. Talk in the salon has always been unkind to Floyd. I've often felt guilty about keeping quiet."

"How do you know him?"

"We met over twenty years ago through the library. He used to comb through research books looking for ways to help his wife through her illness."

"Illness?"

"Emotional frailty is more like it," Miss Donaldson replied, her eyes downcast.

Dean's mother suffered from anxiety? That didn't make her *crazy* like Arlene said. "Why didn't she just see the doctor?"

"She hated doctors and refused medication of any kind."

"Why?"

"From the shame, I suppose. People were very secretive about such matters."

"In the sixties, they used to lock up guys who weren't right in the head," Tony said, tapping a finger against his temple. "Scary business. They drugged up the poor buggers and gave 'em lobotomies."

"Anthony," Miss Donaldson scolded before continuing. "Floyd scoured psychology journals for the names of experts. He corresponded with a number of them. I stored his research files in my office for years. He worried that Bonnie might be upset if she came across them."

"Where are the files now?"

"At his house, I expect. I dropped them off there sometime after Bonnie died."

"Dean never knew anything about this. He asked his father over and over again to talk about his mother," Tammy said. "Floyd owed him the truth. He should have told him."

Tony fired back instantly. "None of us are perfect. Your Dean had a temper, and quite a mouth, from what I understand."

"You're a mother now, Tammy," Miss Donaldson added. "Will you tell Jordy everything about *his* father? Or are there some things you'll hold back?"

After a pause, she replied reluctantly, "Probably the latter."

"Here's something you might not know," Tony said. "One day near the end, Floyd left here early to spend more time with Dean. About twenty minutes later, he came back. So I asked him what was up. He said Dean had a girl in his room. He heard the two of you laughing and talking, plus you'd left your shoes by the door."

Tammy blushed.

"Floyd told me he was glad his boy found someone to talk to, that maybe that girl would be to Dean what Bonnie had been to him. After that, he hung around here later so you two kids could spend more time together."

A tiny gasp escaped Tammy before she clamped a hand over her mouth.

"That sounds like Floyd, all right," Miss Donaldson said.

"He did that?" Tammy said.

"Yes. And he'll take better care of your son than he'll take of himself," Tony said.

Tammy stared at the bar.

"That's a lot to take in, isn't it, Miss King?" Tony said.

She answered with a tearful nod and left the bar.

Tammy broached the front of the diner just as Allan appeared carrying a tray of takeout coffees towards a pickup truck parked along the curb. His painter's cap was turned backwards, and he was wearing unzipped coveralls over a white T-shirt. She levied a watery smile at him.

Allan set the tray on the front seat of the truck and sauntered towards her. Concern replaced his welcoming grin as she drew nearer.

"Are you all right?" He regarded her with such earnestness that she dissolved into tears.

"Hey, hey . . ." Allan held out his arms, and she walked straight into his embrace. He wrapped one arm around her waist and the other around the back of her shoulders. "What happened?"

"Everything. I've completely blown up my life." Her arms looped around his neck, and she pressed her face into the hollow between his chest and shoulder. "My mom showed up at work today."

"Oh."

"And I quit my job."

"At least you have a place to live."

"I thought I could do everything myself." Tammy sobbed. "I didn't know it would all be so hard. Every time I trust people, I get kicked in the teeth. I'm sick of starting over."

"Sometimes you have to be lost to be found, you know."

Tammy lifted her cheek away from Allan's chest and tilted her face upwards. She wanted nothing more than to burrow deeper into his embrace and forget her troubles. He was beautiful and safe. But when his mouth lowered towards hers, a jolt of panic stabbed at her heart. The old Tammy allowed herself to fall victim to emotion; the new Tammy understood the value of caution. At the last moment, she turned her head to one side and they let go of each other.

Allan swept loose strands of hair from her forehead and tucked them behind her ear. "Things will get better. You'll sort it out."

"I will, won't I?" she said, sniffling.

"Of course." His head bobbed as he looked towards the truck. "Well, the guys are waiting for their coffees, so . . ."

"Yeah, of course." She shuffled backwards.

"Wanna lift?"

She stared at the papered-over windows of Harding's Family Clothiers across the street while she deliberated. "That's okay. I should walk." She waited for Allan to climb into the truck cab and settle behind the wheel. "About before . . ."

"It's cool. There's no rush, right?" He turned the key, and the engine began to rumble. "Tell Floyd I'll stop by after work to drop his books off."

Tammy's heart began to ache as Allan drove away. That kiss would have been nice.

• • •

The baby stroller was sitting empty on Floyd's porch when Tammy returned to the house. The front door had been left ajar, and breakfast dishes still littered the kitchen table. She could hear Strum's excited barking in the backyard, accompanied by Floyd's voice. "Look at him run, Jordy!"

Tammy lingered in the front hall for a moment before trudging towards the back door. There was no sense in delaying the news that she'd quit her job.

Something caught her eye as she passed Floyd's mysterious room. An antique-looking key had been left in the lock. She rubbed a thumb over its brass finish and looked towards the end of the hall. No sign of Floyd. She turned the key and pushed the door open to peer inside.

Tammy's gaze swept around the room. The spartan appearance of Floyd's home in no way prepared her for this. The floor had been painted blue, like water, and grey ovals resembling stepping stones had been laid in a path that stretched from the door to the window on the far side of the room. A frenzy of lily pads and colourful fish had been brushed in various clusters across the floor.

Black-and-white photographs covered each wall. Most had been pasted in linear patterns from the ceiling to floor, but some pictures had been tacked in place at haphazard angles. Words and short phrases had been penned in the gaps separating them. Tammy leaned in to examine a wedding picture of Dean's parents. An older couple was sandwiched tightly against his mother while Floyd stood slightly offside by himself. Below was a photo of Bonnie posing on the steps of the Hoffman's porch with Dean cradled in her arms.

Tammy was conflicted over Floyd's privacy, yet she couldn't tear herself away.

In Dean's baby pictures, his mother's face pressed against his as she waved to the camera. An *X* had been scratched across one photo from corner to corner. Dean was playing jacks on the walkway while his mother sat on the porch steps, staring into the distance. Farther into the display, Dean became the lone subject. There he was, running towards Floyd, running away from Floyd, swinging a bat, sitting disgruntled on the library steps, standing at the curb next to Bonnie's parents with a look of trepidation. Tammy inched farther along the timeline of Dean's childhood. At the end of it, she found several candid shots of Dean on the football field of their high school and a few of him competing at a track-and-field event. Still more playing guitar in the backyard.

Tammy remembered a passage from Dean's journal. *Made the team. Played all season. Floyd never showed up for one game. Big friggin' surprise.* Dean never understood. His father hadn't missed a thing; he'd been there all along. But why at arm's length?

Floyd's name was written in black marker across the top of an office box sitting in the corner. Tammy listened for signs of Floyd's return, then lifted the top and discovered a wealth of tightly packed file folders. She thumbed through the tabs. *Dr. Peter Grodzinski.* His was one of the names from the red leather journal hidden in her backpack. The file contained letters he'd written to Floyd. Tammy skimmed the top page. "New mothers participating in the study exhibited manic behaviours within two weeks postpartum." Floyd's notations at the side of the page read, *Medication required.*

The thing Floyd never wanted to talk about—it was Bonnie's mental illness.

Strum padded across the floor and pushed his wet nose against Tammy's face. She turned sharply towards the door, where Floyd stood with Jordy resting in the bend of his arm.

"You're back," Floyd said.

"I'm so sorry," she replied, struggling to fit the lid over the box. "The key was in the lock, so I—"

"You needn't apologize." Floyd hesitated a moment. "Eloise called."

Tammy stood and took the baby from his arms. "Then you know."

Floyd nodded.

"Dean and I had these big plans. We were going to leave Narrow Falls." She wiped tears from the tip of her nose. "Now that I want to stay, what's left for me here? I've made a mess of things. I'm so lost."

"Life can be like that. Sometimes you have to get lost to find yourself."

"So I've heard."

Floyd pointed to words carved into the windowsill. *What light thru yonder window breaks.* "Bonnie's idea of humour. She spent a lot of time in here." His head nodded as he looked around the room. "It helped, I guess."

"Why didn't you just tell Dean the truth about his mother?" Tammy asked.

"To protect him."

"But you and Dean would have gotten along so much better if you'd been open."

"Bonnie didn't want him to know."

"There can be no more family secrets," Tammy said. "Everything must be out in the open."

"There are no secrets left to tell," he said with a gentle smile. "You know everything." Floyd shuffled towards the kitchen.

She wanted to believe him. She wanted a safe place with no more disappointment, a place to be firmly rooted among familiar people and things. Maybe Allan had been right. Maybe this was that place.

"Floyd," she called.

He turned to face her.

"Jordy's birth certificate reads *Jordan Nathaniel Hoffman King.* That's how I registered him in the hospital. He'll always know where he came from and that he's a Hoffman."

Floyd's eyes glistened.

Late at night, after the baby had drifted into a deep sleep and the light no longer shone from beneath Floyd's bedroom door, Tammy slipped from her room. She treaded softly down the stairs to the kitchen and laid his Whitman poetry book and the red leather journal in the centre of the kitchen table.

No more secrets.

29.

The malfunctioning gate at the end of Floyd's walkway hung a dismal face on his newly blessed home. Today, he would unscrew the hinges and the latch, sand rust from the corroding metal, and apply liberal amounts of grease to the moving parts. He strode towards the shed with Strum following closely at his heels.

A length of heavy chain unsnaked itself from the door handles and thudded against the ground after Floyd removed the padlock. He cracked the doors open, and the smell of damp things lying idle flew immediately to his nose. After kicking a wedge of scrap lumber under the outside corner of each door, he followed the dog inside.

A pair of windows on the back wall allowed a faint light to filter through cobwebs and the coiled garden hoses strung from the rafters. He could hear Strum sniffing and scratching at the dirt floor somewhere in the clutter of wooden ladders and yard tools. Bonnie's cruiser bicycle leaned where she'd last abandoned it against a wheelbarrow. With a little effort, he could return it to working condition for Tammy. A bicycle had its practical uses, plus the wicker basket on the handlebars was bound to please her. Women seemed to like that sort of thing. He cleared tin cans of nuts and bolts from the workbench and searched the shelves for used bits of steel wool. Maybe he could build a child carrier for the front of the bicycle, like he'd seen in his parents' honeymoon photos of Amsterdam.

Floyd was searching for the pull chain of the overhead light when the dog loosed an excited bark. He turned sharply to find Doc Gillespie striding towards the shed with one arm raised in greeting. Floyd dusted his hands off and stepped outside to meet him.

"Hope you don't mind me stopping by like this, but I didn't want you hearing this from someone else," Doc said.

Floyd squinted into the sunlight.

A frown creased Doc's face. "It looks like the government is coming through with a loan for the mill."

Floyd's gaze settled on the lapel of Doc's suit jacket while he digested the news. "Are you certain?" he finally asked.

"Quite," Doc replied. "I heard it yesterday. Four serious types dressed in dark suits came into the diner and took the booth behind mine. They talked about a meeting at the mill later that afternoon." Doc's chin dropped, and he clasped his hands behind his back. "A lucky SOB is what they called McLelland. The loan's going to be sufficient to upgrade the scrubber and put most of the laid-off people back to work."

"And R.J. will be a hero for arranging a bailout," Floyd scoffed and turned away from Doc. His boot kicked at some empty paint cans stacked at a corner of the workbench and sent them flying in all directions.

"We don't always get the justice we want, Floyd. But you'll have won a hard-fought battle for equipment upgrades. No doubt there'll be conditions attached to the loan, so mill operations will be held under closer scrutiny, just like you've always wanted." He waited for Floyd to turn around, then looked him in the eye. "Let the ministry exact its pound of flesh from R.J. His wings will be clipped, and for a maverick like him, that's a death sentence."

Floyd grimaced. "If I keep up the pressure, maybe I can wring a morbidity study out of his windfall." He stared at a faraway point and absently pressed a palm against his chest.

"How have you been feeling lately?" Doc asked.

"Why?"

"I'm concerned about you, as a doctor and a friend."

"There's no need." Floyd swayed when Strum's weight leaned against his left leg.

He scratched behind the dog's ear and added, "I have a grandson. He's the spitting image of Dean."

"Congratulations," Doc said. "Forget about this mill business for a while and focus on him."

"Don't worry. It's all about that boy now."

In the middle of the night, Floyd awoke from a restless sleep. The muscles across his chest were drawn tight as lashings, the toll of his worries. He pushed a hand against his sternum and willed the sensation to end.

It wasn't a question of money prickling his nerves. His savings were plentiful, what with the house being paid off years ago and an inheritance left by his grandfather. He'd covered Smith and Harper's legal fees with plenty to spare. On top of that, the post office doled out a monthly pension, albeit reduced due to his premature departure.

The uncertain outcome of the lawsuit was to blame for accelerating his anxiety. Too many people held sway over the course his life might take and the peace of mind he'd be afforded—R.J. McLelland, government officials, Justice Reynolds, and Carl Spivey. Perhaps the most menacing worry was Tammy's power to excise him from his grandson's life, should she choose to. If he were deprived of watching Jordy grow up, there'd be a void nothing could fill.

Since Tammy's arrival, Floyd had been watching vigilantly for traces of Mirabelle's sharp-tongued disposition, but he'd found none. In fact, the girl was exceedingly quiet and not at all given to small talk. On occasions when he'd drawn her out in conversation, they'd discussed benign topics like weather or events in town. Her introversion extended to his involvement with Jordy as well. Or was it mistrust? Whenever Floyd looked at the boy for more than a moment, she'd discreetly place herself between them or concoct an excuse to remove Jordy from the room. So many questions remained unanswered. Where had she been during the stretch of time following Dean's death? Had he known she was pregnant? Had he been pleased? Nervous to press his luck, Floyd convinced himself that the answers were of little consequence. She was here now with his grandson, and that was all that mattered.

Within days of the salon blowup, Phyllis had shared her own version of events with him and Marian. Unwilling to abide Arlene's manipulations any longer, she'd submitted her own letter of resignation a few days later. "Tammy stood toe to toe with her mother, both barrels blazing," Phyllis said proudly. "I wish you'd have been there to witness Mirabelle King being fed a spoonful of her own medicine."

So did he.

An idea unfolded in Floyd's mind. It suddenly became obvious to him that the solution to keeping Jordy in his life was to furnish his mother with happiness and the way to a future of her own choosing. Commercial real estate in Narrow Falls was selling at below market prices, but that would all change once news about the government loan got out. He'd call Marian first thing in the morning. They both had excess funds for investing. Why hadn't this plan occurred to him earlier?

Floyd smiled a smile so wide it made his face ache. He laughed aloud in the darkness and fluffed his pillow. Minutes later, sleep settled over him, and he rested undisturbed.

Over the course of the next three days, Floyd faced the whirlwind of activity with boyish exuberance. The notion of buying the Harding's Family Clothiers building across from the diner enamoured Marian as well. Only a week earlier, they'd been looking out the diner window during a coffee date and commented about what a shame it was that no one had bought Harding's building yet. Such a great location, right on the main street. And folks always commented on the quaintness of the scrolled trim on the exterior of the building.

Once their decision was made, they whisked from the Realtor's office, to the bank, and then to the lawyers, signing contracts and cheques. On the evening the deal closed, they sat together in the candlelit store and clinked glasses of sparkling cider to celebrate the newest dimension of their relationship.

The next morning, Floyd showered and shaved with expedience. He heard Tammy's bedroom door whine open as he stood over the bathroom sink combing his hair. She chatted with Jordy as she passed by the door and went downstairs. Soon the kitchen radio began playing, and Floyd ducked into his bedroom. He dressed in a fresh white shirt and black dress pants with sharply ironed creases. A tie may have been overdoing things, he thought, but what the hell. He deliberated between a red-striped tie and a pale blue one, choosing the latter. Marian would like it best. The clatter of a skillet on the stovetop could be heard above the sputtering of the coffeemaker as he searched for his tie clip. Minutes later, he bounded down the stairs, his newest Manzes laced up and buffed to a high shine.

Jordy thumped a slobbery fist against the highchair tray and grinned when Floyd burst into the kitchen with a hearty, "Good morning, all!"

Floyd poured his coffee and glanced over at Tammy, chiseling eggs from the frying pan. "Smells great."

"Thanks," she replied. Her brows shot upwards when she peered at him over her right shoulder. "Nice tie."

"Thank you." He sipped his coffee, then, as nonchalantly as possible, he said, "Marian will be here any time now."

"Really?" Tammy's voice lifted as she turned away from the stove. "I could make her some eggs."

"We're going out, actually."

Her smile sagged.

"All of us," Floyd added hastily. "There's something important that needs discussing."

Tammy's head cocked to one side. A wave of mistrust swept across her face.

"It's a good news kind of thing," he said. Before he could explain any further, the telephone rang. He offered her a lopsided grin and hustled into the hallway to answer the call.

"Hello?"

"It's Gerald. Are you sitting?"

"What's happened?" Floyd held his breath.

"Clive unlocked the office door this morning and found a sealed envelope lying on the mat. It was pushed through the mail slot overnight."

"Who's it from?"

"Len Rathburn, an engineer from the mill. Short guy, curly hair, bald spot. He sat in the middle of the head table at R.J.'s public meeting."

Floyd resurrected Rathburn's image in his mind. He'd seen the man before that day at the community centre, but the occasion continued to evade him.

"Rathburn claims he's been fudging the results on the effluent monitoring tests," Gerald said. "McLelland's has been pumping enough solid waste into the river to fill the town pool once a week. And the air emissions consistently breach ministry guidelines."

Floyd's mouth gaped.

"That's not all," Gerald continued. "Rathburn has squirreled away copies of correspondence outlining a plan to perform minimal surface repairs to the scrubber—all signed by R.J. McLelland. The maintenance and repair records are fraudulent. The contractors went through the motions, but no meaningful work was ever completed."

"That son of a bitch," Floyd muttered.

"Oh yes, Clive wants me to tell you about aerial photographs that Rathburn's got for us, stretching back to the sixties, when Gene Brookman ran things at the mill. They show an expanding effluent plume of biomass settling on the riverbed. He says the heaviest concentration is along the south shore, from the bridge to a half mile west of the old-age home."

Floyd staggered back against the wall. He remembered now! He'd seen Rathburn at the Brookman estate the night he told Rose about Dean's illness. Rose knew about the cover-up all along. She'd been a party to it.

"You still there?"

Floyd inhaled deeply. "Rathburn has kept it quiet all this time. Why come forward now?"

"His wife has cancer, and it's terminal," Gerald said. "Your speech at the McLelland's meeting was the final nudge he needed to come clean."

"Will he testify?"

"Absolutely. As a matter of fact, we're meeting him later this morning," Gerald replied. "This is the goose that laid the golden egg, Floyd. R.J. McLelland won't know what hit him once Justice Reynolds hears of this."

"We should press for an environmental clean-up."

Gerald laughed. "You'll have lots of time to chase dragons after you cash the settlement cheque."

Floyd hung up the receiver. The evidence he'd spent years searching for had fallen like manna from heaven. Perhaps God existed after all. His head swung towards Dean's bedroom door, and a lump of emotion throbbed at the back of his throat. *If only you'd been here to share in this moment.*

He heard a plastic cup bounce against the kitchen floor. Jordy's protest began as a whimper and promptly escalated to a howl. Tammy lulled him with a sing-song voice. She was lifting him from the highchair as Floyd passed the kitchen on his way outside.

"Everything okay?" she asked.

Breakfast had been laid out on the table with all the frills—napkins, orange juice, and buttered toast. Three eggs, their edges brown and curled, lay on both plates.

"Perfect," he said, tears now blurring his vision. "I'll just be a minute." He stepped onto the porch and gripped the railing. His life as a pariah was about to end. Once Rathburn's story became public, no amount of charm would distance R.J. McLelland from the catastrophic results of the mill's cover-up. Hell, with his authorizing signature on the damning correspondence, he wouldn't be able to claim ignorance or sluff blame onto an underling. All the guns would point at him.

Gravel crunched on the driveway. Floyd opened his eyes to find Marian springing from her parked car. She hurried up the walkway towards him. "Are they ready? Tammy must be excited!"

"She doesn't know."

"How could you resist telling her? I didn't sleep a wink all night." Marian straightened his tie and patted his chest. "Let's go get her—partner."

Floyd's arms circled Marian's waist, and he lifted her off the ground. She squealed in surprise as he spun her around.

"Have you lost your mind?" Marian protested through her laughter. "Put me down."

From the corner of his eye, Floyd noticed Tammy inside the kitchen, holding Jordy in front of the open window. The baby's pudgy hands rested against the screen.

"Grandpa's funny," Tammy said.

Floyd detected a new kind of warmth behind her words, and his optimism bloomed anew.

"Phyllis is here," Floyd announced. From the passenger seat, he could see her peering between the white lettering on the Harding's Family Clothier's plate-glass window. By the time Marian parked against the curb, Phyllis had propped open the front door with a chair. While Floyd escorted Marian to greet her cousin, Tammy removed the stroller from the trunk and gathered Jordy from the backseat.

"It's official." Phyllis dangled a set of keys next to her face.

"I can't believe we've done it," Marian said.

Floyd glanced back at Tammy's puzzled expression, then followed Marian inside. He began to doubt their plan. Maybe he'd been a bit out of his mind. Tammy could say no, and then where would he be? He paced the length of the store, trying to remember the careful wording he'd put together to explain his offer.

Phyllis and Marian were fawning over the antique cash register on the service counter when Tammy pushed the stroller through the door.

"What's going on?" she asked.

"You are looking at my new salon!" Phyllis announced with a flourish.

"You quit Arlene's?" Tammy said.

"Sure did."

"And you're starting your own business?"

"That's right." Phyllis stretched one arm around Marian's shoulders and the other around Floyd's. "It's all because I have the best cousin and friend in the world."

"Marian and I bought the building together," Floyd explained. "We wouldn't have considered it even a few months ago, but now with the government bailout, the downtown will flourish."

"And they're not charging me any rent for the first year!" Phyllis piped in.

"It's only fair. You helped me," Marian said.

"I'll be needing someone to work the reception desk, sweep up, wash hair, and bring the customers tea or coffee," Phyllis said. "Preferably someone with an interest in an apprenticeship. Someone young and brimming with ideas on how to make this place fresh and modern."

Tammy clapped a hand over her mouth. Her eyes were round.

"She's offering you a job," Floyd interjected.

"I accept. I accept." Tammy rushed towards Phyllis and hugged her. "I won't let you down."

"Tell her the rest, Floyd," Marian urged.

Tammy released Phyllis and clutched the handlebars of the stroller.

"There's a two-bedroom apartment upstairs," Floyd said. "It needs a coat of paint and new appliances, but it would be nice for you and Jordy."

"I don't know if I could afford it," Tammy replied in a breathless voice.

"Don't worry," Marian said.

"You and I can fix the place up together," Floyd continued. "Marian has offered to look after Jordy when we're here. Allan wants to help us too when he's able."

"Allan knows about this?" Tammy asked.

Floyd smiled. "You can have the apartment rent-free. And there's another thing. Marian and I would like to take turns caring for Jordy while you're working."

"That's far too generous," Tammy said, raising her palms. "It'll be like I'm your kid."

"Yes, it'll be like you're my daughter," said Floyd. "Fate cheated me out of helping Dean make a start. But now I can do these things for you. And for Jordy. I'd be helping you in Dean's stead."

Floyd could see by Tammy's expression that she was struggling to work something out. "No strings attached," he said. "You'd not be indebted to Marian or me in any way. We'd abide by your wishes in terms of Jordy's care."

Tammy's eyes lit, and she lifted Jordy from the stroller. "Could I see the apartment?"

Floyd's heart was near to bursting as he led her through an archway at the rear of the store and up a narrow carpeted staircase leading to the apartment. He stepped aside at the doorway to let her enter the apartment first.

She walked to the middle of the room, taking it all in—the brick walls, the pine floors, the tall windows and natural light. A small table and two mismatched chairs waited in one corner.

"That door opens onto the fire escape," he said, pointing to the far side of the apartment. "You'll need more furniture, but—"

"I love it."

Moisture gathered in Floyd's eyes "You'll stay, then?"

"Yes."

Floyd rested on a window ledge while Tammy opened and closed cupboard doors on the opposite side of the room with Jordy balanced on her left hip. The baby stared happily and kicked his heels against her.

"You and I never talk about Dean," Floyd said.

Tammy tested the kitchen faucet, then turned to face him. "He's not easy to talk about."

"Dean and I had a tough year," Floyd began. "I guess you'd say the odds were stacked against us. He was angry with me."

"And me too sometimes," she said, leaning her back against the counter. "Miss Donaldson told me you've gone through some difficult times." Tammy's cheeks reddened slightly. "You should have told Dean about all the things you did to help Mrs. Hoffman."

Floyd nodded slowly.

"Did you know about her problem before you got married?"

"There'd been little signs here and there," he said. "She was impulsive at times, but I liked that about her. So different from myself. And when she was lethargic, I felt good knowing I could cheer her up. Once, I saw her mother passing pills into

Bonnie's hand. I didn't ask questions, and she didn't tell me anything. Maybe I didn't want to know." Floyd shrugged. "I was young."

"I know what that's like." She slid her back down the front of the cupboard doors and sat on the floor with the baby nestled in her arms.

"I remember the first day I understood the magnitude of her illness." The past was a movie playing behind Floyd's eyes. "She'd been lying in bed for three days. I tried to comfort her, and still she cried. No amount of coaxing could convince her to eat. Nothing worked, so I telephoned her parents."

"How did that go?"

"Rose marched upstairs straightaway, but Gene took me outside for a talk. It was the first time I learned that Bonnie was manic depressive."

Tammy's eyes narrowed.

"She locked herself in her room when she was sixteen years old—sobbing, refusing food. At the end of four days, she came out. Gene and Rose found drawings sprawled across the walls and words scratched into the plaster. Bonnie was officially diagnosed shortly after that."

"What about medication?"

Floyd could see in Tammy's eyes that she was reassessing everything she thought she knew. If only he'd been so open with Dean. "Pills left her feeling bland and exhausted, so she refused to take them. Bonnie could lie in bed for days or be awake for days on end. I'd often wake up in the morning to find she'd taken Dean somewhere in the middle of the night—to the gorge, the river, or her parents' house."

"Sorry you all went through that."

"My wife was the centre of my universe. I could forgive her for anything."

Tammy looked downward at Jordy's face and brushed a finger against his cheek.

"We didn't discuss her condition with other people; no one in the family did. In a small town, it's best to keep such things private. Otherwise, Dean may have been tormented in school. You know how cruel children can be—and adults too. There are a lot of Arlene Howards out there."

"Do you think it would have been different if he'd known the truth about his mother's problems?"

Floyd shrugged. "I meant to tell him, but there's never a perfect time for difficult news," he said, staring at the wood grain in the floor. "Before she died, Bonnie begged me to never tell him about her mental illness. She thought he'd love her less—maybe even grow to hate her."

"You could have just told him anyway."

"I wasn't convinced he'd gain anything but disillusionment by knowing. By the time I was ready to tell him, it was too late. He'd already left for his grandmother's in Toronto."

Tammy cocked her head to one side. "Surely, you visited him there. Why didn't you tell him then?"

The ground shifted beneath Floyd. He'd promised the girl honesty, and he had to deliver, no matter how painful.

"Actually, I didn't visit him in Toronto," Floyd answered.

"Oh. I just assumed . . ." Tammy said.

"It's not that I didn't want to." Floyd paused to let the words sink in. "I wasn't allowed to."

"But you were his father."

"Not in the eyes of the law."

"I don't get it."

"I signed custody of Dean over to his grandmother."

"But he hated her." Tammy's voice rose, and the baby flinched in his sleep.

"Yes, he did." Floyd's blood pulsed against his temples.

"You wrote him off anyway? He was all alone at the end? Unbelievable!"

"It was the only way I could help him," Floyd said, struggling to control his voice. "His grandmother had social connections and financial means. His odds were better with her."

Tammy hugged the baby tightly and kissed the top of his head.

"There's so much history, so much complication. The solution seems clear-cut in the aftermath . . ."

"What's complicated about it?" Tammy's hands sliced through the air to emphasize her words. "You care or you don't. You fight to the end for your kid or you don't. You sacrifice it all or quit when the going gets too tough." Her eyes grew frantic. "You don't abandon your kid because they're not what you thought they'd be. He was trouble, and you cut him loose. At the worst possible time, you cut him loose and sent him away. Do you have any idea of how frightened he must have been? Away from home and everything familiar, not knowing what to expect—feeling abandoned? Inconvenient?"

"I did fight." Floyd leapt to his feet and thrust his palms forward. "I'm still fighting!"

"Dean warned me. 'Floyd will let you down,' he said." Tammy appeared close to tears. "I trusted you when you said no more secrets. And now this. How could you think I'd allow you in my kid's life when you didn't want to be in your own son's?"

Floyd paced the floor. "Do you think it was easy for me to step away from flesh and blood—the last living soul I was related to; the person I'd been waging battle for, sacrificing my heart, my soul, my peace of mind for? Do you think it was easy to keep the promise I made my wife? She had no idea of the life I would need to give up in order to keep my word. Yet I did it! Given the chance, I'd do some things differently, but I just don't know, where does it end? When do I stop paying for the promise I made to her?"

Marian appeared in the doorway.

"Just when I was thinking you were a good guy, it turns out you're like the rest of them," Tammy said, her chin shaking as she spoke. "A two-faced liar. What's your game?" She paused to glare at Floyd until his shame was complete. "Are you using me to get close to my son? To cure your guilty conscience because you screwed up with Dean? I hate you."

"What do you want from me?"

"Quit the pity party. *You* didn't die."

"Now hold on a minute," Marian said, an index finger drilling through the air. Floyd had never seen her so angry.

He raised a hand to stop her. "It's all right. I had it coming." He faced towards Tammy. "All I want is to live a good life and for Jordy and you to be a part of it.

And Marian too. But, Tammy, you're free to make whatever choice you like."

No one spoke.

"I'm sorry, Marian," Floyd said. He barged through the fire escape door and pounded down the wooden stairs to the alley below.

How could he have been so stupid? *The truth will set you free.* Bullshit. All his life he'd been one step out of beat with people. First Bonnie, then Dean, and now he was driving a wedge between himself and his grandson's mother. All the girl had asked for was the truth. He should have laid his cards on the table the day he showed her Bonnie's room.

Floyd followed along the alley behind Harding's to where it opened onto Water Street and then strode towards Tony's Pub. A car narrowly missed hitting him as he charged blindly across Main Street. The driver blared his horn three times, but Floyd paid no notice.

He yanked on the pub door and discovered it was locked, so he banged his fist against the plate-glass window. Tony appeared, then tapped his wristwatch and shrugged. But Floyd gave a pleading look that softened his resolve.

"A bit early in the day, isn't it?" Tony said after letting him inside.

"Don't care." Floyd dropped onto a stool and planted his elbows on the bar. "I'll have the usual."

"I'm all out of the usual." Tony poured a mug of coffee and slid it across the counter. "Are you going to tell me, or should I start guessing?"

Floyd clenched his jaw and toyed with the handle of the mug.

"You and Marian still on?"

"Yeah, we're fine. Being with her is like falling off a log. The things that come easy are easy. It's the things that require strategizing and sacrifice that are killing me. There's never a good payoff, you know?"

"You haven't had it easy, that's for damned sure."

"Being loyal to the people I love and keeping secrets—it's all too much." Floyd raised his gaze to Tony's face. "My son died hating me, you know? I could have told him about his mother, like he wanted, but I didn't. He thought she was saintly, and

I protected him from knowing otherwise," Floyd said, beating a fist against his chest. "I did that. Even though he wasn't my son, most likely, I loved him all the same."

"Not your son? Then who—"

A knock sounded at the window. Two men stood outside, their foreheads pressed against the glass. Tony waved them off.

Floyd pinched the bridge of his nose between a thumb and index finger. "Carl Spivey. That's who."

"I wish you'd told me this earlier." Tony whisked a towel over his shoulder and braced his hands against the bar. "Spivey can't be the father."

"How do you know?"

"He had the surgery." Tony made snipping motions with the fingers of his right hand.

"What?"

"He bragged about it once in the hockey change room. It must be twenty-five years ago since I played men's league with him over at the rink. Called it his free ticket to screw around."

"You're sure about this?"

"Hell, yeah. Dean was your kid. No doubt there."

Floyd stood on the bottom rung of his barstool and reached his torso across the counter to clamp Tony in an awkward hug.

The Saturday before Halloween, Floyd woke early and made oatmeal for himself and Dean. After breakfast, he climbed the stairs to check on Bonnie and found her asleep and facing the outside wall. Her hair had grown sufficiently that soft curls were forming at the nape of her neck. She'd resumed bathing and dressing in her own clothes. These signposts pointed to better days ahead.

Coughing began upstairs midmorning. She'd be down soon, so Floyd brewed a fresh pot of coffee. When she hadn't appeared a half hour later, he went upstairs to investigate and found her lying in the same position she'd been in earlier. Something didn't feel right. He inched towards the foot of their bed, wanting but not wanting to see.

Bonnie's eyes were closed, her lips parted. A thin rope of bloody mucus hung from a corner of her mouth. A rust-coloured patch spread on her pillowcase and disappeared beneath her cheek.

"Oh God, no," Floyd said, dropping to his knees. When he laid a hand on her shoulder, her eyes fluttered. Then her face convulsed, and she moaned.

"Stop it!" Dean, head down, charged at him from the doorway. His red Superman cape trailed along the floor behind him. He flung himself at Floyd, and his balled-up fists rained down on his father's back until he'd exhausted himself and collapsed in a fit of tears.

By noon, Doc Gillespie's car was roaring along gravel-packed side roads towards Hattersburg General Hospital. Floyd hoped desperately to wake up from this nightmare as he cradled Bonnie in the backseat. "You're going to be all right, sweetheart," he said tearfully. "We're almost there."

The car plunged into a dip in the road. Bonnie moaned, and her muscles tensed. Doc looked away from Floyd's gaze in his rearview mirror and tightened his grip on the wheel. When Floyd had called his house that morning, something about Doc's lack of surprise left him with the uneasy impression that Bonnie's illness wasn't news. Even after he'd arrived at the house and measured her vital signs, he remained evasive when Floyd asked what might be wrong.

Floyd waited until the car pulled onto the paved highway. "How long have you known?"

Doc replied after a considerable pause. "Since August."

"And you still said nothing?" Floyd hissed.

"The telling wasn't up to me," Doc replied, glancing into the rearview mirror.

They were both quiet for a moment.

"Not much farther to Hattersburg now. The hospital knows she's coming. They'll be ready for her."

"How bad is it?" Floyd asked, his voice trembling.

Doc exhaled slowly. "It's in her lungs."

"Cancer?" Floyd gaped from the backseat. This happened to *other* people.

"You should prepare yourself for the worst," Doc said.

"*The worst?* What does that mean?"

"She's dying."

"No," Floyd railed. "That can't be!" He and Bonnie had a son together and a life. As much as she needed him, he needed her more. He couldn't go on without her. There must be a mistake.

At the emergency entrance to the hospital, two nurses hoisted Bonnie onto a gurney and wheeled her through the front doors to the emergency area. Floyd hurried alongside, struggling to keep a hand on Bonnie's arm. "I'll be right here the whole time," he told her. She roused and offered a strained smile. One of the nurses pointed to a bank of orange plastic chairs in the hallway and told him to wait there. Someone would return for him once they had Bonnie settled. The second nurse added to the instructions, but her words were overpowered by a garbled announcement playing over the loudspeaker. The two women pushed the foot of the gurney against a pair of swinging doors and disappeared from view before he could ask any questions.

Floyd dropped onto an orange chair and waited for Doc to finish speaking with a doctor in front of the nurses' station. The Hattersburg man inspired confidence, dressed as he was in the kind of shirt and pants the television doctors always wore. A white cap perched on his head, and a surgical mask hung around his neck. His burly arms folded across his chest while he listened intently to Doc. After their conversation ended, the doctor jetted past Floyd and continued through the swinging doors.

Doc Gillespie came over and sat next to Floyd. "The hospital is going to run some tests on Bonnie, and then they'll advise a course of action," he said. "I'm making the rounds to visit other patients. I'll check in with you before I leave. The process is going to take a while. You might want to get yourself a coffee."

But Floyd didn't want a coffee. He wanted to yell at the top of his lungs and punch something without consequence. He wanted for this day to have never happened and to bring his wife home, happy and healthy.

Bonnie's parents arrived a few hours later. Mrs. Brookman spotted Floyd first. "Where is my daughter?" she yelled at him. "Why is she here?"

Floyd could only stare at Mr. Brookman and think of the mill. Something was wrong there; he'd always known it. The wretched smell it pumped into the air and the yellow foam spewed into the murky water of the river.

Mrs. Brookman squared off in front of him. "Tell me now! You—"

"Rose, let him speak," her husband interjected. He turned to face Floyd. "What is it son?"

Floyd teared up on the word. "Cancer."

"No . . ." Mr. Brookman turned ghostly white and took a seat next to Floyd.

"What have you done?" Mrs. Brookman's eyes filled with grief. "You weren't watching. You should have known."

He *had* been watching—but for the wrong thing. Bonnie's fatigue and lack of appetite had mimicked symptoms of depression. Guilt and self-loathing tore at his mind.

The doctor who'd been speaking with Doc earlier returned to Floyd with his mouth set in a grim line. "Mr. Hoffman?"

"Yes?" Floyd steeled himself.

"I've just come from speaking with your wife. She's adamantly declining tests and treatment."

Mrs. Brookman gasped and clapped a hand over her mouth.

"What does this mean?" Floyd said.

"The best we can do is give her medication to ensure that she's comfortable."

Mrs. Brookman stepped forward with an index finger leveled at the doctor. "March back in there and *make* her take the tests."

"Do something, for godsake," Bonnie's father said.

The doctor looked apologetically. "If only it were that simple. It is her right to decline."

"Young man, do you have any idea who we are?" she said in an imperious tone. Mascara streaks trailed down her cheeks.

"No, madam, I do not," the doctor replied. "But I am clear on who my patient is. It's her needs and rights I serve." He looked at Floyd. "She's asking for you. *Only* you. Examination room three, through the doors and at the end of the hall." He nodded and turned away to fall in step with a passing colleague.

Floyd left the Brookmans behind and pushed through the swinging doors. A pale blue corridor stretched out before him. To his left, an elderly man lay on a gurney and called out for his wife. Farther along the hallway, a frail woman in a faded blue hospital gown inched forward, gripping an intravenous pole for support. Floyd felt as if he'd stepped into another dimension. He peered into an examination room across from the nurses' station. A boy, about Dean's age, slept on a gurney while next to him a woman stood holding one of his hands. When she glanced up, her forlorn expression pierced Floyd. Her sorrow was his future.

The next room was Bonnie's. His heart skittered like a scared rabbit, and his mouth went dry. He peered warily through the door and stepped inside. Her eyes were open. Intravenous lines trailed from the back of her hand to a tiny bag of clear fluid hanging from a pole next to the bed.

"How are you feeling?" Floyd whispered. "Are you in pain?"

"It's bearable. Morphine works like a dream," she answered in a gravelly voice. "Where's Dean?"

"Marian's got him. She sends her love."

"Dean's going to need you," Bonnie said.

"Don't talk like that. You're not going anywhere." Floyd stroked her arm and tried his best to sound brave. He couldn't let her see how terrified he was.

"And you mustn't be angry with Doc. He wanted me to tell you."

"Why didn't *you* tell me? I'm your husband."

"You'd have only worried. But it wouldn't have changed a thing. I knew my odds, and I made a decision. For both our sakes," she said.

"Think of what you're saying, Bonnie. You can change your mind."

"No, Floyd. I won't stay in a hospital, not again."

"But this isn't a Toronto psychiatric ward," Floyd pleaded. He swallowed the lump in his throat. Tears ran freely down his cheeks. "Without help, you'll die!"

"I'm not going to die," Bonnie replied calmly. "I'm going to finish living—on my own terms. At home."

"I'm not a medical person. When you're hurting, I won't know how to stop it."

"That's what morphine's for." She tried to smile. "I have a plan to cover the walls of the happy room with photos of our family—you, me, and Dean. It will make it easier for you. Later."

"How will I live without you? You are the very air I breathe. I don't know if I can do this thing you're asking."

Bonnie turned her face away from him and wiped her eyes. "I need some paper. And a pen." When Floyd hesitated, she said, "Please."

He went to the nurses' station and returned with a pen and a small pad of paper. He placed the pen in her right hand and laid the paper on her lap. She wrote shakily, one word across the paper—*Themselves*—then tore the strip away and passed it to Floyd.

He read it and immediately understood her reference to their favourite Whitman poem. *Only themselves understand themselves and the like of themselves, as souls only understand souls.*

"You've always let me be myself," Bonnie said, her eyes glistening. "Don't stop now."

Floyd nodded reluctantly and tucked the scrap of paper in his breast pocket. "I will carry this with me always."

"Promise me you won't ever tell Dean that my mind is broken."

"Bonnie …" Floyd shook his head.

"He doesn't understand that something is wrong with me or that I'm different from his friends' mothers. Let him remember me as fun and adventuresome. Promise me."

Floyd nodded.

"Say it. Swear you'll protect our son from the truth of what I really am. Promise you won't tell him that I'm crazy. He'll hate me for being broken."

"No one's ever thought those things," Floyd said. "You aren't broken. You're you, and you're perfect."

"Promise me!" she repeated with urgency.

"You have my word." Floyd fought against his tears. "I won't say a thing."

"That's my darling. Now take me home."

30.

A chilly breeze swept into the apartment through the open fire escape exit. Tammy stared glumly at the brick face of the neighbouring building and made no move to close the exterior door. She'd been sitting crossways on the windowsill since Marian carried Jordy downstairs ten minutes earlier. With the back of her head tipped against the inside of the window frame, she listened to the muffled bursts of Marian and Phyllis's high-pitched conversation travelling up the stairwell. Tammy seethed. They had no right to be upset with her when it was Floyd who'd ruined everything.

She found herself wishing Allan were there. He knew how to see the upside of any bad situation. When he was around, she felt better about things. Since they'd come close to kissing, she'd been wishing that a lot.

The baby cried out, and soon after footsteps thudded up the stairs. Marian appeared with Jordy wailing in her arms. "He's hungry," she said, passing him into Tammy's arms.

When Tammy hesitated to raise her shirt, Jordy began rooting against her covered breast. She flashed a look of impatience at Marian.

"You think I haven't seen a baby nurse before?" Marian sucked her teeth.

Tammy lifted her T-shirt, and Jordy latched on to her left breast. "Did you know all along about Floyd signing Dean over to his grandmother?"

Marian pulled a chair next to the window and stared at her before speaking. "You certainly know how to put the damper on things," she answered gruffly.

"Huh, I should have known," Tammy said. She chided herself for thinking Marian a saintly figure. Turns out, she was in on the cover-up too. "Floyd doesn't give a damn about Jordy and me. He's throwing charity at us to wash away his guilt."

"He's *not* that sort of man."

"Wait until the going gets tough or we disappoint him. He'll drop us like a hot potato, and I'll be on my own again."

"You're being completely unfair. There's a story to what happened," Marian said. "You'd feel differently if you knew what Floyd had been facing."

"I doubt it."

"For Pete's sake," Marian said, raising her voice. "Put yourself in his place. Your son is dying. The one person who's made your life a misery holds the key to saving his life."

Mirabelle.

The floor shifted like sand beneath Tammy's feet. She'd been standing on the firm ground of her anger, but Marian was nudging her towards more empathetic territory.

Marian's tone softened. "I know you're a good mother, Tammy. You would do like Floyd and humbly lay your son at that person's feet if it meant increasing the odds of his survival. Isn't that right?"

Tammy chewed the inside of her cheek. "Maybe," she blurted reluctantly. "Yes." Although tears burned her eyes, she refused to let them fall.

Marian folded her hands in her lap and sighed. "I served the Brookmans for over twenty years, the last four of them spent with Rose alone. She crucified anyone who tarnished the Brookman name or thwarted one of her grand schemes. Rose Brookman was all teeth and claws when it came to Bonnie."

"What does that have to do with anything?"

"It's the root of the tree," Marian answered. "Back when the family lived in Toronto, Bonnie's mother introduced her to influential families and steered her towards their sons. But Bonnie would say shocking things in front of guests or refuse to attend her mother's parties. Add to that, staying up all night and sleeping all day. I thought her antics were part of a rich girl's rebellion, but it was more than that."

Tammy listened intently as she leaned Jordy over her shoulder and rubbed his back.

"In the small hours one morning," Marian continued, "a strange car returned Bonnie to the Brookmans' home. The girl was too drunk to stand. Her shoes were missing, and her skirt was turned askew. Rose and I took her upstairs and undressed her for bed. There were fresh bite marks on one breast." She paused to rest a hand against her face. "After that, Bonnie locked herself in her room for days."

"Eloise Donaldson told me about Mrs. Hoffman refusing medication," Tammy said. "I don't get it."

Marian nodded. "In the beginning, she took them. Her spark disappeared. But then I started finding pills tucked in her pockets and under seat cushions. Old problems returned, so the Brookmans decided it would be best to avoid attention until Bonnie's situation was under control. That's when we all moved here, to Narrow Falls.

"And that's when she met Floyd," Tammy said.

"Yes. Rose hated him. He was a civil servant *and* the son of German immigrants, but worst of all, Bonnie loved him more than she feared her mother."

This sounded familiar. "I'm guessing the more Mrs. Brookman lost, the harder she fought to get it back," Tammy said with a raised brow.

Marian nodded. "And the farther she drove Bonnie away."

"And Floyd?"

"Over the years, Rose undermined him at every opportunity—in the marriage, but especially in his relationship with Dean. She even suggested Floyd was to blame for Bonnie's death. Of course, none of it was true."

"Dean believed her. He didn't really like her though."

"Rose loved Dean in a proprietary sort of way. She had to control everything. It was her nature."

Tammy frowned. Dean must have hated that.

"I can never forgive Rose Brookman for how she deceived Floyd in order to take Dean."

"Please tell me everything," Tammy insisted. "I need to know."

"Yes, my dear, you really do."

• • •

Throughout Marian's explanation of Rose Brookman's vendetta, Tammy's chest ached. The more she heard, the more she realized how mistaken Dean had been. He really hadn't understood his father at all. Tammy had no idea that Floyd's mother-in-law had used her money and the law to take advantage of his vulnerability. When Marian told her about Dean's remains arriving at the Hoffman house by courier, tears streamed down Tammy's face.

Floyd's eagerness to be near Jordy made so much more sense now. As if he hadn't been through enough, she'd just crushed him further. What a schmuck she'd been.

Just like Mirabelle.

The prospect of becoming like her mother terrified Tammy. She must apologize to Floyd. Today.

"I'm so sorry," she said.

"Talk is cheap." Marian folded her arms.

New footsteps sprinted up the stairs, and Allan bustled into the apartment. "Hey, how do you like . . ." His voice trailed off when he saw Tammy, and his smile turned into a look of concern.

"Is your uncle downstairs?" Marian asked, rising to her feet.

"Yeah," he answered, still looking at Tammy. "He's talking to Phyllis about renovation stuff."

Marian patted Allan's arm as she passed him on her way to the stairs. He took a seat on the front edge of her chair and leaned forward to brush Jordy's cheek with an index finger. "What's up?"

Tammy broke down into gasping sobs. Her shoulders lurched forward with every new breath. Allan stretched his arms out to relieve her of the baby.

"Hey, don't cry," he said, settling back on his chair. "Things can't be that bad. You've got a great kid and a new apartment, not to mention a great job."

Tammy wiped the cuff of her jacket under her nose and looked at Allan through a fringe of hair. "You knew about that too?"

"Well, yeah. Floyd's been planning your surprise for days."

"I'm the world's most awful person!" Tammy said. "He's been so nice to me, and I crushed him today."

"Whatcha talkin' about?"

"I said terrible things to Floyd. He'll probably never talk to me again," she bawled. "I didn't know. Dean told me stuff, and I just believed him."

"Dean didn't know how good he had it. From what I could see, he didn't want to know either." Allan rested his chin on the top of Jordy's head for a moment. "My old man buzzed off when I was five and never came back. At least Floyd was here, you know?"

"What should I do?" Tammy said.

"Well, what do you want?"

A complete calm washed over Tammy. She sniffled and dried her eyes on the back of her hands. "I want to live without looking over my shoulder like someone's waiting for me to make a mistake. I want to have people in my life who I can count on no matter what. I want to give my son a home and to be the best mother I can be."

"Sounds to me like you've got it all figured out," Allan said.

Just hearing him say those words lifted Tammy's spirits. "Do you know where Floyd is?" she said as she rose to her feet.

"Likely at the pub." Allan pressed his cheek against Jordy's. "Us guys can hang out in your new pad if you want to go over there and patch things up."

Tammy bent forward to kiss his cheek. The fragrance of shampoo still lingering in his hair caught her by surprise. When she leaned away, he caught her fingers and pressed his lips to the back of her hand until she felt the warmth of his breath penetrate her skin.

Allan smiled up at her and let her fingers slip from his. "Chivalry lives on, eh?"

Tammy's heart skipped a beat as she hurried towards the stairs. She heard Jordy coo as Allan sang, "You are my sunshine, my only sunshine . . ."

Everything was going to be all right.

• • •

The weathered faces of two old men were waiting motionless as statues outside the pub as Tammy rounded the corner. They faced towards the river in silence with their collars raised against the wind. The closest man glanced up at Tammy when she tugged on the door handle. "Not open yet," he stated, then took another draw on his cigarette.

Tammy cupped a hand against either temple and pressed her forehead to the window. She could see Floyd hunched over the bar, talking to Tony. She took a deep breath and tapped on the glass. Tony heard her first. After he pointed in her direction, Floyd swiveled towards her, looking startled and perhaps a little worried. Tammy's remorse deepened tenfold.

Tony legged it to the door and invited Tammy inside. "You got five minutes," he told her, reaching into his shirt pocket for a pack of cigarettes. He shrugged at the other men as she shuffled past him. "First drink is on the house," Tony announced. His lighter clicked softly as the door eased shut behind her.

Tammy trudged into the dimly lit pub with some idea of what she wanted to tell Floyd—that she was sorry, for starters, and that she'd had him all wrong. Her heart felt as though it were being wrung out like a wet cloth. When she stood before him, the only words she could muster were, "Marian told me."

"Everything?" Floyd said, staring straight ahead at the bottles lined up behind the bar.

"I didn't mean what I said back there. The pressure has been getting to me, I guess." Tammy struggled to constrain her emotions. "People have been either smothering me or trying to get rid of me. And then Dean . . ."

Floyd's thumb traced the rim of his coffee cup.

"I don't know who I am if other people don't tell me," Tammy continued. If she demanded honesty from Floyd, she needed to tell the truth too. "For the first time, I'm making choices without someone in the background trying to control me." Her voice dropped to a whisper. "I cared for Dean, but the truth is, he tried to control me too."

Floyd swung his head towards her, his eyes full of sadness.

"My parents were so ashamed when they found out I was pregnant. They shipped me off to Hattersburg. I ended up at my aunt's, but she kicked me out. Her boyfriend set me up, and now she believes a bunch of stuff about me that's not true."

"I get it, believe me," Floyd said. His gaze strayed over her shoulder and rested there for a moment before he looked her in the eye again.

"I'd like us to get along," she said. Tears flowed freely down her face.

"We're not so different, you and I. Each of us has done whatever was necessary to protect our sons." He patted the barstool next to his. "'Only themselves understand themselves and the like of themselves, as souls only understand souls.'"

"Whitman, right?"

"I suppose you've read him?" Floyd cocked an eyebrow.

"A bit," she said. Her face burned red as she climbed onto the stool.

Floyd's gaze flicked past her to the front of the bar again, and his head tilted slightly to the right.

"Is something wrong?" she asked.

His attention returned, and he looked directly into her eyes. "What is it that you want? Do you want to leave town and get away from your parents? Do you want to leave Narrow Falls behind? Just tell me because I can't keep guessing and being wrong about what people need from me."

"First off, I want to stay in Narrow Falls. And secondly, I'd like to take you up on the apartment, if you're still offering."

"Consider it yours," Floyd replied with a relieved smile.

"Thank you," she said, fiddling with a coaster on the bar. "Dean might not have shown it, but I know he loved you. Otherwise, he wouldn't have been so angry with you."

Floyd's mouth wavered with emotion.

"I don't know how I'll ever repay your kindness, Floyd."

"Family helps family," he replied. His gentle smile straightened into a frown when he looked past Tammy's shoulder again.

She spun her barstool towards the window. Outside the plate-glass window, a man wearing black-rimmed glasses and a beige trench coat towered over Tony.

Floyd stood next to Tammy and squinted. "Looks serious. They've been talking for a while."

"What's Superman doing here?" she asked.

"He's a reporter . . ."

Tony flicked his cigarette at the ground and yanked the door open. "Floyd, you're gonna want to hear this." He turned towards the newspaperman. "Mike, come in here and tell him what you just told me."

The reporter strode past Tony with his right hand extended. "Mike Hornby from the *Sentinel.* I heard you speak at the community centre." He reached into his coat pocket and pulled out a pencil stub and a rolled-up notepad.

Floyd shook his hand. "And this is Tammy."

Tammy lifted her chin and made herself taller.

Hornby nodded at her and hastily switched his attention back to Floyd.

"Hurry up and tell him!" Tony said.

"What's going on?" Floyd asked.

"R.J. McLelland has been forced to step down as CEO of the mill," Hornby announced. "The board voted him out this morning."

"No!" Floyd said. His eyes widened.

"He's been caught at something," Mike said. "I don't have all the facts yet, but I will."

"I'm sure of it," Floyd said.

"There's more," Tony said. "Mike, tell him about the other business."

"The results of the ministry's environmental study will be released to the public next week," Hornby continued. "Word is things aren't looking good. My sources are hinting at confirmation of an environmental disaster." His brows raised above the top of his glasses. "That means a lot of finger-pointing and looking for answers.

Len Rathburn, that engineer from the meeting, he's resigned too. All the rats are abandoning ship."

"This is gonna help your case, Floyd. You'll be rolling in dollar bills when this is over." Tony patted Floyd's back.

Floyd's eyes widened. He knew Rathburn's input would change things, but he hadn't allowed himself to hope for such an avalanche of repercussions.

"You were right about everything," Hornby said. "Care to comment?" His pencil stub hovered above the lined paper, and he looked up at Floyd with anticipation.

"Not really. You should talk to my lawyers."

Floyd locked his eyes on Tammy's face. She could see him vibrating with pride.

"What are you going to do now?" Hornby asked.

A slow smile curved Floyd's mouth. "I'm going to go home and celebrate with my family."

The following morning, Tammy came downstairs, lured by the smell of coffee wafting up from the kitchen. Strum was resting on the mat inside the front door. His tail thumped against the floor when he saw her coming. She scooted through the kitchen door and surprised Floyd and Marian. They'd been holding hands across the table, but when they saw her, their hands dropped into their laps. Marian's cheeks grew red, and her eyes sparkled like a young girl's.

"Sorry," Tammy said as she filled a cup.

"No need," Floyd said. "I was thinking that you and I could head over to the apartment in about an hour. We should make a shopping list of supplies we'll need from the hardware store."

"And I can watch Jordy while you're out," Marian said.

"That'd be great!" Tammy replied. She grabbed an apple from the counter and returned to her room. Jordy lay in his crib gnawing at a slobbery fist. Tammy wound his mobile and settled on the bed. "Mommy's going to make us a beautiful home, something just for us." She crunched the apple and flipped through the hairstyle magazines Phyllis had leant her. She was on her way with a place to live, a job, and a new family. For the first time in her life, Tammy King felt unstoppable.

It took forever for the hour to tick away. She'd drained the coffee cup, fed Jordy, and changed his diaper, yet twenty minutes remained on the clock. Strum barked, and she heard the familiar creaking of the front door. "Grandpa's ready early," she told Jordy as she scooped him from the crib along with his favourite teddy bear. "Let's find Marian," she said, kissing his cheek. With the baby in her arms and a purse slung over one shoulder, she crossed the landing and set off to the kitchen.

Two steps down, she heard someone in conversation with Marian. Tammy trapped the teddy bear between herself and Jordy, then bent forward, hoping to identify the visitor. She could only see the bottom half of Marian's body and, on the other side of the screen door, a pair of legs clothed in dark navy pants, the kind men wore with a suit.

"I'll get Floyd," Marian said clearly. She treaded along the hallway towards the back of the house and flashed a worried look up the stairs as she passed by.

Jordy whimpered.

"Shhh." Tammy laid a finger across his lips. When she shifted the baby on her hip, the teddy bear slipped from between them and bounced end over end until it came to rest on the bottom step. Tammy sighed heavily when Jordy began to cry. The screen door screeched open, and heavy footsteps plodded across the floor. She slowly descended the steps and came face-to-face with Reverend Findlay.

He bent forward to retrieve the teddy bear from the floor and adjusted his glasses. "I believe this must be yours," he said. He pushed the bear against Jordy's chest, then wiped his hands on a handkerchief drawn from his pocket.

"Reverend Findlay . . ."

"Yes, your mother told me I'd find you here. I see things have changed since we were last scheduled to meet,"

Tammy held Jordy firmly. "I am my son's mother, and it will stay that way."

"So it would appear," he said, "although for your sake and his, I encourage you to keep an open mind."

A low growl sounded just as Strum brushed against Tammy's legs. Suddenly, Floyd was at her elbow.

"Findlay," he said. "What do you want?"

The reverend's eyes turned cold as stones, but his smile never wavered. "How long has it been since we've conversed, Mr. Hoffman? Two years? Five years?"

"The last time we *conversed* was at my wife's funeral. Ten years ago." Floyd's tone was stern. "And the time before that was at our wedding. I don't believe I much cared for you on either occasion."

Reverend Findlay's head jerked back. "I forgive your rudeness."

Floyd snorted. "State your business and be on your way."

"My *business,* as you put it, is twofold. First, there is the matter of the baby's christening."

"Is this my mother's idea?" Tammy asked.

"She is anxious about the child's spiritual well-being, given your current arrangement. We'll need to work out an appropriate choice of godparents, of course." His lips pressed together when he glanced at Floyd.

Tammy's blood boiled. "If and when I decide to have Jordy christened, it won't be by you."

"That's been dispensed with," Floyd said. "What's the second matter?"

The reverend cleared his throat. "I understand you keep your son's remains in this house."

"What of it?" Floyd replied.

"I presume you plan to inter him at the church cemetery next to his mother. Were she here, Rose Brookman would not rest until this was set right. I am willing to make the necessary arrangements on your behalf and prevail over a proper ceremony."

"Dean's fine right where he is."

"The boy should spend eternity next to his mother," the reverend said.

Tammy bristled. "If he has to spend eternity anywhere, it should be in a place where he and his mother were happy together, not in some cold cemetery."

Reverend Findlay had no time to recover from her comment before she stormed past him and flung the screen door open. His face turned deep red. "Good day, then." He cast a withering look in Floyd's direction and left. Strum followed him onto the porch and growled from the top step until the reverend turned onto the sidewalk and disappeared from sight.

"Well done, you!" Marian said. "He won't be coming around here anytime soon."

Adrenalin pumped through Tammy's veins. Never in her life had she spoken so directly or been praised so highly.

Floyd wore a faraway look.

"Are you okay?" Marian asked.

"You're right," he said to Tammy, "about where Dean should be."

"Really?" she said.

"It's hard to let go of that last piece of someone you've lost. I've been holding on to it so tightly. But now, in a very real way, my son has returned to me through Jordy. I'm ready to let go of his ashes. It's time he was with his mother."

It was midnight when Floyd's Volkswagen Beetle turned onto the old logging road leading into Brewster's Gorge. The car rocked back and forth as it dipped into ruts hardened in the road. The headlights shone a few yards into the darkness and illuminated the trunks of trees hugging the road.

Tammy looked over her shoulder to where Jordy slept, harnessed in his car seat, and a lump rose in the back of her throat. Moonlight filtered through the tree branches so she could see his peaceful face and the soft gleam of his father's urn buckled into the seat next to him.

A bright light swung through the back window and flashed in Tammy's eyes. Marian's car had turned onto the road behind them and now followed close behind. When Floyd eased onto the shoulder at the entrance to the gorge, she stopped her car behind him. Tammy could see Allan wave from Marian's passenger seat.

Floyd pulled the keys from the ignition and rested his fists on his knees. "Are you ready?"

"Are *you*?" Tammy replied.

His eyes glistened. "I believe so."

Outside the car, the air was crisp and clear. Even in the dark, Tammy could sense the newness around her, the budding trees, the promise of a new life. She was here with these people, and they were about to do something important, together.

Allan approached with a length of patterned cloth draped over one arm. The head of his nylon guitar case bobbed above one shoulder as he tromped towards her through the dew-covered grass. Floyd passed between them on his way to see Marian at the trunk of her car. He held Dean's urn snugly against his chest with one hand and a camping lantern in the other.

"Hey, man," Allan called out to Floyd

Tammy raised a finger to her lips.

Allan raised his shoulders by way of apology, then whispered, "If you're cool with it, I'd like to carry Jordy." He shook the cloth out and stretched his arms wide.

"What is it?"

"A tribal sling for carrying babies."

"I don't know . . ."

"It's great. Mom used to tote me everywhere in this thing. I'd really like to do this."

"Are you sure?"

"I'll carry in front so I have a hand on him all the time," Allan said. He held his hands out to demonstrate. "I won't let him go."

Tammy hoisted Jordy from the car seat and placed him against Allan's chest. He balked at having been awakened by the cold air but quickly settled back to sleep.

Allan looked down at Tammy as she arranged the sling across Jordy's back. "They love it when they can feel your heart beating." His expression turned serious as he searched her eyes. "How you feeling? It's a big night."

She was swimming with emotion, some of which she wasn't sure how to handle. Allan was making her heart flutter when she should be feeling mournful. "I'm doing all right," she replied. "What next?"

"Pass one end of the sling around my waist and the other end over my shoulder, then tie them together in a good knot in the middle of my back."

When she finished, Tammy lifted the canvas strap over her head and shoulder and let the guitar case rest against her back. "Is this right?"

"Looks good to me," Allan said, pulling the hood of his sweatshirt onto his head.

Floyd's lantern enveloped himself and Marian in a circle of light. She stood against him with a blanket draped over her right arm and a wicker picnic basket at her feet. Their breath appeared as fleeting clouds in the night air.

Marian extended a flashlight to Tammy. "It's pitch-black out there. Be careful," she said. "I wouldn't want to see you hurt."

Tammy hugged her tightly.

"What was that for?" Marian asked.

"Everything," Tammy replied with a catch in her voice. "Just everything."

Floyd and Marian shared a satisfied smile. He reached out to squeeze her hand before leading the group onto the overgrown path.

Tammy's senses registered details beyond the reach of her flashlight beam—a waft of pine, the splish of water. She didn't need to see the trees to know they stood tall against the sky. She didn't need to see the river to know it flowed ceaselessly. It was time to trust her instincts.

Floyd, Marian, and Allan were all good people. *She* was good people. She could raise Jordy to be a proper kind of man. Hadn't Allan's mother done the same? Tammy would never be like her mother because she hadn't lived her mother's life. Her journey would be what she made it and because of whom she'd let into it. She couldn't fear the dark so much that she never stepped into it.

Tammy looked back at Allan. One hand cupped the back of Jordy's head, and the other was under his bottom.

"He's asleep," Allan said proudly.

His affection for her son sent a flash of emotion through Tammy's heart. The shadows hid his face inside the sweatshirt hood, but she felt certain he was smiling.

As the tangle of brush began to thin on either side of the trail, the sound of fast-moving water grew louder. After a few more yards of hard-packed ground riddled with granite rocks and exposed pine roots, they reached the river. The water sped past at an alarming speed. They kept to a narrow footpath that hugged the bank until they reached a bend strewn with rocks the size of fists. Tammy could feel them through the thin soles of her sneakers.

Floyd and Marian stopped and waited for Tammy and Allan to catch up. Floyd lifted his lantern. "Is everyone all right?

"We're fine." Tammy's eyes rested on the urn. It was impossible to look away. "Is this the spot?"

"No. It's about ten minutes more to the falls."

"Surely, you're not going to climb them," Marian said.

Floyd's gaze dropped to the urn.

"It's dark, and the rocks will be covered in frost," she continued.

"What if Marian and I stand at the bottom and shine the flashlights up?" Tammy said. "You should be all right,"

Floyd pointed to Allan. "And if I use my coat to tie Dean to me like that, I'll have both hands to climb with."

"I suppose," Marian said.

"Well, all right, then." Floyd beamed.

At points where the trail widened, Tammy walked alongside Allan, shining the flashlight ahead of them. Their shoulders pressed together, and on several occasions she stole discreet glances.

"What's Marian got in the basket?" he said.

"Cheezies, peanut butter, and root beer. All Dean's favourites."

"Huh. I really like her. She's good for Floyd."

"There's someone for everyone; that's what they say," Tammy replied.

Allan's right arm dropped to his side. His knuckles grazed the back of Tammy's hand as they walked.

"I really love the apartment," Tammy ventured.

"It's great. Close to work," he said, "and my place."

Tammy adjusted the guitar case against her back and looked pointedly at Allan. "It's funny, you think you'll never forget the *first* place you lived." She hoped the lift of her brow would imply that she was speaking in riddles—not really meaning first homes, but first loves. "It seems like the best," she continued, "but it's all you've ever known."

Allan studied her for a moment, then slyly added, "So how can you really know it's the best?"

"Exactly," she replied with exuberance. "But then you get out there, and you find there are other places to live."

"With rooms that feel familiar."

"Or windows with a different view," she added. "Before you know it, you forget why you liked the first place so much. And you're glad you moved."

"We're not really talking about apartments, are we?"

She smiled up at him. "Nope, not at all."

"I think you're going to love your new place," Allan said. He reached out to squeeze her hand.

"I think you may be right." Tammy squeezed his hand in return.

The party soon arrived at a clearing where local teens often gathered to drink beer during the summer months. Two logs had been laid at right angles, and where they met, there was a circle of rocks containing charred firewood.

"I can hear the roar of the falls," Floyd said. "Let's leave our things here. We can come back afterwards and start a fire."

Minutes later, they arrived at their destination. The falling water shimmered where the flashlight beams touched it, and the froth glowed where the flow dropped into the river below. Floyd stood alone at the water's edge. No one spoke.

He passed his lantern to Tammy and the urn into Marian's hands, then removed his jacket and fashioned the body into a sling to cradle the urn against his stomach. Marian knotted the sleeves together behind his back. Once everything was secure, they all lifted their faces to take in the rise of rock he was about to scale.

Floyd turned towards Tammy, Allan, and Marian. She thought he might say a few words, but instead he held Marian's hands and kissed her tenderly. He edged past her to Tammy. He hugged her and kissed her forehead. There were speckles of water on his eyeglasses. "Thank you for loving my son," he whispered shakily.

Next, he embraced Allan. "You're a fine man. Dean was lucky to have you as a friend."

There were no tears until he bent to kiss Jordy's cheek. Floyd sniffled, then, head down, he began his climb of the rock face.

Tammy held the lantern above her head to shine light on the placement of his feet. Marian directed the second flashlight to points farther up the wall. The climb went smoothly, with Floyd advancing in a calculated manner, rock after rock and hand over hand. He soon completed the climb and was standing at the top of the falls, silhouetted against the night sky. He slipped the urn from inside his coat and held it in both hands for several seconds before raising it to his face.

"Ohhh," Marian wept.

Tammy's throat tightened, and her heart ached. Allan's hands rested on her shoulders, and she could feel Jordy's back between her shoulder blades. Hot tears spilled from the corners of her eyes as her heart welled with emotion.

Floyd knelt on a ledge overhanging the river and held the urn over the edge of the falls. Dean's ashes poured out like sand pulled into the torrent of plunging water. But some bits lifted with the breeze, like the leavings of paper burnt in a fire, to float through the beams of light.

THE END

Acknowledgements

I would like to thank the following people for the inspiration, feedback, information and support they've offered: Valéry Brosseau, Kylie Burns, Joel Campbell, Angela Durante Dukát, Kelly Ferguson, Renée Sgroi, Jenny Sorenson, and Daniel Walker.

I also extend deep gratitude to the guiding hand of Jenny Quinlan, my insightful editor from Historical Editorial; and to my invaluable critique-group family, fellow writers Cryssa Bazos, Connie Di Pietro, Tom Taylor, Andrew Varga, and dearly-missed Jay Stewart.

I would also like to thank Zach Tuinman, the fine artist whose painting graces this book cover; Lynde House Museum, provider of his creative inspiration; and Eric Tuinman, my partner in publication and the best second chance I could ever dream of.

About The Author

Gwen Tuinman was born and raised in rural Ontario, and now resides on an urban homestead in Whitby, near Toronto. She graduated from Trent University with a B.A. in Psychology and from Brock University with a B.A. in Education. Gwen is the creator of The Wild Nellies, a collective of diverse womxn creatives whose events raise awareness and funds for charities that help women escaping domestic abuse. In 2019, The Denise House/Sedna Women's Shelter and Support Services recognized Gwen as a Woman of Courage. *The Last Hoffman* is her first novel.

www.GwenTuinman.com

(Author photo by Angela Durante Dukát)

9 781999 175924